BROWN SUGAR ESPRESSO MARTINI

AUBREY TAYLOR

Book Cover by Aurora McGaughey
Book Illustration by SunshineCovey

Editing and Proof Reading by Becky Clapham and Jessica Norton

Illustrations by Aubrey Taylor

First Edition 2026

Contents

SUICIDE AND SUICIDAL THOUGHTS
(OFF PAGE AND CONVERSATIONS)
SEXUAL HARASSMENT
(CONVERSATIONS ONLY)
MILITARY PTSD
CHILDHOOD PTSD
EXPLICIT SEXUAL CONTENT
ABUSE (FROM A PARENT, CONVERSATIONS ONLY)
GUN VIOLENCE (CONVERSATIONS ONLY)
Take breaks, get some water,
snuggle your loved ones and pets.
Be kind to yourself, being a human being is tough.

A Happy Playlist for My Sad Girl.

Wake Me : Bleachers
Absolutely : Nine Days
Don't You Give Up On Me : Jonah Kagen
Sally, When The Wine Runs Out : ROLE MODEL
Better If Worse : HAFFWAY
Sinner : Benjamin Steer
Riot Girl: Good Charlotte
Friends That Kiss: Kyndal
She Likes Sports : almost monday
Drive: X-Ambassadors
Real Love Baby: Father John Misty
I'm Not OKay (I promise) : My chemical Romance
Texas Sun: Khruangbin, Leon Bridges
Ripple (Soft version) : Good Neighbours
On Your Way Home: Patrick Droney
Summertime: My Chemical Romance
Angeleno Moon: The Fray
What's It Gonna Take?: thebandfriday
Angel of Mine: Odhran Murphy
Peach tree: Ethan Regan
Riccochet: Rise Against
The Reason: Hoobastank
Girl Almighty: One Direction
Redemption: Skizzly Adams, Lissie
Give & Take: John Marc
I Believe in a Thing Called Love: tiLLie
Hand in My Pocket: Alanis Morissette
Back To Us: Ike Dweck
Authomatic: Half-Alive
All The Small Things - Blink-182
Run Baby Run: Boston Levi
Good Man: The Federal Empire

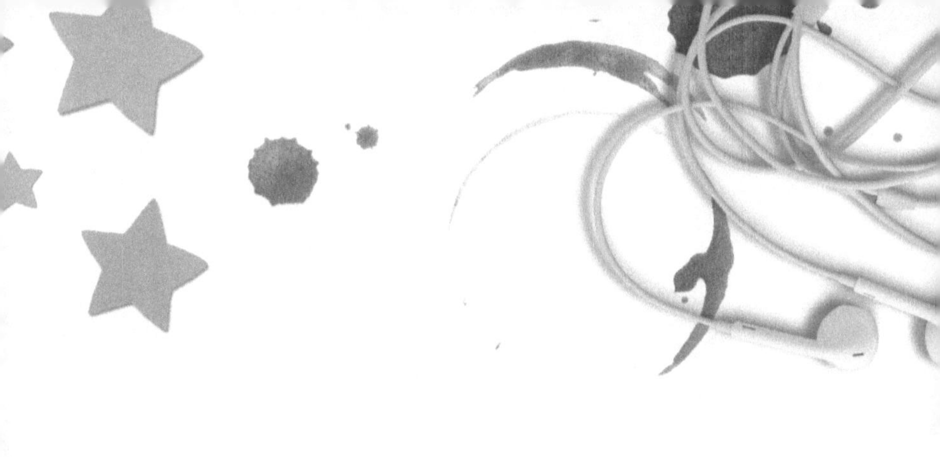

> STRONG IS BEAUTIFUL, STRONG IS POWERFUL.
> SEXY IS WHATEVER YOU WANT IT TO BE, AND I HOPE MORE GIRLS
> CAN FEEL HOW I FEEL.
> **- ILONA MAHER**

To all the women who are finding their self worth
in a society determined to keep us
quiet and meek.
Your voice and your strength matters.
It's time to change the world.

Rhea

Y ou know how they say, "when it rains, it pours"?

Well, when the tenant in the condo upstairs leaves their bathtub faucet running for six hours and is unreachable because they're on a plane to Cabo, it pours.

"Oh, Rhea." Sunday stands beside me in her adorable red rubber boots, holding a mop. I'm so distracted by the water flooding my condo that I don't even realize she's arrived. When I called her I thought maybe it would be a smaller problem, but as the caretaker tries to access the upstairs unit the tub continues to fill, and now there is a solid two feet of water destroying every square foot of my place.

"I loved that couch," I whine, my voice cracking a little. The long black velvet couch I bought with my first real paycheck is soaked through to the wood supports, and both it and I look like a rained-out cat.

"Neil Lancaster fingered me on that couch." Sunday offers up the grossest memory she can come up with to make me laugh.

All five foot three of her beams with a certain kind of light; the kind you find at sunset during music festivals or at sunrise when you're still riding your bike around with your best friends at fifteen, at four a.m., during summer vacation.

"Ew," I laugh.

She gives me a nudge, "pretty sure he finger-banged you there too, so don't even start with me."

"He was such a cute little man-slut. I almost miss him." I nod, trying not to be absolutely depressed about my drowning living room. "He was British, right?"

"Irish," Sunday corrects me. "He was so good at it."

"It was the extra length on his middle and ring finger..." I stare across the living room sadly at the water still leaking down the wall. "His last name always threw me for a loop." I sigh.

"It was very *English*... Have you heard from the caretaker?" She asks, leaning the mop against the wall. "This is bad." Sunday looks from me to the damage and back to me.

"You think? My favorite couch is ruined, I just replaced the flooring, and I only got half my art off the wall, so my signed CM Punk poster is destroyed!" I say as calmly as possible. "This sucks."

"Okay, okay... maybe it's not that bad?" She holds up the soggy frame and chews on her lip. The poster itself is curled and warped inside the frame, and as she sets it down, the nails pop off the bottom, and the glass slides out, hitting the water with a heavy slosh.

"Sorry." She grimaces.

"It's okay, can't make it any worse."

"At least with the front door open, the water is draining into the parking lot?" She smiles at me.

"It doesn't matter, it's everywhere. My room, the kitchen, the bathroom. Everything is underwater," I say, "this is not what I meant when I said I idolized Shrek's swamp for its solitude."

"You did say that," Sunday gently laughs.

I wish I could see it like that, but I can't seem to find a light in all the destruction around us. "The association emailed me saying that they'll have someone in here to assess the damage as soon as the condo is dry."

"That's going to take weeks," she scoffed. "Let Kaia talk to that old twit, what's her name again?"

"We're not quite at *threatening* them yet," I brush her off. "Can I crash at your house for a couple of days?" I ask her, and she nods immediately.

"I'm going to try to collect what dry things are left, and I'll meet you for warm-ups in an hour?"

"Are you sure? Can I stay and help?" She suggests.

"I'll be fine, I'd rather be alone in my sadness for a bit anyway. And that mop isn't going to do much," I add, giving her a soft, limp smile.

She stands there for a couple of minutes longer, hesitant to go.

"I got it, promise. I can handle it," I convince her, shoo her out the door, and get to work. I turn back to the condo and the tears start to fall, but I have too much work to do to break down, so I keep moving.

I grab the dry duffel bags from the top shelf in my closet after wading through the water and shove what clothing isn't drenched inside, along with as many boots and sneakers as I can fit. I take the bags right out to my Bronco, grateful that I still have her, and head back inside for more things. My DVD collection is underwater, and so is the expensive leather armchair with its pretty silver studs. Everything smells like a damp dog, and it's overwhelming to say the least.

I swallow tightly, trying to control the panic attack that's bubbling up in my chest, and continue to move through the house. I unplug the fridge begrudgingly, cursing myself for filling the damn thing with food the night before, and then return to the bathroom with my last bag to grab everything I can from there.

Taking pictures of everything for insurance breaks my heart, and my camera roll goes from photos of the girls and me to my newly minted swamp. I hate myself for not spending the extra money on the bigger condo to avoid having upstairs neighbors, but the damage is done, and there's not much I can do now besides be sad.

My laptop is the last thing I take, safe and dry on the kitchen island before wandering down the drenched steps to the driveway. The caretaker is coming down the stairs when I toss my belongings into the backseat, and his expression is tight with concern.

"I'm sorry, Ms. Drake, that's an awful call to get." He swipes his hat off his head and ruffles his hands through what little grey hair is on top of it. "I'll make sure they get fixed up as soon as they can."

"Thanks, Leon, I appreciate it. Say hi to Hattie for me?" I say, popping the shiny black handle on the Bronco.

"Of course," he says.

"Oh–if you can salvage my posters..." I add.

"I'll do my best, Ms. Drake. Have a good game." He turns back to the soggy condo and leaves me to stare at the open front door for a moment longer.

At least it can't get worse.

When I finally get to the field, the girls have already changed, and the stands around the open-air field are starting to fill with people coming to watch the game. It's our first time out of the indoor arena we use to avoid the cold weather at the start of the season and the smell of grass and fresh air is a welcome break from everything.

Cosy stands talking to Coach, looking over her shoulder as I return from the locker room, stretching out in my gear. I pop my mouth guard between my teeth to chew on as I start to fix my hair back into a tighter braid.

"Sunday got us up to speed," she comes over to me and tells me to spin around with the wave of her finger. "Lower," I squat down so she can reach my head with our height difference. "You alright?" She asks as she tightens every strand carefully.

"Yeah, it just sucks." I grind my teeth together, trying not to think about how not alright I am.

"Well, you can stay with any of us," she offers, "and anything we can do to help. We're in. They opened a new thrift shop in Lorette. I'm sure we can re-furnish the condo in no time with a little elbow grease."

"Thanks, Bones," I hum. It does make me feel better knowing that, no matter what, the girls have my back through the mess. She finishes the braid, and I stand up to my full height. "Today's game is going to be rough." I chew on my lip. The Devils rugby club is coming off a couple of hard losses and has a point to prove.

"Yeah," Cosy swallows tightly, "and Kaia's in a mood, so keep her close."

"What happened?" I ask.

"Christian has been ignoring her calls for three days," she says with a small sigh. "Let her get out the rage, but stop her before anything goes too far?" Cosy suggests, and I nod.

"I can handle that," I agree.

"Good." She starts to walk back toward the group of players, and my eyes trail to the opposition's bench, where they all seem to be in foul moods as the clouds pour in and the rain starts to fall.

"Great."

The rain stings my face as I come to a halt in the grass. The wind kicks up the smell of dirt, blood, and sweat into my nose as the sound of a sharp whistle cuts through the noise. My fingers tingle from the cold air, and my chest is tight from the lack of oxygen, but I can feel my heart racing in my chest. *Rhea!* I can hear my name being called, but it feels out of reach. *Rhea!* It isn't real, nothing more than a whisper. *Rhea!* The scream comes again, and I shake free of the dazed state, slamming headfirst into a wall of rain and a field of players.

The play is dead, and Kaia is in the dirt, *again*.

They've been targeting her all game with their biggest players.

"Get up!" I haul her off the ground. The downpour makes her skin slick and her cleats slosh through the mud, but she finds her footing and shoves away from me. Two dark braids whip around her sharp features as she searches the field with violence tight across her jaw.

"They're cutting inside," Cosy yells from her position. Mud coats her red ponytail, it stains her jersey, and drips down her thighs into her cleats.

She tugs on the elastic around her hair, tightening it as we shuffle back into our line. With only a minute left on the clock and tied at fourteen, it's anyone's game, but we need it more.

Across the line Lacy is glaring at me, her cheeks red and her expression dead set on murder. She's one of the bigger girls who play for the Devils. To my right, Sunday, our smallest player, taps the ball against the side of her cleat before giving it a hard kick. Our line moves in unison down the squishy turf, Cosy stepping out of line just after half to slot herself right behind Kaia as she spins clumsily to get away from an attacker.

I push harder, willing my legs to move faster. I file in behind Kaia, rolling my hands into her shorts in an uninterrupted motion, lifting her from the ground without effort to give the advantage and pocketing the ball into her arms.

That's my girl.

It's tricky but worth it to take possession back if we can.

Kaia pops the ball to me to avoid the next hit.

"Alright," I grunt, dropping low to wrap it up into my chest to protect it from the oncoming trouble. Lacy is on a mission, but she forgets herself and her size. She may outweigh everyone else, but not me, not even soaking wet. With my shoulder in her stomach I rock her back off her feet, pushing the ball out to Kaia, who's waiting with a path. She now has the space to move the ball another twenty yards before she's grabbed from behind and tripped into the ground hard.

Cosy is on top of it all before I can even unravel from Lacy to follow Sunday up the field as Kaia extends the ball out between feet and arms. I surge forward, using every ounce of my strength to dig my cleats into the over-saturated earth. I need to catch up to Sunday. She's fast, but she can't outrun everyone. She needs a wall and an escape plan. I watch, still a few feet out, as Sunday launches herself sideways and skips forward through the mud into an open lane.

"Run!" Kaia screams, fueling her already insanely quick steps.

The rain makes it hard to see, but as I turn to my right, Kaia is caught off guard by a late hit that knocks her back onto the ground as Sunday crosses the line and the clock winds down to six seconds. I move to help Kaia, who is shoving the forward who took the cheap shot. She raises her hand, and her expression turns vicious as Cosy yells from behind me, adding to the already intense amount of noise.

"Fuck you, Abby!" Kaia shoves, her feet sliding around in the mud as she gets up and hauls back to hit the forward in the face. The follow-through is abruptly interrupted as Abby lunges forward, wraps her up, and walks her backward aggressively before slamming her back into the dirt. They roll around the pitch as the referee jogs over to get in the middle, only to stop on her heels when she sees Kaia is involved.

The distraction gives her the upper hand; she flips Abby into the mud with a splash, pinning her there between her thighs as she continues her assault. Kaia pulls back and hits her hard; the sickening snap of knuckles meeting cheek echoes through the white noise of the rain.

"You cheap-shot-taking-cunt!" Every word is another punch. By the time she runs out of breath, Abby is bleeding from her nose as Kaia pulls back her arm with the intention of hitting her again, and I step in and wrap her up around the waist to pull her off the forward.

"Stop! She's not even fighting back." I hold her body tightly against my chest as she squirms violently with adrenaline. "Kaia!" I snap, and like a popped balloon, all the fight explodes from her in that instance, allowing me to see her back on the ground.

"Muzzle your damn dog, Mitchell!" Their captain barks at Cosy.

"Keep yours on a tighter leash, McKenzie!" she hollers back and flips her off, making her way over and snatching Kaia's hand to look at it. "Locker room now," she whispers, giving Kaia the look. Cosy's all too good at it after three years playing on the same team with Kaia. An unspoken bond that when Cosy makes an order, she follows it. She's probably the only person who has that type of authority over her. "You can let her go," she says to me, and I nod, but I can feel the enraged energy that's vibrating from her strong but small frame.

My hand snaps out, catching her by the collar of the jersey and holding her in place as she snarls a few choice insults as Abby crawls off the ground.

"Okay, well..." Cosy sighs, waving us both off. "I tried."

"Come on, Killer," I say to her, practically lifting Kaia off the ground by the damp fabric and directing her toward the building we use as a locker room during away games. The door slams behind us, and with it, the violent rainfall is shut out.

"That's definitely going to get you suspended," I say with a barely audible laugh and let go of her.

She stomps across the room, over the tiled Hillcat logo and past the row of lockers to the sinks along the back wall. She runs the faucet and shoves her hand beneath it without saying a word while I rub the palms of my hands into my eyes to clear away the water sticking to my lashes and sink to the bench with a tiny huff.

"You alright?" I ask, and before she can even answer, the door swings open, giving neither of us a second to cool off, and Coach files in with Cosy behind her. Kaia turns immediately, leaning against the sink and crossing her arms, no doubt preparing for the bad news.

"Six games," Coach says.

"Six?" Kaia flips her lid, "What do you mean six? Abby hit *me* late!"

Cosy puts a barrier between them, mostly for Coach's sake.

"One game per punch," Coach explains, "the ref is Abby's sister, Kaia."

"Boo-hoo!" Kaia groans.

"You pissed off the wrong person." She puts her hands on her hips, "I tried to get it lowered, but they aren't budging."

Somehow, it had gotten worse.

Brighton

The Hollow is coming apart at the seams.

It's a rare night when it isn't at capacity, but tonight feels different. Two very different crowds have filled the bar, creating a powder keg just begging for a spark. The hockey-game crowd is happy, drunk, dancing, flirting, finding dark corners to enjoy the night, while the first-responder crowd has just come off shift, looking to forget the horrors of a massive downtown fire.

Something has to give; I just wish it wouldn't be inside the walls of my bar.

I throw a towel over my shoulder, dip two glasses into the ice bin, and set them on the countertop behind the bar. My hands work on the drinks while my eyes scan the crowd for trouble, and my head throbs from lack of sleep.

"I asked for a double vodka, Bright!" One of the mouthy firefighters, Derek, tosses his half-empty glass onto the bar, and it spills over the girls minding their business next to him. He shoves his boxy shoulders between stools, practically knocking over the guy next to him, and slams his hand on the bar.

"And I gave you water, *Derek*," I say without skipping a beat, my jaw tight with annoyance. The lights flicker across the heavy red drapes and upholstery of the Hollow, illuminating everything in a hazy, warm glow while still keeping it dark inside, other than the soft white glow from the bar.

"I come to your bar to drink, not to pay fifteen dollars for water!" Derek raises his voice, and beside me, my twin brother, Boone, chuckles under his breath.

"You haven't paid for the last three drinks, Derek," I remind him and give the waiting girls their rum and Cokes one at a time with my right hand. They take off as quickly as they can, and Derek slides into the opening, following me as I move on to the next waiting body around the rectangular bar.

"So what, you're cutting me off?" he yells over the swell of pop music.

"Unless you're keen on your station peeling you off the road with a Halligan, then yeah, Derek–I'm cutting you off," I say, turning to the guy beside him. "What can I get you?"

"This is bullshit, Bright!" he continues to argue as the guy orders two beers. I pull them from the fridge behind me, popping the lids off against the counter and sliding them across the bar. "Is this because of the Sunday thing? I told you, man, she's not my type."

"It has nothing to do with you calling my little sister *ugly*. This is because I don't want your blood staining the concrete outside. It's bad for business. But Derek," I say, angling over the bar to remind him how much bigger I am than him and to steady my left hand on the countertop. I anchor myself and get in his face, lowering my voice. "If you don't fuck off, it's going to be a good enough reason for me to cave your face in," I warn him with a smug smile. "You get *water*, or you *get out*."

Boone pushes up behind me as Derek takes a second to decide his fate before stumbling back away from the bar with a few choice swear words.

"He turns into such a mean drunk." Boone clears his throat, and I unclench my entire body.

"He's an asshole sober." I shake my head and turn toward an explosion of cheers and hollering.

"Girls are back." He slaps my shoulder. "At least that's some happy news. They beat the Devils." Boone hovers beside me, his hair as dark and unkempt as the scruff on his jawline, in his black Hollow t-shirt, cropped just enough to show off his torso of tattoos and body hair.

"Just barely," I grumble. "Go clean some glasses or something." I wave him off.

"You can't boss me around, I own this place too," Boone scoffs, flipping me off.

"I'm three minutes older and three inches taller. I can do whatever I want," I offer him a tight smile.

"Real mature," he laughs, but hauls one of the full trays over his shoulder, chatting as he makes his way through the crowd to the kitchen.

I leave the bar to Judd, who has handled a tougher crowd, and make my way over to the booth as the girls slide into it. I look to the table over, and Derek is glaring at me with his friends, his expression vicious enough to burn a hole through me. It's only a matter of time before he starts shit, and we have to throw him out.

"Good game tonight, girls," I say, crossing my arms over my chest to hide the violent tremor currently coursing through my left hand.

I run my eyes over Sunday, checking for any major injuries, but find nothing on her and am met with an annoyed look that makes me chuckle. Sunday is four years younger than Boone and me, with dirty blonde hair that she dyed as an act of rebellion to stand out from the pitch black color of ours. But she has the same big green eyes as Boone and that same goofy smile. They're both big golden retrievers, wearing their hearts on their sleeves and walking around in need of constant protection.

I wish they made it a little easier.

"Did you actually have it on?" Kaia snaps with a smile. "Or did the Huskies game take precedence?"

"You were up behind the bar," I confess, and she rolls her eyes. "First round is on me," I offer as an apology. Unfortunately for the Hillcats, the hockey game brings in more bodies, and the Hollow, for all its worth, still runs on money.

"Hey, Bright," Sunday speaks up as I turn to go get their drinks, and I know she's about to ask for something because my name comes off her lips sweet as honey. She's been using that tone to get what she wants her entire life.

"Yes, Sunday," I wait for it.

"Do you think you could set up the karaoke machine?" She leans on the table and flashes that signature smile up at me.

"Tonight? No." I scoff, and her smile turns agitated. "Are you out of your mind?"

"Bri," she whines, and I shake my head.

"Absolutely not." I stand my ground. "You guys already get it on Thursdays. I'm not opening it up just because you flash puppy eyes at me. *Wrong brother.*"

"Oh come on, Thing One!" Kaia starts to whine with her.

"Sorry for a second there, I forgot you had a stick up your ass!" Sunday groans, and her friends laugh, but I just sigh. "Where is Bobo?"

Bri and Bobo, horrible nicknames given to us by Sunday, when all she could do was hobble around the house in a diaper, screaming for attention.

I hate it, but at least I'm not Bobo.

"You aren't running to Boone because I said no," I warn her.

"Yes, I am, and you can't stop me without it causing a show, so..." She uses the table and stands in the booth, hopping over the back and landing in the lap of a drunk fire guy with a tiny giggle before she darts off through the crowd in search of our brother.

"Thanks for the help, guys." I look at the rest of the girls.

"Bros before hoes," Kaia snorts.

"She's trying to cheer Rhea up," Cosy says, leaning back and stretching her arms up as she rolls her neck side to side.

I look from her to Rhea, sitting in the other corner, picking at the curled plastic on the old drinks menu. She looks sad, maybe more distracted than usual. Her raven hair is messy around her hardened jaw, multiple dainty piercings glimmering under the bar lights, and noticeably absent is the broad, pearly smile she usually wears.

I groan at the sight of her, pathetically busying her mind.

Always a sucker for a sad girl.

"Drinks," I say, tapping the table with a finger before backing away. "And karaoke..." I add, and Kaia gives me a small nod. *Anything for Sunday*, I tell myself, which subsequently means anything for any of them. "Just let Day think it was her doing." I wave the towel and keep walking back to the bar.

"Hey Judd," I call to him as he finishes up with the customers he's talking to and turns.

The Hollow uniform fits him tighter across the chest, and the back is printed with large red font that says I'M A CHEAP DRUNK. A few years ago, Boone took it upon himself to create a uniform despite my saying multiple times that we're a dive bar and didn't need them. Now the staff members walk around in black shirts with the Hollow logo on the front and a collection of idiotic sayings on the back.

And with the intent of pissing off Boone, I only ever wore the one that said 'THING ONE.'

"What's good?" I'm still getting used to the British twang in Judd's voice, and every once in a while, it catches me off guard, remembering he's not an East Coast boy.

"Can you get drinks to table six for me?" I ask him, and he looks over my shoulder to the Hillcat table with a scowl. "Hey, make two for Cosy that way when she pours the first one on you, she'll still have something to drink." I pat the bar and slip through the crowd to the stairs that lead up to my apartment.

Boone stops me on his way out of the kitchen, "You alright?" He asks, and I nod.

"Forgot my phone upstairs," I say, and Boone sees through the lie but lets me go anyway. I take the steep black stairs to the apartment, unlocking both locks before slipping inside and closing the door behind me to breathe. I uncurl my hand from my jeans pocket and watch it shake. The tremor is getting worse. I breathe in for four, hold it, and breathe out for four. Holding my hand out and begging it to stop so I can return to work.

"**J**udd should not be allowed access to liquor. What the hell is this?" I choke down the drink, and it hits my stomach like firestarter. Sunday returns with a wicked smile on her face and slides into the booth next to me.

"Bobo is setting it up," she squeals and slams back one of the weird-colored drinks. "Oh god!" She spits booze everywhere, causing Kaia to scream in laughter and Cosy to throw napkins at her. "Judd made these," she says before anyone can explain. "The sympathy hire has gone too far." Sunday frowns, completely disgusted.

We all look over to watch Judd juggle three drinks while he flirts with a cluster of girls around him. The Hollow shirt is a size too small, and his sandy blond hair is darker at the roots, messy, and licks at his neck. He winks one of his glassy blue eyes and carries on through the crowd with a subtle flex to his massive arms and a lazy smirk on his lips.

"It's a shame he's so pretty to look at." Kaia slumps against the table, poking the terrible drinks. Cosy scoffs and pats her on the head. "This is all yours, baby girl," she says, pushing the glass across the table to me.

"Don't make me?" I scrunch my brows and give her the biggest, watery eyes I can manage.

"This is your pity party, remember? He was trying to cheer you up with his house special," Kaia reminds me.

"I hate you," I say to her, grabbing it and slamming it back with a loud gag. My phone buzzes on the table, and an email about my condo comes through, only making me more depressed. I shove it away, and Cosy picks it up to read it.

"Shit," she scowls and shows Kaia, who leans in with her eyes unfocused on the phone. "They're giving you a six-month timeline for repairs."

"Which means it'll be closer to a year," Kaia says. After the game, she showered and left her long brown hair to air-dry, and now it's wavy around her sharp features. There's a soft pink hue to her tawny skin from the booze, and she looks up at me with sympathy in her eyes. "I'm sorry, Reaper. I know you loved that condo."

"It's chill," I shrug. "It's just a house..."

A house I bought with my own money after years of renting. At nineteen, I'd moved out of my parents' house, in desperate need of space from the chaos that my family embodies. Don't get me wrong, I love them. They're everything to me. My mom and stepdad are incredible—four younger siblings, Reid, Remi, Shana, and Toby. And too many animals for one house, but it's always loud, someone is always creating noise, and sometimes... I just need the quiet.

The condo is my first real home. Three years there, and it was finally starting to feel like mine...or at least it had. *Don't cry again, not here.*

"Hey, sport," Boone says, his hand squeezing my shoulder. "I don't know if anyone told you, but it's actually illegal to be sad after I fight Bright to set up the karaoke machine, so if you could like..." I tilt my head up to see him standing behind the booth, and he smiles at me, digging his tattooed fingers into his dimples, "turn that frown upside down?"

"You're a dork," I say, shaking my head.

"It worked, though," he winks, turning his attention across the table, "now go scare some of these drunks out of the Hollow with your beautiful singing voice, Kaia."

"You're an asshole," she purrs and flips him off, but slides from the booth and pulls a reluctant Cosy with her. Boone forces Sunday up and out, and I watch as they disappear through the crowd.

The speaker squeaks as Kaia gets her hands on a mic, and the entire crowd at the Hollow flinches until it rights itself. She wastes no time finding her favorite Nelly Furtado song, no doubt just to piss Boone off, who's watching from a spot behind the bar with a smile on his face. It doesn't matter what she does; it will never make him love her less.

"Here." A tall glass slides across the table; vibrant pink and slushy. I look up as my hand wraps around it and my mouth finds the straw. Brighton leans against the booth with his hands in his pockets, his eyes on the stage in the corner of the bar with an annoyed expression that's forced because the corner of his mouth curls up and his right foot twitches like he wants to tap along to the beat.

"I thought you didn't bring out the blender on hockey nights," I say quietly, enjoying the perfectly mixed drink. There's even a poorly drawn sign behind the main bar that says "*No blended drinks when the Huskies are on.*" A rule laid down after Sunday exploded watermelon daiquiris all over the bar one night; it smelled like rum in the cracks of the nearby booths for months after.

"It was already out," he lies.

I take another sip, my eyes never leaving him.

Brighton is handsome, and even though they're twins, it's not in the same way Boone is. All rugged and scruffy. Like a goofy, tattooed grizzly bear. No, Brighton is a black bear. Sleek, all sharp edges and quiet anger. He still cuts his hair like he's on active duty, but it's a little longer on top now and lends to soft, loose curls he fights to keep back out of his stormy blue eyes.

He's hardened muscle, old sun burns, and scars from years of service, softened around the edges from being home. What little I do know about him all comes from Sunday or Boone. Unlike his siblings, he's reserved and barely speaks to anyone.

The Hollow is as busy as it is because of Boone's friendly, border-collie energy and nothing else. He finally looks over his shoulder at me, and I quickly adjust my stare to Kaia, but out of the corner of my eye, I can still feel his gaze on my skin.

Looking down at the slushie margarita, I smile sadly and try to enjoy the sweet taste of it before I collect myself and join Sunday for a tipsy rendition of Hand in My Pocket by Alanis Morissette that has the front row of the crowd cheering for us. For a second, I actually forget that my entire life has been disrupted, sinking into the energy that the girls were putting out. I do my best to completely forget until I'm another three drinks down, belting slurred lines of a Queen song.

"You know, despite not having a house to go home to, today wasn't so bad," I say, leaning over the booth to take a glass of water from between Kaia and Cosy. Sunday is a few tables over, flirting with a paramedic loudly just to rile up her brothers, but the crowd is finally starting to die down, leaving mostly the regulars and a few drunks. I'm sweaty, tired, and too tipsy to drive home, but I'm not so sad anymore—and that's what matters.

"We got a lurker," Kaia says, her eyes trailing a booth over.

"Fuck, I hate that guy," I groan, seeing who she's talking about. Derek Trysen, one of the meathead firefighters who frequents the bar, is circling Sunday. *Again*. It's a game he likes to play. He's well past thirty, with a greasy curly blonde mullet, beady dark eyes, and still thinks that pulling a girl's hair is flirting.

"I can't hit another man in this bar for not doing anything. Thing One will flip." Kaia sighs, looking over her shoulder to Brighton, who's surprisingly also watching Derek circle like a shark.

"I could use the outlet," I say, and Kaia's eyes flicker to mine with excitement, "he feels bad for me, I can probably get away with it."

I could take Brighton Black one-on-one.

Sober...

"I like sad Rhea, she's a wild card." She slaps the table a couple of times with her hands, and every ring across her ten fingers clangs loudly.

"Give me some of those." I hold out my palm, flat.

"God, that's hot," she moans and starts to shuck them off so I can slip them on. I keep my eye on Derek, who's getting suspiciously close to Sunday, and like clockwork, his hand comes up her back and her head snaps to see who's touching her. She looks him over, the dirty look on her face dark enough to kill. Both Kaia and Cosy snort at her expression.

"Oh, that's going to start shit," Cosy angles to watch.

"Stay here," I say, moving through the crowd. Luckily, I'm taller and can see over most of the heads bobbing around, keeping my gaze fixated on the two of them. The guys she's sitting with and chatting to are aiming to get restless, shifting in their seats as Derek puts his hand on Sunday again.

She shoves him back, and two of the guys at the table are up and out of their seats. Sunday waves them off, but the distraction leaves a split second for Derek to get handsy, and his palm grips her ass hard enough for her to yelp and shove him again, but she's so little against his large frame that he doesn't even budge.

By the time I get to her, the paramedic dude-bro behind her is jostling her around to get to Derek, and she's in the middle of a full-blown fight.

"Let go," I snap at the paramedic who doesn't listen at first until I reach out and yank on his hair hard.

"Ow! What the fuck?" he says before turning to see who did it. "Sorry, Drake, I didn't…" he clams up and releases Derek's shirt, giving Sunday room to slip out of the chaos and back against the booth.

"Yeah, you sure didn't." I smile. That's the normal reaction, being a girl standing at over six feet and formed from years of rugby and training turns the heads of men, and not in the good kind of way. I'm pretty used to them being more scared of me than turned on, and I don't mind. *They can't handle me anyway, and scaring them shitless is more fun than sex.*

I turn around to face the idiot who grabbed Sunday and cock my head to the side, looking at him. Out of the corner of my eye, I can see both Boone and Judd approaching as Brighton watches on from the bar. I have a choice to make: let them handle it or do it myself.

Derek opens his mouth to defend himself, but I'm in the kind of mood to hit first and ask questions later. *Handle it myself then.* My hand comes up, and before Derek can even register the movement, my closed fist collides with his face, and the bar erupts in gasps and chatter.

Blood pours from his nose, and an explosion of pain ripples across my knuckles, but when he drops his hands, pride bubbles up in a sharp, wicked laugh at the sight of the ring imprints littering his skin.

"Okay, that fucking hurt," I choke under my breath. *Why is his face so hard...*

Derek looks at the blood in his hand and back up to me with vicious intent. He charges me, but I'm quicker and drop my stance in preparation for his attack, wrapping my arms around his middle and pushing him back into the crowd. His back hits a table, and glass goes flying. He tries again, his movements sloppy with unbridled rage and his feet slipping in the spilled drinks beneath him.

"Oh fuck off, you water buffalo! We were just having fun!" he grunts and tries to attack again.

"Let it go, Derek." A hand wraps around the back of his neck as he makes to hit me, and Brighton hovers behind him, fingers digging into his skin. "It's bad enough you're a creep, don't stick around to get your ass kicked in front of all these people."

I expect him to make a girl joke, but Brighton doesn't; he just squeezes Derek tighter when he tries to fight the hold. He gives it one more go, but Brighton hauls him backwards, "Get. Out."

Derek scrabbles away, his idiot friends on his tail, and Brighton looks at Sunday, "I'm good. Nothing he hasn't tried before." The muscle in his jaw ticks at her answer, but he looks to me, his eyes doing a quick scan.

"Good here too," I say quickly to get him to stop, unprepared for the tingle of warmth his gaze gives me. "Fine, promise. Super chill!" I spit out between my laughter.

When Brighton finally turns away, he runs into Boone, who says a few things before starting to clear out the bar. I look down at my hand, flexing it sorely and slip off the rings one by one and shove them into my pocket before they get swollen on.

"Nice punch," Cosy says, coming up beside me and tilting her head back. "His nose will be crooked even after a trip to the emergency room.

"I wish it would stop him from being a creep," I say, the adrenaline still coursing through my veins. *Fuck, I love punching men.*

"Just means you get to punch him again in the future." She winks at me and backs away to find Kaia.

"You're not wrong," I call out with a tipsy smile on my face.

Brighton

erek barks insults all the way around the corner and out of sight. "I'll clear out the front," Boone yells, and slaps my shoulder on his way past. I scan across and spot the Hillcats that stuck around, huddled in a tight circle, talking, and lean on the bar with both hands flat to the surface as I watch them.

Rhea handled herself well—better than expected—and I admire her for sticking up for Sunday. My sister may be tough; she may come into the Hollow covered in bruises from rugby or exhausted after a twelve-hour shift. But she's still my little sister, and those are things I can't stop from hurting her. Creeps inside my bar are a different story. I try to keep my distance, give her space—but tonight, with Derek... Sometimes I wish self-control weren't my best trait.

I wet my bottom lip and stare at the liquor above my head, calling to me like a bad habit. Rum makes the tremor stop, but it would make everything else worse. I roll my neck out and listen to the string of complaints as Boone clears the bar forty-five minutes before closing. There's an impossible knot between my shoulders, created from tension and the weight of my own bullshit.

"Brighton?" A voice breaks through the thick blanket of stress fog and settles at my feet. I look down to see Rhea standing there, cradling her hand. *No one really calls me that anymore*, I want to say to her, but she speaks again. "Do you think I could get some ice?"

"You hurt yourself?" The words slip out with a hint of concern, and I grind my teeth together to keep my mouth shut.

"It's not that bad—"

"Killjoy!" Boone cuts her off with a sharp bark of the name they call me on the field to get my attention, *'it's because you're a fucking buzzkill, Bri. Loosen up.'* I turn to see him at the other end of the bar, waving me down. I close the gap, running my hand through my hair as I go, trying to get straight before my mind wanders too far and I can't get it back.

"What?" I snap, leaning into his gravity.

"Cosy is too drunk to drive, so I'm going to play taxi driver," he says, "let Rhea know to meet us out front in five?"

I look over my shoulder at her, still standing by the bar. She looks smaller than usual as she tries to hide the pain on her face.

"I'll take her," I blurt out.

"You'll what?" Boone's face curls up in confusion.

"I should check out her hand, just in case. I don't want her suing the Hollow cause she broke something and can't play rugby." I say.

"Suing—" Boone stares at me like I have five heads. "Never mind. Just don't screw any of Sunday's friends. That's not a mess I'm equipped to clean up," Boone says quickly as if I'm the brother with that kind of agenda.

I narrow my eyes at him. "I've never tried to fuck her." The look has him confessing like he can't hold it in.

Boone's been in love with Kaia Keegan since he laid eyes on her. She strutted into our house like she always belonged there after only knowing Sunday for a single day. I remember when she was all pigtails and attitude. Not much has changed, not her attitude or the way Boone loves her. She was strictly Sunday's annoying best friend for a long time. It wasn't until later that Kaia demanded his friendship, too. Boone crossed a line that day, and we all knew he'd never come back from it.

I personally hate it. I hate seeing him sad that way, but he knows what he wants, and settling is something Boone has never been good at. So torturing himself is the only answer in his mind.

"Yeah, following her around like a kicked dog is so much better," I grumble, and his jaw clenches tightly. "Go. I got this Hillcat. Lock the door on the way out, take the rest home."

"If something happens to her, you're dealing with Sunday," Boone warns.

"She's five foot three and weighs a hundred pounds, even full of booze," I say, acting scared, but Boone pulls a smile to my face, and some of the tension seeps out.

"She bites," he reminds me, pointing to the Sunday-shaped scar on his arm; it's one of the only places not covered in tattoos. Boone says it's a branding and deserves as much respect as the story behind it, but I think both my siblings are full of shit.

"Take her home before she starts gnawing on the furniture." I grab a few bottles of water we keep under the bar for the staff and hand them to him before he leaves.

I inhale, rolling out my shoulders before I turn back to Rhea, her massive brown eyes on Boone as he goes. I know what an adrenaline high looks like. A lot of the guys overseas slip in and out of them like it's second nature because over there, being on high alert will save your life. But she's standing alone in the Hollow, nursing a bruised hand, half-cut on cheap drinks and too many shots.

I take a second to think about it before filling a bucket of ice and moving out from behind the bar. "Follow," I say, and she snaps out of her trance, her head tracking my every step.

"Are you going to kill me?" Rhea asks. "'Cause I think I could take you..." she stops to hiccup before she finishes, "but I'm down a hand, and if I'm being honest for a whole minute, I thought Boone was standing beside you."

"My first aid kit is upstairs," I explain to her.

"Right." She narrows her eyes at me, "...just Brighton here."

"No one calls me that, it's just Bright," I tell her.

"Has anyone ever told you that you *aren't* very bright?" She narrows her eyes at me and snorts, "Okay, that makes you sound stupid, but I didn't mean it like that... I mean like..." she giggles, and the sound makes my jaw clench. *Please stop.*

"Spit it out," I tell her, just trying to get her to focus.

"I meant like..." Her feet shift against the floor and echo through the empty bar. "It's so quiet in here..." She gets distracted and looks around. "We are *super* alone, cool..." She giggles again, and the sound is surprisingly sweet and unexpected from a woman who looks like her.

Rhea Drake is all sharp curves and even stronger lines. She's six one, maybe six two, with a body built to contest most of the guys on the men's rugby team. She snaps her fingers at me and then hisses when the pain trickles up her arm from using them.

"And I'm the stupid one between the two of us," I huff.

"I meant that you aren't bright in *aura*," she explains.

"Aura?" I stare at her.

"You glow really dark red, almost *black*. Everyone has one. Sunday glows butter yellow, and Cosy is blue!" she says, and it's then that I realize she's lost the plot and there's no coming back from her tangent. "They even change! Like human mood rings." Her face gets sad again as she remembers something.

"Alright. Let's go get that hand looked at, and you can tell me about this aura thing..." I say. I have no idea what she's talking about, but it works because she follows me to the stairs. "Just be careful, they're steep," I tell her, and let her go first.

The last thing I need is her slipping and falling down the stairs. I keep in time with her, and as I reach the top, I tell her that it's open. She looks back at me nervously, and I sigh, stepping up to share the narrow step, chest to chest, before I pop the door open. She's staring at me when I turn my head back. Even in the dark, she's bright like a star. *Have you always been this warm? Too close, Brighton. Take a step back.* She smells like booze, sweat, orange, and sage. It fills my nose and makes it hard to listen to myself when she's staring at me like that. I watch her throat bob roughly as I gently nod my head toward the open door.

"In you go," I say, swallowing the unexpected warmth.

I close the door behind us as she wanders into the apartment. It's industrial, like most of downtown Harbor is, with exposed brick walls, metal in the high ceilings, and cold, dark flooring. I'm not much of a decorator, and the only thing in the apartment is a large rug that my daughter, Daisy, picked out when I moved into the place. I think it's ugly, but she loves it.

"I like your rug," Rhea says.

I close my eyes with a sigh. *Of course she does.*

"Sit down," I instruct, and she sinks onto the old leather couch with a pout. I grab the first aid kit from under the sink, a bottle of water, and a towel from the cupboard, along with the ice, to bring back to her. I lower to the coffee table across from her and rest on it, holding out my hand to her. "Let's see," I say, and she allows me to take it. Two busted knuckles, but the hand doesn't seem to be swelling too badly, other than that. "I'm going to clean those cuts," I tell her, and she looks like she's going to be sick.

"Anyone ever tell you that you suck, Killjoy?" She hiccups again.
Often.

"What color is, uh—" I dig in the bag for the antiseptic wipes, ignoring her protests, "—Kaia?"

"Like a hazy pink," she hisses as I touch the wipe to the open cut. I hold her wrist tighter to keep her from pulling away. "Same as Boone," she slurs, and I give her an eyebrow. "I don't pick the colors, I just see them."

"Water." I hand the bottle to her from beside me, and she scowls like she might argue with me, but I stare back, and she quietly concedes to being taken care of. "What about you?" I ask her as she struggles with the bottle between her knees. I reach out and unscrew the lid for her, still holding onto her sore hand.

"I can't see my own," she scoffs, bringing the bottle to her lips.

"Oh, sorry, I didn't know there were rules to seeing invisible color clouds…" I groan, almost cracking a smile as I clean the other hand.

"Ow," she grumbles, the sound coming from the base of her throat. "Reading auras is a serious thing, Brighton Black." Her face is twisted into a grouchy, pain-licked expression. "The color of your *invisible cloud*," she mocks, almost spilling her water, "means something important!"

"Alright, Hellcat. Simmer," I warn her, and she smiles at the nickname, making that tingle of warmth make a secondary appearance in the depths of my chest. She might actually be the most agreeable person I've ever met, and that's saying something for my sister's friends.

"You said Sunday is yellow. What does it mean?" I ask her as I finish with her hand and give it back. I lay the towel in my lap and start piling the ice into it with my hand as she inspects the cleaning job I did.

"Warm, authentic," Rhea says, taking another sip of water. She pushes a piece of her thick, black hair behind her ear, "— joy. Sunday radiates joy."

"I can't argue with that." I tie up the towel in a knot to close the ice inside. "Hand." I put my palm up for hers, and she slowly obliges. I could just as easily give her the ice to hold herself, but I'm selfishly enjoying our conversation, as silly as it might be. "And the pink?"

She stares at me for a long moment, no doubt trying to decipher whether or not I'm messing with her or really want to know.

"Come on, tell me." I encourage her.

"Unconditional love, but super sensitive to others' emotions, and it makes them wild cards," she says with a shrug when I nod. Not exactly as dead-on as Sunday's, but pretty close.

"And dark red?" I ask her, prodding at what had started this whole conversation. She's searching my face for something, but I can't quite figure it out. I want to ask her when she opens her mouth again. Red is bad, I can see it without her even explaining.

"You've been really nice to me, Brighton, and I'm feeling much better. Maybe I should just—" She pushes from the couch, but the booze hits her like a brick wall, and she gags once, almost trips, and then sinks back to the couch.

"Why don't you just lie down here, and I'll take you home once I get all this cleaned up?"

"Yeah." She nods, "That's a..." She starts to clumsily kick off the boots she's wearing, but the zippers are stuck, so I lean down and run my fingers along the back of her calf, pulling it down and off her foot. She curls up on the couch without finishing her sentence and is out cold before I can even tell her that she can't sleep here.

"You're an idiot." I tilt my head back and scold myself for even bringing her upstairs.

"Stable," she hums in her half-awake state, and I look down at her, hair splayed across her face as she wiggles deeper into the couch. "But...angry. So angry."

I couldn't tell if it's adorable or annoying that she talks in her sleep, but I cover her with the patchwork blanket hanging over the back and leave her there to sleep.

I t's dark, smells like toast, apples, and that candle Cosy gave me as a housewarming present—one I've been too scared to light in the last three years. I roll over, leather crunching beneath me, as I slowly open my eyes and find myself in a house that isn't mine, on a couch that is definitely not mine.

I hook my good hand over the back and lift myself just enough to peer over the edge. "*Oh,*" I gasp softly, seeing Brighton half-naked in...*his*... kitchen. Right. I punched someone last night—Derek! And now I'm sleeping on Brighton Black's couch in my socks, and *holy shit, my hand hurts*. I look at the swollen, irritated knuckles and curse drunk Rhea for doing whatever she wants.

My eyes flicker back up, running down the broad expanse of Brighton's bare back. Unlike his brother, his tattoos are a little more sparse but just as impressive. Across his back, inked in heavy black between his shoulders, is a raven with its wings spread wide and talons poised for attack. Just below is an impressive scar that seems to nestle into the lower half of his shoulder blades and curl to the front of his body in a twisted, almost beautiful curve. His arms are painted in various black-and-gray tattoos, leaving patches of his tan skin open down to his wrists.

He turns, and I sink against the couch, but he's wearing headphones and doesn't even look up from whatever is in the pan he's holding. Starting at his shoulder, coming down over the left side of his chest is a bundle of daisies that float across his heart. A stark contrast to his

28

back, light and dark. Only complemented by the long chain that tangles around a pair of dog tags.

Brighton clears his throat, and I realize I've been caught. Heat rushes to my face as I sink back into the cushion to die a slow, embarrassing death. I hear him shuffling around for a few moments before his footsteps grow louder and the coffee table creaks loudly. When I roll over to face him, he's got a shirt on, *thank god,* and is holding a plate of food.

"Hungry?" he asks.

Say no, Rhea. Put your shoes on and get a cab.

"Starving," I say with a tight, uncomfortable smile. He hands me the plate, pushing off the table and wandering back into the kitchen as I pick up a burnt piece of toast and shift on the couch to get comfy.

You're sitting in your best friend's older brother's apartment without your shoes while eating toast on his couch. What the fuck is wrong with you?

"Coffee?" he asks. From this angle, he looks a hundred percent more intimidating. I nod gently and take the mug from him, reaching out with my bad hand, only for him to shake his head and wait for me to take it with the other. "Do you want something for the pain?"

Sure, yeah, actually instead, you can just shoot me now because explaining this to Sunday later is going to kill me anyway.

"That would be... awesome..." I grind out. I'm practically choking on thick shame.

"Rhea, we didn't have sex," he says sharply, staring at me like I should know better. "You passed out drunk on the couch after ranting about some color thing you do." He explains, but all I can focus on is the rogue curl falling against his forehead.

"Oh, thank god." I gasp and set the plate on the table with a gentle thud. "Auras."

Brighton shakes his head and wanders away, "Yeah, that's the party trick."

"So nothing else happened?" I ask, turning on the couch to face him in the kitchen. He leans his back against the counter and takes a drink of his coffee.

"You might have broken your hand?" he shrugs. "You should go in and have it looked at."

"Why were you naked, then?" I interrupt.

"Shirtless," he corrects, scowling. "It's what I sleep in," he adds, his eyebrows scrunched up. "You're in my home."

"Right," I agree with that. "And it's fine. I'd know if it was broken. Been there, done that."

Brighton watches me carefully, not saying a word as I ramble through the embarrassment and look around the apartment for my boots. He points with his coffee to the front door, and there they are, sitting neatly up against the wall. I nod, standing and stealing a piece of toast off the plate to slip between my teeth.

"I'm sorry about last night, getting drunk probably wasn't the smartest decision considering everything that's happening, but it sure felt good in the moment," I say, looking at my bruised hand. "Luckily, I have an excuse for the principal about my hand and won't be out of a job and a condo..." A pathetic laugh bubbles from me.

"I heard," he offers with a tight jaw. "Loveday is pretty good at renovations if you need someone to do repairs—"

"I don't even know how I'm going to afford all of this bullshit, I'm going to have to get another job that doesn't interfere with school hours and rugby..." I sigh, rambling on and completely forgetting that I'm standing in the middle of his living room.

"Thanks for, uh..." I gesture at the couch.

"Thanks for punching Derek," he says, setting down his coffee. "Hey." He closes the gap between us as I try to pull on my boots with one hand. I swear, take a deep breath and try again.

"Sit." He palms the back of the stool at the island and turns it toward me.

"I'm not letting you put my shoes on, I'm full up on doing embarrassing things in front of Sunday's brother," I groan and keep working at the boot, two seconds away from leaving in my socks.

"I'm the one who took them off you. Now *sit*." It rolls off his tongue as a gentle demand, and when I look up, he nods at the seat, not taking no for an answer. I pad over to the stool as he switches spots, grabs my boots, and squats down in front of me. Even on the stool, his shoulders sit level with my hips, and he looks up at me like it's the most normal thing in the world to be putting my boots on.

It's fine that Brighton's face is level with your fucking vagina, Rhea. Everything is totally normal and fine.

"You can pick up shifts at the Hollow," he says, swallowing hard as his finger pulls at the first zipper.

"I couldn't work a bar even if it was only opening beers and flirting with men, Brighton," I huff, and a tiny smile forms on his stern face.

"Bright," he corrects me, "and we need more security on game nights. And you happen to have a better right hook than my current guy, so..."

"A bouncer?" I snort. "You'd pay me to hit men?"

"I'd pay you to make sure no one is causing trouble," he warns slowly as he palms my calf and slips the second boot on, his hand eclipses it and makes it look tiny in his grasp. *That's not an easy thing to do.*

"Why?" I ask him as he zips it.

"You look after Sunday." He inhales and rises to his full height as I slip from the stool. We come chest to chest, and I get the faintest feeling of deja vu as his eyes flicker downward. He clears his throat and steps back. "You can start tomorrow night, there's a hockey game."

I nod and move toward the door, "Hey, you wouldn't happen to have a spare room?"

"Don't push it." He shakes his head and waits for me to take a few steps before closing the door behind me.

Every time the bell rings, it vibrates through my skull, and I'm counting down the hours until I can wrap up here and get fresh air.

"Ms. Drake." Annie—an oddly short seventh-grade girl who reminds me of Sunday—stands at my desk.

"Hey Annie," I sit up a little straighter and lean on my sticker-bombed desk. Being the most disrespected teacher in the school, *as well as the most loved*, is a hard gig. Teachers don't take me seriously because I teach art, but my room is a space for anyone. Kids who can't handle the school cafeteria 'cause it's too loud at lunch, ones I find sitting in the hallway, because they were kicked out of class. Most just use my room as a study hall during free periods.

I also have the biggest room in the school, next to the gymnasium, and that always comes up in conversation at staff meetings and during teacher development days. I have free rein of the space, and unlike most rooms, it's darker inside. I replaced all the bright white lights with dimmable ones, and art covers every ounce of the walls. Kids are allowed to paint and repaint the tables if they have an idea, and art is more than just marks and exams.

It's expression and emotion.

"I've been working on this for weeks, and I can't get it right. Can you tell me what's wrong with it?" She hands me her notebook, and I suppress the small grunt of pain as I take it with my sore hand.

It's a sketch of an elderly lady feeding ducks at the park. I recognize the tree from the space down past Main, Twindleway Park. It's got a big pond and a dog run that Cosy loves to use.

"Why did you choose her?" I ask her, looking over the messy pencil sketch.

"Uh," Annie pauses to think.

"There must have been a reason," I encourage, admiring each little duck she took the time to create.

"I guess I liked that she was so old, feeding a bunch of baby ducks..." She chews her lip, and her shoulders sag like she said the wrong thing.

"Then there's nothing wrong with it," I hand it back to her.

"There has to be," she sounds disappointed.

"Nope." I shake my head. "You capture her age with grace in these lines, and every duck you drew has its own personality, Annie. It's beautiful."

Annie stares down at it, and I can tell something is still bugging her.

"What did you think was wrong with it?" I ask her as the second bell rings for late students. "Why don't you stay here and think on it? You have... English next?" I ask her, and pick up the phone on my desk as she nods. "I'll let Mr. Disson know you aren't feeling well, and you can hang out here with the seniors, maybe one of them can help you figure it out?"

Annie nods a little more enthusiastically that time.

"Mr. Disson," I say as he answers on his end.

"What do you want, Ms. Drake?" he snaps, and I can hear the dust spit from his crusty eighty-year-old lips.

"Annie Gaul is supposed to be in your English class right now, but she projectile vomited all over my room three minutes ago and is being sent to the nurse's office."

"Sure she did," Mr. Disson grunts.

"Are you calling me a liar?" I challenge him, and he says nothing. "Excellent. Have a good afternoon." I hang up the phone, "If you see him, give him a two-step wobble—sell the dizziness." I laugh, and she cradles her notebook closer to her chest as she backs away to find a quiet spot to sit, as most of my senior class floods in and finds their own.

"Wow, creeping in on the second bell, how downright cool of you all…" I tease and push from my desk to start class. "I want you all to make a card, including a poem for someone special in your life, and I expect to have twenty-one cards on my desk tomorrow addressed to me." I joke, and the class gives me a few pity laughs. "Get to work," I say, and inhale to keep my hangover at bay.

I sit down, checking my cell phone to see a few missed messages from my Mom and a few from the girls. And one from my brother.

REID

Mom's being a nutcase again. Send help.

I stare at the message, and the headache only gets worse. It's probably nothing, but I'd swing by the house before practice to check on him anyway. I set the phone face down, looking over the class once before laying my head on the desk and counting to ten to keep from vomiting.

"How does it feel?" Kaia turns my hand over in hers, "who taped this?"

"Uh," I swallow, looking around the busy locker room. "Me."

"Liar." Her eyes snap to mine. "I've seen your tape jobs with my own eyes, and even with two good hands, you're like an unattended toddler." She narrows them on me, and I feel the burn from her glare.

"Stop it," I grind out.

Kaia cocks her head to the side and gives me the look.

"Brighton."

"I knew it!" She squeezes my hand, and I hiss at her. "You dirty slut," she says, holding tighter. "Tell me what happened, right now!"

"Nothing, he cleaned the cuts, wrapped them up, and I blacked out on his couch," I confess, "when I woke up, he was half-naked in the kitchen cooking me breakfast, and he helped me put my boots on. Did you know his hands were the size of two of mine?"

"Yes," Kaia says instantly, "back up, half-naked?"

"Half. Naked." I emphasize.

"God, I bet he's fucking packing under that shirt. I've seen Boone. Those brothers are built for roughhousing with wild animals." Kaia groans, letting go of my hand.

"Imagine a Discovery Channel show of just them, half-naked, wrestling bears." I tease.

"They *are* bears." She moans louder. "Wait, you said he put on your boots..." Kaia refocuses on the conversation.

"I tried...more than once to do it myself, but couldn't get them on, and he wouldn't take no for an answer!" I slump over and put my head against her shoulder. "Sunday is going to kill me."

"For what? Her brother is a big boy." Kaia laughs. "A *very...very* big boy." The moaning returns, and I pinch her arm to make her stop. "Ow!" She slaps my hand, "You don't have to tell her what happens in the upstairs of the Hollow, stays there."

"I do, though," I say, "he offered me shifts at the bar to help pay off the renovations that I'm going to have to do to the condo."

"I've known those men since I was seven years old, and you got Bright on his knees, at your service and offering jobs?" Kaia starts laughing like it's the funniest thing she's ever heard, but I don't find the humor in the situation. "Never in my life did I think he was capable of being wrapped around someone's finger; he probably keeps hunting knives in every pocket just to cut the strings and yet..." She stares at me with big brown eyes and an expression on her sharp face that screams over exaggeration.

"It's just a job, Killer," I warn her before she starts to fantasize too much. Once that starts, she's impossible to reel in, her imagination takes hold, and she starts messing around in everyone's business with plans that no one asked her to make. "I know that look, it's a couple shifts at the Hollow."

"For now," Kaia hums, standing up and hauling me off the bench with one hand. "When's your first shift?"

"After practice," I say tightly.

"Sunday!" Kaia barks. "Rhea is starting at the Hollow tonight so she can drive you over for your shift instead of me!" she says, backing away and darting out of the locker room before it can explode.

"I'm going to kill her," I grumble under my breath and turn to see Sunday, in all her adorable glory, looking at me, confused. She finishes her braid as she closes the gap between us and makes a face. "I needed to pick up a second job to help with the renos, and there was a bouncer position opening up. Brighton offered it to me tentatively..." I say, waiting for Sunday to flip out.

"Brighton?" She giggles at the way I say his name. "Kaia's probably pissed 'cause she's asked a billion times and he always says no." Sunday teases, "I, on the other hand, can't believe it took this long to get a carpool buddy," she squeals.

"So you're not mad?" I ask, a little scared that she might be, and hiding it well.

"Reaper, this is going to be so much fun," she says and skips from the locker room onto the field.

I join the rest of them on the field as Coach starts to give us the rundown of what the next couple of weeks will look like. Kaia still leaves a space for Addy at her left, and it makes me a little sad to know it'll always be there. Addy had left for California the summer before; it's been nearly six months without her, but she is thriving in San Francisco on the team there. We were all just trying to get used to the Addy-sized hole she left in our chosen family.

"Drake, what the hell happened?" Coach points to my hand, and I tuck it behind my back sheepishly with a tight smile on my face.

"Would you believe me if I told you that I fought a cougar to save a baby duck on the side of the road on the way to work this morning?" I ask, and she narrows her icy blue eyes on me. "Bar fight, at the Hollow."

Coach sighs. "Please stop getting in fights on and off the field."

Kaia groans, "It was at Sunday's defence."

Coach looks at all of us and raises an eyebrow; the implications of her repeating herself are clear. No more fights. She runs practice hard, whether or not she's trying to make me feel punished, the drills put me on my ass, and by the time the sun starts to set over the fields, I'm completely drained of life. My arms and legs burn like I've been running for days, and my lungs are screaming for reprieve as the girls join me to stretch.

"I'm going to shower, and then we can head over?" I say to Sunday, who gives me a quick nod and rolls over in the grass to stretch out her hips. I climb from the ground, my muscles jelly as I struggle to get to the locker room. Inside, it's quiet, most of the players are still on the field, and I take the opportunity to get clean for the first time in twenty-four hours.

The water runs hot and feels good on my skin as I toss my fingers through my hair to loosen the braids and get the dirt out of each strand of pitch black hair. I close my eyes, and Brighton, half-naked, flashes across my vision. *Shit.* I open my eyes and stare at the faded teal tiles of the shower room wall, and then look around before closing them again to find him standing there.

The tattoo stretches across his back as he moves around the kitchen, and I continue to shower with my eyes closed to keep the image there a little longer. He turns and looks at me over his shoulder, and the door to the locker room slams shut, causing my eyes to shoot open.

I reach out and turn the handle to the right.

Cold. I need a cold shower.

Brighton

S unday and Rhea crash through the front door of the Hollow twenty minutes before puck drop, and I instantly regret hiring one of my sister's friends. I remember quickly why I haven't allowed it before: Sunday is going to be a menace.

"You're late," I say, cleaning one of the high bar tables that surround the dance floor as Boone sets up the projector in the corner for the game.

"Coach ran us hard because Rhea's a dumbass," Sunday giggles, throwing her bag behind the bar.

"Punishment for being a tough guy." She holds her hand in the air and smiles at me. I roll out my shoulders and go back to cleaning. Ignoring them both and their excuses. Sunday walks Rhea through some of the easy stuff, like where to put her crap and where all the important things are behind the bar. It's all things Rhea knows from being around for so long, but Sunday insists. I keep my eyes on them as they move around the Hollow, stopping periodically to talk to people flooding in from the streets to catch the game.

The Huskies are looking good, better than they have in a long time, and if they want to make the playoffs, they'll need to keep that energy up. They were playing Pittsburgh tonight, and it'll be a hard-fought game. I personally don't care, win or lose, people will drink.

"Brighton?" Rhea's voice floats over the white noise from behind me, and I turn to see her standing at the end of the bar as I fill the ice buckets.

"Bright," I remind her, and she winces but nods. "What do you need?"

"Where do you want me tonight?" she asks.

"Uh—" I clear my throat. "Just keep an eye on the girls tonight. Sunday, Maggie, and Ida are working tables. If anyone gets handsy or rough, toss them out. No warnings, just get rid of them."

"I can handle that," she says, looking around. She's wearing a tiny black crop top that scoops around her muscular, tattooed arms and shows off the dark ink on her stomach above the waist of her skin-tight black jeans. "Did you hear me?" she asks, and I look up from her boots to meet her gaze. "Do I... like need a name tag?"

"That could be fun! Think of all the stupid shit I could put on mine!" Boone interjects from behind me as he hops down from the stage and rounds the bar. "I actually have something for you," he says to her, and starts digging in a bin on the floor. He holds up a Hollow T-shirt that doesn't look big enough for her and flips it around to show her the back.

"I make grown men cry?" Rhea says, cocking her head to the side. For a second, I think she might say no. The alternative is worse. She whips off her tank top, standing in the bar in nothing but a sports bra, and she does this stupid grabby thing with her hand. Boone laughs and chucks it at her so she can pull the T-shirt over her head. She motions scissors with her fingers as Boone pulls them out and starts laughing as he helps her cut off the bottom half of the already tiny shirt.

Fuck me.

"It's perfect, Bobo," Rhea coos, and Boone stands back to admire his work.

"Not quite," he says, his fingers pick at the now ratty hem around her taut abdomen. I bite down on my tongue to suppress the unreasonably jealous groan that rumbles at the base of my throat. Boone pulls the fabric away from her ribcage and cuts two narrow slits in the sides that flatten into rough diamond shapes as the shirt stretches back over her skin. He does the other side to match and puts the scissors between his smile as he backs away to admire his work.

"What do you think?" At first, I think she's asking Boone, but she's staring at me with her arms out at her sides.

I swallow tightly, watching her bare, tattooed stomach rise and fall with each shallow breath she takes as she waits for me to answer. *I'm going to kill Boone.*

"Cat got your tongue, Bri?" He teases like he can feel my thoughts imploding. I want to flip him off, but that would tell Rhea exactly what I'm thinking, and that's quite possibly the most dangerous answer possible.

"It's not workplace-appropriate," I clip.

"Perfect," Boone says with pride. He takes her hand and gives her a twirl before tying the discarded length of her shirt around his forehead to push back his unruly brunette hair.

"I can change if—" Rhea asks, clearly concerned by the tight expression on my face, but I can't tell her I'm not pissed off with her, because that would mean admitting all the other reasons why I'm trying to keep a straight face.

"It was a joke," I say, "as long as you're in a Hollow shirt, you're dressed for work." She shrugs, seemingly satisfied with that answer. "And Reaper, no drinking if you're working," I warn her, and take the chance to pull myself out of her gravity. If I stood there any longer, I'd burn a hole through her.

I start to restock the bar, and as the Hollow starts to reach capacity, I take a second to scan the crowd for her. She's leaning against a booth, talking to some of Kaia's firefighting buddies with a smile on her face, but her body language suggests she's telling them off. Boone rests against the bar with his arms crossed as Sunday slides up to sit on top.

"That's unsanitary, Day. Get down." I smack her thigh with the back of my hand, but she doesn't budge.

"She's doing really well," she says, reaching for a bottle of water. "Some of them in the back were getting rough and almost knocked over Maggie, but she calmed them down really fast."

"Good, that's why she's here," I say in a clipped tone. "Game's turning sour, keep an eye on table nine, and the line back there." I point to a group of guys along the wall who are more drunk than I'd like. As I say it, Rhea pushes off from her spot and crosses the bar to two of them, shoving once before she grabs the larger one by the back of the collar.

All three of us watch as she cocks her head to the side and smiles brightly at him. It's not a friendly smile; it's the kind that says *I could kill you if I wanted to,* and it makes Sunday giggle like an idiot beside me.

Thankfully, the noise comes from her because the heat that licks across my chest is embarrassing and shouldn't be there. I curse myself for helping her the other night because it's easier to keep myself separated from Sunday's friends by avoidance, and I had let Rhea walk right in the front door. *Get your shit together, Brighton.* I flex my hands and dig my fingers into my bicep as she herds the group of men out the front door as the Huskies score to win the game with seconds left on the clock.

The Hollow erupts in cheers, and somewhere in the bar, a loud crash sounds, causing my entire body to seize up in defence. Boone's hand wraps around my bicep, his grip tight enough to ground me in reality before I can even think about slipping.

"Breathe," he says, scanning the bar. "It's just a tipped table. I'll go help Rhea."

He says it, but it's harder than that to fill my lungs, and it feels like someone dumped ice down my spine. My finger itches for a trigger like my hands are still permanently attached to a weapon. I blink slowly, and it's not until that first, deep breath that Boone's grip disappears.

I didn't even notice Sunday slip from the counter, but she hands me a cup of water and helps two girls with their drinks, her eyes constantly drifting toward me in concern. I hate that they have to be on guard like that, or maybe I hate that they're so good at it after all this time. They shouldn't have to be the first line of defence between me and the PTSD that blankets my senses at any small moment of trouble.

It's just a tipped table.

In my head, it never is. To my reflexes, it's gunfire.

"Focus, Major." Ghosts of my past flicker across my mind and paralyze me.

I inhale slowly and bring the ice-cold water to my lips, downing it all and letting the frigid temperature shock my system out of defence mode. I nod to Sunday, who's still staring while she works, and she gives me a small smile in return. Six years of tours, back and forth, balancing the line between warzone and what should be normal life. But the lines blur, and normal life quickly becomes a battlefield, and my siblings are the only people willing to stand in the contact zone.

I spend hours reminding myself that I did this for Daisy, joining the military, doing what I did. I did it for her, and now the fight continues to hold myself together long enough to show her that I could be a good dad on home soil, too. I have to make all the blood and sweat worth it. *So much blood.*

My fingers itch for a drink.

"Brighton?" Rhea's voice makes me huff with relief. Her timing is impeccable, and it's going to drive me insane.

"Bright, Rhea. It's Bright," I remind her, and her dark brows furrow. "What?"

"Where's the broom?" she asks, her fingers rapping against the black bar top.

"Not your job," I say with a shake of my head.

"There's glass everywhere," she argues, and it takes everything in me to keep a straight face. She doesn't look as sad as she did the other day, her eyes have a little color back in them, and her cheeks are rosy from the heat in the bar.

"Boone will sweep," I say above the chatter.

She opens her mouth to push the subject, but studies the expression on my face and thinks better of it as Sunday slides in front of me to grab a few menus from the slot below.

"Why don't you both throw an order in and take food upstairs to Daisy?" I say to Sunday, who gives me a sweet smile, her little hand squeezing into mine before she hands the menus off.

"Are you sure? There's still an hour until close," Rhea asks.

"Everyone needs to eat, and you threw the only rowdy people out. It's dead in here now," I say without looking around. I can tell by the noise that it, in fact, is not a dead bar, and she stares at me like I'm insane, but once I make up my mind, it's rare that I budge on a statement.

"Go," I say as Sunday comes around the bar. "I'll bring it up when Boone has it ready."

Rhea

"Bri's apartment is about as boring as you'd expect..." Sunday leads me upstairs to her brother's apartment, and I'm tempted to blurt out that I've already been inside, but I keep my mouth shut as she pops the bottom lock.

The smell of apple hits my nose again, mixed with something deeper and spicy, and I realize that it's Brighton's cologne. I close the door behind me softly and kick off my boots, sticky from spilled drinks, just in case there's glass on them.

"Daisy Bell, where are you?" Sunday calls out and disappears down the back hall. I hear a soft knock and a door far away clicks open as I slide onto a stool at the island. I stare across the gap to the kitchen sink and try to combat the memory of Brighton's impressive back as it threatens to sneak in.

I pull out my phone in a feeble attempt to distract myself from my surroundings and find a photo from Addy in the group chat. She looks so happy, and I try really hard not to be sad about it. Distance is hard, and as happy as I am for her, I miss her.

I type up a reply as Sunday returns with her niece in tow.

Daisy is a small carbon copy of her dad, but she looks like Sunday more than anything. With long blonde hair, big green eyes that clearly belong to her mother, and a grumpy scowl that definitely does not. She pulls her headphones out and sets them on the island to wave to me.

"Hi, Ms. Drake," she says.

"What did I tell you about that?" I shake my head. "Outside of school, it's just Rhea."

"Right." She offers a tight smile that mirrors her dad's annoyed face and grabs a bottle of water out of the fridge.

"Hey Daisy, what's that room?" I ask her and point to the one that's off the living room.

"Dad's office," she shrugs. "But he never uses it. I don't think I've ever seen him even go in there."

"Doesn't he have an office downstairs?" Sunday scowls.

"Yeah, I don't know. I think he's just being a weirdo," Daisy says, like that's a normal response.

"I didn't know the apartment had three bedrooms," Sunday says. "I always thought that was a closet."

"It's not very big in there. He keeps it locked, though."

"It's locked?" Sunday whips her head back to Daisy.

"Dad's *weird*," she says with a small laugh. I'm about to bring up the question of renting the mystery room again when Daisy's phone vibrates on the island.

"Are you still talking to that boy?" Sunday asks, derailing the conversation, snatching up Daisy's phone, who instantly flips out and reaches for it back.

"Auntie Day, don't," she snips, and Sunday laughs. "Please."

"Awfully defensive for a little girl who claims to be innocent. What are you, hiding on here?" She asks. "Is that little shithead sending you inappropriate texts because I promise not to tell Bri?"

"Oh my god," Daisy gags.

"What's your password again? What could be so important that you have to lock it down?" Sunday grumbles playfully.

"World domination. And pictures of paper road trip maps." Daisy was quick, and it made me giggle as Sunday admitted defeat and handed the phone over.

"My brother's obsession with maps is getting out of hand, and you enable it!" Sunday rolls her eyes and snaps her fingers at Daisy. "That glove compartment is a safety hazard."

"He unfolds them in his lap on drives and stares at them with this face on," Daisy makes a funny expression that's not angry but perplexed, as the front door clicks open and Brighton wanders inside with three plates balanced in his long arms. "It's funny watching him use them."

"What's funny?" He says in a gruff voice, sliding the plates to the counter.

"Your face," Sunday quips and reaches out for her burger. "Thank you," she says quickly and slides Daisy her plate. Brighton looks down at mine and pushes it toward me with a tiny nudge, and I give him a nod. Boone piles the plate high with spicy sweet potato fries, and the black bean burger looks delicious to my empty stomach.

Before I can even be grossed out about the tomato, Sunday reaches over and takes it off my burger to put on hers. Tomatoes are the one food group I cannot wrap my head around, wet little things that taste like nothing and make everything soggy. But for all my quiet complaints about them, I can't even bring myself to ask for the burger without them. Some deep-rooted fear of being a bother to someone has seeped into something as stupid as asking for no tomato. I sigh and try to ignore it and Brighton's intense stare as I start to eat.

After we finish, he washes the dishes while Sunday says goodnight to Daisy. Then we head back to Sunday's. My little pile of belongings beside her bright orange couch is depressing. I curl up on the tiny sofa, to the sound of my phone vibrating with messages from my family, and the tears flow, making my pillow wet as I fall asleep.

"You can't move that far," Cosy says and points to the board on the table. "You've got thirty feet," she says to me, and I slide the miniature back away from the monster we're fighting in Dungeons and Dragons. I chew on my lip and try to figure out another way to get Kaia's character out of the trouble we're in, but come up short.

"I cast suggestion," Sunday says, rolling her dice. "The hag hears the most beautiful trap music playing in the distance and starts to dance. She loves the music so much she may never stop dancing," she reads to them with a smile on her face. A natural twenty stares up at us all, and Cosy looks over her books.

"It hits." She shakes her head. "I hate that spell." She always says that, but she also never gets mad at Sunday for equipping it because it makes her happy.

"Can she do that?" Addy's boyfriend, Jensen, says over the iPad.

"Go away fuckboy," Kaia snips. "You were not invited to this session."

"Don't be like that." He smirks at her, and she flips him off. "I miss you too, Kaia," Jensen hums and kisses Addy's temple before disappearing off-screen.

"It was a good move, Sunny," Addy says, leaning over on her books to get closer to the camera.

"Thank you." Sunday sits a little taller as Cosy tries to figure out her next move as dungeon master. "Does anyone want another margarita?" she asks, tapping the table with her fingers. "Since our hag is dancing," she giggles as Cosy begrudgingly nods yes.

I follow Sunday through her dining room toward the kitchen and slide onto the counter as she starts dumping things into the blender without measuring. *That's why we're always so drunk.*

I try to stretch out my back, and when I reach my fingertips to the sky, it cracks loudly with a pop that makes Sunday turn her head to look at me.

"Was that your spine?" She sounds disgusted, and her face matches with a horrified look.

"Yes," I say, trying not to laugh or *cry.*

"Are you okay? Why did it make that noise?" She pauses midway through making drinks and stares at me.

"I'm sleeping on a sofa made for Smurfs..." I raise a brow and smirk.

"It's not that small." She rolls her eyes.

"You also don't own a single curtain," I groan, pointing to the massive floor-to-ceiling windows.

"It's aesthetic, and I like the sun!" She argues. "You cave troll!"

"They're east-facing windows!" The sun floods through them at five a.m., and while I am a morning person, I have never been *that* kind of morning person.

"Have you made any progress on finding a place to rent for a short term?" She asks. I know if I asked her, she wouldn't care how long I slept on her couch, but I can't do that to her. We both need our own space, and Sunday especially. She tended to get overwhelmed and anxious after too much social interaction, and while me being in her house right now didn't do that. It will build, and eventually she'll either break down or go insane quietly, so she didn't hurt my feelings.

"No," I choke out. "Everything is a year lease or hotels, which would get expensive fast when I'm already paying a mortgage and now renovations."

"You were the only person with a two-bedroom," Sunday sighs. All the other girls on the team either lived together or in studio apartments. There's no space for me anywhere.

Except...

"At least I have a job now." I shrug, "Well, a second one. That was really nice of Brighton."

The use of his full name made her face do that weird thing again. "Yeah..." I watch as she lines up the cups on the counter.

"How often does Daisy stay with him? Her mom lives in Harbor, right?" I ask.

"They trade weeks," Sunday says slowly, "she works over at the stadium."

"Cool, cool," I say with a nod. "And like, why doesn't Boone live with him?"

"They'd kill each other under the same roof." She says, not really paying attention to me. "Bri is all military, even now. Boone is..." She looks over at me and sighs. "Well, all *not*."

"Yeah," I agree, not having any clue what that means aside from Boone being a lunatic.

"I don't really blame Bobo, though," she continues, "Bri is hard to live with."

"Is he, like... a sloppy guy?" I ask her with my head tipped to the ceiling to avoid the burning gaze coming from her.

"Hey," Sunday says to get me to look at her. "What's with the twenty questions about Bri? You don't have a crush on him, do you?"

"No, no!" I raise my hands to further my point. *Well kinda.*

"Rhea," she narrows her eyes at me.

"Seriously, no crush!" I open my mouth to argue more, and she silences me with the violent sound of the blender churning over.

Her eyebrow cocks, and she dares me to start again.

"Do you think that room is really an office?" I ask her when the sound is cut, and she stares at me, confused. "In your brother's apartment. The locked room?"

"That's what this is about? I have no clue, it would be a miracle if you managed to get him to rent it to you," Sunday says.

"Why?" I ask. I didn't really know a whole lot about Brighton outside of what I've been told. Unlike his social butterfly twin, he kept his distance from us, was polite but short, and never hung around long enough to hold a conversation. It was like Sunday, and Boone had stolen all the extroverted energy and left him with the leftovers.

"Bri doesn't really like people in his space," Sunday explains, "like more than a usual person, and there's a lot to it, but I don't think he's roommate potential."

I think about that for a moment, the conversation I had with him the other night felt normal, but I was also very drunk, so maybe I'm imagining things. "But there's a chance I could convince him."

Brighton

"How do you handle that?" Rhea asks, sitting at the bar, shoving sweet potato fries between her lips while she listens to music. She pulls out one earphone, and the cord bounces on her shoulder. The Hollow is shut down for the night, and I'm running through the closing chores while Boone cleans the kitchen.

"What?" I grunt, shoving a door closed with my boot. It's becoming a consistent challenge to keep my eyes off her, but when she wears tight black pants and tiny fucking t-shirts, it's impossible not to admire every sculpted curve of her body.

"The empty sound?" she asks when she's finished chewing.

"Silence?" I furrow my brow at her. Only Rhea would find an issue with the quiet.

"Yeah, that." She snaps her fingers. When I don't respond, she takes it upon herself to fill said silence with her voice. "I won't even volunteer for after-school activities because it's scary. Makes everything feel haunted."

I pause, stocking the new bottles of vodka. That we can agree on, when everyone is gone, and the Hollow is empty... It does feel haunted. It's when the memories claw their way back into my skull and paint everything red.

"You're afraid of the dark?" I ask her with a huff, trying to seem normal. No one needs to find the skeletons that clank around in my closet.

"Nobody is afraid of the dark, Brighton," she scoffs. It's funny to see a woman so sure of herself pretend like she wasn't afraid of the monsters under the bed. She's Rhea Drake, for God's sake; people move out of her way when she moves through a crowd. I've seen the tackles she makes; *the monsters under her bed should be afraid of her.*

"Bright," I repeat myself for the hundredth time.

"People are afraid of what could be in the dark… It's the lack of control—the endless possibilities." She speaks absentmindedly as she picks up the burger and swallows tightly. I gaze down at it in her hands and notice Boone put tomatoes on it again, but I never hear her ask for it without them.

"Control the darkness." I shrug like it's a simple answer. "If you aren't afraid of what will come out of it, then it doesn't matter anymore."

"Oh yeah sure, good advice, Terminator." She rolls her eyes at me, giving me a phony salute, and takes a bite, chewing slower than usual. It's clear she's struggling, but I'm not going to say anything about it. Fighting with her about tomatoes isn't on my agenda tonight.

"What did you call me?" I pull out a few bottles, a piece of paper, and a glass, setting them on the counter. I still need to come up with the specials for next week before bed.

"You know, big as a black bear, cold as steel, meaner than a rabid animal, impossible to kill…" Her sentence trails off when she notices me staring at her. "I'm starting to feel like that's a nickname Kaia gave you in secret."

"Yeah," I say in a clipped tone. It's barely two minutes of silence before she's asking ridiculous questions again.

"What are you doing?" she asks, setting down the uneaten half of her burger. I look up from the bottles of liquor to her and find those massive dark eyes staring back at me, the red lights from the Hollow glimmering around inside like stars.

I clear my throat. *She's your little sister's best friend, and these hot flashes are because you haven't touched a woman in two years. Get it together.* If I just keep reminding myself of that, it will be easy to get the rest of my body to fall in line.

"Changing the drink menu for next week," I say to her, and she smiles.

"Literally the best day of the month is when you change the specials." The way she blurts it out is endearing, and she pushes up, dropping her headphones onto the counter and slamming her hands on the bar top to see the piece of paper.

"This is classified information, Hellcat." I hold the paper away from her and watch her cheeks turn pink as her eyebrow raises. "You know, a Hellcat. A bad-tempered, *violent* woman."

"I kind of like that." She shrugs it off and I realize that she's telling the truth. *You're a strange little thing.* "And please, I work here now. That should give me some kind of special insight!" She grabs for the paper, leaning further now, and if she loses her balance, she'll barrel roll into the back of the bar, so I move closer to get her to stop.

"It's blank." I show her.

"Do you decide on a whim?" She sounds excited.

"It just depends on how I feel, I guess..." I say with a shrug.

"Oh, the girls will get a kick out of this, straight and proper Brighton Black, creates the drink menus on a vibe!" She giggles.

"Hey. No." I raise my hand to her, "What happens when we lock the Hollow up stays here. You can't be spilling trade secrets," I warn her.

"You made that sound kinda cool, so I'm not going to argue, but just know it's adorable that you do it," she says, a little softer. The teasing in her voice is neutral as I back away from the bar top again.

"Do you want to help?" I ask her. *I shouldn't ask her.*

"Unless you want to kill customers and have to buy new glasses, I should probably stay on this side of the bar," she says, patting it gently and sinking back onto her stool.

"There's no one here to poison, Rhea," I say, and I can see the gears turn over as she considers it.

"It's probably not a good idea." She gives her head a shake and turns back to her fries, but it's pretty clear that she really wants to try.

"Don't be a chicken," I say to her.

Her eyes snap to meet mine, "I'm not a chicken."

"You're acting like one. What's the worst thing that can happen? You break a glass?" I scoff. "Sunday breaks two a night."

Rhea's teeth sink into her bottom lip. I flex my hand at my side to keep from reaching out to stop her from doing it, but she rises from the stool and takes a deep breath. I don't say a word as she rounds the bar and comes to stand next to me.

"What's the drink you made me the other night?" She asks after a moment of weird silence.

I run my hand over my mouth and try to think. I know exactly what I made her, but saying it quickly would be an admission of my scattered, lingering, and very inappropriate thoughts of her. It's also not a drink that suits her; it was just fruity with too much vodka to make her brain foggy enough to forget her bad day and smile... but I know which one will suit her.

"I'll be right back," I say, and don't wait for a response before I'm moving toward the kitchen. Boone is moving around, scrubbing down the steel tables with a rag in a sleeveless Hollow shirt with his headphones on.

"Hey!" I bang my hand on the end of the table, and he jumps out of his skin.

"What?" He slips the headphones off in a clumsy panic, and I realize that I've scared him for a different reason. He thinks something's wrong.

"Shit." I pause, breathing in. "Sorry. I just need you to turn on the espresso machine for me."

"You really need to work on your entrances." Boone finally takes a breath. "I've taught you how to use that more than once." He points to the giant brewer with a sigh. "It's also two a.m.," he adds, but moves around the table to the second counter and puts his hand around the back to flip it on.

"I'm just running through the tests of this month's specials," I say. "And that thing has a mind of its own."

Boone stops to give me the *'you've been to war, and the espresso machine scares you'* look, and I scowl deeper at him. He raises both hands and goes back to making the espresso for me. Before long, the entire kitchen smells like coffee.

"Two shots," I say to him, and he narrows his eyes on me. "I'm teaching Rhea."

"Oh, you're *teaching Rhea,*" he mocks. "That's the second time this week that you're entertaining one of Day's friends after close."

"She was eating dinner and asked to help," I say.

"Sure," Boone smiles, "does she need a drive?" He asks.

"No, you just finish up here and get home." I can see from his expression that he wants to comment again, but instead he sets the cup on the counter in front of me and waits, watching my hands.

"They're getting worse," he says. "The tremors, why?"

The anniversary is coming.

"I don't know," I hold out my hand, and it's shaking again.

"Go plan your drinks, but I'm taking you to the doctor—"

I open my mouth to argue that I don't have the time for that, but Boone glares me into submission and points to the espresso shot. I nod, only noticing then that he'd put it in a taller glass, and even though my hand shakes, I don't spill anything as I wander back out to Rhea. She's staring up at all the booze with her arms crossed, but she hasn't moved an inch.

"Did you just stand here the entire time?" I ask her, coming around and setting the shot down.

"You said you'd be right back." She shrugs and leans over to smell it. "Is that espresso?"

"Did you even taste the drink I gave you, or just—" I joke.

"No way you made me something else." She cuts me off with the sweetest smile. "It was pink, and..." she stops to think about it, "...bl ended! I wasn't that drunk!"

"Right," I say, reaching out around her to grab two glasses from the top shelf between my fingers. She stills as I move, and our faces get close again as I slide them off the hook and bring them back around. This whole time, I'd thought her eyes were brown, but they have soft speckles of green mixed into the chocolate tones. "Mm," I hum, turning away from her and setting the glasses down.

"What else was in it?" She leans against the counter with her nose in the cup.

"Vodka," I say, popping the cap as my hand grabs a metal shot glass from under the lip. I don't need it, but if she wants to learn, she's going to. I set it down for her, letting it slip from my fingers to the counter, where it rattles as it balances. "In the fridge, there." I point, and she turns to look, "There's a bottle labeled BS."

"It's labeled bullshit?" She looks up at me as she leans over and pops the door open.

"Brown sugar," I correct her.

"Less fun," she grumbles.

"How is bullshit more fun?" I scowl and take the bottle from her as she presses the door closed with her boot.

"For a second there, I was starting to think you had a sense of humor," she teases, and reaches around to tie her hair back in a bun at the base of her neck. It's then that I notice the few scattered, light-handed tattoos that creep up over her shoulder and kiss the base of her throat.

"Wrong twin," I say, holding my tone, but she smiles again, and I take it as a win.

"Thank goodness we dodged that bullet," she ruffles, shaking out her arms like she's preparing for a game. I look her up and down, and an amused smile almost forms on my lips at her funny personality.

"And what bullet would that be?" I shove two shakers into the ice bin before setting them on the counter.

"How about you stop asking questions and teach me how to make this without killing the girls. Maybe I can surprise them at the next Dungeons and Dragons night..." she trails off.

I remember the first time that Sunday told us she was starting it, neither Boone nor I could believe it. And I think that was the general consensus from everyone, but it also makes sense because Sunday is the type to fall in love with every book she reads and cry at every television show she watches. Role-playing with her friends is a natural progression, but it's still hilarious to think Hillcats sit around a table once a week and play with tiny figurines of elves and warlocks.

"How sweet do you want it?" I ask her, holding the bottle over the opening.

"You decide," she says, and I know there's no meaning behind it, but the way she says it is sweet and soft.

"Three-fourths of an ounce," I explain, squeezing it into the cup blind, handing it to her, and pointing to the shot glass on the counter. She listens, under-pouring a little and letting the syrup slide into the shaker. I hold my breath as she licks her finger clean and reaches for the vodka with her other hand. "Two ounces," I tell her.

I follow suit, free-pouring it again, and use half the espresso in the mug before handing it to her.

"That's it?" she questions, looking around at the simple ingredients.

"And you haven't even broken a glass yet," I tease, warranting a soft scoff from her as I push the lids of the shakers on. I give them both a good bump and hand one to her. "Hold it tight. You don't want to smell like coffee, and neither do I."

"I just—" she motions with her arm, and I nod as she starts to shake it faster. I follow suit but take the time with my free hand to move the glasses closer to her. It's addicting finding ways to make her smile, and the one she's wearing now is bright and void of any sadness that lingers beneath the surface usually. "It's so cold on my hands," she says, stumbling a little with it before she finds the rhythm.

I pop the shaker apart and pour the contents through the strainer into the martini glass without a second thought as she struggles with the lid of hers.

"It's stuck," she practically whines, and I take it from her, smacking the side hard with the butt of my hand. It pops free, and her eyes go wide. "Oh." She mumbles, her eyes on my hands, taking the glass and strainer from me to pour her own. She spills a little, picking up the glass and running her tongue along the side to collect the overpour. Her eyes peer up at me over the glass, and she lowers it away from her mouth sheepishly.

"How is it?" I ask her, trying to ignore the heat burning in my chest from the unfiltered side of her.

"Delicious," she takes another small sip.

"And no one died," I say, still watching her.

"And no glasses broke," she adds, with a soft smirk.

"Luckily, I would have had to take that off your paycheck," I say to her.

"Ruthless," she scoffs.

"I'm the mean twin, remember?" I smile at her, it's genuine, and it feels weird on my face.

"Seriously though, who calls you that?" She steps forward a little, and it takes everything in me not to meet her step for step, but I stay totally still. "I'll beat them up," she offers.

"You think I can't take care of myself?" I feign offence.

"I never said that!" She stumbles over her words, and the martini sloshes around in her glass. "Shit," she swears and brings it back to her lips to down a little more of it.

"Careful." I reach out and straighten the glass in her hand as she panics to keep it steady. "Messy," I huff under my breath. My hand brushes against hers, and she stills instantly, her breathing shallow and loud in the quiet space.

"Hey, Brighton?" she whispers, and I don't correct her this time because it seems no matter how many times I tell her, she just is incapable of only saying Bright. She sets down her glass, and I can tell she's dancing around asking me something as she plays with the rings on her fingers.

"Yes?" I respond after she goes quiet.

"I know you have a spare room and—"

"Nope," I cut her off quickly to keep her from even thinking I'll entertain it.

"Please? I'm sleeping on Sunday's couch, and I can't do it anymore! She's the size of an American girl doll, and my back is screaming!" She instantly enters begging territory, and it makes it increasingly hard to deny her what she wants. "I promise I'm a good roommate, I'm clean, I'll buy my own food. I'll do my own laundry and help around the apartment!" She steps forward out of instinct, and I don't flinch away from her because I like the closeness; it's soft and volatile. Even thinking about letting her sleep in my apartment is a bad, *bad* idea. There's a list of reasons explaining why, but all I can think about is how sad and desperate she looks.

If she says please again, all bets are off.

"Please."

Shit.

"Under one condition," I break like a cheap piece of wood the second it leaves her lips. She nods, listening, "You start calling me Bright."

Rhea starts to laugh wildly. It's loud and full of more life than I've ever heard. When she stops, her cheeks are red, and she's so close to me I can smell the espresso on her breath.

"Deal."

The sheets smell like Brighton.

The sheets smell like Brighton. Shit.

I pry one eye open and pray I'm not forgetting something, but I'm in bed, and it's empty. It takes a second to remember that I'd finally convinced Brighton to let me rent his spare room and that last night I insisted on staying despite only having my rugby duffel with me. I just needed one good night of sleep, and considering I woke up forgetting what time zone I was in, I can say it's a success.

I slip out of bed and double-check the living room before sneaking over to the bathroom and running the water. It's a good size for an apartment, but plain. Bright, white and clean. I peer up at the shower head and grin. It's high on the wall; unlike at Sunday's, where it's made for short people and turns cold the second I step under it. Living with Sunday is never an issue; the problem is that her house is not made for a six-foot-tall woman. It's like moving around in a doll's house.

Before getting in, I dig around and find a towel in the closet behind the door. Everything in the closet is organized by bottle, labeled in clear boxes, and folded perfectly. "God, he really is the Terminator," I whisper, grabbing the towel and hanging it up. The water is so warm, and before long, I'm standing beneath the stream, proud of myself for begging Brighton long enough that he cracked. Working at the Hollow, I'm privy to different sides of him I didn't see before, ones I either ignored or was too drunk to care about.

But he's really a sweet guy, softer than I was imagining him being. It's obvious that he's still pretty apprehensive about having me rent the apartment room, but I'd prove to him that I could be a good roommate this week, and then he'd have no choice but to let me stay until my condo is livable.

I realize instantly that I'm lacking just about everything I need to get ready for work and curse myself for being weak last night at the promise of a bed. Every tiny upset is a further reminder that I just want to be home in my own space. I step out of the shower, dig around until I find toothpaste, and use my finger to brush my teeth as best I can before slipping back into my pajamas and hanging the towel on the hook.

There's a brush in my bag and a change of clothes, so I start to make a list in my head of what I need to do before work, but when I open the bathroom door, my thoughts are derailed. Brighton is in the kitchen, much like I found him the first night, but this time he's properly clothed.

"Oh, so you do own shirts," I say, turning off the bathroom light.

He shakes his head with a huff, but doesn't turn to look at me as I pad across the cold apartment floor on bare feet. I notice at the end of the island is a fresh mug of coffee, and before I can ask, he points to it without pausing what he's doing at the counter. I take it between my fingers and inhale the smell before lifting it to my lips for a sip. My eyes follow him as he grabs a couple of containers from the fridge, and from my position at the counter, I can see just how organized he is. Everything inside has a place and a label, just like the bathroom. This may be a terrible idea after all. *Confirmed, I'm bunking with the Terminator.*

"What are you doing?" I ask finally, just trying to break the silence. It's not that it's awkward or tense; I just have a hard time sitting in silence, no matter the situation or the people involved.

"Making lunch for Daisy," he says after a moment.

"Wow, Sunday never made me lunch." I groan playfully and drink more of the coffee. Brighton looks over his shoulder at me as he shoves food into her little lunch bag.

"I'll get you keys made today for the front door," he clears his throat, "but I have to be out in twenty, so if you could..."

"Oh yeah," I slide back from the counter, almost spilling my coffee, and straighten out. "I can take Daisy to school, if that makes it easier for you?" I offer.

Brighton stares at me for a second, considering this before setting the bag at the other end with a bottle of water. "Yeah..." he says. "You sure?"

"We're going to the same place," I remind him.

"That's right, you... teach... gym?" It takes him a minute, and the muscle in his jawline flexes tightly as he guesses totally off base.

"Art," I chuckle.

Please stop doing that thing with your jaw. It's making it impossible to focus.

"Sorry, Day tells me all of this stuff about you guys, but she talks in circles." He runs a hand through his messy hair, and all the muscles in his arm ripple in the most distracting way.

"It's okay, I don't really scream *art teacher*," I point to myself and realize I'm wearing a sports bra and my rugby spanx, and suddenly feel very exposed. "...I'm going to go get dressed."

Living with a man is going to take some adjustment.

"I'll go get her up," he says, his eyes trailing over me before snapping up with the turn of his head.

The morning students flood into the art room, and it's clear from the moment they start huddling that something is going on they don't want the teachers to know about. This happens on occasion; they get restless over some gossip, and everything else in their lives takes a backseat, including school.

I clear my throat, "You guys gonna let me in on the intel or ignore me the rest of the morning?" I put my hands back on my desk and lean against it with my legs out in front of me. Garth, one of the hockey boys, turns with a smirk.

"Nothing to worry you with, Ms. D." He smirks, but when Daisy wanders into the room with her friend Lori, the room goes silent.

"Mmm." I narrow my eyes at him, and he shrugs, taking his place at the back table with his buddy. I tap my fingers out over the table and stand up to do a circle as they pull out their projects they've been working on for the art exhibit at the end of the year. I stop at the table of boys, and the whispers die. "Can I see what you're working on?" I ask.

"I left mine at home." Henrik, one of the kids struggling through every subject, is quick to spit out an excuse.

"Yeah, Ms. D, unfortunately, we were all at Henny's house last night working hard on our projects, and we just worked so hard into the night that we forgot them at his house." Garth smiles at me like it's supposed to make me believe him.

"Oh, Garth." *You stupid little fuck,* I think and roll my eyes at him. "Guess you all need to start new projects," I say, leaning over the table while looking at the six of them. "Or me and Coach Marchan are going to have a really nice conversation about your asses sitting on the bench this hockey season."

Their smiles drop.

"You shouldn't swear, Ms. D." Henrik dares to say.

"And you shouldn't lie. Guess we're both breaking some moral codes," I respond dryly. "Go get your extra books from the back, and they stay here. I want to see art by the time the bell rings, boys." I pat the table before wandering away.

Daisy and Lori sit quietly across the room, with their sketchbooks and canvases strewn out on the table, working through scraps of magazines and massive boxes of junk. Daisy tucks a chunk of blonde hair behind her ear, and for the first time, I can see her father in her. Her focused face is similar to the look he gives me when I'm talking too fast, and it makes me smile as I pull a chair around and sit on it backwards to investigate what they're doing.

"How's it going?" I ask, leaning over to peek at what Lori's sketching. "Is that a bullfrog?"

"I'm going to put him in a Halloween costume, but I can't decide if he's a devil ears and tail guy, or if I should dress him up like Shrek…" she trails off.

"Definitely Shrek." I laugh. "He'd look pretty cute with a *stay out of my swamp* sign." I circle a blank space on her page, and she looks up at me with a smile. "And you, Daisy?" I ask her, not realizing she has her headphones in and the volume turned up. Lori taps her, and she removes one, "What are you doing for the dream project?"

"Uh." Daisy chews her lip.

It's a simple project that I set almost every year because it's one that students usually run with in the funniest ways. They're meant to take something from their dreams and put it down on a piece of paper in any way they want to convey it. Most just draw or paint something, but every once in a while, I get a student like Daisy who works a little harder. Her brain works a little faster and a little more creatively than the rest of the kids.

She's got a base of scrap paper, randomly glued to the page, and at first glance, it looks harmless, but then I realize most of the scrap paper is dark red, yellow, or a heavy blue color. She's sketching on top of the mixed media, and I can't really tell what it is because of the different tones, but her fingers are covered in pencil, and she throws her arm over it when she sees me inspecting it.

"It's stupid and not finished," she says quickly.

"Alright," I say, throwing my hands up. One of the older girls, Carly Stepson, parades into class ten minutes late, cutting off my train of thought, and Daisy's expression goes from concentrated to terrified as the girl wanders over to throw her arms around Garth. "One ruler apart, Carla, you know the rules." I snap my fingers at her.

"It's Carly," she says, not letting go of her boyfriend.

"I know," I smile at her sweetly, but the venom is clear. *God, I hate teenage girls.* "Back up."

"Sorry, Ms. D. I didn't realize it's that time of the month for you," she says with a smile.

Teenage girls are vicious. "Even if it were, it doesn't change the rules of my room, and you're already late, not working on your project, and fraternizing. So..." I narrow my eyes at her, still turned in my chair. "Sit down, and get to work, or you can do it in detention after school."

"Why can't you just send me in the hallway like a normal teacher?" she groans, letting go of Garth and finding a chair.

"Because it's so much fun ruining your life." I tsk and roll my eyes.

Turning back to the girls, Daisy's eyes are down, pointedly away from Carly, but it's clear she's listening to the entire conversation because she presses play on her phone after a few seconds of silence. I chew the inside of my lip and look at the rowdy table with a bad feeling.

Brighton

"This place reeks of death," Boone huffs and picks at the sleeves of his shirt before deciding to roll them up around his arms.

"It's a hospital," I scowl.

It'd been a while since we'd been in one, but it never fails to make him uncomfortable. It's the only time he gets antsy. Sometimes I don't even know why he offers to do this stuff with me. *Threatens. He doesn't offer—he threatens.*

"What time is your appointment again?" He asks, looking down at his phone.

"One," I tell him, just like I've told him every hour for the last six.

"Ten minutes," he responds, like I'm the impatient one.

"You know you didn't have to come with me," I say.

"If I didn't come, you wouldn't come." He argues, and he's not wrong. The only reason I'm sitting here consoling his feelings is because he made sure I got in the truck. The problem is, the issues with my hands aren't something the doctors here can do anything about. It's mental. The closer I get to that day, the worse it gets. Even now, in the middle of the day, my left hand rattles against my thigh no matter how I try to calm it.

"You can wait in the truck, Boone," I tell him, and he instantly shakes his head.

"No, I promised Sunday I'd be brave." Boone makes it sound endearing, but I stare at him like he's nuts.

"You told Day?" I sigh.

"He sure did." Sunday stands across from me, in her stupid bunny scrubs with her hand on her hip.

"Shouldn't you be in the ER?" I ask her.

"Maybe." She narrows those judgmental green eyes on me and demands answers. "What's going on?"

"Nothing," I brush her off. Boone snorts. "Shut up."

"Bri," Sunday's voice drops into a territory I know well.

I lift my hand from between my legs and show her.

"It's back." She steps forward to get a proper look at it, and I nod.

"It's worse," Boone rats me out. A loud announcement comes over the hospital speakers, and I take a second to breathe as we wait for it to die down.

He's not wrong; it is worse. The closer we get to the anniversary, the more they shake. It's no different than any year, but for some reason, this year, this far out from everything that happened, it's like my brain is replaying the memories louder. Unable to forget all the bloodshed, and it wants to remind me on maximum volume that I'm guilty.

That's what the shake is. It's guilt.

"Why didn't you tell me?" She asks when the silence returns, no longer looking at my hand but at me.

"Because of that." I nod at the unreasonable motherly glare she gives me in the wake of finding out my secret. *It's back.* Like the tremors are some kind of unspeakable monster. "It'll die down again in a couple weeks, we all know it, but Boone wanted to come, so here I am."

"Are you going to let them X-ray you this time?" She questions.

"Do you know how expensive that'll be? No." I shake my head. "It's not my muscles, Day, I'm healthy as ever. That's exactly what he's going to tell us today."

"Okay," she concedes. "Then therapy."

"I'm not having this conversation again," I shut her down as firmly as I can. A few people she knows shuffle by, and she entertains them with small talk for a moment before turning cold again. It's a version of Sunday we rarely see. *All work, no play, Day.*

"You never want to, but it's clearly the solution. You have to talk to someone about what's going on up there, to fix that." She points at my head, then my shaking hands.

"The therapist is as useless as the X-ray."

Sunday huffs, completely unimpressed by my answer.

"You know what." She laughs under her breath. "I have too much work to do to argue with this idiot. Just get a scan, please."

"Sure Day." I agree, but when the doctor asks, I'll say no. When she wanders away, Boone turns his head to me and sighs.

"You're not gonna get the stuff, are you?" He groans when I shake my head.

The doctor tells us exactly what I expect: there's no apparent damage, and I'm in good physical shape, and then he proposes running a few tests. I politely decline them all.

"One of these days, Sunday is going to drug you, and you're going to wake up in a fucking care home for the mentally unstable," Boone grunts as we wander back to the truck.

"Better than her picking at shit she can't fix with stubborn willpower." I climb in and slam the door as he follows.

"You know she learned that from you?" Boone turns to me in his seat. "She's just trying to look out for you, the way you looked out for us."

"I don't need you guys to do that," I tell him.

"Hey," he clips, and his voice is more serious than before, so I give him the proper attention before turning the engine on. "I'm your brother, and being born three minutes ahead of me isn't an argument you can use here. Let me help."

I stare at him, the scruff, the chaos, the gentle nature that rolls off him, and my brain just screams to keep him out of harm's way. To keep him at arm's length from whatever the fuck is stirring around in my brain. I've leaned on them enough; it's my shift to protect.

"I just need to get through these couple of weeks, and it'll be fine," I tell him, and I know he's not buying it because his lips twitch with the urge to fight it.

"Eventually, something is going to give, Bri," he says quietly. "It's easy to put out a small fire, but whatever you got going on, it's bigger than that, and if you snap— None of us is equipped to put out a wildfire."

"I hear you."

"I don't think you do," he snorts, "but I said my piece. Can we pick Daisy up early and get tacos?"

I nod and start the engine. "Yeah, we can do that."

The school is quiet when we arrive, and Boone stays in the truck as I wander through to the office. The girl at the desk is sweet and figures out what class Daisy is in, calling down to the room so I can go get her. I snake up through the hallways to the second-floor science lab to find her causing trouble with Lori. When she sees me at the door, she smiles, actually smiles. It's big and genuine, full of excitement for her jailbreak as she collects her bag and shuffles from the class.

"Uncle B wants tacos," I tell her as I shut the door and hold my hand out for her backpack.

"Mom's going to flip if I skip school for that," she laughs, handing it over.

"I'm not scared of your mother," I groan and adjust the small bag on my shoulder. "What is in this thing?" I scowl at the weight.

"Rocks," she declares with a straight face. "I just need to grab something," she says to me and picks up her pace down the hall to a room at the end of the hall. The door is covered in crap, and the room is practically completely dark, but Daisy disappears inside, and I stand in the doorway to sneak a peek at what's beyond the frame.

"Brighton?" Rhea's voice is sharp, lower than normal, and confused.

I clear my throat. "I didn't realize…"

The sign on the door is covered in crap, but it still reads ART ROOM in bold letters that have been painted over. I turn to look at her as she approaches from behind her desk in a long dark skirt, a white t-shirt, and some sort of harness thing that buckles across her stomach. Her hair is down today, curled around her face in all different directions. It's the softest I've ever seen her, and it's distracting.

"What are you doing here?" she asks, crossing her arms under her chest.

"Daisy has an appointment," I say.

"You don't have to lie to Ms. Drake." Daisy returns and pulls her backpack away from me to shove a messy-looking book inside. "She's the only cool teacher in this school."

"Oh." I nod. "You must be proud of that distinction."

"Quite," Rhea beams. "It's hard work to get a bunch of teenagers to admit you're cool, don't be sour because I earned it and you're just someone's dorky dad."

"Dorky?" I huff, feeling lighter than I have all day. "Take that back."

"She's right, you are kind of dorky. You own like thirty maps..." Daisy grumbles under her breath.

"At least they're organized, look at this place," I say, pointing lazily to the chaotic classroom.

"Freedom of expression," Rhea and Daisy say in unison. *Weirdos.*

"I'm outnumbered here," I admit defeat.

"We're going for tacos," Daisy tells her, handing her bag back to me.

"Jealous," Rhea playfully hisses at her, and I watch the interaction with a foreign smile on my face. "Although Mr. Crockett is kinda cool," she argues.

"Yeah, but he teaches Gym, and *smells* like it."

"Fair point," Rhea laughs with her, "don't have too much fun."

Daisy dips out of the classroom, but I stay rooted for reasons beyond my comprehension. Rhea stares at me like I'm insane, and for a long moment, the world feels a little less suffocating.

"Do you need anything else?" She asks me after a second.

I shake my head, shaking the feeling off at the same time, before digging into my pockets, "Here." I hand her the set of keys I promised her.

"Oh, thank you." She takes it, and her fingers brush against my palm. "Say hi to Bobo for me."

"On it," I note, backing out of the classroom but never taking my eyes off her.

"That one," I say, lifting the beer to my lips and pointing with my other hand to the board. "I put my axe between his eyebrows." Cosy waits for me to roll my dice, and it hits a seventeen with a plus three advantage. She takes it as a death blow and moves on to Sunday, who's making faces at Adeline through the laptop.

"How's couch surfing?" she asks me after Sunday takes her turn.

"Actually, I found a room to rent," I say, sliding Kaia a note under Cosy's nose. Cosy eyes me, suspiciously. "It's nothing..." I smirk.

Kaia unfolds the paper and cackles before looking over the board and flipping through her notes from the last session.

"You did?" Adeline's eyebrows lift on the screen.

"Yeah—Bri's letting her stay in his spare room," Sunday says before I can. After Brighton had caved and said yes, the first person I'd called was Sunday. I wanted to make sure it was okay with her before I moved in with her older brother, but she hadn't seemed bothered. If anything, she encouraged the idea, saying that it would be good for everyone, including Daisy.

"You're living above the Hollow?" Jensen's voice comes from the background, and Adeline mutes her camera, scowling at him, and then smiles. "Sorry, leaving," Jensen says, his voice becoming nothing but an echo as Adeline returns to the conversation.

"At this point, you should just let him play," Cosy says with a soft smile.

"Yeah. For the time being, I just hope that the renovations don't take as long as they're predicting," I say, as Kaia enacts our plan. Cosy has us pinned down in an abandoned house that Adeline just *had* to explore, and now we are being attacked by a horde of goblins.

"What's the timeline?" Adeline asks.

"Six months minimum," I groan.

"That's brutal," Cosy mutters, and I'm not sure if she's talking about the length or whatever is happening in the game.

"And your brother is terrifying, Sunday," I say. "Did you know he has everything labeled?"

"Yeah, like right down to his underwear," Sunday laughs, her focus on what Kaia's doing behind the mundane conversation. "I give it a week before you're at each other's throats."

"What's that supposed to mean?" I pout.

"You're a slob," four voices chorus at once, and we all start to laugh.

"No offense, Reaper, but you've never been neat a day in your life," Kaia says while rolling an eighteen, plus two with her stealth. She manages to get around the goblins without being noticed and slits the queen's throat without skipping a beat.

Sunday swiftly steps in with her dice, rolling a fifteen and saying, "I'm going to cast 'Animate Dead' on the goblin queen."

Cosy groans. "Next campaign, I'm making all the monsters harder."

"Sure you will," Kaia purrs.

"The spell hits, and the Goblin Queen takes a massive breath as she wakes, completely under Mirage's spell for the next twenty-four hours."

"Are they reimbursing you at all? For damage—time—anything?" Adeline asks me, as Jensen sets a plate on the table beside her and hangs over her shoulders to listen.

"I don't know yet." I shrug, a little defeated and definitely over having this conversation with everyone. "It's just a waiting game now."

"If you need a good lawyer..." Jensen says, and Adeline pinches his arm, making him yip before retreating out of frame again.

"Thank you for the offer, but I'm hoping it doesn't come to that. I just want to get through the next couple of months with my head down." I say, and the girls agree, but Kaia stares at me with mischief in her eyes.

Yes, that includes keeping Brighton Black a ruler's distance away from my underwear.

"If it doesn't work out with Bri, you can always go back to stealing our couches; door's always open," Sunday reminds me.

"I'm not looking to add back pain to my list of worries right now," I tease her, and she rolls her eyes at me, lifting her drink to her lips.

"We should make a bet." Kaia slaps the table with her hands. "How long Bright and Rhea will go without—"

"Killing each other," I cut her off because I can see her actively trying to start crap.

"That's what I was going to say." She smiles at me, shifting in her chair to straighten out and get serious. "So who wants to play?"

"I'll bet twenty that it doesn't last the week," Sunday is the first to chime in.

"I give them a month," Adeline pipes up.

"Twenty-three days," Jensen yells from off-screen, and Kaia laughs.

"Really?" Adeline glares at him over the laptop.

"Cosy?" Kaia looks over to her as I sit silent and let them get it out of their system.

"Two months. Reaper stays clean for three weeks—then she slips and drives him to the brink of insanity."

"Wow, thanks for the vote of confidence, you guys." I shake my head and finish my beer. "What I really need is advice on how to survive him."

"Stay out of his hair," Sunday says quietly, "only be in the apartment for sleeping, it's not like you aren't busy."

"Avoidance," I laugh. "Perfect."

"Oh, come on, Rhea, you have to admit this entire situation is hilariously awkward. It's Sunday's brother," Cosy says.

"Kaia and Boone have *zero* boundaries, and I'm the one making things weird?" I groan and nearly snap my pen between my fingers as I lean back in the dining room chair.

"Bobo and Killer don't count; they've never had boundaries," Sunday says without looking at me. "*This is weird.*" She waves her pen in my direction. "I'm still stuck on how you even convinced him."

"Did you give him a Hollow Special?" Kaia asks with a laugh, and we all give her disgusted looks. "What? I meant her charm!"

"Sure you did," I sigh, "I just asked him...more than once..."

"In the voice?" Sunday narrows her eyes. "You did the voice, didn't you?"

"I might have done the voice on the last one," I conceded to her interrogation instantly.

"Yeah, a stone statue couldn't resist that voice," Kaia purrs, "Thing one was screwed." She adds, leaning over the table, and her eyes flicker to meet mine. "Means he has a weakness."

"Or I just annoyed him enough for him to break," I argue.

"Have you met either of his siblings?" Cosy snorts, and Kaia snaps her fingers in agreement. "He's quite possibly the only person in the world who uses the word no with them."

"Hey, sometimes he says yes to me..." Sunday protests and looks around the table.

"And then he immediately does what he says he wasn't going to do," Adeline says, sipping on her beer. "Admit it, Sunny, Bright is the living definition of a brick wall."

"He's just..." Sunday rolls her eyes. "Fine, but someone had to say no to us! Our parents were never around to do it, he's stone cold because someone had to be!" She says, a little upset that we're teasing Brighton.

"We love that grumpy groucher, Sunny." Kaia reaches out and gives her a pet on the head, "The entire situation is..."

"Perplexing," Cosy finishes her sentence.

"Yeah, well, it won't last long if you four have any say," I groan. "Can we finish the session? I'm exhausted." I say, a little over being teased as well.

The girls don't drop it for the rest of the night, going back and forth with theories about why Brighton had said yes to me renting the room, but in all honesty. I think he was being nice because I forced his hand. Sunday sends me back to the Hollow with my bags and a grocery bag of snacks for Daisy. The Hollow is still busy when I pull the Bronco into the back lot, and I cut the engine but sit in the front seat with my eyes closed for a little while. The sounds of the city are some of my favorites. Guessing how everyone's night is going by the distant laughter and hollering.

My phone vibrates, interrupting the quiet, and the screen flashes with my mother's face. I lean over and answer the call, "Hi, Mom."

"Rhea! Your sister told me about the condo. What in the world happened?" she asks. The main reason I hadn't called her about the condo yet is that she'd been adamant that it was a bad purchase. I think part of the reason she hates it is that she doesn't want me so far away, but the distance is exactly the point. My mom is eccentric to say the least.

"It flooded," I say, not really sure what else she wants if Remi already told her. I knew I shouldn't have texted that fifteen-year-old snitch.

"Why didn't you come home? Where are you staying? We can move Reid into Remi's room to make space for you!" She starts to ramble.

To make space for you.

"No, no, you don't have to do that. I'm staying with a friend. Don't take Reid's room from him; he earned that," I say, remembering how excited my brother was to have his own room when I moved out. "And Remi doesn't need to find out what teenage boys do in the dark just yet," I add lightness to my sad tone to keep her from thinking I'm upset with anything she's said.

"I wish you had called me," she says, and I realize that I've failed in my damage control. "And Gabe could have helped."

Gabe is my stepdad, a funny guy, really good to my mom and younger siblings, and has two kids of his own from another marriage. Shana and Toby, both really cute kids. Nine and six. It makes for the most chaotic family dinners. Remi is the youngest of us at fifteen, and Reid turns seventeen this fall.

"I'm truly good, no help needed. I heard that Reid got accepted into the Hockey program?" I say. "That's good, if he makes it through, it pays for his university, yeah?"

"Oh, he's so excited, Rhea," she instantly becomes distracted from my problems with the question. "Those hockey boys he loves... uh..."

"From the Huskies?" I interject, "North and Carter."

"Yes! I knew that! Mercer North and Kenji Carter are running the practices this year," she says.

"Damn," I scoff. They really pulled out the big guns.

"They're training the next wave, at least that's what Reid keeps saying about it. He's the youngest boy to be accepted, and he said three girls got into the program. Isn't that amazing?" One of the line cooks pops the back door open for a smoke, letting the light from the Hollow spill into the dark parking lot. Mom continues to talk as I make my way from the Bronco, the moment of quiet lost completely. I gather everything from the back, balancing it all over my shoulders and in my arms.

"Hey, Rhea!" she calls, and I give her a whispered, "Hey," as I sneak in the back door and up the stairs to the apartment.

"They practice Thursday to Sunday, four days, isn't that insane. I don't know when those big fancy players even have time to win hockey games!" Mom says.

"Real superheroes," I say, completely disconnected from the conversation. Reid had told me all of this already, but Mom would be damned if she didn't believe it was her story to tell. "Hey Mom, I'm beat and have practice in the morning, so I'm going to let you go."

"Oh, I'm sorry, Rhea, I didn't even realize what time it was. We'll see you on Friday for dinner?" she asks quickly.

"Yeah, Mom, I have a game, but I'll be over after," I say.

"Oh, maybe we'll come to the game! Make a whole day of it." She claps on the other end, says her goodbyes, and hangs up.

I stare at the phone and sigh. She's been saying that for three years.

They'd made time for two games in total over that time. It's not Mom's fault; she tries her hardest, there's just a lot going on in their house with four smaller kids and no spare time. I settle myself against the wall, promising myself that tomorrow I'll put everything together and away, but for now, I just want to crawl into bed and forget about today.

Morning comes faster than I expect, the light shining through the heavy navy curtains Brighton hung over the windows. I look up at the clock and am grateful my body got me up in time for a shower and some toast before school. I crawl from bed and decide on food first, going to the fridge for something I could steal until I get my own groceries after work today. On the top shelf sits a paper bag beside Daisy's lunch kit, labelled in scratchy dark marker with my name. I smile at it softly, my fingers gripping the door of the fridge a little tighter. Brighton had made me lunch. It seems so silly and trivial to feel fuzzy over something as simple as a bag of food, but it's more than that to a girl who's never had her lunch made for her.

He's just being polite, Rhea, you whined about it yesterday. It means nothing.

I'd spend the rest of the day trying to convince myself of that.

Brighton

"The new binder is slick." Boone drops it on the table next to my head as I kneel with my sleeves rolled up, trying to reconnect the karaoke machine to the projector. There are about fifty too many people all yelling at me at once, and the bar is already packed with rowdy, drunk first responders coming off shift.

Boone's been up my ass all week about getting the karaoke binder finalized, and because he has the musical knowledge of a nine-year-old, I had to put a new one together while juggling everything else. What I didn't tell Boone was that Rhea helped. Well, she took it over, if I'm being honest. I left the binder on the island one morning, and she begged and begged for an hour until I gave in. All week I've been cursing him for even asking, because it meant fighting with her over songs, but the look on his face makes it worth it, and suddenly I'm not so pissed off.

"Move this," I grunt and tap the speaker with my shoulder.

Boone listens, shifting the weight to the left, and gives me more space to get my shoulder between it and the wall. I pop the wires together, and the projector flickers back to life.

"Fuck, I hate this thing, and I hate karaoke night," I say, pushing off the ground to clean my hands free of the dirt.

Boone claps his hand over my shoulder, "For a man that loves his bar, you sure *hate* running it."

"Screw you." I shake free and make my way over to the bar as some of the waitresses working the outer ring of the bar hand out the sign-up sheet for the turn order. The unfortunate part of tonight is that it never fails to bring in a massive crowd of people wanting to spend a shit ton on drinks and singing all of my favorite songs terribly.

Tonight of all nights is a necessary Hollow event, and my least favorite of them all. I serve the people that Judd is running behind on and throw Sunday out of the bar to help with tables before she gets into the shots, but the entire time I'm working, my eyes are scanning the bar for Rhea.

It's not like she's hard to lose; everyone gives her a wide berth as she floats around, making sure people are behaving, stopping to chat with faces she knows before moving on. Her hair is loose around her face and hides all the tiny tattoos that I know exist on the back of her throat.

I swallow hard.

"Bri!" Sunday's voice cuts through the noise, "grab me three pitchers, Pilsner."

I get them ready for her, prepared to help her carry them, but am only left impressed as she balances all three in her small hands and disappears into the crowd. When the karaoke begins, I try to sink into my own head and far away from the sound of people singing out of tune.

Sometimes I think Boone is right; running a bar is quite possibly the stupidest decision I've ever made, but arriving home, fresh off that plane... discharged with nothing to my name but Daisy. For the first three weeks, all I did was walk up and down Main Street, Harbor, just trying to find a reason to be around. I tried with Riona, but she couldn't do it and I don't blame her. So I didn't have an apartment, staying with Boone was killing me, and Sunday hovered like I would kill myself at any second. And damn did I consider it—almost every single night for two months. I sat with the option staring me in the face from the kitchen table, always picking nights when Boone and Sunday worked...

But like the miracle she was, Daisy knew somehow. The phone would vibrate on the table, and her sweet little face would appear to remind me that she was the purpose for all of this pain. That I'd survived the worst of it.

The walks grew longer and turned into runs that led me to new parts of the city. Sunday introduced me to Cosy, and I started taking dogs out with me, giving me even more reason to keep moving. After two years of circling and knocking on death's door, I sold the gun. That was the biggest step I took. My skin itches even thinking about it now. But it had to go.

One morning, a few years after being home and completely out of routine, I ran in the opposite direction, toward the sunrise, and found a building, barely standing, and it was like it vibrated. I stood out on that sidewalk staring at the emptiness of it, every broken window, graffiti-covered wall, and tarnished floor. Something had called to me, cut through the noise, and given purpose to the aimless wandering.

Boone didn't question it.

He threw in half the money and spent every free hour he had helping me rip it apart and build it from the ground up. Seven months later, about two hundred grand of money neither of us had, and a stupid idea that we could do it with no experience, *the Hollow was born*—a reason to keep working, a reason to keep breathing. If I were moving and providing for Daisy, I would have purpose. That had been enough when I was overseas; it had to be enough now.

It's been seven years.

I can't go back to the old Brighton.

My hand shakes around the bottle, and I set it down on the counter, trying to steady my breathing, when I catch her out of the corner of my eye.

"Don't you just love tonight?" Rhea says from my left, scooping a water bottle from the corner of the bar.

"Drunk people butchering my favorite songs?" I groan, and she stares at me with a funny face. "What?" I mumble uncomfortably.

"You're such a grump. Pretty sure you're a fake music lover," she says, looking genuinely perplexed by it. I don't say anything more to her because my name is called for drinks, and by the time I'm done, she's gone from the bar and across the room, smiling at a table of firefighters. I inhale slowly, trying not to let it get under my skin that she doesn't smile at me like that when my eyes catch Boone.

He's staring at me like I'm an idiot, and I shake my head before getting back to work, trying to ignore the implications in his glare. I manage to keep my head down for the majority of the night, focusing on the bar instead of the noise. That's the hardest part of owning the Hollow, all the noise. The first few weeks after opening had been exhausting; controlling my reaction to every little noise took a toll on my body.

Sunday and Boone learned quickly. She's adamant they didn't, but I'm convinced they both went to group therapy to deal with me, and whether or not that's true. I'm grateful every day that they haven't given up on me. Without Sunday, I wouldn't have Daisy. During deployment, after she was born, Sunday was the driving force for Daisy being around our side of the family. She worked hard to keep her niece around, for me... for herself. My siblings were the real heroes of this story; I'm just the reason they needed to grow up faster.

The best thing I can do for everyone is just keep moving.

As the night goes on, the numbers in the bar start to dwindle, and it grows quiet with only the regulars floating around talking with one another. Sunday and Rhea sit at the edge of the bar, chins propped in their hands, fluttering their lashes at me.

"What?" I snap, setting down a tray of clean glasses.

"Now that it's dead in here, do you think that we could..." Sunday starts, and I shake my head.

"You're working tonight, no singing," I warn her, swiping a towel off the counter and drying my hands.

"Aw, come on, Bri—just one song!" She drops her voice in that tone she used to use when we were younger and widens her eyes at me, but my gaze flickers to Rhea, who's sitting quietly with the softest of frowns on her face. *Fuck.*

"One song," I clip, and Sunday turns to look where I'm staring, her brows furrowing as Rhea slides off the stool, excited.

"Bri." Sunday doesn't move. Her tone is soft and confused, and I realize I'm an idiot.

"Go. This won't happen again..." I say, trying to ignore the concern on her face. She's clearly not thinking about karaoke, and my heart stills in my chest at the look she's giving me.

"Nothing's going on, Day. Stop staring at me." I sigh, but she doesn't move.

"You've got a lot going on... tread lightly," Sunday says, more possessively than I've ever heard her be, and I know she's talking about my past, all the things I've done, the trouble I've caused, but...

I won't be that version of myself again. Never.

And nothing is going on between Rhea and me. She's just a pretty face.

"I gave her a room to rent, a job... Why am I the bad guy?" I scoff.

Rhea calls her name, but she doesn't budge. "Don't do anything stupid," she says quickly, pushing off the bar, "*Please.*"

"Scouts honor." I give her a half-hearted salute and watch her back away from the bar. I can tell she's still wary, but Rhea is shaking the new binder at her, and she puts her focus back on her best friend. I flex my hands in the towel and try to ignore the unfamiliar guilty feeling that gnawed at my insides.

Boone slid behind the bar and threw a plate of fries between us before hauling himself up on the counter to sit. I turn to scold him, but he's pointing to the fries, "Eat." He mumbles with a mouth full of potatoes.

I grab a few, noticing that he's brought out a cup of the hot mustard for me, and dip them inside. It's not until they hit my tongue that I realize how hungry I am. "Thank you," I grumble and continue eating.

Under Pressure by Queen starts over the speakers, and it's like an instant balm to my frayed nerves. I relax a little against the bar and watch as the girls figure out what parts they want to sing, but the second Rhea opens her mouth, everything else fades away. It's like she's the only one up there, and when the music brightens, she does too; it's the happiest I've seen her since the day I met her.

Seven years ago, Sunday came home and decided that she was joining the rugby team. Both Boone and I said no, more than once. Sunday had suffered from grand-mal seizures from the day she was born, terrifying and exhausting. She managed it as well as anyone could, better than either of our parents did. Boone and I had become her primary caregivers the minute we were legally allowed to. It was the three of us against the world. *Always.*

Rugby was a rough sport. Neither of us played, but we knew that much. But Kaia had joined the team, and Sunday wanted to follow. We argued for weeks about it, and Sunday signed up anyway. She was twenty-two, and we couldn't stop her. Instead, we joined her. Practices usually held in tandem with hers meant we could be on the parallel field, never too far away but just enough that she could feel the independence she craved.

It's all we could do, we just had no clue that with it came a group of friends that Sunday had always needed outside of us. Kaia had been around for a long time, but Rhea, Cosy, and Adeline completed the circle. Raised by two idiots, Sunday needed girls.

She spins around with Rhea on stage, happier than ever, and I suddenly realize her concern. This is her life just as much as it is mine, and putting my nose where it doesn't belong is bad for everyone.

I can be Rhea's friend.

Her roommate.

She smiles at me, and the thought wavers just long enough for Boone to huff.

"What the fuck is that?" He laughs when I turn my head to him.

"It's nothing," I say with a shake and grab some more fries.

"If that's nothing, I'd hate to see it be something," he says. "She's singing directly at you!"

"They're just having fun, Boone. Fuck off," I say to him, but he isn't wrong. Rhea's eyes are still glued to mine, and the smile on her face is bright as she sings the lyrics to one of my favorite Queen songs. *Screwed. You are so very screwed.*

"I should have seen this coming," he hums.

"What?" I snap as he shovels more fries in his mouth.

He cleans his hands of salt, chews, and then points, "You would have a crush on the scariest Hillcat."

She's not scary.

"When did we start talking about Kaia?" I tease, and his face hardens.

"Sorry, the scariest Hillcat when Kai's not in the room," he corrects himself and forces a smile on his face. It's been getting worse; the itch to start shit with Kaia's boyfriend is coming to the surface more often than not. But Boone tries to be respectful of her choices, and only God knows why. From what I know of Kaia's boyfriend, he's a douche, works in the business sector, has never gotten his hands dirty in his life, nose is constantly stuck in his phone or someone else's asshole.

I don't care who Kaia dates; I just wish it didn't hurt Boone so much to watch it happen.

"Go back to the kitchen, you animal. You're getting salt everywhere," I say, shoving him off the counter in an effort to ignore how the idea of having a crush made me feel.

Friends. Rhea and I are *friends*.

Rhea

My thighs are on fire, and my chest rises and falls in uneven lulls that do nothing to help me catch my breath. We rarely get outplayed on the field except for when we come face-to-face with the Northside Rugby Club. The NRC is a bunch of very fast, very nasty athletes who always put on their best show.

"Patty is going to go left, watch that lane," Cosy says, her red braids in tatters from the rough game. Kaia is already bruising around the thigh where they caught her and slammed her down hard.

Kaia stomps twice in the dirt to get Sunday's attention, and the two of them communicate without words. It's second nature to them: when the ball leaves the opponent's hands, they both take off faster than anyone, weaving down the field. Kaia is on her tail and picks her up by the shorts just enough for Sunday's fingers to reach the ball before the other winger. Once back on the ground, she spins to her right, knowing Patty is covering left, and kicks off that foot.

Cosy manages to get between Sunday and the oncoming attacker, slowing their route, opening a pocket—but leaving her right side completely open. She sees the player and whips back, popping the ball up and behind her into the open arms of Kaia.

"Easy!" Kaia screams, kicking her feet into motion and dodging the next attacker. Cosy, Kenna, and I work hard to keep behind her as we follow Sunday up the flank, keeping separated enough that if Kaia runs into trouble, Sunday has the lane.

But the trouble is two yards out, and there's no way she catches Kaia with how fast she's moving. Kaia's head flicks over her shoulder, and a wicked grin spreads across her face as she bunny hops between the posts and sets the ball down.

Cosy reaches her first, giving her a rough hug and grabbing the ball for the ref. With the conversion, it puts us three tries ahead, and the NRC looks pissed. There are still two minutes left on the running clock, and we move back into line as quickly as we can, itching to get one more try. If we rattle them today, it means they'll start to waver in future games, and man, it feels like flying.

"Yukon," Kaia yells, and Sunday sighs. "It'll work," she argues just as quickly as Sunday taps the ball and sends it flying through the air.

"It never works," Sunday calls out, splitting the line into a crooked Y formation, leaving me in the back line to follow up. It blocks the team in from both sides, and as soon as they catch the ball, we're all over them. One by one, they're forced to lay the ball down or pass it out, and eventually there's only Patty and me. One versus one, heading straight toward each other like two trains.

I press my tongue against my mouth guard, making sure it's in place, and surge forward faster. The ball is tucked carefully under my arm. I know it's a gamble that I'll no doubt get yelled at for, but as Patty lunges for me, I drop my shoulder inside and lift with my knees. Her feet slide in the soft ground for no more than three seconds before she's scrambling on her toes for purchase. I push harder, almost back to full height, and Patty grunts as her feet leave the ground. I've only got a few yards, and all I have to do is get the ball on the ground over the line.

I scream as my muscles stretch and flex beneath my skin, juggling her weight and my grip on the ball as I step forward faster. She's trying to find the ground without letting go of her hold on me, but she's too far off it to do anything for another six yards. I drop her suddenly, shifting right as she scrambles to keep her balance, clawing at me as I spin away from her and her teammate across the line with a hard thump as my body hits the ground to score the last try.

Everyone is screaming, and the girls pile on top of me, hollering and cheering as the whistle blows to end the game. The NRC girls shake our hands with long faces, Patty stopping briefly as she reaches me.

"You're an animal," she says with a smile. "Only you could pull that off," she compliments, clapping her hand on my back as she starts to move again. Kaia is standing to my left with her shorts hiked up as far as they can go, her face contorted grossly as she pokes the red and purple bruise that seems to span her entire thigh.

"That's going to be fun in the morning," I say to her, fingering her shorts and tilting my head to get a better look at the bruise.

"You're telling me, I have a week of doubles on the rig. They're going to have to roll me out of the station in a wheelchair," she hisses.

A flash goes off, and Sunday pulls the disposable camera away from her dirty face. "It's one for the book," she waves it around. "Still doesn't beat the great back bruise from the opening game, but it's a close second."

"I hope one day the police have a reason to raid you, only to find that creepy bruise binder you keep." Kaia groans, letting her shorts unroll as she straightens out and puts all her weight on the other leg. If there's one thing I admire about Kaia, it's her ability to complain once and move on. She thrives in taking care of her shit, despite the state of her body. The idea that if she stops, she'll die is lived out every day in the roughest possible way. "I want a bacon cheeseburger, buffalo fried pickles, and at least fourteen shots of booze in my body as of thirty minutes ago."

"That does sound amazing right now," Cosy huffs, running her fingers through her hair as she loosens her braids and shakes out her hair.

"I can't, I have a shift in two hours, and I need a nap," Sunday says, following us back toward the locker room.

"That's the fourth game in a row, Sunny. I thought you weren't picking up after game shifts anymore," Cosy asks.

"I've kinda got used to the quiet?" She says, pushing open the door. "The ER is always a mess, but it's a lot quieter later at night. Not to mention it usually lines up with your shifts, and you always bring in the most insane patients. Keeps me on my toes," Sunday pinches Kaia's ass and pulls off her jersey before heading to her locker.

"I'm in," I say, pulling off my own and sinking to the bench.

"You live there now, of course you're in," Kaia giggles. "Have there been any more *incidents?*" She says it quieter, like it's supposed to insinuate something more than just shirtless sightings of Brighton Black.

"No, we're friends," I say, thinking about the fact that he's been making my lunch all week, and try not to blush. He's quiet and respectful, he's always out of the apartment before I get up from bed, and even though I can hear him moving around while I'm in the bathroom, he's always down in the bar when I get out and leave for work.

Yesterday evening, after school, the pile of dirty clothes I had been collecting in the corner showed up folded and clean on my bed in a brand new laundry basket that didn't belong to me.

"The Terminator did my laundry," I add, just to keep her satisfied and quiet.

"Like all of it?" Kaia stares at me.

"Folded and separated." Our cleats click against the tile flooring as we kick them off.

"I wonder if Bright is a panty sniffer." Kaia flips the script, and I practically choke on my own spit.

"Yeah, cause this isn't awkward enough for me," I groan, rubbing my hands over my face.

"I'm just saying, guys like that always have weird kinks. " She shakes out her hair, and it whips me in the face.

"Guys like what?" I ask, a little concerned.

"You know the silent serial killer type," Kaia explains. "Quiet, mysterious, a little mean, and too pretty to be *that weird* and that antisocial."

"I think he just likes his privacy," I defend, and Kaia's eyes spark with mischief.

"Yeah, most serial killers do," she smiles.

"Wasn't Ted Bundy a social butterfly?" I challenge.

"Ted Bundy wasn't hot, definitely not like Brighton is. There's something messed up going on in his head, Reaper. He's twisted and quiet; it's dangerous." She strips from her jersey and shorts and stands in her sports bra and Spanx, "Make no mistakes, I want you to climb that mother fucker like a tree, but just make sure that's *all you do*."

"What's that supposed to mean?" I scowl.

"You fall in love with every tall, dark-haired man you see, and Bright is not the one," she warns. "Honestly, the only thing that's missing is the ugly mustache. You know better than anyone he's fucked up; if he wasn't, we'd know more about him. Sunday brings up Boone constantly; we *know* him. Why doesn't she talk about her very handsome second brother as much?"

I strip down and wrap a towel around myself, my mind drifting to horrible places. We wander to the showers as Sunday leaves for her shift, and I chew my lip thinking about what Kaia said.

"Do you think he's dangerous?" I ask, turning on the hot water.

"No," Kaia answers quickly, "if he were, they wouldn't willingly allow Daisy to stay there. I just think he's messed up worse than the Black siblings like to put out there."

"Maybe it's not our business," I say, trying to calm my own thoughts down as I wash out my hair.

"Sure, before, but lines are blurred now that you're sleeping under his roof." She adds, grimacing at the bruise on her leg one more time.

"You make me sound like a piranha," I snort.

"Worse, you're a slut who hasn't had sex with a man in like five months. You're like a sexual predator," she says.

"Ew, don't call me that!" I turn away from her and reach for the soap along the back wall. "I'm not sleeping with Brighton Black. He's a roommate and a friend."

"Who's probably packing a weapon and a nasty set of bedroom kinks," Kaia adds, and all I can do is groan.

An hour later, Boone is sliding plates across the table to us at the Hollow. I pick at the plastic on the drink menu along the corner that covers the intricate logo beneath. A skeleton hand holds a cup of whiskey with the first responders' red cross spray-painted roughly behind it all and framed in a simple circle. I always wondered if it was hand-drawn, and with Kaia in my head, suddenly, I'm wondering if Brighton is an artist beneath all that mystery. Picturing him with a pencil and notebook doesn't do it for me, though, and I push the menu out of my reach and pull my burger close.

"Good game today, pussycats," Boone says, and Kaia gently stabs him with a fork. "That last push was insane, Reaper." He points to me, completely unfazed by her, as he gets called from another table. "I'll have Maggie bring some drinks around."

Once he's gone, Kaia collects the pickle from her plate, holding it out for me, in trade for my tomatoes, but when I lift my bun, there aren't any. She looks at me and then frowns with a tiny shrug, still offering me her pickle without trade. I stare at the bare black bean burger in confusion, looking around at everyone else's to see that they all had tomatoes. I look over the booth and find Brighton's gaze on me from the bar.

He's wearing his Hollow shirt, and his dark hair is brushed off his stern face. His jaw does that infuriating ticking as he watches me, but he nods and goes back to work the second I make eye contact, like he was embarrassed to get caught staring. *I'll figure you out, Brighton Black, just please, for the love of all that is holy, do not be a serial killer. I don't know if I can be attracted to Dexter.*

"Shit, the drink menu for the month is incredible," Kaia waves it in my face, and I give it a proper look.

The Reaper: Brown Sugar Espresso Martini made with top-shelf vodka, a house-made BS syrup, and freshly brewed espresso.

"The Reaper?" I huff, and Kaia gives me that knowing look. He could have written out brown sugar, but he's left it BS on purpose, and it makes me smile.

"Roommates, just *friends*," she mocks and goes back to her meal.

Every time I undo the zippers on my boots, I feel his stupid hands on my calves—and panic. I kick them to the side and follow the noise of my siblings through the house, finding them all at the island doing their homework while Gabe makes dinner.

"What up, shitheads," I say, kissing Toby's bright red head. He's not doing homework, but he is creating some of the worst artwork I've ever seen in my life. He looks up at me and smiles, pushing my arm away from his head, and refocuses.

"Hey, can you look at this?" Remi asks from the other end, and I move around, getting a small wave from Gabe as I lean over what my sister is working on. She's the mirror of me, with dark hair and a wide, goofy smile that counterbalances her big, sad brown eyes. She's working on a comic strip for a book report on The Outsiders.

"It's cute," I answer honestly, "they need a little more gruff, though." I point to the drawing of them in the brawl. "More dirt, more blood," I instruct. "Where's Reid?" I ask, standing up and giving Shana a kiss on the head to match Toby's as she works on a math minute sheet.

"Right here," Reid saunters into the kitchen with Mom on his tail in a huff. His dark hair is plastered to his forehead with sweat, and he narrows his bright green eyes at me. The only sibling who got Dad's eyes and a constant reminder of what we had all gone through at his hands.

"Hey, slow down," I say to Mom as she misses the table with her purse and it crashes to the floor, making Remi jump out of her skin. I put my hand on her shoulder and wait for Mom to take a breath. "I went to pick up your brother from practice at school, and he wasn't there!"

The panic in her voice is palpable. Reid groans.

"I threw on my headphones and jogged home as a cool down," he defends himself. "She's insane."

"I've warned you before that you can't do that! You have to tell me where you are!" She chokes up and loses her cool again.

"He's not going to fucking grab me off the street, Mom!" Reid slams the fridge shut and stomps away, leaving everyone in the kitchen wide-eyed and concerned.

Gabe pulls the pan off the stove and moves toward Mom, ushering her from the kitchen. I take over the cooking, dumping the ground beef into the sauce mixture and checking the pasta before turning to my siblings.

"So, who else got into trouble today?" I ask gently, and the three of them stare at me, terrified. Remi's chest is thumping, and I feel bad for her because I can't comfort her racing heart with my own. "Oh, come on, I won't tell Mom and Dad. Give me the goods," I beg them.

A smile creeps onto Toby's face, "Oh, I know you did something bad, what was it?"

"I let Lady Gaga out of her cage, and I can't find her," he shrugs, knowing full well that Mom hates that fucking snake.

"I still can't believe you named your snake Lady Gaga," I laugh.

"It's all he watches on YouTube, day after day. Lady Gaga." Remi adds with a smile. "Dad put garlic bread in the oven," she says, and her nose sniffs the air. "It's burning," she adds.

"Shit," I swear. "I mean, shoot." I pop the oven open and, without thinking, shove my hand inside to grab the pan. On contact with the heat, my skin burns, and suddenly, shit isn't the worst thing they've heard. I flick the faucet on as Gabe comes wandering back into the kitchen because of the commotion and grabs the pan from the oven as I run my hand under cool water.

"Are you alright?" he asks me, sliding the nearly burnt bread onto the stove top to cool.

"Yeah, barely got me." I lie. There's a nasty, irritated line cutting into the palm of my hand and between my thumb and pointer finger where I grabbed the pan. I inhale slowly, pushing away the stinging pain and forcing a smile on my face. "You made spaghetti?" I ask him.

He nods, giving me one of his signature smiles. Gabe is a stout man, with more personality than strands of hair on his head and a heart big enough to love three misfit children and their high-strung mother. It's hard to remember a time when he wasn't around, or even the moment he had joined our lives. Mostly because it means having to think about my father, which isn't something I freely ever want to do. He's the exact opposite of my biological father, soft around the edges, encouraging and kind, sometimes annoyingly so.

"Go clean up for dinner, the first aid kit is in the bathroom, and I'll get the hooligans to the table." He pats me on the back gently and guides me out of the kitchen. As I go, I collect whatever dirty clothes I find and chuck them in the basket at the bottom of the stairs.

I can hear Mom pacing in her room as I reach the top, but I choose the source of the problem instead of dealing with more of her tears for the evening.

"Knock knock." I push Reid's door open. He's lying on the floor staring at the ceiling with a frustrated expression. "She's trying," I say to him, sinking to the floor beside him and assuming the same position.

The glow-in-the-dark stars Gabe had super-glued up there for him when he was seven are still holding strong. When Reid had panic attacks or nightmares, we would lie here and count them until he fell asleep again. So many nights spent on this floor, wondering if he'd ever get to a place where his brain didn't attack him in his sleep.

A place where the memories we didn't ask for would fade to black for good.

"No," he argues, "Everyone else is trying, she's still the same."

"Fear is a hard emotion to shake," I say, but I can feel his upset through the carpet we lie on. "She's just scared, and you're her kid. It's like a motherly instinct or whatever."

"He's not going to pick me off the street or from school, and I'm seventeen, I can defend myself from him," he argues.

I swallow tightly. The problem with Reid's logic is that he couldn't. I was seventeen, being put through walls and down stairs; that's why I got strong. So I could fight back. I dig my fingers into the carpet to keep the anxiety at bay and remind myself just how strong I am. He can't get me now, can't get us, he's gone.

"He's gone," I say out loud to Reid, "but it doesn't mean it can't come back. You know, most teenagers would love a chauffeur for a Mom."

"I just want to be a normal teenager, Ree," he says, his voice straining as he uses the nickname he used to call me when he was little. He turns his face to me, and he looks sad.

"You get to be one because Mom survived, the least you can do is let her drive you around." I remind him.

"We all survived, not just her. She wasn't even there that day, and you don't have a twenty-four-hour surveillance on me," he pouts.

I dig my phone out of my pocket and hold the screen up that shows his location, "air-tag, in your backpack."

Reid blinks slowly and then looks at me. "Right." He sighs, rolling over and sitting up. "I'll go apologize," he says, "but she's gotta relax a little, I can't do this with her for much longer."

He's saying all the things I said to myself before I moved out, and I get it. I understand his frustrations and worries, but he would be okay, and he's safe because of her concern, not despite it.

Thirteen years ago, I shot my Dad.

I sit up and watch Reid wander from the room.

Thirteen years ago, I shot my Dad to *save my brother.*

My hands tremble against the carpet as I start to count the stars on the ceiling.

I could still see him straddling Reid's tiny body in the backyard. Reid hadn't done anything wrong... he just swung the stick too hard, and the puck hitting the shed sounded like a gunshot. Dad flipped a switch, and Reid was the enemy. Everything had happened so fast.

He survived, no charges were pressed, and he was put in a home for men like him who needed more help with their PTSD. He went in, and we never heard from him again— until Mom got the divorce papers in the mail. He had served almost twenty years in the military, and the trauma consumed him so badly that when he was triggered, everyone was a threat. Including his wife and children.

For thirteen years, we've all waited for him to find us, to remind us why we were afraid of the dark. Some days are better than others, but Mom is always on edge, especially with Reid.

"Are you coming down for dinner?" Remi's head pops into the room, and her smile instantly makes the noise quiet.

"Help me up, I'm old and turning to dust," I whine, and pretend to be heavier than I am.

"Ree, you weigh a thousand pounds!" Remi grumbles.

"Wow, now I'm fat." I slap her hand away playfully and scramble to my feet, chasing her through the upstairs and allowing her giggles to push away every bad memory that seeps in.

"Major Black. Nice of you to join us." Landon leans against a column, watching the guys set up chairs in the old church. "Haven't seen you in a while."

"Haven't needed to be here," I respond stiffly.

"Sorry, I forgot you suffered memory loss and forgot the last ten years of your life," he teases dryly. *You always need to be here.* That's what goes unsaid. And he's not wrong. Neither is the silence. In it, I can hear my hands shake with unresolved trauma, and the dark corners are spreading again at a speed I can't manage to keep up with.

But there's another person in my home now.

I can't let it get out of control.

Sergeant Landon Gaboury fought the same tours I did—twenty years older than me, twice as hardened. We never fought together, but he was around at the same time as me. He's all gray lines and wrinkles, tired from life and what it's thrown at him. He's a good shoulder to lean against when everything goes to shit. He keeps a level head, clear eyes, and never misses a beat.

"You look tired," I say just to get under his skin, and he scoffs.

"Fuck you, Black." He huffs. "How's the daughter?"

"Thirteen," I shrug. "Some days she wakes up and remembers she hates me, so that's fun."

It's the opposite of fun. It's torture and unpredictable. I hate it.

"Sounds like she's keeping you sharp," he says with a knowing smirk. He has three kids of his own, all grown, I think. He never really talks about them, but it was always his driving force. Do better for them, create a world for them.

His motto became mine.

Do better for Daisy. Create a world for her.

That's the point of all this. I cross my arms and watch as a few of the guys argue over whether the circle is even or not, but Landon claps his hands and interrupts them. He hands me a coffee that I probably won't drink and wanders over to take his chair. Everyone files in after him, finding a spot to bare their souls in the most raw way possible, and we all go quiet.

"You know how this works," he says to them. "I'm not going to force you to talk; being here is a step you have to take yourself. So is telling your story. If you aren't ready today, try next week."

A few of them stomp their boots in response, a habit from basic training that a few guys held onto later in life that they just can't shake. There are a few new faces around the circle, and I can't tell if they've been coming for a while and I just haven't been here, or if they're fresh meat for Landon to mind warp into spilling their guts.

There's a reason he's the liaison for the army now; he runs these group sessions all day long, seeing sad faces, hearing heartbreaking stories. But he's damn good at getting people to talk.

"We can sit here in the silence too," he says, setting down his coffee and fixing his eyes on me, but I just shake my head. *Not today. Just leave me be.*

One of the new faces clears his throat. He's a squirrely-looking kid with fiery red hair and brown eyes that bounce around like he's seen some shit. We all have but... It's like he's still seeing it—still in it.

"Private Dixon," he says, coughing nervously. "On stress leave from active duty. Two weeks ago, I watched my entire team go up in flames and I...uh...well, they..." he stutters. "They said group would help, but I kind of just feel like a pussy," he admits, and some of the guys laugh despite how serious it is.

"How many guys?" Landon steers the conversation back.

"Nine." Dixon swallows hard. "IED."

"How did you survive?" One of the rougher guys, Patrick, leans forward and asks.

"We were loading the truck," he stops again, dropping his head, "they liked to play tricks on me, it was like making me one of the boys…" he says. *Hazing*. Not unusual. "Every time I tried to get on the back, they'd pull forward. It was a game we played…"

"Sounds like you're a joke." Patrick crosses his arms and scoffs.

"Patty, I suggest you wait your turn unless you want to tell everyone about how you used to bootlick every officer you came across for a promotion?" Landon doesn't even turn his head away from Dixon when he offers up the threat. "Keep sharing," he says to the kid.

Dixon can't be more than twenty; it's clear how young he is in the way he talks and holds himself. Patrick has him rattled, but I watch Landon pull him out of his shell.

"They pulled too far forward the last time and hit the IED," he confesses. He's only here to talk about it because they were bullying him. I exhale slowly, controlling myself as Dixon continues. "The ones that didn't die from the impact caught fire," he says, looking down, and it's only then that I notice he's wearing gloves. "I tried to get them out, but," he turns his palms over and stares at the leather—no doubt covering the burns. "Group is supposed to help with the screaming," he blurts like he hadn't just told a story that dark, but we all nod and agree in our own way.

"It does." I clear my throat. "Eventually."

Landon looks at me, giving a small nod of thanks, and turns his attention back to Dixon. As the night goes on, the tremor in my hands gets worse, and eventually I have to set the coffee cup on the floor because it's spilling onto my jeans.

I help clean up the chairs as Landon says goodbye to the last of the guys. When I put the final stack away, I find his gaze on me.

"Have you gone to the Doc?" He asks, pointing at my hands as I shove them into my pockets.

"I am the doc." I brush him off.

"Don't do that, Black," he warns. "You came tonight for a reason."

"Just needed familiar company," is my excuse, but Landon doesn't buy it.

"You're my most cagey one. You've been to forty-six meetings over the years and never told a single story."

"I don't have any to tell," I say. It's a delicate lie.

"You have more than anyone, Brighton." He uses my full name, and it makes me think of Rhea. A smile creeps onto my face, and he clocks it. "What's that?"

"What?" I shove it down.

"You smile less than you talk, so what's that grin for?" He asks again.

"Just thinking of someone," I admit, and it's a simple enough lie that he'll think I mean Daisy, maybe... "It's nothing. Do you need any more help?"

"I could use some honesty. I can't help you if you don't talk to me," he pushes.

The church feels so empty with just the two of us in it, but I lean against the column and cross my arms. "Nightmares are back," I say tightly. "The usual shit to keep them locked up isn't working, and it's causing this." I hold out my shaking hand. Landon stares at it and nods. I can never tell what he's thinking, and I wish I could. It's almost always good advice.

"It's trauma manifesting. You need real therapy," he gives the one answer I don't want.

"Figured you'd say that," I huff, pushing off the column and moving toward the front door.

"You walk yourself in a circle long enough, Bright, you'll start tripping over your own steps," He says as I push out into the night air. I spend the walk home thinking about what he said, and it doesn't matter how many times he's offered therapy as a solution; I know it won't work, so why bother?

How is a shrink on a couch going to walk me through something they've never experienced? Do they know what it feels like to feel constantly drenched in others' blood? Do they wake up soaked from sweat, reeling from the same nightmare over and over? How many deaths have they seen, dead bodies have they carried? Do they walk around with a soundtrack of kids crying for help?

No, I'm not going to be taught breathing exercises by someone whose nightmares consist of a barista using oat milk instead of two percent. Fuck that.

I unlock the apartment door and find Daisy at the island with Rhea. She never does her homework in the kitchen. It's always in her room, behind locked doors with her music on full blast.

"Hi," I choke out, removing my boots and hanging up my keys.

Rhea looks up from what she's doing and gives me a small wave. My eyes snag on the bandage around her palm, and my brows furrow at the sight. Daisy starts to pack up her things, vacating the area the second I get home, as per usual, and I fill a glass of water for myself.

"What happened?" I ask, even though I shouldn't. *Not my business.*

"Fistfight with a baking sheet," she says, setting down her pen. She's grading something, but I can't really tell what.

"Who won?" I ask, reaching under the cabinet for the first aid kit.

"Baking sheet. The garlic bread was delicious, though." She laughs softly. I put out my hand for hers, and she hesitates.

"Black Residence rule number sixteen: you let me perform first aid. I don't need you getting an infection under my roof," I tell her, and it seems to quell her nervous concern because she lays her hand in mine.

"There are rules?" she asks as I unwrap the messy bandage with a scowl. The burn isn't minor; it spans across her soft hand and looks sore. "You never said anything about rules."

"I'll make you a list." I toss the old bandage in the garbage and grab a clean cloth to clean the burn gently. She flinches from the warm water, but I hold her wrist with just enough pressure to keep her in place. When I'm finished, I wrap it again and let her have her hand back.

"Next time, hurt a different body part. I'm sick of staring at your hand," I say before thinking, and then regret my word choices as a tiny smile forms on her face. "I didn't mean it that way." Pathetic—damage control, and we both know it.

Rhea tries to hide her amusement as she slides from the bench. She gives me a tiny thank you and retreats to her room, leaving me alone. And it's not until she's gone that I realize that the room had been so quiet with her in it.

Brighton

A week later, I'm sitting in the grass across from Judd, stretching out my calves, when Boone slumps down between us with a groan.

"You okay?" Judd asks, raking dusty brown hair back with his fingers before dropping to all fours and sinking into a knee stretch.

"Barty is back for the Bears," he says, rolling out his neck. "I'm so sick of that guy's face."

I look over to the Bears' side of the field, and sure enough, Henry Barton is running passing drills with another player. He's been out with a groin strain for a few weeks, and playing against the Bears has been enjoyable without him.

The Harbor Hogs aren't exactly the most professional team. Sure, we play hard and are good, but a lot of the guys on the team are here because they needed a hobby. We have a few imports, Judd Loveday—Lovey to the boys—is one of them. A center from the United Kingdom, he's fast, big, and enjoys the sport. He came over with a program to help the sport grow and he's extremely knowledgeable when he's not being a dumbass.

But Henry Barton plays like he has something to prove. It's sweaty for no reason, and it gets under Boone's skin like nobody's business. My brother watches him like a hawk as Judd rambles on about something in an accent I barely understand half the time. I roll out of the grass and wander back over to the bench to get some water before the game starts, and look up to find every single Hillcat in the bleachers.

Sunday waves excitedly, and I lift my bottle, trying to ignore who's sitting on her left.

Rhea's wearing the tiniest crop top I've ever seen in my entire life. So small that every time her tattooed stomach rises and falls, I catch a glimpse of the lacy black bra she's wearing beneath. She talks to Kaia with a smile on her face and picks at the tears on her black jeans, completely oblivious to half the players staring at them. I grind my jaw down and turn my eyes back to the field, praying that today's game is rough enough to lay me out permanently so the torture that is Rhea Drake can stop.

Across the way on the second field, a team of workers is changing the bulbs on half of the game lights that usually illuminate the field for night games, and there are a set of unmarked trucks in the parking lot. I reach over and pat Raul on the shoulder, "What's all that for?"

"They're doing some midnight foam run thing this weekend, set up started today." He explains and finishes taping his calf.

"Alright, Captains," The referee blows his whistle, and the game comes to a slow start. If we're honest, the Hogs don't really have a captain; it's just whoever wants to go through the torture of listening to the game-day speech. Judd draws the short straw and marches across the field to get it started as Boone starts chirping at Kaia behind me.

"Pay attention," I grab him by the collar, and he stumbles backwards but manages to flip her off before we take the field.
The Bears take possession. The clock starts.

Tolia, one of our smaller guys, is quick off the line and manages to get to the ball before anyone else. He's immediately met with contact, but drives his shoulder hard into the attacker and pops the ball backwards to Judd, who takes it cleanly, sidesteps the next guy, and eats up another ten yards. He's pushed to the outside of the field, but I'm there to take up the slack, and the second the channel closes, he flicks the ball out, and it finds my hands. Two guys are coming at me, one a half-step ahead, forcing me to hesitate—then my stall trips him up and leaves a hole between them to slip through.

My calves burn in the best kind of way as I find the pocket and take off and leave the nearest guy behind, scoring the first try of the game. The exercise, tangled with the adrenaline, feels incredible, and I realize this is why we play. To forget everything else. I toss the ball to Chris, our fly-half, and jog back to where I belong with sweat dripping between my shoulder blades.

By the time the whistle echoes out, we're down two, and everyone is ready to collapse in the heat. "It's too hot out here today." I palm a tossed water bottle and drink down the water before chucking it to the next guy.

"Hey, man, no one asked you to show off that early. You set the tone for the game." Judd is leaning over on his thighs in line as the ref blows the whistle, and I laugh at his disgruntled comment.

"It's been seven minutes, boys," Kaia yells down from the bleachers.

"And six tries. Bugger off," Judd groans.

"I've seen toddlers put in more effort, Lovey," she harasses him, and he tries to ignore her, but she's just too good at getting under his skin, and it's not just him. She's got the attention of at least four other players.

"Says the girl who hasn't scored in two games," he clips back.

"I don't have to score every game; we have a whole team of winners," she teases. "It's not our fault you boys have one golden egg."

Her gaze snaps to me. I shake my head, unamused by her shit and too gassed to give her anything back. She smiles at me viciously.

"What, no smart remark, Killjoy?" she hums, using my nickname, and all I can do is turn my back on her. "It's been more entertaining watching them change lightbulbs," she teases, and I hear the rest of the girls laugh.

"Seven more minutes, give them nothing but hell." Judd pulls us together.

It takes all seven minutes to secure the win; every second counts as we pull ourselves through the heat exhaustion and up the field, inch by inch. The Hillcats make themselves loud and clear as the clock ticks by, and I think the heckling actually makes them play a little harder. The fear of Kaia having more ammo is terrifying enough to make Boone run faster than he ever has.

"Slow poke!" Kaia yells as we jog back to our line for one last push up the field.

Boone's lips curl into a smirk, annoyed and amused by her all at once, and maybe a little turned on, which makes me roll my eyes.

"Pay attention," I snap at him, and he waves me off as the ball flips into motion. Luckily, his focus is quick, and his eyes flicker to the ball. He surges his body forward and slams hard into the player who has it, pushing him back a few steps before he collapses to the ground, forcing a wide right field scrum before the ball is shoved from between the bodies.

It rocks free of the player's hands and tumbles along the ground. The Bears stumble to get control of it, flicking it out, but it slips through the fingertips of their winger, and Judd is there to scoop it out of their possession. He moves quickly, coming to a wedge as Boone and I wrap behind him, giving him a split second to give Boone the ball. The attackers trip over each other, and Boone slips through the lane, untouchable as he picks up speed and leaves them behind.

His chest is pumping as he sets the ball down, and we take the game by six points. The best thing about Boone is that he makes the smallest things feel enormous. Like a recreational game of rugby, there are no stakes, no trophies, no television broadcasts. And yet, Boone screams at the top of his lungs like an animal, catching a rip in his jersey and tearing it more as the Bears wander around him, disappointed in themselves. The celebration starts immediately. Judd throws Boone over his shoulder and claps him hard a few times before setting him down. I watch him point over to the bleachers, making sure that Kaia has seen every step.

"You know, for your size, you're pretty fast," I tease him as he pushes around Raul playfully. He tosses his arm over me, and we find ourselves in line to shake hands. The Bears are respectful until we reach Barton—his face set in a hard, mean line.

"For a second there, I thought you were going to have to pull in some ringers," he says to us, and Boone scoffs.

"You can never just take a loss, can you?" Boone squares his shoulders.

"That was barely a loss, Black." He steps into my brother's space, and I tense.

"Not what the scoresheet says—unless you play rugby as well as you read?" Boone laughs, but I can hear how on edge he is with every word.

"You still following Keegan around like a kicked dog?" Barton needles.

"I always forget you're friends with that spineless piece of shit." Boone shakes his head. Kaia's *current* boyfriend, Christian, will always be a sore spot that Boone pretends isn't.

"It's pathetic," he says under his breath and steps forward.

"Say it with your chest, Barty. I can't hear you," Boone tenses.

"I said, it's pathetic," he hisses, and the next step he takes warrants my intervention.

"Step back from my brother, Barton." There's no lightness to my words, only a command, and it makes him turn his head toward me. My hand shakes at my side, and I ball it to keep it from doing it any further.

"What do they call you guys again? Thing One and Thing Two? Is it because you're idiots or because you share a brain cell?" He chuckles, still trying to get under our skin. I scoff, ready to beat his ass for less. "I'm not starting shit. Calm down, Bright."

"Back." I don't raise my voice. "Up."

"Alright, hey! Hey..." Judd is the first to step between the three of us, and he easily walks Barton back away from my brother. "Cool off," he says, turning back to us. "We won. We go home with the Hillcats. He goes home to his hand."

"Maybe if he's lucky, Christian will help him out," Boone claps back, and the laughter that falls from his lips is more natural this time. His shoulders go slack as Judd slaps him on the stomach and wanders back to the bench.

"If you're quicker off your left foot, you'd have that opening faster." Kaia is standing with her arms crossed in the bleachers, and Boone smiles up at her.

"Be quiet, Killer, we all know I'm faster than you. I don't need fancy foot tricks to take off." Boone is quick to silence her, knowing that it's only going to rile her up more.

"Oh," she smiles, sick and wide across her face. "That's cute."

"Aw, baby girl, that was so close to a genuine compliment," Boone fires back. The flirting never stops. "You're good, Kai, but you aren't that good. You'd never catch me," he argues.

Everyone simultaneously groans and grumbles around them.

"Is that a challenge?" Kaia narrows her eyes at him and climbs down from the bleachers. Her five-seven frame is average, but pitted up against Boone's six-three, she's dwarfed.

"Please don't, I'm exhausted..." I say, rubbing the sweat from my face with the bottom of my shirt, when I drop it, Rhea's staring at me like I just dropped my pants. *Subtle.*

"No, Boone thinks he's better and faster than me." Kaia's tone is vicious, and her dark eyes are cutting through him like a knife as she speaks. "So let's prove that once and for all..."

"I'm not racing you. I just played a full game." Boone scoffs and ignores her deadly expression as he runs a towel through his sweaty hair. He lets it fall around his neck, and both tattooed hands tug on either side as he finally looks down at her.

"So go take a nap," she hisses. "Hillcats vs the Hogs. Tonight."

"Half our players work at the bar tonight, Kaia," I remind her and dig through my duffel bag for my phone. Daisy is at home by herself, and while I know that she's old enough to be there, the worry still remains, and checking in on her periodically helps.

"After shift. Three a.m." She shrugs.

"No," I say it at the exact moment Boone agrees. "Are you serious? This is childish."

"I'm not letting you run that pretty little mouth without consequences," Boone says to her, never looking over at me because if he did, he would see how pissed off I am.

"Three a.m.," Kaia says again.

"I want new siblings," I mutter and swipe my bag off the bench to head to the showers as the Hogs and the Hillcats stare each other down like assholes.

Rhea

"Wait, which one is it?" I ask Kaia as I dig in the trunk of her Impala. She brought a duffel bag of face paint and neon body spray after swiping the keys to the field panel off the coach's desk.

"Yeah, that one, it's like a purple color," she says, tying her cleat. Cosy yawns beside me, and Sunday shoves the bottle of cinnamon whiskey toward her.

"Wake up," she demands, and Cosy takes a swig.

"I'm only here because someone promised me I could assault Loveday," she says with heavy eyes.

"Not half asleep, you can't," Sunday laughs. "Another," she says, pushing on the base of the bottle to tip it back into Cosy's throat.

"Go hand these out," Kaia says, shoving a handful of face paint at Sunday. "Reaper, with me. Let's go do some illegal shit."

"My favorite," I giggle and follow her closely as we traipse across the parking lot to the utility shed. "Do you think they'll be pissed at us?" I ask as she pops the lock quietly. We slip inside, and I fish my phone out to help her see as she finds her way over the box that's labeled 'lights'. She unlocks it, flips on Pitch A's lights, and before I can ask if it worked, the Hillcats erupt in cheers.

Outside, everyone's war paint glows under the hazy black lights for the midnight foam run, and suddenly, the night gets a lot more fun. I pull my hair back into two even buns at the base of my neck and check to make sure that I have my mouth guard in my pocket before we take the field. Because the jerseys we all wear are similar, most of the Hillcats are ready to play in their sports bras and tank tops. It gives us the perfect opportunity to add more color to our arms and chests, and makes us glow like trouble.

In the black light, it's hard to even tell that the Hogs showed up, but as we get closer, we find them standing around talking in a huddle, almost imperceptible in the darkness. Boone turns, his expression souring—but Kaia silences him before he can open his mouth.

"Here," she says, tossing a bag to him. His face lights up when he opens it, and he pulls out their own stock of face paint. He gives her a lopsided smile and starts handing it out, because beneath all the bickering, they're always on the same side.

"It's not going to look as cool as yours," he frowns, waving his giant hand at her, "I need your delicate hands, Killer."

"Oh, sure, now you're all sweet talk." Kaia's tone changes, and she takes the pastels from him.

Most of the guys are helping each other, but Brighton clears his throat from beside me and hands me a package. "You're an art teacher, aren't you?" he says gruffly, and I'm surprised he showed up at all. He didn't really seem like the type to break his routine.

"You want me to...?" I take it from him with a smile, and he turns in my direction. It's an odd thing to be taller than most of the men around you, *all the time.* It usually means no heels, no platforms, *no fun*—lots of self-confidence issues. Watching Brighton Black sink onto his heels, bend his knees, and fold his arms to come eye level with me brings a burst of girlish euphoria blooming in my chest.

Oh. He stares at me, the black lights making his stormy eyes even sharper, and I try to remember what he wants.

Breathe, you stupid slut. You are a strong, independent woman; he is just a man.

"Are you going to—" He starts, and I startle free of my thoughts.

"Hold still," I say, steadying his chin as I drag bright purple paint across his taut cheekbone, right over the faint scar there. "What number are you?"

"You don't know my number?" he says, deadpan.

"I— No," I confess.

"One." He says, lips still pressed in a straight line, jaw still impossibly tight.

"Duh," I curse myself for not being aware. *Thing One. It's literally written on everything, Rhea.* On his other cheek, I draw the one and leave it at that.

"Thanks," he says, waiting until my fingers leave his chin before he snatches the paint and tosses it to Boone. "Let's get this over with. I'm exhausted."

"Wait, wait—" Kaia holds up her hands and makes sure that all eyes are on her before she continues to speak. "Stakes."

"Yeah, you lose, and Boone gets the title of the fastest," Brighton says.

"Don't be boring," Sunday giggles as she helps Judd paint his number on his bicep in neon green.

"I want something important," Kaia says, like she already has something in mind, and Brighton groans with impatience. "I want the Boone Burger."

"You order that every game night, why is that important?" Judd asks with maximum confusion.

"No, *I want it*. If we win tonight, the Boone Burger becomes the Hillcat Burger." She stares at Brighton as Boone's face scrunches up in annoyance.

"Deal," Boone says, already grinning.

"You idiot," Brighton groans at his brother's undying confidence.

"They aren't going to win." Boone turns to him, and I can feel the heat coming off his skin from beside me. It's so hot I back away and fall in line with Cosy as the Hog's huddle to discuss their strategy.

We create our own and listen as Cosy gives us a game plan. "We won't beat them in size," she notes, and Kaia rolls her eyes. "Not even Reaper can take on the twins. It's just logic; we have to beat them in speed. Do not get caught by either of *them*," she says, and Sunday scoffs. "They're stronger than you, even if your ego doesn't believe it. The way we win this is by using our brains and running our rodent plays."

The rodent plays are simply that, quick, sneaky plays that focus on not getting caught. We all nod, understanding her instruction, and put our hands into the middle of the huddle with one loud cheer.

"Hold on," Brighton puts his hand up. "Who's refereeing this crap? Because you're a cheater, Kaia Keegan." He points directly at her, and she blows him a kiss.

"That would be my job," a voice comes from behind Kaia. "Sorry, I'm late." He slides into the line, giving her a little fist bump, and salutes Brighton from beside her. "Hey, Brighton."

"Fuck," he swears.

Cael Cody, former shortstop of the Harbor Hornets baseball team stands there in all his blond buzz cut glory with a wicked smile on his face, in a pair of gym shorts and a white T-shirt that glows under the black lights. Brighton's jaw tenses uncomfortably.

Kaia and Cael have been causing trouble for months since meeting through Addy's boyfriend Jensen. I shouldn't even be surprised she brought him tonight, but it's like she knows something the rest of us don't.

"Does he even know anything about rugby, Kaia?" Boone grumbles.

"I gave him a crash course," she says sweetly, her eyes lighting up when Cael smirks at her, and I don't blame her. I'd let that blond menace ruin my life. "Don't be mean to this angel; he came here as a favor," Kaia teases, and Cosy snorts.

"Yeah, don't be mean to me. I'm here to have *fun*." Cael's smile grows, but his eyes are daggers when they land on Brighton. I look between the two of them, and it seems Cael is getting more enjoyment out of it than Brighton.

"Whatever." He rolls his shoulders out and turns to whisper something in Boone's ear, who only nods slowly before throwing the ball toward Kaia.

"You kick," he says, and the teams fall into line as Cael starts the timer on his watch.

"Seven minutes," he says, standing between the lines with a whistle between his fingers. "Play dirty," he smiles, looking at us.

Before anyone can argue with his logic, he blows the whistle. It's immediately clear the Hogs aren't taking this lightly when Judd pockets the ball, lands, and plants his whole hardened body into the turf, leaving poor Margie—totally unprepared for full contact—hits him like a bug on a windshield. She handles it with grace, wrapping around his core and digging her heels in as hard as she can to slow him down.

He flips the ball out, and it finds Boone without contest, but Kaia is quick and slips away from the pack to lunge at him. He fights her off, but it's not enough; he fumbles the ball in his attempts to get her off him, and they both hit the ground hard. Sunday finds the loose ball, threading through two of the Hogs to find the open lane. Kaia springs up and stomps a foot beside his head. He laughs loudly as mud sprays across his face and watches as she takes off to catch Sunday, who's speeding toward the try lines without pause. Raul lunges for Sunday, catching her by the waist, but she pops the ball out, and it finds Margie, who throws herself over the line to score.

Raul rolls over in the dirt, and one of the other players hauls him up as Sunday kicks the ball for a point. She turns with a malicious smile on her cute little face as it soars through the posts. She and Kaia start to dance without music, shimmying around each other in a circle while we move back to our lines.

"Oh man, think of how many Hillcat burgers the Hollow is going to sell," she hums as Sunday falls into place and taps the ball to her foot, kicking it out to the left and right into Judd's arms.

Cosy is quick, though, and gives him a taste of his own medicine with a hard block that knocks him back a step and scares him bad enough that he tosses the ball out to Laurie, their smallest player and fastest.

Kaia sees it too, and before Laurie can create space, she slams into him, wrapping her arms around his hips and walking him backward until he trips over his own two feet and collides with the dirt. The ball pops free, and Cosy gets her hands on it before Tolia. She fumbles it for a moment but tosses it wide to a waiting Sunday.

I spot Brighton and Judd in my peripheral, and click my teeth before pushing the pace to get in front of them. If anyone is going to block them, it's my body, but Judd is fast, and Brighton is falling in line with every strong step he takes.

Fuck.

The black light shines over every sharp line that makes up Brighton's face, the way his jersey sinks into his tense muscles, and how his shorts ride up on his powerful thighs. I nearly trip over my own legs, but catch myself just in time to slam into him and derail his path to Sunday. We collide hard, roll through the turf, and skid to a rough stop as Boone hurdles our tangled bodies and makes for his little sister. Brighton freezes, his entire body flexing beneath me, and I'm suddenly too aware of his skin against mine.

Too warm, too close. Get it the fuck together, Rhea, we aren't making out with Sunday's brother... He licks his bottom lip. *Making a mental note to Google how to become Brighton Black's tongue later.*

"That was dirty," I hear him say but my eyes are still locked on his lips. "Rhea," he snaps and starts to move. I come to my senses and kick free of him roughly, now covered in the paint from my skin, and scramble to my feet after Boone. "You gonna call that penalty, Cody?" Brighton barks as we run, and Cael shrugs.

"I saw you trip over your own two feet! You should tie your shoes better," he clips and keeps moving.

Brighton has at least three inches on me in his step as he rushes past me to support his team. Cosy jogs beside me, doing a once-over before continuing past to catch up with the rest of the players. Sunday wastes no time bringing us up by another six points, and Boone curses loudly as Kaia turns to him and gives him a wink.

"Say it," she snaps at him, her smile bright.

"Never," Boone palms the ball off the ground as Cael blows the minute warning whistle and causes panic. He moves quickly, and the ball is in play even quicker. We barely have time to position, and the ball bounces hard off the ground ten yards behind Josie before flicking out of bounds.

"You fucking—" Cosy spits, knowing precisely the play the Hogs are trying to run. Kaia quickly explains to Cael what's happening. Josie stands out of bounds next to Raul, and Cael positions himself between them, blowing the whistle before any of us are even ready for it.

Brighton doesn't flinch. He hauls his brother up over his head while Kaia and I scramble into position, but Boone's arms are longer, and he pulls the ball toward him with one hand and slaps Kaia's with the other.

"You can't win this, Killer." Boone teases her, and takes off as Kaia hits the ground with a feral look on her face.

Brighton

As soon as Boone's feet hit the dirt, he's gone and Rhea struggles to let go of Kaia fast enough. She trips for a heartbeat before digging into the dirt and finding her stride to catch up with my brother. She tries, but there's no catching him with the head start. She reaches for his shorts, but he spins away, skips a few steps, and slides over the line for the try.

He picks himself and the ball off the ground, pointing at Kaia and returning the smug wink she had tossed him earlier. I shake my head as Cael blows the whistle to call the five-minute break, and we all gather for some water.

"Don't get cocky," I warn Boone and hand him the water bottle. I look over my shoulder, and Cael is smiling, chatting away with Rhea. My jaw tightens uncomfortably. "That gremlin's not calling bad hits. Keep it clean."

"I'm fully aware we're down, Bri," he says to me, snatching it away. "Maybe if you spent less time rolling around in the dirt, making out with Reaper, we'd be winning."

I stare at him. *She'd hit me hard. I hope she's okay.* I fight the urge to look over my shoulder again just to check. *Is it Cael or is it her that has you so unbalanced?*

"Just play. Stop showing off," I warn.

I fix the sleeves on my jersey, rub the sweat from my palms, and stare down Cael until he blows the whistle again. It's all I can do to keep my focus. Rhea laughs about something with Kaia, and it feels like it's been weeks since I last heard that noise. Every day that goes by, her sad girl smile chips away at what resolve I have, and I find myself softening to her more than I respectfully should.

"Just play," Boone mocks in my ear as we line up.

I run my hand through my hair and take count of the opponents. Kaia is twitching at the end of their line, her body itching to move.

"Try to keep the tackles fair, Black," Cael drawls as he passes, twirling that stupid fucking whistle. I want to choke him with it. He blows it loudly, and the second half of the game starts. The ball bounces back and forth between the teams for a moment before Cosy wins clean possession and starts to move it up the field.

Judd cuts me off to take Cosy down, and I let him—because before he can even get his hands on her, the ball gets shucked wide into Rhea's arms. Her long legs pump fast the second she comes in contact with it. I side-step, encouraging my body forward as she barrels toward the gap between Chris and me. She's going to slip right by because he's slow and clumsy, barely able to stop the ball as it flies by him, and Rhea stiff-arms him straight in the chest.

Shit.

"Get her!" Boone hollers from behind me.

I didn't need him to tell me what needed to be done. I'm just not even sure I can catch her at this point. Unlike Boone, I can admit when someone is faster than me, and Rhea, despite her strength difference, carries herself most gracefully. I chase after her, seeing the win slipping from our grasp, the closer she gets to the line.

My thighs scream by the time I get in range, and I launch from the dirt, knowing that if I miss the wrap-up, it's over. I'm the only person close enough to stop her. My hands find the soft skin of her stomach and yank her hard against my chest. Our feet tangle. She gets three more steps before we're hurling toward the turf. My shoulder explodes from the contact as I wrap her up and we roll clumsily through the grass. We land with her on top of me—her chest in my face, that wicked grin already there. She pops her arm up, ball still in her grip, and taps the grass above my head with it.

"Thanks for the help," she says in a whisper that shudders through my entire body.

"Yeah," I groan as she pushes herself off me with her nails digging into my chest. "No worries, Hellcat," I grunt, pain biting through my shoulder.

"It was a good tackle," Judd's voice echoes from my left, and his hand comes into view first, helping me off the ground. "She's just freakishly tall," he says.

I grumble something under my breath, and Judd takes that as an agreement as we flood back to our spots down fourteen. The rest of the game goes worse, the second moral drops, and we realize that we're the inferior team; the guy's adrenaline deflates. Boone does his best to get them back, and we score another try, but Kaia follows it up by running the entire pitch. She hurdles Raul without pause and flips over the line because she's just as much of a show-off as Boone.

Cael blows the whistle to end it, and we stand around out of breath and out of confidence, but Kaia is on a mission. She stomps across the field to where Boone has sunk into the grass on his knees, trying to get air into his lungs.

"Say it," she says again, both hands on her hips.

"Never." He shakes his head, and she squats down to get level with him.

"Say it," she demands.

"I fucking hate you," he grumbles, but there's a dopey smile on his face.

"No, you don't," she's quick to counter, and she pokes him in the chest. "Say it."

"You're better. And faster," he pants. "Happy now?"

"The happiest," she sings, springing up from the grass.

Boone groans at the thought of moving that quickly after playing two hard games today, and I relate to the pain on a cellular level. He pushes from the grass, and Kaia yelps, running away from him, and their laughter fills the quiet night. I roll back into the grass and stare up at the pitch black sky for a second as I try to recenter myself. Despite how much I had protested the night before, it had turned out pretty fun. It's been a while since I'd actually been out of the house.

"At least they'll sleep well." Rhea laughs at the two of them playing like little kids as she walks over to me and offers me her hand to pull me from the grass. She watches Boone catch up to Kaia and haul her over his shoulder. When she looks back at me, she offers me a tired smile that turns into a yawn.

"Do you need a ride home?" she asks after a minute.

"Yeah, actually. Boone brought me and..." I get distracted by the paint smudge streaked across the top of her breast, staining her sports bra.

"What?" She clocks me staring instantly and panics, looking down at herself. She starts to laugh wildly at the sight of it and shrugs, "You're not exactly clean yourself, Terminator."

I look down at myself and see what she means. The paint from her body is smeared all over my jersey, shorts, and skin, all transferred from her body when we collided. It takes me a second to register: she didn't say my name.

"I hate that nickname," I groan, caught off guard—then a huff that's almost a laugh escapes me.

"Oh." She turns red from embarrassment, and her voice gets really low and slow as she says it. I realize that she looks scolded by the comment, and that's not how I meant it, because honestly, Rhea can call me whatever she wants as long as she says it like that.

I scowl at myself, and she catches the expression, only furthering the sad look on her face. *Fuck.* I force a tiny smile, and she just shakes her head as we make our way over to her car. She jogs over and grabs her keys from the passenger seat of Kaia's Impala and rejoins me awkwardly standing with my bag waiting, then heads for a vintage, shiny black Bronco that stops me short.

"Is that a '69?" I ask her, pointing to the vehicle, and she nods, her brows furrowing at my surprise.

"It sits in the Hollow parking lot. How have you not noticed it?" She says, popping the window on the bed so I can throw my bag in the back.

I walk around her and open the driver's door, staring at her over the door as she comes to the other side with a smile. "I don't actually go out back," I admit. "I park my truck down the street where it's free."

"Of course you do," she says with a small smile. I close the door and wander around to the passenger side. "You own the building." She questions.

"I don't own the parking lot," I argue.

The second I open the door, the smell of girl, art supplies, and sweaty gym gear hits my nose, and I look over the top of the Bronco at her. "What the hell?" I look inside at the absolute mess of the interior. The back is completely piled with her belongings and school stuff, and there are so many shaker cups and energy drink cans on the floor, I can't even tell what color the floor is.

"How old are you?" I grumble.

"Twenty-nine," she says, her tone confused.

"Not seriously—never mind. This is disgusting," I say to her, kicking a spot free for my feet as I climb in. "You're disgusting," I mutter as she starts the engine.

By the time we get home, it's already five am, and I can already tell that Rhea is hungry because she beelines up for the fridge.

"Don't," I say to her as she reaches for the handle.

"Why not? I'm starving," she whines.

"You're covered in paint. Do not touch anything but the shower faucet," I say, pushing off my cleats and dropping my duffel bag. "And clean that when you're done," I warn her. She looks down at herself and shrugs, slinking off to the bathroom. While she's in there, Daisy emerges from her room, sleepy and bleary-eyed.

"Morning..." she yawns. Of all the things she got from her mother, being a morning person wasn't one of them. That she got from me.

"You hungry?" I ask her as she eyes the paint that stains my uniform.

"Yeah," she leaves a headphone out as she slides onto the stool and rests her head in her arms to watch me. "Where were you?" she asks.

"Your uncle had a rugby thing," I try to lie.

"He made a bet with Auntie K again, didn't he?" She smiles at me, and I can see her mother so clearly in the expression.

"Mmm," I hum and nod, throwing a pan on the stove before grabbing the bacon from the fridge. I get everything going and trade places with Rhea as she scurries back to her room to get dressed. The rising sun shines through the small bathroom window, illuminating the water droplets she left behind. And the paint, so much paint. I sigh with an annoyed smile and wipe the floor, clean the counter, and shower before taking the time to clean myself off.

When I return—wet hair, clean skin—Rhea is sitting on the recliner that faces the kitchen with Daisy between her thighs on the floor. Her fingers brush through Daisy's hair with such ease as she carefully and intricately braids it back off her face into a single, tight line.

"Your dad is pretty good at rugby, but man, Kaia out there, she was so cool tonight," Rhea says, and I scowl. "You should have seen it, everyone was covered in neon paint."

"Like glow bowling?" Daisy asks.

"Exactly, and the Hillcats won so..." Rhea whispers.

I check on the bacon, shaking my head at their conversation, but find myself watching the process and wishing that I were the person Daisy asked when she needs her hair braided. Almost jealous of how easily Rhea manages it. I can't really hear what they're saying, but Daisy smiles up at her and hands her an earbud. Rhea's face scrunches up for a second, and her head turns to the side as she listens, but something surprises her, and she shakes her head in disbelief before handing the headphone back.

Daisy thanks her for doing her hair and wanders from the kitchen to get ready for school before breakfast. Rhea finds a spot at the island while I make toast. I get everything together, turning to give her a cup of coffee, only to see her with her head against the countertop, fast asleep. I set my mug down and stare at her for a second.

Friends would make sure their friends are comfortable... and not sleeping in dangerous positions? Right?

I move around the island, still at war with my own thoughts, and scoop her up against my chest. I don't move her far, but the feeling of her sleepy, weightless body against mine sends those unfamiliar sparks of possession through me. My skin practically cries out for her as I lay her on the couch and move away from her. I cover her with a blanket and stare down at her, still completely out of it.

Just. Friends.

"I 'm not sure." I hold a sundress up from my closet for Sunday and Daisy to judge. Both of them shake their heads, and it's funny because they look so much alike at that moment.

"Where did you even get that?" Sunday scowls.

"What's wrong with it?" I look down and hold it up to my shoulders.

"Rhea. It's yellow."

I look at the soft striped yellow and laugh. "Maybe my mom bought it?" I say, also confused.

"Who is this guy anyway?" Sunday asks, shooing me aside to raid my wardrobe.

"Miles Tenley," I say as she hands me a dark burgundy top and continues to dig. "He works over at the station with Kaia."

"Oh—the brunet with the pretty hazel eyes." Sunday pulls my black denim jacket off the hanger. "Go casual, he's probably just going to drive you across the city to a different bar."

"True," I say.

"Daisy, go get your stuff so I can take you to your mom's." Sunday looks over at her niece, who barely hears her with headphones in but nods and disappears. "Is this a take-all-my-clothes-off date or a serious, get-to-know-you date?"

"Get-to-know-you." I pull off the dirty shirt I'm wearing and pull on the low-cut one that Sunday handed me. It hugs my stomach and looks nice under the leather jacket.

"Boring," she says, smiling anyway. "If you need anything, call. I don't trust any of those firefighters," she winks.

"Kaia vouched for him, but honestly, I think she vouched for a quick fuck, so..." I laugh and shake out my hair so it's less stiff. "The last three guys were dicks," I sigh, tugging my jacket straight.

"The only men I trust are my brothers," Sunday says, dead serious.

"How hard is it for a guy to be a decent human being?" I ask, and she snorts in disbelief.

"These?" Sunday holds up a pair of boots that would make me four inches taller, and I shake my head. The last thing I need is to be taller than the guy on the first date; that's asking for a disaster. "You know the rules: if he doesn't pass the vibe check, you get the hell out of there. I give you full permission to fake a medical emergency on my behalf," she presses her hand to her chest and gives me the sweetest smile.

"Oh yeah, so here's the thing... You eat your burger weird, and oh my god, wow, my best friend just collapsed...I have to go!" I mock panic, and she hands me a pair of sneakers that are flat in absolute despair and laughter. "Thank you," I say, and she steps back like she's styled a mannequin.

My phone rings on the bed.

"That's him. I should go." I give her a peck on the cheek and shove my phone into my pocket.

"Debrief later," she warns as I head toward the front door.

"Where are you going?" Brighton asks from the kitchen, eyes flicking between us.

"Reaper's got a date," Sunday says, leaning on the doorframe and waving me out. I clock the stern look on Brighton's face, but he doesn't say a word as I open it and leave. Miles is waiting in his truck, and the first red flag is that he doesn't even look up when I open the passenger door myself.

"Hey," he says, still staring at his phone. "Sorry. Work emergency."

"Is the station on fire?" I joke, and he shakes his head like I'm serious. I decide silence is safer, and it's another five minutes before he starts the engine and pulls from the curb.

"Kaia said you like Japanese food?" he says, cutting off a hatchback to force his way into the left lane.

"Love it," I perk up a bit, pretending not to be terrified by his aggressive driving and the lack of music in the cab.

"So you've been to Japan?" he asks, driving through the next red light as it turns.

"No, never. I wish," I say, and he scowls. He's cute enough, with brown hair that's cut close to his scalp and a light scruff around his jaw. His brows are heavy, and his lips have yet to leave the thin line they're in.

"So you like *western* Japanese food," he says in a tone, and finally looks over at me.

"There's a place outside the city, in one of the smaller towns. A family moved from Japan—"

"Right," he cuts me off. "Well, I got us a spot at that Indian restaurant over off Nineteenth Street."

"Oh, I like Indian too," I say, unsure why he even brought up the Japanese food topic if that isn't what we're doing, but I try to go with the flow. The parking lot is busy when he pulls in, and he parks his truck over the line, taking up two spaces, causing me to sigh as he slams his door closed. He's halfway to the door before he remembers I exist and slows, because half of me expected him to open my side for me.

"Kaia didn't say you were tall," he says, his eyes raking down me like I'm a display. I should have seen that coming, because why would Kaia care, and why should he? But it's always an issue. His brow furrows again.

If you continue to stare at me like an animal in a zoo, I will key your truck in front of you.

"Sorry?" I say instead, and he shrugs but opens the restaurant door for me. Inside is just as busy as the parking lot. The table is so small my knees wedge under it, and there's dried gum stuck beneath the edge. Miles puts his phone on the table, screen up, and it lights up, showing about thirteen messages all coming through as the waitress asks what we'd like to drink.

"I'll have a beer, and she'll take a glass of red," he says before I can open my mouth.

Wine... How am I supposed to drink Satan's piss with a straight face?

He does the same thing when she comes back around to take our food order, and I'm two minutes from telling him that my entire family has died in a freak tsunami just to get away from him. I sip on the disgusting wine, just trying to get some liquor in my body, and watch as he rechecks his phone.

"So you work with Kaia?" I ask him, and he nods. "Have you always worked with her, or are you a new transfer?"

"New," he says quickly. "You teach... drawing?" he asks.

"High school art." I correct him and swallow down the entire rest of the glass in one gulp. He looks at the glass when I set it down on the table and smirks.

Shit, now you think I want to get drunk and have sex with you.

"Art was always my least favorite subject; I never really saw the point of it," he confesses, and I'm not surprised.

"What was your favorite?"

"Gym," he says quickly. "Played just about every sport I could," he says.

"I play rugby," I say.

"Oh yeah—fake football, with Kaia right?" *Yes, with Kaia. Why don't you ask her out on a date so I can watch her throat punch you?*

"It's not football," I try to keep my cool, but dealing with a guy like this would require about ten more vodka shots and a lobotomy.

"You tackle and score touchdowns. It's the same thing, only not as cool," Miles scoffs.

"Tries," I correct, and he narrows his eyes at me. "Do you have any hobbies now?" I ask in a pathetic attempt to keep the conversation going. The only way to get him to talk is to talk about him. And this is exactly how the rest of the date goes: if he does ask me a question, he ignores the answer for his phone. I learned he likes travelling but only to all-inclusive resorts on singles packages, and he doesn't listen to music because it's distracting. *Right, because God forbid something steals his attention from his phone.*

At the end of the night, I pay for my meal, *and* the wine I never ordered before we end up back in the parking lot.

"Tonight was nice, but this isn't going anywhere," he says, still staring at his phone.

Oh, thank fuck he doesn't want to have sex.

"You're a little high maintenance for me, and frankly, Kaia made it seem like you were cool, but I don't see it..." He looks up at me, and his expression is blank, like he genuinely believes he's letting me down easy. I lick my bottom lip and hold on to the intense rage that bubbles up in my chest at his smug face.

"Do you think you could drop me off at home?" I ask politely.

"Actually, I'm heading the other way—party," he says. "So call a cab. Let's keep this parting clean of any drama." He turns away from me, and I nod, an unimpressed scoff falling from my lips. "It was nice to meet you, Reanne."

"Rhea," I correct. He doesn't even hear me.

I stand there staring at him as he pulls out of his double space, almost hitting the person behind him, and takes off out of the parking lot.

"Holy shit," I laugh—so loud it turns into a near-cry. I tug my phone out of my pocket to call Sunday and find it dead. Only making the threat of tears worse. I literally only brought my phone... *If you didn't have such a crippling fear of cab drivers from podcasts, you'd be fine right now, you big baby.* I turn back to the restaurant, wandering back inside and asking the busy girl behind the counter if I can use the phone. She shrugs and sets it on the counter for me, but when I go to dial Sunday's number, my brain blanks on the last four digits.

"Eight-four-one..." I mumble to myself, the need to cry getting worse, and then I remember that I shoved one of the Hollow business cards into the back of my phone last week when a cute paramedic wrote his number on it. *I was so fucking drunk...I should have called him for a date.* I dial the number and wait; it rings more than once, but someone answers, and through the noise of the loud bar, I hear him.

"This is the Hollow, Bright speaking," he says.

"Brighton!" I blurt, relieved.

"Bright," he says like he's annoyed, but I can hear the smirk in his voice. "Why are you calling the bar Rhea? Aren't you supposed to be on a date?"

"Yup. With an asshole. Can you find Sunday and get her to come to the Indian restaurant on nineteenth? Like ASAP?" I ask him, and he grumbles something.

"Stay put," he says. The line goes dead.

Brighton

I shouldn't have grabbed my keys.

I shouldn't be speeding across town, barely stopping at the lights.

I shouldn't even be fucking worried.

But her voice is in my head, and her sad eyes have gotten under my skin,
so...

I turn the corner to the restaurant and sigh.

Rhea Drake looks smaller than I've ever seen her, perched on the curb, wiping tears from her cheeks in the dark when I pull up. She doesn't look up, even when I open the door.

"Of course you'd be in the shadiest part of town," I mutter, climbing out. She looks up at me, and the tears fill her eyes.

"You were supposed to send Sunday," she says, swallowing hard. She's been crying for a while because the black mascara is smudged beneath her eyes, and her cheeks are a horrible shade of pink. I grind my teeth, trying to be her friend and not a jealous idiot—despite the wave of it that hit when she left the apartment earlier.

"And you're supposed to be smarter," I joke, and she sighs, but the tiniest laugh falls from her. She takes my hand. It's small in mine as I pull her up and guide her to the passenger door. She doesn't make eye contact as she climbs inside, but she mumbles something about my truck being spotless, and I can't help but laugh as I shut the door.

When I get into the driver's seat, she's messing with the radio, and only her sniffles can be heard over the sound of skipping radio stations.

"Stop." I hold a hand out, and she flinches anyway. "Here," I say, digging into the center console and unlocking my phone for her before fixing the Bluetooth she messed up, and letting her go through my collection. She stares at it for a second and then starts to scroll through the playlists with a funny look on her face. "What?"

"You actually have decent taste in music," she admits and looks up at me. It's nice to see that she's stopped crying, but it still itches at something deep inside of me, locked behind all the doors that are labeled '*just friends*'.

"How is it possible that your statement sounded like an insult?" I pull the truck to a stop at a red light and take the phone from her to pick a specific playlist. "This one," I say, putting the phone away. It's a mix of old and new—soft rock and folk I've collected over the years. One of my favorites.

She's quiet again, and I hate that I can't figure out how to pull her from her shell. *Be her friend, you know. The word you keep repeating to yourself every time she smiles at you.*

"What happened tonight?" I ask, turning back toward the Hollow.

Rhea grimaces as she flips her dead phone over in her hand a few times. "It was a blind date. Kaia meant well, but I think Miles was more interested in her than me," she explains. "He spent the whole night on his phone. When he finally looked up, he used it to comment on my height."

"You aren't even that tall," I say. *She is,* but she gives me a small, defeated laugh, and that's all that matters. But as soon as it appears, it's gone again, and I don't know what to say to make her feel better. All I can do is get her back to the Hollow.

"And then he ordered me red wine," she gags, and I stifle the laugh in my chest.

"You hate wine." The words slip out before I can stop them, but her smile is back. She stares at me, not through me, and it makes my ears get hot. *Please stop.* "Firefighter?" I keep my voice light. "What's his last name?" I try to distract her from the fact that I know exactly what she likes to drink, and it's never been red wine.

"Tenley, I think?" She sighs.

"Sounds pretentious," I mutter. I hadn't heard the name, which only means that if he works with Kaia, he's a new face. One I had the urge to hit. *Reel it in Brighton. Friends don't feel like this.* She can take care of herself. *Sure, that's why you sped all the way to the restaurant.*

She shifts in her seat at the sound, and it takes everything in me not to snap when she props her dirty shoes on my leather seat. "Yeah! You know what he said to me?" She shakes her head, and the smell of her shampoo floods my nose.

"What?" I ask, just to keep her talking.

"He called me high maintenance!" she scoffs, "Me?"

"I mean... You did make me drive half an hour across town," I say, and her expression hardens.

"I called for Sunday. It's not my fault you came!" she cries out and crosses her arms.

"Why didn't you just take a cab?" I ask her, turning onto the next street, and she loses her balance a little.

"Do you know how many women get assaulted in cabs?" she grumbles, and her bottom lip juts out.

"Says the woman who was crying on the curb in the dark." I clear my throat with a smirk on my face.

"Not the same thing," she argues.

"Sure, yeah," I nod.

"It doesn't matter. I should have just gotten a cab. I'd rather disappear forever than suffer the shame that is my best friend's brother *turned roommate*," she says like it's an insult, "picking me up from a bad date downtown only for him to scold me all the way home." She throws her hands through her hair and rests her head against the seat of the car.

"Day was called into work," I tell her.

"Oh," she says, prying one eye open to look at me.

"And I'm not scolding you," I say with a scowl, "you should just be more careful."

"I bench press more than most of the guys on your team. I would have been okay," she brushes me off, and I can't argue; she probably does, and it's probably pretty impressive.

"You didn't even bring a purse or whatever," I point out.

"I thought you weren't scolding." She pushes back as the song changes to something she knows, and a tiny squeal leaves her throat as she leans over and turns the sound up. I stop grilling her for information but make a mental note of his name so that I can ask Kaia about the guy later, knowing her, the second she finds out he abandoned Rhea on the side of the road, she'll have him strung up by his balls, but... I also need to know.

She sings to herself as the lights illuminate those sad eyes with each passing mile back to the Hollow. Part of me wants to just keep driving her around because between the music and the movement, she seems to be calming down a little, but I see the bright red sign of the Hollow up the street, and so does she.

"Hey," I say, pulling the truck to the curb just outside with the intention of driving it around the block after I let her out. She unbuckles her seatbelt and stares at me with her fingers wrapping around the handle. "Tonight wasn't your fault. And any guy who treats you like that isn't worth your time." I aim for friendly, a big brother talking to his little sister's friend. Her head tilts slightly, and the softest smile she's ever given me forms on her mouth. *Atta boy, that definitely worked the way you wanted it to.*

"Thanks for the ride, Brighton."

"Bright," I correct automatically, and she just slips from the car without another word.

I drive around the block four times before deciding to rejoin society, but my mind still lingers on her heartbroken expression sitting on that curb as I walk back into the Hollow. She's in the back booth with Cosy and Kaia, her face buried in an espresso martini, and it brings a small flicker of satisfaction to my chest knowing that she found comfort.

Whether it's her friends... or the drink I stupidly, selfishly named after her.

I pull out my phone and text Kaia.

Who is he?

Kaia looks up, scans the bar, and lands on me with a sick, vicious smile, and I know that she's having the same thoughts I am.

Rhea

I haul the boxes of cat food from the back seat of the Bronco and into the shelter. "Where am I putting these?" I ask Cosy, who's behind the counter.

"Just in the storage room. I have to go through them and make sure nothing's expired." She's wearing this adorable gingham top and a pair of jean shorts with her red hair tucked into a matching bandana. The entire outfit makes the guy across the shelter, playing with kittens, stare every time she leans over the counter to wipe the corners.

Her cherry red outfit is such a contrast to the teal walls of the shelter, and she's like a beacon for attention because of it. The shelter is her baby; if she's not on the pitch, she's here. She bought it three years ago when it was a failed Hookah shop, stripped everything down to the bones, and rebuilt it exactly how she wanted it—taking care of every animal in Harbor. She never says no, never lets an animal go hungry, and she proves every day that the world might be a horrible place, but it's full of wonderful people.

If she takes in any more animals, she'll need more space. The three rooms she has are already near capacity, and the front of the store is starting to collect a few random species that I don't even think are legal to own in Rhode Island. But she loves every single one of them the same. It's endearing and inspiring.

The dude is practically drooling, so I drop the box loudly to startle him before wandering over to her. "You have an audience," I say, nodding toward the guy.

"Not my type," she grumbles without looking up.

"What exactly is your type?" I ask, leaning against the countertop and playing with the rack of cat toys hanging in my face.

"Not that," she cements. The guy isn't bad; he's shorter with dark curls and one of those bushy mustaches that look like they tickle.

"You don't like a little carpet burn?" I ask her, and she finally stops cleaning to toss me a look. "What? Maybe if we get you laid, you won't be so mean in DND."

"I get laid a lot..." Cosy laughs. "I don't need your help, and I'm not mean. The monsters are perfectly suited to your level."

"Boring," I yawn and throw my head back. "You got any hamsters in this place?" I ask her.

"Why..." she eyes me. "If you plan to let one loose in Bright's apartment, count me out. I don't need to be sleeping with one eye open."

"Boo, you whore," I whine, and she laughs.

"How's Lady Gaga?" Cosy asks, wandering back through the shop.

"I still can't believe you gave him a snake for his birthday. My Mom had a hissy fit over it." I groan.

"Worth it." Cosy snorts.

"He's fine, Toby lets him out of his cage on a weekly basis, and the house descends into chaos, but they don't have issues with mice anymore..." I shrug.

"So are you here because you're hiding from a Saturday with them or because you want to be?" She asks me as she starts to dig through the box. I lower to the floor next to her and help with one, checking the bottoms for expiry dates and setting aside any questionable ones.

"Want to be," I sigh. Then—because I'm honest—"also hiding. Two birds, one stone. Mom has Reid all up in knots—and you know him, he's a dick.. So he pushes buttons, she gets worse, and then he closes up more. It's a vicious circle I don't want to be trapped in," I explain.

"That's the problem, though, Reaper." She looks up at me. "You *are* the middle."

I push over my tower of cans and groan, "This is why I moved out in the first place. Because I don't want to be."

"You let them depend on you way too much. Maybe it's time you stop answering every time she calls crying?" Cosy suggests.

"That would involve starting a fight I don't have the energy for." I chew on my lip. I'm just not ready to quit cold turkey, even though the stress is building again.

"Find it," Cosy says. "Before she starts walking all over you again."

"What if I don't answer one day and it's something serious?" I ask her.

"Your mother is a grown ass woman, Reaper."

"I know. I know that. I just..." I trail off. "My siblings aren't, and if she's falling apart, who's there for them?"

"You aren't *their* mother either," she adds, "but I get that. You feel guilty, you want to pick up the pieces that she's unable to carry, but it shouldn't be at the expense of your own mental health," her voice goes soft. "Throttle your help. Give them what you can when you're around, but don't overextend yourself because you feel guilty."

I open my mouth to say something, and the front door chimes, "I swear if that sketchy guy stole a kitten I'm—" her words die on her lips, and a smile forms. "Look what the cat dragged in."

"Hi." Daisy stands in the doorway with August and Lori, all three of them looking like they're searching for something.

"Where's your Dad?" Cosy asks her, and Daisy rolls her eyes.

"He dropped me off, but I didn't tell him August is here..." she eyes me.

"I'm no snitch," I say, raising my hands.

"I hope it's okay that I brought them?" Daisy shifts in her t-shirt and jeans. She looks cute, but is very nervous to have August around. Lori, on the other hand, is completely unbothered and is sticking her hands in a bird cage close to her.

"The more hands, the merrier." Cosy wipes her hands and stands. "Hey, you want to help them? Might clear your head?" She turns to me.

"Sure," I say with a shrug and follow her out to the front of the shelter.

"Usually, Bright and Daisy walk the dogs on weekends," Cosy explains.

"They do?" I say, surprised, and Daisy laughs. "That's cute."

He would.

"They need adult supervision with them, so do you mind going to the park with them?" She asks me, and I nod. I could use the chaos it brings to make me feel less guilty about not being at home today.

"Hell yeah, Ms. Drake!" Lori lowers her voice and yells, causing all the animals in the shelter to go crazy.

"Who are we taking?" I clap my hands together. Cosy smiles and collects a few leashes and a few dogs, one of the three kids, and two for me.

Roger, a border collie with three legs, Bucky, a black lab, and Sugar, a senior bulldog with a funny attitude that only disappears around Bucky. We make our way down to the park, and the second we're inside the dog run, the kids have the dogs running in circles.

I find a bench to sit on, and the second I do, the phone vibrates. *Mom.* For a split second, I think about answering it, letting her rant, getting it over with for the next few days, but I don't. I listen to Cosy, *don't overextend yourself,* and I click ignore to enjoy the afternoon air with the kids and the dogs.

"Hey, Rhea?" Daisy's voice comes out of the blue, and I set my phone down to see her wandering toward me.

"What's up, D?" I ask her as she sits on the bench.

"Do you think Auggie likes me?" she asks, and I tense at the question. *This is a little outside of my pay grade. As a teacher* and *a roommate.*

"Uh," I clear my throat and follow her nervous gaze to Auggie chasing Sugar in a circle as Sugar chases Lori. "I think he's a good kid... and he gets really good grades."

"If I wanted my mom's answer, I would've just asked her again," Daisy sighs. I look back at her and find her staring aimlessly; she's clearly pretty frustrated.

"It's hard to tell with boys," I start, "you have to be careful. With all of them—even the nice ones," I explain. "But I can tell you what I do know about having a crush, and if he does any of these things, then maybe it's worth talking to him about it." I lift my leg and tuck it under myself as I turn on the bench toward her. "When a boy pays attention, he knows your favorite songs, your favorite foods, and your *least* favorites. They open doors for you and always make sure that you get home safely. When they make jokes because they know you'll laugh at them, or they can be silly around you."

"Like, they act differently around you in private?" she asks, and I narrow my eyes at her.

"Not like that!" she groans. "Like... texting. And in the band room. Auggie... talks a lot but only to me. He's quiet around everyone else."

"Exactly like that," I say, deadpan. Daisy smiles at me, and her body relaxes a bit.

"And if he has a silly nickname for you that only he uses..."

"Oh... he calls me Leda," she says and looks over at him. "He said it's one of Jupiter's moons."

"Can't be sure, but I've never had a boy call me anything like that, so it's safe to say the boy has a crush. But you didn't hear any of this from me." I point between the two of us and eye her until she pretends to zip her mouth closed.

"Thanks, Rhea." She stands up from the bench and goes back to playing, but not before stopping to say to me. "Not to make things weird..." She lowers her voice. "But Dad calls you Hellcat."

He does.

"Just a stupid nickname, Daisy. It's not the same. Now, go play before Sugar starts a revolt against Auggie and Lori." I shoo her off and shake my head as the sound of him saying it tickles the back of my thoughts. Roger takes her spot on the bench and puts his head in my lap. "It's just

a stupid nickname," I murmur, scratching between his eyes. "Right?"
Roger whines, which is wildly unhelpful.

Brighton

"It's next week, right?" Sunday asks as Rhea types on her phone. She's been like this since the date, quiet, sullen, and uninterested in almost everything, putting on a show when people are looking too closely and forcing a smile to her face for her friends. It's starting to drive me insane. She's been pretending like all the crap Miles said to her didn't bother her, but a week later, she's still chewing on the insults like they're leather stuck between her teeth.

"Yeah. Museum downtown. Starts at seven," Cosy says, picking at her lunch.

"Who are you bringing as a date?" Sunday asks her, and Judd drops a container of limes hard on the counter, earning dirty looks from all of us in the practically empty Hollow. Saturday afternoons are usually dead; people come in for lunch, but it's mostly regulars or randoms that come in off the street for food.

The Hillcats sit at the end of the bar, picking at lunch and chatting about God knows what—until the HSAs come up. The Harbor Sports Awards are for athletes within the city, spanning from professional to semi-professional, as well as college teams, and more community out-reach.

It's usually a stuffy event that Boone caters, but it's too many bodies and too much chaos for me to handle, so I stay and take care of the bar. We've had a system for the last few years, and it works perfectly.

"Probably Dad," Cosy says with a smile. "He loves those dinners."

"Oh my god, please bring him. After last year, we need that comedic relief," Sunday gasps, "when he and Kaia got so drunk they ended up in the fountain and nearly got arrested—but he flirted his way out of it because the museum security guard was going through menopause *and* a divorce!"

"I heard about Josephine for weeks," Cosy gags.

"Think of the breakup drama if she still works there." Sunday giggles, shoving some fries in her mouth. "You have to."

"Alright, alright," Cosy concedes. "Who are you bringing, Reaper?" she asks Rhea, who finally looks up from her phone—like she's just noticed the food in front of her.

"No one," she says and lifts the bun of her burger out of habit and finding it without tomatoes. "It's always a hassle, and guys always want something out of it..." Her eyes lift to me, and her thoughts are so loud I can practically hear her thinking as she smiles. "Hey, Brighton?"

"No." I set down a beer and look away before she can see the amusement in my eyes.

"You didn't even wait for me to ask the question," Rhea pouts.

Don't.

"If it involves dancing, suits, noise, music, or people," I list, "no."

"Be my date," Rhea says.

"No."

"Just as friends!" she argues. "You're the only man in Harbor tall enough!"

"No." I fight back and continue to serve some of the people sitting around the bar with a polite smile.

"Boooo," Sunday cups her mouth and yells.

I give her a dirty look, and she leans back on her stool to cross her arms.

"You'd really leave a girl dateless? I thought we were friends now." Rhea pokes the bear because she likes the sound it makes when it growls, but I shake my head no again.

"Boone goes every year," Cosy quickly adds, and I grumble under my breath as I make my way down the bar to where they sit.

"He *works* the event. That's different from attending," I remind her and lean on the bar with both hands to stare the three of them down.

"I know you own a suit," Sunday narrows her eyes at me.

"Doesn't mean I want to wear it, Day," I clip, curling my fingers against the counter. I give her a serious look, and her shoulders roll forward in defeat as Rhea huffs.

"It's okay. It was a long shot. Forget I asked," Rhea says. "I have physio in twenty, I'll see you guys at practice later?" She looks at the girls once, then disappears through the bar.

"She goes alone, you know," Sunday says later that night, leaning over the bar. She's sandwiched between two people trying to talk while waiting for me to make her a tray of fruity drinks for a bachelorette party.

"What?" I look up at her as I palm two shakers.

"The HSAs, every year her family tells her that they're going to be there and they don't show up," Sunday says.

"So then she's used to it," I brush off Sunday, trying to ignore the fact that maybe I feel a little bad for Rhea.

"Yeah, maybe. But she shouldn't have to be," she argues, and the girl next to her is starting to get impatient with the interruption.

"She'll be fine, Day. Maybe she should just tell her family they suck. She's a big girl," I strain out the martinis. The Reaper has sold more this week than any special we've run in five months. I can't tell if I hate it or love it. But making them will be the death of me.

"You are so dense! She doesn't want to hurt them. She takes care of everyone else's feelings, who takes care of hers?" Sunday snaps as I arrange the drinks.

I take care of her. The thought is intrusive—violent. It sits at the back of my throat, threatening to expose me. I swallow roughly and sigh.

"Why are you pushing this so hard?" I ask. "Aren't you supposed to be all *stay away from my brother*?"

"When have I ever been like that? Kaia's been in love with Bobo since..." Sunday can't even fathom the math. "Besides, you and Rhea are roommates. You're friends. Aren't you?"

She doesn't say it like an accusation; it's more of a statement designed to push me into doing something stupid. Sunday disappears with the drinks, and I have fifteen minutes of silence from her nagging before she slips behind the bar and starts again.

"I'm going to fire you if you don't leave me alone." I groan and slide two beers to the bar top for the guy in front of me as Sunday leans against it to catch my eye line.

"Going as her date for the HSAs is something a friend would do; it's not like you have to stick your lightning rod anywhere," Sunday complains.

"Are you delusional?" I hiss under my breath and start to wipe down the counter aggressively to get the image out of my brain of Rhea...

Naked. Rhea naked.

"All I'm saying is that she could use the support," Sunday whines, brushing her hair behind her ear and turning to help the girls at the end of the bar, calling for help. She circles back around, and those green eyes burn a hole into my back.

"Don't all the Hillcats go? That's her support system. She doesn't need arm candy, Day." I hesitate. "She's just... lonely." It slips from my mouth, and it's meaner than I expect it to sound.

"One, you are not arm candy." She looks disgusted, "and two it's different, everyone brings someone. Family, a partner, a friend..." she says.

"So set her up with a date." I groan and turn away from her, but Sunday isn't done with me yet.

"You picked her up from the last blind date. Men are horrible, Bri. They don't care about what the night means to her. They just want her horizontal so they can forget that she's taller than them," Sunday snaps.

You're making it really hard to keep my distance from her, and you have no idea.

"She's winning an award this year, they get told in advance so they can prepare something just in case. She knows she's winning it and still expects no one to show up for her. It's not about the fanfare, Brighton," she snaps, and I know I'm in trouble when she uses my full name. "Be her friend."

"I didn't ask for any new friends," I say, my response short and cold.

Sunday stares up at me for a moment longer before she's called to help at the table, but the lingering effects of that pleading stare stick to my skin and bother me long after she's gone.

Brighton

Daisy doesn't even talk to me on the way home from school. She grabs a donut from Boone as she stomps through the kitchen, offering him a sweet thank you before disappearing upstairs without even a wave goodbye. I hate not knowing what I'm doing wrong.

"At least she's eating?" Boone leans against the counter, eyes tracking the hallway she disappeared into. He holds out the tray, and I shake my head. "Alright. She's the *only* one eating. What is wrong with you?"

I shake my head because it's nothing Boone can fix, but he's going to try, and it preemptively annoys me. I'm Daisy's Dad, and I should be able to figure out what's going on in her head, but every time I try, she shuts me out. Sometimes it's easy to blame her mom—even though I know I shouldn't—because it's the simplest excuse to slip into.

"She's been like that for two weeks. She's even making me drop her off at Cosy's. I don't even get to walk dogs with her anymore." I confess. "The most I get out of her is a thank-you for making her lunch."

"Manners are intact, that's a good start," Boone responds, throwing a heavily tattooed hand through his hair. "This is going to piss you off, but... she's acting like you."

"You're right, that does piss me off." I snap and turn my head to look at him properly.

"Means she's got good integrity," he backpedals.

"I don't like not knowing. What if it isn't me? What if something else is going on and she doesn't feel safe enough to talk to me about it?" I grumble.

"Do you want me to talk to her?" he asks.

"No, I *want* her to talk to me," I emphasize the issue for him as a few of the kitchen staff start arriving for the dinner wave.

"Yeah, you're impossible," Boone sighs. "Give me ten. I'll make her a quesadilla, and you can try bribing her for information."

"Thank you." I groan as he finally gives in.

"Two peas in a pod," he grumbles and starts cooking. I wait at the entrance of the kitchen, watching everyone move around the bar. People usually arrive a little earlier for dinner unless they're planning on staying for when the Hollow becomes a true pub with loud music and louder drunks. *This is my favorite part of the day—the calm before the storm.*

I close my eyes just for a second, trying to rearrange all the thoughts flying around in my mind, but all I find is the familiar darkness—proof of how unstable I still am.

"Here," Boone breaks the silence and holds out a plate and a can of Sprite. "Oh," he says, turning away and popping open a fridge, "take these." He drops two small closed containers in my hand, both full of jalapeños. "She likes extra."

I nod, trying not to react to how much it pisses me off that *he* knows that about her, closing my hand around them and wandering up the stairs to the apartment. I lock the door behind me with a spare finger and can instantly hear the music pouring from the crack beneath her door and smell a soft lavender scent moving through the apartment that makes my jaw clench.

I knock once, waiting to hear proof of life. Nothing. So I twist the knob and ease the door open. Daisy is sitting at her desk with her phone in front of her, doing homework.

"Is that a quesadilla?" she asks, her nose betraying whatever she's angry about.

"Yeah," I say. "Extra jalapeños."

She narrows her eyes at me, and I know she sees through it all.

"Boone sent them up," I confess.

"I know." She confirms as I set the plate down on her desk.

"Where did you get that?" I point to the candle lit on her desk.

"Uncle Ryan and C get me one every birthday, from Auntie," she says, and I stare at the light purple candle. *Of course they do.*

Riona's brother is Ryan Cody. Coach of the Harbor Hornets, and Cael Cody's father. The family from hell. The only person in that family that ever treated me like one, was Lorraine. Cael's mother, but a lot has changed since she died and I don't think even she would look at me in the same light. I swallow hard at the thought, angry any everyone but myself for a moment but I can never let her see that rage toward them because they treat Daisy like gold and that's *all* that matters.

"Smells nice," I manage. I back away—clearly uninvited—as she pops the tab on her Sprite and turns away from me. "Hey Daisy," I say to her, stopping before I leave her alone completely.

"Yeah, Dad?" She doesn't look at me, but at least she responds.

"Is something going on?" I ask her. "Anything I can—"

"No," she's quick to shut me down.

"Are you sure?" I wait, watching her pull apart her food and load it up.

"I'm fine. I have homework to do," she clips, and I take my leave, shutting the door behind me.

Something is wrong, I can feel it, but without her cooperation, there's so little I can do short of calling her mother or asking Rhea for information; she teaches her art... she might know something. But that just makes me a busybody and breaks what fickle trust Daisy does have in me.

Speaking of, as I come back into the kitchen, Rhea comes through the front door, drops her duffel, and kicks off her shoes. She's got her headphones in and is singing at the top of her lungs like the world can't touch her. I cross my arms and lean against the archway to watch her spin around the kitchen in her socks with a smile on her face. *The worst part?* A smile creeps onto my mouth, and I can't stop it.

She jumps out of her skin as she turns to see me watching her, and the headphones get tugged from her ears roughly. "Hi." She says, completely out of breath.

"Hi." I shake my head and brush off the amusement to get ready to open the Hollow for the evening, but I stop at the door. "Do you know if anything's going on with Daisy?" I ask, despite my better judgment. "She seems to talk to Sunday more than me, and she's been a little off lately."

Rhea's eyes flicker to the hall and back to me. "Not that I know of? Maybe it's just teenage hormones?" She smiles.

"Yeah, maybe..." I take her answer, but it doesn't do anything to soothe how I'm feeling.

"What the hell is this?" I slap my phone down on the steel counter, and Boone turns to look at the screen with both hands in the air, covered in seasonings. It's been two weeks of Daisy sulking around like someone kicked her dog, and she still won't talk to me. It's been so bad that my finger gets itchy over her mother's number, but then I chicken out because I'm not ready to have that fight.

"Uh," Boone's face scrunches up as he reads, "can you... Can you get my glasses?" he asks, and I reach over to the top of the sink and flick the tortoise shell frames open and slide them onto his nose. "It's an email from Daze's homeroom teacher. She wants you to come into the school at your earliest convenience for a conversation..."

"I know that Boone," I snap. "What the fuck does it mean?"

"Means you need to go to the school, Bri," he scowls, "if you're gonna be a dickhead, stop asking for advice." He turns away from me and goes back to the chicken he was messing with for lunch rush. "Go to the school, I'll be here," he says when I don't move.

"Yeah... yeah," I shake free of my bewilderment and fish my keys out before leaving the Hollow to drive across town to the high school. The streets are pretty empty for almost lunch, and the car park's already thinning out. A deep sigh leaves me when I see *her* vehicle parked two rows over, and all I can do is tighten my grip on the keys as I make my way inside. The office points me in the right direction, and before I even enter the room, I can hear the conversation that's happening.

"He'll be late, if he shows up at all. You might as well tell me what this is all about." Riona's voice is as icy as her glare as I come around the corner and stand in the doorway. "Speak of the devil," she snaps, her blue eyes piercing through me.

"What's going on?" I ask, ignoring her jab as Daisy keeps her eyes on her lap.

"Mr. Black, please." Daisy's teacher points to the chair. A mousy-looking man with thick frames and thicker lenses. His hair is brushed over to make it appear like he's not losing it rapidly, but his scalp is shiny against the fluorescent lights above us.

I look at the tiny chair and scowl. "I'll stand."

"Bright," Riona scolds. I hate the way she says my name now. It stings when it touches her tongue and leaves a bad aftertaste in her mouth. "Just sit."

"It's okay, Ms. Cody," the teacher plays the mediator in a war long over. "I needed to speak to you both today because there seem to be issues going on in the classroom that are preventing your daughter from her studies."

Both of us look at Daisy, who refuses to make eye contact.

"Issues?" Riona takes control of the conversation as per usual.

"Daisy seems to be having trouble with a young man in another," the teacher explains, and Daisy scoffs, but Riona doesn't seem to notice. "Today marks the sixth time in the last two months that the two of them have been caught in heated exchanges."

"Can you stop reciting Shakespeare and get to the point?" Riona snaps with a smile on her face, and it takes everything in me not to laugh at her demanding nature. It's why I fell in love with her, and ultimately why I was scorched from her life. She didn't give second chances, and frankly, I didn't deserve one anyway.

"Daisy has made several claims that this student is harassing her with the help of some others, but—"

"*Several?*" I step forward, uncrossing my arms, and the teacher shrinks in size. The word 'harassing' instantly boils my blood and makes me want to find the kid myself to show him exactly what harassment feels like.

"Enough," Riona clips, and I tense. *This is why you're left out of these conversations. Your only tactic is violence.* "Why are we just being brought in now if this has been going on for months?" she says in a much more diplomatic tone.

"That's what I would like to know," her teacher says. "I've sent notes home and haven't received replies until today, when I sent the emails."

Riona looks over at her finally, and I can feel the worry rolling off her shoulders.

"What's his name, Daisy?" I ask carefully. *Nothing.* I turn to the teacher and glare, "What's the student's name?"

"Garth Robertson," he finally breaks.

"Has Garth laid a hand on Daisy?" I ask carefully. I see his eyes flicker between Riona and me, his fingers shaking against the notebook open on his table. *He has.* I don't get a reply, though; it's like I'm not even in the room.

"And have you spoken to Mr. Robertson's family?" Riona asks, turning away from our daughter.

"Uh..." the teacher stumbles, and I shake my head.

She's going to eat you alive, you spineless coward.

"Right," Riona pushes up off her chair and braces herself on the desk with both hands, as she leans in toward the man, and he leans back to keep the distance. "Here's what we're going to do: I'm going to take my daughter home because it's clear that you and this school have zero policies in place to protect her from bullies like Mr. Robertson."

"Ms. Cody..." he stutters and looks to me for help, but I just stare at him. *You're on your own.*

"What *you're* going to do," she begins, "is write up a formal email to Mr. Robertson's parents and let them know that I want to have a meeting with them present to discuss exactly what's going on and how we can move forward in a manner that benefits both students. And you're going to do it the second I leave this office, because if I don't hear back from you by the end of the day, I will have Mr. Black return tomorrow and stand over your desk until it's finished."

"Will Mr. Black be at the meeting?" The teacher asks, and Riona glares. "I need to know whether or not to wa—" he stutters, the word warn ripe on his trembling bottom lip. "Whether or not to include him in the email."

"Mr. Black will not be at the meeting." Riona is cold about the delivery because it's not for the teacher; it's a warning for me. *To stay far, far away from the school and from them.* "Daisy, go get your things from your locker, please."

She doesn't even flinch, still silent in all of this as she rises from her seat and starts out of the classroom. I don't hesitate to follow her as Riona digs her card from her purse and lectures the teacher on calling her directly instead of passing notes.

"Daisy," I call out, keeping a slow pace behind her as she walks through the school to her locker. "Daisy," I say again. "Come on, Squish." I use the stupid nickname her aunt gave her the day she was born, but it makes her stop and look up at me. "You alright?" I ask after a second.

She inhales slowly, shakes her head as she steps in my direction, and it takes everything in me not to crumble as she tucks herself into me for a long hug. I wrap my arms around her and squeeze, only letting go when she gently pushes on me for release. But I don't let her get far, I tuck my hand around the back of her head and stare down at her.

"You gotta talk to us," I say to her quietly, and open my mouth to pry more when a throat is cleared to our left.

Rhea stands in the doorway—black jeans, old band tee knotted at her stomach. It's always startling to see her in teacher mode. The tags around her neck click as she steps forward into the hallway and closes the door to her class behind her.

"What's going on? Are you okay?" She asks, and I go to respond only to realize she's talking to Daisy. *Of course she is, you oversized chipmunk.*

"I'm good, Ms. Drake," Daisy says quietly, and I let go of her and shove my hands into the pockets of my jeans. Her eyes finally meet mine, and I can see the worry there, clawing at her better judgment to keep quiet, but she's growing just as attached as I am.

Shit.

"Why did they call your Dad then?" She pushes Daisy, who shakes her head and sighs.

"Garth," Daisy and Rhea groan at the same time for clearly very different reasons.

"If I weren't your teacher, I'd give that kid a swirly," Rhea grumbles. The smirk that forms on my lips dies just as fast as the loud clicking of Riona's heels cuts down the hall toward us.

"Run," I mouth. Rhea's brows knit in confusion as she turns to see why I said it.

"Mom," Daisy says as she comes to a slow pace, no doubt ready to bark orders at all of us, "this is Ms. Drake. My art teacher." Riona turns to Rhea and offers her a smile I've never seen in my life.

"I've heard so much about you." Riona extends her hand, and Rhea shakes. "Ms. Cody, Daisy's mother." The recognition flickers across her face, and she tries to hide it, but Riona is too quick. "Yes. *That* Cody."

"Small town," Rhea manages to get out, but it's very clear that she wants to ask a hundred inappropriate questions.

"Very," Riona says, her voice tighter than before. She turns back to Daisy, looking her up and down, "Have everything?" She asks, and Daisy nods.

"It's my week, Riona." I try to swallow the possessive growl in my voice, but it's silenced with one sharp, vicious look.

"I'll bring her by the Hollow tonight. I'd like to have a conversation with her." Riona lowers her voice to keep the conversation private, and Rhea does her best to avoid it completely.

As if this isn't awkward enough, being read to filth by my ex with her watching. You're pathetic, and she sees that now.

"Is this not a conversation we should *all* be having, together?" I say.

"You lost that privilege years ago, Bright." *Death blow.*

"Yeah, put the gun down, Riona. I get it," I swallow. "I'll see you tonight," I say to Daisy as Riona wraps an arm around her and leads her from the school. It's another two minutes before Rhea finds her voice again.

"What was that about?" She asks, and I run my hand through my hair as I turn too fast and end up practically chest to chest with her. I expect her to flinch or jump at my sudden movement and our closeness, but she doesn't move; she just stares up at me, waiting for an explanation.

"Brighton," she says.

"Sorry," I grumble. "I don't know. Daisy won't talk, and her home-room teacher's tiptoeing around that Garth kid." I put my arm out in the direction we came and sigh.

"Mr. Dickson," Rhea rolls her eyes.

"Mr. Disson," I correct with a small laugh.

"Dickson," she emphasizes. "Garth Robertson is a shitty little fuckwit with a god complex."

"Where have I heard that name before?" I ask her, trying to keep my cool.

"He's a Robertson," she says, like that should explain everything. "Hockey legend turned Mayor of Harbor."

"He's Ricky Robertson's kid?" I scoff and shake my head. "I used to fucking pummel that asshole in high school," I say, and her smile grows, "you're being liberal calling him a legend."

"He's Harbor royalty," Rhea laughs, and I realize she had been mocking him the whole time. "And so is his spoiled son. His girlfriend has decided that Daisy is her new chew toy, no clue why, they're good at sneaking around and playing nice. But Garth and the hockey team have taken it upon themselves to start crap with Daisy's best friend when no one is looking."

"Lori?" I ask, and she nods with pride that I know who she's talking about. It stings, having them all think I'm standing on the outside of their circle, but I know my Daisy.

"I'm pretty sure something happened with Lori and Garth over summer break, and now it's a sore spot for the girlfriend." Rhea shrugs.

"How is Daisy involved in all this shit?" I ask, confused as to why she's the one in trouble and not the shit head.

Rhea stares at me with her eyebrow cocked, "Have you met any of the people in Daisy's life?"

"What?" I scoff.

"She was raised by wolves, Brighton. She's involved because if they were picking on Lori, it would have ticked her off. And Daisy has thicker skin. She fights back for her friend." Rhea explains and waits for it to sink in. *Raised by wolves.* Boone, Kaia, Riona. *Fucking pack animals.*

"So she's in trouble for standing up for Lori?" I say in disbelief.

"Yup, and I can't do a damn thing to stop it..." she trails off.

"When I asked you yesterday if you knew anything was going on?"

"I only had speculation. I figured that Mr. Dickson had already brought you into the loop. I'm sorry, Brighton."

"It's fine." It comes out rougher than I mean it to. "I'm sorry. This is just..."

"I get it." She stops me. "I have to get back to class," she says as a smirk curls on her face, and I know she's up to something because her cheeks are pink and her eyes are glassy with mischief. She pops the door to her class open, and the sounds of chatter and laughter pour out.

"Hey, Hellcat," I call before she disappears. "Don't do anything stupid."

"No promises," she hums at me as I turn to walk away, and the echo of her students teasing her about her visitor blankets my heavy, angry footsteps.

I'm pushing bins closed and washing paintbrushes in the back of the classroom when two sets of footsteps barge in and the door slams shut. Before I can announce myself, Garth's voice snaps through the room—angry, hushed..

"What the hell did you tell them? Why am I in trouble?" he snaps. "It's your stupid friend making up lies!"

"You know they aren't lies," Daisy's voice comes next, and I freeze. "You're in trouble because you're a jerk."

"Shut up," he groans, "Lori keeps telling people I forced myself on her, and it's bullshit. Carly is all up in knots, and it's your stupid friend's fault. If she would just tell everyone the truth, none of this would be happening!"

"Maybe you should tell the truth!" Daisy gets louder, and I smile—until a tiny squeak cuts through it. "Let go of me, Garth, or I'll rearrange your teeth."

I clap my hand over my mouth to stop the laugh that bubbles up at her clapback because I know it's all Kaia. She would be so proud.

"Garth." I step out from the washing station, my gaze dropping to his hand locked around her arm. "She asked nicely."

"That wasn't nice. And she started it." He lets go and backs away two steps.

"In here, that won't work—and you know it," I say, and he swallows hard. "What's going on? And I don't want an excuse."

"Daisy and Lori are harassing me," Garth clips—too quick, too confident.

"How?" I ask him, begging him to expand on it.

"Lori's obsessed with me! She thinks she's my girlfriend, and she's turning into a stalker!" Garth raises his voice as I walk toward them. I nod to Daisy so she takes a couple of steps back from him.

"Doesn't sound like Lori?" I say, confused. "Can you expand on that?"

Garth groans. "This is bullshit!"

"Language, please," I warn him, "and if you're having issues with Lori, we can schedule a meeting with both your parents to discuss them."

"No!" Garth is quick to shut me down. "I just want her to stop!"

"Here's what we're going to do," I uncross my arms and lean back against my desk. "You're going to leave Daisy and Lori alone," I say. He opens his mouth to argue. "And that includes making sure Carly does, too—until the meeting with Daisy's parents."

"That's unfair, this isn't my fault!" He whines, and it takes everything in me not to laugh. *You're all the same when caught, what horrible learned behavior.*

"Well, from what I can see, you're in my classroom, and if I find out that you hurt Ms. Black in any capacity, even the tiniest bruise, Garth. I will make sure that the meeting is about your aggressive behavior toward female students." I remind him who the teacher is, and he presses his lips into a thin line.

"My dad will deal with you," he threatens, and I finally can't restrain myself. I laugh.

"Get to class, Mr. Robertson, before you say something that lands you in detention for the rest of the school year."

"Ms. D," he whines.

"It's Ms. Drake, and I gave you an instruction."

Garth stares me down a beat longer before throwing Daisy a dirty look and disappearing from the art room.

"Are you okay?" I ask Daisy the second he's gone.

"Yeah, he's a loser. I could take him," she says, squaring her shoulders like she means it, and her confidence makes me smile.

"Listen." I wait until she looks at me. "I know these things aren't solved by adults, no matter what happens in that meeting. Garth probably isn't going to stop, and neither is Carly. But this room is a safe zone, so instead of fighting him..."

"Come here." She finishes my sentence, nodding once. "Okay."

"Thank you, I don't need you suspended because he's a little douchebag." I flick the bottom of her chin with my finger, and she smiles at me.

"Language, Ms. D," she says quietly, mocking me with that soft expression before adjusting her bag "thank you," she adds as she shuffles out the door to her next class. By the time lunch rolls around, Kaia barges through my door with an evil grin on her pretty face. *I needed that mischief today more than ever.*

"Putting all vegetables on a sub should be illegal, Reaper." Kaia stands in front of my desk with a wrap of her own and in her paramedic uniform.

"Did you put tomatoes on this?" I ask her, opening it up to double-check.

"Don't insult me," she snaps and slides onto the desk across from me. "You have to be quick. I left the new guy in the rig, and I don't wanna give him the 'baby in a hot car' treatment, this early into our working relationship."

"Right," I say, as if that's the most reasonable thing that's come out of her mouth before.

"Daisy got hauled into the office. She's been scrapping with this asshole of a kid for two months over something that happened with Lori." I stop to pick off a banana pepper and toss it between my teeth.

"The best friend?" Kaia asks, nibbling on her wrap.

"Yeah, and Garth Robertson."

Kaia snorts, "Did you see Ricky's new campaign for a *'Better Harbor'?"* she asks me. Harbor has been a mess and usually I'm not one to get involved but it's been effecting our lives too, teacher funding, the budgets for the paramedics and hospitals, they're even gunning for Cosy's shelter... It's exhausting having to fight for our town against people who are supposed to make it feel like home. Ever since the trial concluded, it's been a constant string of old white men making promises they can't keep. I don't trust any of them to protect Harbor; our little town deserves better.

"Yeah, pretty sure he's still hoping that his butt buddy, Charles Shore, is going to get off scot-free and ride in on a white horse to save his mayorship," I groan. "Anyways, I can't do anything about it, not without getting fired."

"Oh, please," Kaia giggles—like I've just handed her a stack of cash and told her not to spend it all in one place. "Hold on." She stops me, pulling out her cellphone, calling someone, and putting it on speaker between us. "Boonie," she purrs when the line connects. "Reaper needs our help."

"Yeah, Bright just stormed through the kitchen like he wanted to burn down the whole town. What the hell happened?" he asks over the sound of the Hollow in the background.

"Go outside, you nitwit. We can't hear you," Kaia orders, and like he could read her mind, the back door slammed louder on the other end of the phone.

"Garth Robertson—"

"Fucking Ricky's kid!" Boone cuts me off with a loud gag noise.

"Focus," I laugh, because I'm not any better, and Kaia rolls her eyes as if she didn't just do the same thing when his name was mentioned. "He's been taunting and harassing Daisy, but the school can't do anything about it because of who he is and because she's been retaliating how and when she can."

"That's my girl," Boone hums. *"What do you need from us?"*

"I mean..." I look up at Kaia.

"A conversation, we can have a conversation with Ricky about all of this," Boone cuts off Kaia's devious thoughts without even being able to see her. *"Kai,"* he warns. *"A conversation,"* Boone repeats—like saying it twice will stop Kaia's brain from spinning.

"Sure," she says, but it's clear she has other plans in mind.

"He's the mayor, we can't just beat the shit out of him," Boone warns her.

"*You* can't," she scoffs. "Jail time will only help my reputation."

"Not funny," I say to her, and she smiles wickedly. Between the three of us, Kaia is the least likely to spend any time in jail. Christian would have her out so fast her head would spin, but it's the thought that counts.

"A little funny," she whispers and takes another bite of her lunch. "So like what? We just go down there and *talk* to the guy?" She asks.

"Yeah, and we bring the shipment of eggs I just got delivered," Boone laughs.

"Stop flirting with me, Boonie," Kaia's voice goes low and teasing.

"Never," he responds quickly.

"Have you seen my brother?" Brighton drops a case of beer on the bartop and eyes me like he already knows the answer. "He's been M.I.A. since lunch, and I can't get him on his cell."

"No clue." I shrug my shoulders, adjusting the way the shirt falls over one side. "Maybe he's just taking a much-needed break from the Hollow."

"Okay. Now I know you know something," Brighton growls and points a finger at me. "What did you do, Hellcat?" His voice gets all husky and deep like he's trying to whisper, but it still comes out as a gruff shout.

"I didn't do anything." I avoid eye contact, but my phone rings in my back pocket, and I look down at it with a grimace.

"Who is it?" He asks, leaning over the counter to see the screen. "Does that say Harbor Police?" he snaps.

"Maybe..." I back away from the bar and out of his reach as I answer the phone. "Hello?" I answer it, keeping my eye on Brighton, when he's mad, the Hollow shirt threatens to tear at the seams around his throat and biceps, and I should be scared. Instead, I'm an idiot—horny, desperate, and doomed.

"Reaper, I need a favor."

"Kaia?" I practically yelp. "Where are you?"

"Lockup." She tries to stifle the laugh, but it escapes anyway. *"You should be honored. You're my one phone call. I didn't even call Christian."* She tries to sweet-talk me.

I watch as Brighton pulls his phone out next and scowls at me. His face contorts, and it's pretty obvious he's talking to Boone because I can hear him in the background of Kaia's phone call, trying to explain himself.

"Will you come get me?" she asks over the commotion. Brighton hangs up faster than I do, and I know I'm in trouble.

"If Brighton doesn't murder me for getting you both thrown in jail, sure. Be right there," I whine and hang up the phone. "Listen..."

"Get in the truck," Brighton snaps, already moving. I follow, and he opens the door for me, waiting until I'm inside to slam it with strange precision before getting into the driver's seat.

One quick Google search tells me exactly why they're in jail. "Um," I squeak.

"What?" He breaks his eye contact with the road to look at me.

I swallow the nerves and start to read. "Two unknown assailants egg the mayor's house after a heated debate on the front lawn."

"They did what?" Brighton slams on the brakes at the red light, and I slide forward on my seat. "Put your seatbelt on," he clips, and I don't hesitate to follow instructions. "I shouldn't have gotten you involved," he says quickly. "And you shouldn't have gotten them involved. This was my problem. My Daisy."

My face scrunches at the possessive nonsense of it.

"What now?" Brighton questions as he pulls into the police station.

"Daisy isn't just yours," I say quietly, and climb from the truck without listening to what he has to say. I understand that he's her dad, so by blood, Daisy is his, but he's wrong, which doesn't happen often. Daisy belongs to a village, and offensively, he believes differently. Even if it's a moment of lashing out because he's pissed off with me.

The officer at the counter has us sign some paperwork, and Brighton pulls out his wallet to pay for the bail. She leaves us in silence for nearly twenty minutes as Brighton stares at the large no access door waiting for his brother.

"I'm sorry," I say quietly, squaring my shoulders. He opens his mouth to say something when the door clicks open with a loud buzz, and the two criminals wander through.

Kaia's sporting a nasty bruised cheek and wearing an oversized t-shirt that is clearly Boone's because he's in a dirty black tank top and looks much more pleased with himself than Brighton.

"You brought him?" Kaia whines. "Now we're going to be in trouble!"

"You got thrown in jail, Kaia. You were already in trouble," Brighton snips. "What were you thinking?"

"Probably shouldn't admit to anything inside the police station," Boone whistles and throws his arm around Kaia before parading out the front doors. Once we're in the parking lot, Brighton asks again and pops the tail on his truck. "Up." He pats the tailgate, and Kaia obeys without hesitation. In true fashion, he has a first aid kit in the emergency duffle and grabs her by the chin to look at the cut on her cheek.

"Explain. Now," he barks.

"Turns out the reason Garth is a shit head is that it runs in the family. Ricky wasn't very remorseful about his son's actions. He assaulted Lori." Boone leans against the truck and watches his brother carefully as he cleans the cut.

"He admitted that?" I ask.

"Sort of," Kaia tries to look at me and Brighton turns her face back to him. "He referred to it as a private misunderstanding and that boys will be boys."

"So you punched the mayor?" Brighton growls.

"Kaia punched the mayor," he corrects, and Kaia smiles brightly. "I punched his security officer," he admits.

"What did you say to him?" I ask them both.

"Well, after we egged his Mercedes—" Kaia starts, and Brighton tightens his grip on her face. "Ow." She snaps, and he lets her go. "He came out hot and denied his son's involvement in anything that Lori is claiming. Which means something bad happened, but after he was punched it loosened up his jaw muscles. Boone reminded him how much of a motormouth I am. And that if he pressed charges, I'd make sure that everyone knew what kind of person his son is."

"Turns out Garth is on his last strike," Boone says, angling Kaia's face with a finger under her chin as Brighton backs away. "He's being sent to boarding school at the end of the semester." He inspects the cut, and his eyes meet mine. "Problem solved."

"So why did they throw you in jail?" Brighton asks.

"For show. Can't punch the mayor without consequences, Brighty," Kaia purrs.

"Don't call me that," he grumbles. "And get in the truck."

Boone helps Kaia down, and they wander around to climb into the back together as Brighton closes the back with a loud slam.

"Thank you," he says, wetting his bottom lip like it costs him. I don't say anything back because I'm still upset with his nonsense, but I let him open the passenger door for me, and this time he doesn't close it in anger.

"Oh, Rhea, I love that color!" Mom coos from the other side of the video call. The phone is propped up on the dresser as I slip into the floor-length dark blue satin dress. It hugs everything, and the thin straps at the top crisscross over my exposed back, connecting to the swooping waistline around my hips that settles just above my tailbone. I can tell she doesn't like how much skin it shows, but I work hard for this body, and I want to make sure everyone else knows it, too.

The muscles in my back are tense from being nervous, and there's about fifteen crumpled pages on my bed from trying to write some speech that would make people remember my face. Everything sounds so stupid and so fake, and I gave up hours ago before getting ready for the awards.

"What are the other girls wearing?" Mom asks, and if she'd ever made time to come to these things, she'd know that every year we pick a color and all find dresses that match the color. This year is blue.

"Other shades of blue," I say as I change out the plastic spacers in my ears for something fancier.

"Oh, you'll all look so pretty," she says, her focus on something else as she talks. "I'm so sorry we can't be there, Rhea. You just know how expensive the tables are, and Gabe is at work, so there's no one to watch the kids while I'm out." I tune out her excuses as she continues to talk and make sure that all the pieces of my dark hair are lying right in the soft curls I formed them into.

"It's okay, Mom. I get it." I say, trying to sound sympathetic to her guilt. "It's not that big of a deal anyway, it's the same as every year. Stuffy speeches about sports, drunk hockey players hitting on people, the coaches all hogging the karaoke machine at midnight," I talk until she stops whining about not being able to come, and expertly hide how much it is bothering me that she's not. But if she knew about the award, then she'd make this ten times worse and still not have the time to show up for it. But in reality, winning Best Female Athlete is a big deal, *a really big deal.*

"What shoes did you pick out?" she asks after a few moments of me shuffling around, looking for my necklace without luck.

"I was thinking about wearing my heels, the black ones," I say, wandering out to the living room to grab them from the closet. I had them all in my room, but the Terminator took them all and organized them into their own space at the front door. Part of me is grateful; the ones I did save from the condo were crushed in a cardboard box at the foot of my bed. *I just wish he'd ask before he went all Marie Kondo on my belongings.*

I grab the heels from the closet and set them out.

"The four-inch ones that you wore to graduation?" she asks me. "Those made you tower over everyone in every picture you took, Ree," she says, meaning well, but it feels like I've been pinched. "Don't you want to look nice in photos tonight? If you wear those, most of the girls will look like twelve-year-olds next to you. Where are the flats that we bought you for the wedding?"

"When I was a teenager, Mom? In the garbage." I laugh.

"All I'm saying is that a nice pair of flats will complement your outfit and not make you stand out in the crowd too much. They're more feminine, and you'll be more comfortable!" She argues with the best intentions.

"Yeah. You're probably right," I say, and put the heels back to trade them for a cute pair of sandals that match the dress. "I should go, Mom, the girls will be here soon."

"Oh my gosh, yes, I won't keep you! Please take photos!" She starts to ramble off a thousand questions, and I field most of them before hanging up. My hands hang at my sides as I tip my head back, breathing through the sting behind my eyes before turning my eyes back on the flats at my feet.

I turn around to set my phone on the island to lace them up, and Brighton stands in the archway to his room in a full suit. It's a classic black with a white dress shirt and a perfectly knotted black bow tie, and it fits him in all the right places like it was made exactly for his hulking frame. He's showered, and his hair is freshly cut; this clearly isn't the Brighton from the Hollow, but whoever he is tonight... It's a hell of a surprise.

You're going to have to change your underwear if you keep staring.

Brighton clears his throat, and it startles me out of the trance he put me under.

"What are you doing?" I manage.

"Not a word," he says, walking out into the living room past me. "That was in your shoe box," he says, nodding at a silver necklace laid neatly on the island. The exact one I'd been looking for earlier. "And wear these." He sets the heels at my feet before straightening out.

"Are you sure?" I ask him, and the look he casts over his shoulder is icy, but it's not meant to scold, it's meant to encourage, and I can see that now. *The difference.* "Heels, alright." I concede and slip into them.

I swallow tightly as he grabs his keys from the wall and shoves them in his pockets before coming back to stand in front of me. He's still just as tall as me, and I can't help but smirk. He absolutely notices the amusement on my lips because he nods in satisfaction, reaches around me, his hand brushing my arm, and grabs the necklace.

"Turn," he says, and I do, careful not to startle him out of the ridiculous favor he's about to do me. His fingers gently push my hair over my shoulder before he carefully latches the necklace, and it falls perfectly against my chest between my breasts.

"Thank you," I say, letting my hair fall back against my shoulders.

"Mm," he nods as I grab my clutch and my phone. The drive to the museum is quiet because I don't exactly know what to say to him, but he hands me his phone to pick a few songs for the ride, and it quells the rumble of nervousness in the pit of my stomach for a beat. "You like this?" he asks when an Olivia Rodrigo song comes on.

"You don't?" I scowl.

"There is, in fact, better pop music out in the world," he argues, and that stubborn strand of hair that never stays put falls free and rests against his forehead in the movement.

"Don't worry, we'll fix those musical tastes in no time," I tease.

He smirks but doesn't comment as he pulls the truck around to the valet. He hops out, and I go to follow, but he gives me a dirty look as I open the door.

"Don't," he says, holding out his hand.

Did he just scold me for opening my door on my own? I try not to mess up my lipstick by chewing on my lip, but it's hard when this version of Brighton is a gentleman. I'm starting to understand why my mother fawns over James Bond. If this is what she sees... I swallow tightly and try to ignore the mess of emotions causing a storm beneath the surface. I freeze at the bottom of the stairs when the cameras are flashing and all of a sudden feel ridiculously nauseous at the idea of climbing them with every eye in Harbor on me.

I can't do this.

I can feel the panic rising at the base of my throat, and it's going to explode violently if I don't get control of it quickly. My hand shakes in Brighton's, and his stormy eyes are locked on mine with a warm intensity as he tries to figure out what's going on without me spelling it out to him. I want to, but the words are caught behind the need to vomit.

"Back in the truck," Brighton says gently. "Hellcat." Then, when I don't move, firmer: "Get in the truck." He snaps each word so he knows I'm listening and holds my hand, stepping me backward to help me back into the passenger seat before taking his keys from the valet and climbing in.

"Brighton, I have to be here," I choke out as he pulls away from the curb.

My hands rattle around the clutch in my lap, but I tilt my head up and try to pretend there are stars to count on Brighton's roof. One at a time, I picture them stuck there, in all shapes and colors, and slowly my breath returns to my lungs. He drives two blocks down, makes a right, and drives back up the service road that leads to the back of the museum. He parks in the dark and helps me down onto the gravel like I'm breakable.

"Careful." His voice is low and cautious with me as he wraps my arm into the crook of his elbow to navigate the path. He knocks on a big metal door, and after a little while, it pops open. I recognize the girl from the Hollow, and she gives Brighton a confused smile as he thanks her and brings me inside. He wanders over and fills a glass with water before handing it to me.

It helps. I can breathe again.

"You done being high maintenance?"

I turn my head to get mad at him for saying that, but find him smirking at me, and I realize that he's making a joke.

"Oh, ha ha." I roll my eyes, and he takes the glass from me. I take another long breath in again and nod.

"Out loud," he says, and something about his tone steadies me.

"I'm done being high maintenance now." I laugh at him, and he raises his eyebrow with a tiny nod before turning his body so we're shoulder to shoulder. He leads me out to the party, bypassing the press and the anxiety to bring me straight to my teammates.

"What the hell was that?" Kaia asks as we approach. Christian looks unimpressed already, but at least he's dressed nicely. Kaia's in a skin-tight navy blue lace dress that shows off the matching bra and underwear beneath.

"You look hot," I gasp.

"Don't use flattery to avoid the question, Reaper." She pokes me in the shoulder.

"I didn't want the valet driving my truck, so I took it around back. Checked on Boone," Brighton cuts me off as I open my mouth. "Do you want a drink?" He asks me, his arm leaving mine as he steps away. I nod, and he takes his leave, but not before stopping abruptly, "Come on, Christopher, I'll buy you a beer."

"It's Christian," he snaps, looking over Kaia's shoulder.

"I know," Brighton says without missing a beat, but Christian follows and leaves us to talk.

"It's an open bar..." Sunday whispers, confused.

"What really happened?" Cosy eyes me, she's wearing baby blue, and it fits her perfectly. It pushes up her breasts and hugs her waist in the right spot.

"Wasn't prepared for all the press outside, we came in the back," I admit.

"Okay, well, we're inside now, you look like a goddess, and you managed to get my brother in a suit," Sunday praises. She's in the most adorable indigo pant suit without a shirt underneath, and out of the four outfits, she's got the least amount of clothing on but looks sharp and mean. I love it. "So let's make the most of it."

I roll my shoulders back, forcing that confidence through me. I take a second to forget about the sadness and shove through the disappointment that stings at the corners of my eyes. *Do this for yourself and no one else.*

"Let's fucking party." I push a grin to my face, and the girls start cheering.

An hour later, after dinner and a string of horrendous speeches, the girls and I are messing around on the open dance floor to a mix of late-2000s club music and passing around the crystal plaque with my name etched on it.

The sadness is at bay, and I feel like I can fly... *which may or may not be the gin talking, but at this point. Who cares?*

I slip from the circle to find water, and Brighton is standing against the bar, talking to Boone with his hands in his pockets and his eyes on the room. I watch him for a second, taking in the way his jaw tightens when he hears a loud noise and loosens when his brother says something. He's perplexing and confusing, all while being one of the most straightforward, no-nonsense people I've ever met.

He pulls his hand out of his pocket, leaning over the bar, and pops the lid on a water bottle with his thumb before handing it to me.

"They're going to break that." He nods to Kaia, twerking on the glass award in Sunday's hand as she pretends to slap Kaia's ass with it.

"Oh well," I shrug and start to laugh again. "They're having fun. Do you even know what that is, Killjoy?"

Brighton sighs.

I try not to care. The speech left me sweaty and uncomfortable under a row of hot lights and unable to see the faces that mattered. Not to mention telling a story about the struggles of being a female athlete to a room full of rich, white men who didn't understand the plot point was infuriating. Next year, they would be praising some other girl, younger and faster than me. *Don't get me wrong*, I want to be proud of my accomplishments, but it's hard when I'm constantly cheering myself on in a society that doesn't give a shit about women's sports.

Addy would be furious: *"Make them give a shit, Reaper."*

I wish she were here tonight to see this. I think about pulling out my phone, but don't want to risk the drunk tears to do it. And just like that, the sadness creeps back uninvited. Mom hasn't even responded to the picture of the award. I take another slow drink of water to bring myself back from the ledge. I wish the girls didn't have to carry the burden of making me feel loved; it's not their job, and they do their fair share of hollering, but... It's different knowing their families would be here for them tonight. They'd drop everything for them.

Like the girls do for you. I smile, staring at them, still being lunatics. This is what matters, this is *who* matters. So if they break the award, who cares, because knowing the girls, they'll glue the pieces back together—just like they've done with me.

Brighton stares at me like I'm insane, and I probably look like it.

"Do you want to dance?" His voice cuts through the thoughts, and I realize that the music has slowed in the distance.

"Uh," I look around to see that all the girls have found partners. Sunday is dancing with Cosy's brother, Van, and she's found a cute, older basketball player to lean her head on. Kaia is noticeably missing, but the chances that Christian is causing shit somewhere are high, so it leaves me alone.

Always too tall. Always alone. I hate this. I shouldn't have worn the heels.

"Take them off then," he says, and I turn to look at him.

Shit, I said that out loud. I need to work on that.

"Oh yeah, cause that won't draw attention," I sigh.

"Offer's only being made once." He was serious.

"It's okay, you don't have to," I say, forcing him to be here is already a lot, and I don't want him going out of his way the rest of the night.

"Don't tell me you can't slow dance." He stares at me. The jab is harmless, but it settles against my chest because it's not just that I don't know how. I've never been asked. Brighton studies my expression, and his jaw tightens, but he extends his hand to me. I watch as his approach to the situation shifts. "You dragged me here tonight, the least you could do is stop being a coward and dance with your date."

The tone he uses makes it clear that he reads me like a book, turning it around on himself—like I'm doing him the favor. I look down at his hand, scarred and having seen so much of the world, and it makes me terrified to take it. It shakes gently, a tremor he can't control. He gives me grace and waits, but I can tell he's trying not to fidget because his entire body is rigid.

"Take my hand, Hellcat. *Please.*"

When we finally meet eyes, the storm is gone, and his blue eyes are calm, waiting for me to take a risk, so I slide my hand against his with a tiny, nervous groan.

"Shoes?" He gives me an unimpressed nod, and I laugh, kicking them off. He scoops down and grabs them with his other hand before holding them out to Boone over the bar and leading me through the sea of bodies to the dance floor.

"Here." He places my hand on his shoulder. "And here." His other hand slides into mine, pressing our palms flat together. He pulls me closer to his chest and slowly starts to move his feet, giving me time to follow his feet as he glides us around in a soft circle to the music.

"Rhea, you have to let me lead," he murmurs when I trip over him again.

"Sorry," I grumble and try to pull back from him. "We don't have to do this. It's stupid."

"It's a square," he says and tightens his hold on me. "Follow the play. One," he ignores my protest to abandon the dance and side steps with one foot leading, "two." He moves that same foot back, "three." He steps to the other side and, on four, moves forward.

My movements start to become less clumsy, and eventually, we're moving together in a smooth rhythm with many fewer mistakes.

"Where did you learn to do this?" I ask.

"Men are resourceful, Rhea, especially when they want to impress someone." It's meant to be nonchalant, but my muscles go tight at the thought of him doing it for a girl. "What?" he asks, noticing the shift.

"I guess, I just never took the Terminator for the kind of guy that would learn to dance to get laid," I let out a tiny laugh, and his hand tightens around mine.

"Despite popular belief and vicious rumors," he tilts his head down to catch my eyes, and I feel the heat rise on my neck. "I'm not made of cold metal and robot organs," he smirks.

"Was that a joke?" I snort, and he spins us in a quick circle that leaves me struggling to keep up, but that's the point because his hand slips down my back and rests against the bare skin. I'm suddenly very aware of every scar, every callous that stains his palm, and I can barely breathe.

"Being able to dance doesn't make me soft," he explains, his eyes back to scanning the room around us. Always watching. At first, I thought it was him just being careful at the Hollow; things usually go wrong in a matter of seconds, and drunks can be unpredictable. But as I get to know him, I realized that it's not that at all.

He watches for danger. It's instinct. It's the trained behavior of a man scared of the world.

"I never implied you were soft," I tease, and he spins me around in the other direction. *Brighton Black is anything but soft,* my brain screams as I dig my fingers into his bicep to keep upright. All the shots and drinks are starting to get to my head, but the dancing is amplifying the dizzy feeling in my chest and head. "It's a welcome surprise that you can dance. I'm sure that it's a good party trick to get the girls." I say with a small laugh. "Mission accomplished."

"I learned for Daisy," he says quietly, like it's obvious, and I turn my chin up to look at him again.

"Oh." The information catches me off guard in the most genuine way, and I hate how muted the music becomes in my ears when he meets my softened gaze with his own. His jaw ticks, and before he speaks again, his tongue wets his bottom lip. "I knew eventually she'd need me to know how, and I wanted to be prepared."

"That's much sweeter motivation than I expected," I admit. "Maybe there's a beating heart beneath all that metal after all." I move my hand to poke his chest.

"Don't tell anyone," he says, grabbing my wrist to trap it against him and leaning my entire body back toward the ground in a low dip. "I have a reputation to uphold." He pulls me back up against his chest as the music swells—and then he just looks at me.

I open my mouth to be an idiot. The liquor gives me the worst kind of confidence, but before I can say something stupid, he spins me outward toward where the girls have started to dance together again and lets go of my fingers before backing away into the crowd and disappearing.

Cosy's brother offers to take the girls home at the end of the night, and as much as I don't want him to, I nod. I didn't come as Rhea's date; I came as her friend, and I think I was successful in making sure that she had fun. My job for the night was over. I pull off the tie and toss it into the front seat of the truck with my jacket as Boone brings out a tray of leftover food and a couple of beers. I pop the tailgate for him, and he sets it all down before taking a step back, letting the silence settle for a moment.

"I don't know why you cater this thing," I say to him, popping the beer and handing it to him. He hates this gig more than anyone, forced to wear a tight black chef's coat that covers his tattoos and buttons uncomfortably at his throat. His hair is brushed back off his face, and he looks like a functioning piece of society. *He looks like me.* "We don't need the money."

"Mm," Boone swallows a long pull of beer and scowls. We both know why he actually does, it's to keep an eye on Kaia. "He got drunk tonight and was flirting with girls at the bar all night—*in front of me.*"

Boone lets go with a defeated laugh and downs the rest of the beer. "One of these days it'll be me catching him doing something stupid instead of her, and I'll kill him, Bri."

"I should probably buy a shovel." I shrug, and the next laugh that leaves Boone is lighter and more genuine to his easy-going nature. "You alright?" I ask him.

"I will be, eventually." Boone nods, his hair falling around his face from its brushed-back, professional-looking form. "I can see it in her; his days are numbered."

"You've been saying that for six years, Boone." I take a swig of my own beer as he pops what looks like a crab cracker into his mouth.

"I know my girl," he says, and I believe him. "She's fed up."

That's a scary thought, Kaia Keegan at the end of her rope.

"Reaper looked like she was having fun," Boone notes after a long beat of welcome silence. "Can't believe you put that on for her." He points to the dress shirt.

"I did it because Day wouldn't leave it alone," I scoff.

"That's such a load of crap," Boone laughs, poking me in the chest with his finger. "You came because you have a crush on Reaper."

"Nope," I shake my head. "Friends. I came here as her friend."

"Rhea Drake has plenty of fucking friends, Bri, none of them spin her around on the dancefloor until she's dizzy and weak in the knees." Boone pushes with a wicked grin, and I hate the way the memory warms the base of my chest.

"She drank half a bottle of gin tonight. The dizziness wasn't me," I argue.

"Nah, Bri. You're rewiring something in that girl's brain whether you mean to or not," Boone says. Too observant for his own good. "Just don't do it if you don't mean it."

"What's that supposed to mean?" I scowl. I'm not doing *anything*.

"It means make sure you know what the word *friend* means before you cross any lines." Boone smiles at me, and I want to argue, but I hear him, and I nod. "You should listen to me. I know a thing or two about being a friend..."

"Hah," I bark, "you poor, sad son of bitch."

"She looked like a fucking angel tonight."

"Kaia Keegan has never been an angel," I argue, and Boone gives in to the statement without a fight.

"You know I couldn't imagine doing that to Day," he says after a few more snacks, and sets his beer down to clean off his fingers. "Just not showing up. Especially for something like this? If she won that award tonight, I'd drag Dad down here at gunpoint just to make him witness the incredible person she grew up to be."

I draw in a short, painful breath of cold air between my teeth.

"We can just stop at gunpoint and leave it there. He doesn't really deserve the rest," I say.

"Yeah, I guess he doesn't..." Boone chews on the thought.

Our parents weren't the greatest, even before we figured out what was going on with Sunday. Dad only got worse after that. Spewing garbage that she just needs to get her head right and believe that he's not sick. Such bullshit.

"But I get what you're saying." I lean against the tailgate. "I heard her talking to her Mom on the phone, and I couldn't do that, to Day... to Daisy?" I huff. *People really need to stop making her sad.*

"Yeah, well, luckily, we all have you." Boone nods, "and Day has never felt like that, ever, Bri. And it's because you took care of us."

"Like a bull in a china shop," I laugh, and he smiles.

"Semantics," he huffs, "it's why we push so hard, you know. Because we know, we might not have always gotten it, but we know now. How much did you carry after Mom and Dad bailed?"

"You were just kids," I say.

"*We*," Boone corrects. "We were all just kids, but you stepped up, and it's our turn to do that for you. With your hands, with Daisy." He sighs, "But you have to let us. You can't do it alone, even if you think you can."

"I'm doing just fine, Boone." I shut him down.

"You can say that shit to Sunday all you want, Bri, but I *know* you aren't." Boone steps forward and pokes me in the chest above my heart. "We're pretty different a lot of the time, but we're still connected, and I feel all that hurt radiating off of you, but you won't just find a way to let it go." He pauses, "Isn't it heavy?"

It's unbearable.

"Don't give me the twin link nonsense. I hate that crap." I try to turn it in a direction that's lighter and doesn't feel like he's backing me into a corner.

"Brighton." He pushes, and I know I'm trapped.

"Yeah, it's fucking heavy, Boone." I snap. "But it's mine."

"It doesn't have to be," he argues in the most nonconfrontational way he can. "You can let it go, or at least try to talk about it."

"I go to group," I scowl.

"And never talk…" Boone raises an eyebrow. "And you've been missing because that Landon guy called me to see if you were still around."

"Fucking…" I sigh. "I'm going. Landon's a nosy asshole."

"I want to trust that, but I don't," Boone says. "Because I know you, and the second you feel like you're being forced to do something, you turn tail."

"That's not true." I scoff.

"Riona." Boone stares at me coldly. "She pleaded for you to go to therapy, man. Publicly, more than once, and I've never seen that woman beg."

"Don't," I warn him. I wasn't having this conversation with him.

"Ri would have laid down on a sword for you, Bri…" He trails off because we both know it's true. Riona was always too good for my ass, and it became blindly apparent when I returned home. "But you made her question her intelligence, her strength. All because you won't talk to anyone, you don't even have to talk to us."

"I'm sick of this back and forth," I groan.

"Yeah, well, so are we." Boone shrugs. "But I'm not going to stop because I've seen you at your lowest and I refuse to see it again." He sounds so unbelievably sick of me.

"Yeah."

"Did you book that therapy appointment?"

"No," I answer honestly, because I won't be doing that. No matter how hard they push me. No matter how much guilt eats at me, it's not going to change a damn thing.

"Stubborn dickhead." Boone scoffs.

I roll over in bed to reach for my water bottle, but my sleepy fingers catch it awkwardly, and it tumbles from the dresser to the floor. "Shit," I sit up and lean down to grab it from the floor, but lose my balance and end up on the ground with it in a pile.

"Of course it's empty," I groan as I open it. *Drunk Rhea, you are useless.* I push off the ground, my legs and arms sore and heavy from all the booze, and make my way to the kitchen. Brighton would scold me for filling it out of the tap, but I'm too tired to care, and the light from the fridge is too bright at three am. I turn the water on, running it as cold as it will go and struggling with the tight lid on my bottle for too long before it pops open.

At this point, it would have been better to die of dehydration.

I yawn loudly and stick the bottle under the water when I hear a noise to my left. I pause, listen, and turn my head slowly to look through the darkness of the apartment, but don't find anything.

Or at least nothing I can see. Comforting.

"Brighton?" I whisper when the noise happens again. I turn off the water and set the bottle on the counter to investigate more. Padding across the tile floor to the pitch black hallway where the noise is stemming from, it rattles again, like someone trying to unlock a door.

I peer into the darkness and listen, but it's silent, which is almost instantly worse than the unknown noise. I put my hand on the archway and lean forward more, not quite willing to explore it completely.

"Hello?" I say, *yeah, because if there's something in the dark, it's going to answer you, Rhea. Dumbass.*

The rattling is gone, and I straighten out, thinking maybe it was the tap shaking? I look over it and scowl, but as I go to walk away, I hear the noise again—this time louder, almost urgent, and it causes me to step forward in the darkness further.

As my eyes adjust, I realize that Brighton is at the end of the hallway at Daisy's door, rattling the doorknob but not opening it, and my chest tightens.

"Brighton?" I say to him, but it's like he doesn't hear me. His torso is drenched in sweat, and he's all but banging his head against the wooden door as he violently tries to get inside. "Bright?" I try, it feels weird having his name roll off my tongue like that, but the situation is uncomfortable, and I don't know what else to do.

He doesn't stop his methodical movements, almost like he's stuck in a trance he can't get out of. I step closer, my body rigid and on guard as he abruptly stops shaking the knob, but his lips start to move, and he grumbles something under his breath for a moment before the rattling starts again.

He's stuck in a loop.

He's sleepwalking.

"Ok, um..." I roll out my shoulder, trying to wake myself up a little more before approaching Brighton and reaching out to touch his hands. "Hey Brighton," I say quietly, trying to get him awake without startling him, but it doesn't work, and he whips his head toward me. His dark hair is messy and plastered to his forehead with sweat as he advances on me, and I stumble back through the hallway out of his reach.

"Hey! Hey, hey," I put my arms out, almost tripping over the couch from his sudden movement. My heart is racing in my chest so rapidly that it feels like it's trying to rip itself to shreds in fear. Panic surges, and the reality of the situation begins to bleed into memories of my childhood like they're one messed-up video reel on repeat.

"Brighton!" I yell, grateful that Daisy isn't home this week to hear me screaming. My eyes flicker over his shoulder to the hallway. Why *is he trying to get into her room?*

His footsteps are heavy against the floor, and despite my better judgment, I screw my eyes shut for a split second to remind myself where I am. Every dangerous thought flickers through my head—*no, no, he's a good dad.*

I don't know how to stop someone from sleepwalking! I try to breathe, but it feels like his hands are already around my throat, and I can't tell the difference between my memories and what's real until I smell Brighton's cologne. *This is real.*

My eyes fly open, and I put my arms out behind me to feel my way around in the dark as he advances. "Brighton," I lower my voice as he charges at me. I'm basically pinned down against the island with very few options to put space between us. So I do the opposite.

"This is idiotic," I whisper, before meeting him in the middle and wrapping myself around his torso with a tiny yelp of fear for what he might do. I squeeze tightly and wait for him to freak out, but he freezes, his entire body going solid. I hold my breath, waiting for the worst, but he just stands there for a long, terrifying moment before he clears his throat and his body starts to relax.

"Rhea?" His voice is dry and scratchy as I tilt my head up to look at him, slowly uncurling my fingers from his sweaty skin. I quickly step back from him until my back hits the counter. He looks confused as he reorients himself and figures out where he is.

"Did I hurt you?" Is his next question, and it surprises me because he didn't, but it's the second thing that worries him after coming to his senses, and it tugs weirdly at my chest.

"I'm fine," I say slowly, "are you okay?" I ask him.

"I uh—" He stops and turns around, looking at the living room before his exhausted eyes land on me. "I—" he tries again, and nothing comes out, but his hands are shaking violently at his sides. His brows furrow, and his jaw is so tight it looks painful as he watches the tremors in disgust.

My own heart still races at a painful pace, but at least my brain doesn't think we're in danger anymore. The splinters of my father are gone, and only Brighton stands in front of me, sad and confused. *Shit.*

My heart goes still, then starts to break away in tiny flakes at the sight of this normally sturdy man, *shaking.* Every inch of him is shaking.

"Let's get you back to bed?" I suggest uncomfortably, completely unsure how to diffuse the tension and drifting away from the counter to stand in front of him. I offer him my hand, and he looks down at his own, trembling before he takes it and inhales sharply like the contact burns.

I lead him down to his room, and it's exactly as I expect. Clean, organized, white sheets, a gray blanket, and a single fan in the corner to keep him cool. I smile to myself, not bothering with the light as I pull him back to bed and help him in. "I'll get you some water," I turn to leave, and Brighton's hand catches my wrist.

"How did you..." He breathes out, still sitting up in bed. He wipes his face with his other hand and hangs it there for a moment, only his ragged breathing echoing through the dark room. I stare at his hand around my wrist and keep my focus on that as Brighton collects himself. "I'm sorry."

"For what?" I stop, confused, and he catches the look I give his hand, because he quickly releases my wrist and folds his hands into his lap beneath the blanket, out of sight.

"Not telling you about the sleep walking," he chokes out the words, and he's never sounded so unlike himself.

"No harm done," I smile at him, but he doesn't return it. *Other than some crippling trauma—but that's not your problem.* "Does it happen often?" I ask, unsure what to do.

"No," he says, "I mean... I don't know."

"You were trying to get into Daisy's room?" I say, and he looks up at me with a heartbroken realization.

"It's nothing, I..." he sighs. It's a strange thing to watch Brighton Black stumble around on his words. Not that he uses many normally, but to hear him struggle with his explanation is odd, and does nothing to quell the overwhelming empathy that's currently strangling me to death. A smart person would walk away, take a beat, give him space. But I've never really been good at that—the whole space thing. My brain has always needed answers immediately so I can fix the problem; if the problem doesn't exist, neither does the anxiety. The worry, the fear... the dread.

"This is childish, and it's three a.m. You can go back to bed," he says.

I don't move. "Tell me?" I ask, sinking toward the bed with caution as he watches my movements but doesn't tell me no. I sit at the end, curling up my legs and wrapping my arms around them.

"Locked doors," he says. "I don't know what it is about them, but..."

"Is it PTSD?" I ask him, and his head snaps up. I try not to flinch, but my body reacts, and I see his brows pinch together in the darkness. "Military brat," I say, watching as the air leaves his chest in one thick wave.

"I didn't know," he says. He looks around him and gently palms the top blanket on his bed to hand to me as my body shivers from the fan blowing on my back.

"My Dad was in the Marines my entire life," I admit. It's strange talking about him, and the tightness in my chest grows. "He used to... sleepwalk? But it was different, it was during the day."

It's psychosis. That's what the doctors told Mom, extreme trauma to his brain and nervous system turned him into a lunatic. *'He needs to be in care twenty-four hours a day and medicated for the time being.'*

"Even more reason to be sorry," Brighton interrupts my thoughts. His voice is more quiet than I've ever heard it. "You didn't rent that room to babysit some fucked up Jarhead."

"I'm the one who intruded on your sleepwalking quality time for water," I say with a small laugh, trying to lighten the situation, but he doesn't even smile. "Besides," I say, shifting on the bed and tapping his foot with mine. "What are friends for?"

He nods, seemingly needing to hear it as his eyes flicker to the open window and rest there like he's daydreaming. It's quiet for a long time, and part of me is worried I'm not catching the social cue to leave, but then he speaks again.

"It's not PTSD," he says, but it's pretty clear that it is.

"Okay." *Dad used to say that too.*

Brighton's head turns back, and he stares at me with the simple answer, his eyes so bright and sad against the darkness. I can tell that he's trying to figure out how much to tell me, what to keep a secret, and what to share.

"Sunday liked to lock doors," he says, clearing his throat. "Even before she was diagnosed with the seizures. It was scary 'cause she'd lock herself in rooms."

I fold my hands in my lap and listen, scared to spook him back into awkward silence.

"As we got older, our parents divorced, and things got harder. Just childhood crap," he sighs, "Boone and I ended up taking over guardianship of Sunday."

I didn't know that. Sunday's never told us that.

"Our Mother was never really equipped to deal with her medical issues, and our Father believed it was mind over matter, or that she just wanted more attention, and if Sunday believed the seizures weren't real, then they'd stop," Brighton explains, and I can see how uncomfortable he is talking about it. "There were a couple of incidents when we were younger, but the worst one was the week after we moved into our apartment. We were eighteen and eleven, just kids trying to figure it out. Day went to take a bath and locked herself in the bathroom."

His voice trails off, and his head dips like he's ashamed of the rest of the story.

"She was there for a while, and I went to check on her, but she didn't answer, so I kept trying the door, and Boone kept the keys on his belt..." his story becomes little pieces that I'm expected to connect. "She had one of the worst episodes she's ever had. By the time I got into the bathroom, her muscles had spasmed so badly that she was drowning herself."

I tense. I can't even imagine a world without Sunday, and to have to experience that first hand like that... "But she's alright," I say quietly, and he looks up at me finally.

"*Yeah*, she's alright." He inhales slowly, like it hurts to do so. "Locked doors..." he says again. I stare at him for a second before turning my gaze to the ceiling, counting invisible stars to slow down my heart. "Why do you do that?" Brighton asks, and I tilt my head back to him, and he's watching me carefully.

I swallow hard, staring at him. It's *my* turn to figure out how much to tell *him*.

He's been honest.

Brighton

"Glow-in-the-dark stars," she says, brushing a piece of hair behind her ear. Every move she takes is a helpful distraction. My mind is a war zone after midnight, and I'm still trying to talk myself off the ledge. But Rhea doesn't seem bothered by the fact that she found me wandering around trying to unlock doors. Lying to her felt wrong, but I couldn't bring myself to be honest.

The story about Sunday is true. But it's not the worst of the PTSD, not even close. It's the tip of an iceberg that I lost control of a long time ago. But Rhea is just trying to help, and I can't fault her for that. Tonight had been scary for everyone. I looked down at my hand, the tremor was still there, and hiding it wasn't going to solve anything. *What if you had hurt her?* My jaw tightens. I need to be more careful.

"Huh?" I say, blinking up at the ceiling.

"No, not in here," she laughs softly. "I have a step-dad," she explains, "Gabe." Rhea smiles at the thought of him, and it loosens some of the knots in my chest. "Reid, my younger brother, used to get panic attacks, and one of the things he did to calm down was count things. But it's hard in the dark when the nightmares start..." She trails off because she's speaking from experience. That much is easy to read. "He needed something to count when the lights were out, so Gabe stuck hundreds of stars to his ceiling, and it kind of just became a thing. I look up, close my eyes, and no matter where I am, the stars are there to count."

"Rhea," I say softly. I want to ask her. I *have* to. "Why did you need to count them?" It's an odd sensation drawing a line in the sand, keeping her at arm's length when she makes it so easy to want to comfort her. *Enough. You can't think about it like that. She's Sunday's best friend.*

She stares at her hands, and she decides to tell me faster than I had about my own invisible scars. *Focus on anything but her eyes. Or the way her entire body is shaking.* "Our Dad was sick, really sick." Her eyes are full of water, and I instantly regret asking. "He used to..." She swallows, "see us as the enemy."

Fuck.

I go completely still, and it feels like even my blood has stopped pumping. Her father was one of *those* cases. The kind where the guys come back so messed up that day-to-day life isn't possible anymore. Severe PTSD that destroys lives, and it's usually too late to help them. Most end up homeless, or worse, taking their own life.

"When Reid was little, he was playing in the backyard with my Dad, and something snapped in him; he almost killed my brother that day. But..." I watch her sigh; whatever else she has to say is heavy. "Dad was the kind of man to have guns in the house, even against the wishes of my mother, and he had been outside cleaning a few, watching my brother hit pucks with his hockey stick. I picked one up, and her face scrunches up as she tries not to cry about it. "I clipped him in the stomach. I was sixteen."

"You shot him?" I whisper.

"At the time, it felt like I'd killed him, but I know now the bullet went through and through, he got taken to the hospital, and I never saw him again. But Reid has never forgotten that day, and neither have I," she says quietly, "I slept in his bed for two years after, so even though Gabe put those stars up for Reid, I grew kind of attached to them."

And I attacked you in my sleep tonight. I swallow how I feel, unwilling to let her see it because it isn't her guilt to carry. What I did was out of line, normally, but Rhea waded into the deep end of her own trauma to save me from drowning, and my only thank you is lying to her about what's really going on. I grind my teeth together and try not to think about it.

"I'm sorry I scared you tonight," I say after a long silence, only the sound of the city waking up as background to our breathing.

"You didn't have control of that," she brushes off my apology.

"Rhea," I say her name, and she looks up at me. "I'm sorry," I repeat myself with her looking at me, so she knows I mean it.

"Maybe I'll get you a bell," she teases, her eyes still sad but a soft smile forced to her full lips. The look in her eyes is the only way I know she heard me.

"Get out of my bed, Hellcat." I kick out my foot, and she giggles but slips from the mattress to return to her own room. It's only when I hear her door click over that my hands relax from their grip on my sheets, and I allow myself to feel the guilt.

Music plays from Daisy's room, and I know she doesn't have her headphones in because I can hear it, so I knock on her door and wait two seconds before pushing it open. "Hey, Squish," I say, and she looks up from her binders on the bed.

I wander in with her grilled cheese and set it on the end before sinking to my knees beside her bed to look at what she's doing.

"Math," she groans.

"Ew." I share her sentiment on the subject. I've never been overly book smart, sure, intelligent enough to bust my ass through courses in the Marines and pass what I needed to become a medic, but it wouldn't get me anywhere, and I couldn't apply it to much besides basic first aid. The most I've done is treat Rhea the last few weeks because she's the clumsiest, most aggressive woman I know.

Every day since our conversation, my mind has wandered to her, what she was really thinking that night she found me stumbling around in a daze—but she hadn't said anything to me, and I can't tell if that's better or worse.

"How are things at school?" I ask Daisy.

"Uh—" she sighs, reaching for her grilled cheese and scowling at the lack of accompaniments.

"They're inside it," I tell her, and watch her pull the bread apart to put eyes on the jalapenos. "Answer the question," I poke.

"Lori skipped the last couple of days. I think she's scared of Carly. But Garth has left me alone, so that's good." Daisy shrugs, "I guess it's something."

"Wanna know a secret?" I lean closer, and she smiles, mirroring my gesture. "They're shipping Garth out to some private school 'cause he's a shithead."

"Really?" Her smile grows, and I nod.

"Apparently, no one wants to deal with him, so school will feel safer now, and I'm sorry that you had to fight this one on your own." I drop my tone so she hears the remorse in my voice.

"It's just dumb boys, not war, Dad." She tries to make me feel better. "And Auntie K taught me all the important sore spots in a fight."

"Oh, of course she did." I sigh, "You know you can talk to me... about this stuff? About drama and—"

"Boys?" She laughs with a mouth full of cheese and bread.

"Yeah, those things." I roll my eyes for her amusement.

"Mom says you're the worst boy she's ever known," Daisy smirks.

"Your Mom's a liar," I smile at her and shake my head. "All boys are the worst boys, just..." I inhale slowly. "Be safe. Protect yourself. And *talk to me*." I stress the last point with an authoritative tone.

"Promise," she nods as I push from the bed. "Hey, Dad?" I pause at her voice and turn to look at her. "Do you think you could take me to the music store?"

"Heaney's?" I question.

"Yeah, Mom and I pass it all the time, and I want to look at the instruments," Daisy says. She looks so much like Riona in that moment that it makes my heart slow, and I nod.

"I always knew you'd want to learn to play the Oboe one day," I joke, and Daisy starts to laugh, disgusted by the thought of it.

"No, I want to learn to play the guitar!" She says, "Please?"

"We'll see," I say, but there's no chance I don't drive her down there the first chance I get just to see the look on her face. *Anything for you.*

Brighton

"We're at capacity," Judd says in passing, banging his hand on the bar top to get my attention. The shirt he's wearing says, *MISSIONARY SO WE CAN KEEP FIGHTING,* and he's wearing a dark blue bandana to push back his unruly sandy blond hair.

"Already?" Boone calls out, and I shrug. "Where's Rhea?"

"Tagging the firefighters," Judd says, nodding toward the group of men clustered around her in the back hallway. I grind my teeth, watching them crowd her as she wraps bright red bracelets around their wrists. *She's doing her job.* Or at least that's what I'm trying to tell myself.

"Remind me again why I agreed to this?" I slam the fridge door closed beneath the bar and turn to Boone and Kaia.

"Because of that," Kaia says with a wicked smile on her face, the bruise on her cheek is fading, but the sentiment of what she did for me, for Daisy, will last forever. It's been a week, and I've only gotten one vague text from Riona: It's resolved.

No thanks to your diplomacy.

I turn to see him, leaning against a booth, talking to some of his buddies a few feet from Rhea. Her shoulders are tight, and her eyes flicker occasionally in his direction when he laughs loudly or makes a comment to someone in the group.

A week after the date Boone came to me on Kaia's behalf, throwing down a Harbor Fire association calendar and pointing to it like I was supposed to understand why. *"They need a venue to host this year's competition on the calendar,"* Boone said, and I shrugged. Told him that they could fuck off and find somewhere that needed the business. But then he told me who was on the list of contestants.

Now they're invading my bar—and her space. But there's a reason. I need eyes on that piece of shit, and now that I've seen him, all I want to do is wrap my hand around his scrawny neck and squeeze.

"Right," I mutter, turning back to them.

"Keep it together, stick to the plan," Boone warns.

"No drinks. Dry all night," I repeat.

"Separate him from his friends. Keep him busy," Kaia purrs with a smile. "And the girls will handle the rest."

"Don't get caught, I don't have the money to bail you out again." I point at her with a towel gripped between my fingers and palm to steady my hand. I shouldn't have agreed to this at all but it's better than beating the shit out of him myself and then explaining why I did.

"Yes, sir." She salutes as she slides from the stool and disappears into the crowded bar.

"I've got two grand in savings," Boone says, suddenly less confident.

"We're going to need a lot more than that if all three of them end up in lock up," I grumble, and he agrees, "go help Rhea," I say.

"Why? She's fine?" Boone scowls.

"They're crowding her. She's uncomfortable," I clip, not looking up at her, and just hoping that Boone follows the order.

"What about that is uncomfortable?" He laughs, leaning over the bar with his eyes on her across the room. I follow his gaze to find her laughing and flirting with one of the guys; his hand swallows her wrist while she fights the sticky backing off the bracelet. She's wearing that tiny, shredded Hollow t-shirt and a tiny pair of black, patchwork jean shorts that stick to her thighs. If her purpose is to get attention tonight, she has it. *From nearly everyone in her vicinity.*

"Boone," I snap. "Go make space."

"Fuck me, man. You're a piece of work," he scoffs, but listens this time and wanders away. The crowd parts for him, and he takes his time to talk to people who say hello, but eventually he slips in behind Rhea and leans against the wall. He asks her for a stack, and she hands him some with a smile. It's only when the firefighter breaks contact with her that my shoulders relax, and Boone smirks at me, spotting the change in my muscles from across the way.

"Hey man," a voice calls to me, "can I get a beer?" I turn to see that scummy shit bag standing at the end of my bar with his hat pulled down over his hair and his eyes raking over the tiny, barely legal blonde girl next to him. *Right.*

"Sure," I say. And walk away. I push around to the kitchen and find a moment of solace in the back. I pop open the fridge to grab a water and slam the door behind me before leaning against the counter and closing my eyes.

"Brighton?" I flex my hand around the bottle as I bring it to my lips.

"Yeah?"

She's standing there, with a tentative smile on her face and those big, sad brown eyes as the bar rages around her in the background. It's nearly impossible not to make note of all the intricate ways her tattoos flow together when she's wearing so little clothing: the inky details that swirl and stain her shoulders, arms, and stomach, all like giant works of art that seem to highlight every strong muscle in her body.

How do you do that—look pretty under fluorescent kitchen lights?

"The fire guys are all tagged, Judd is just setting up the host, but I think they're ready to start so I'm going to watch the area around the stage." Rhea angles toward the opening of the kitchen with her arm out and her back muscles flex. It's the most graceful part of her, almost mesmerizing to see her inky skin stretch to accommodate them.

"What's that?" I ask, pointing to the pen on her inner arm.

"Turns out not all the firefighters are assholes," she says with a tiny smile that shouldn't bother me. *That's mine.* I press my tongue to the roof of my mouth. *You are out of your fucking mind, Brighton Black.*

"I'm not picking you up if this date goes bad," I warn, trying to ignore every other thought in my brain.

"I promise to charge my phone this time," she brushes it off, and I find myself wishing she didn't. *Grow up. You're friends. That's what you do, you let your friends date people. Rhea wouldn't give a shit if you dated someone.* "What?" she says, and I stare at her for a moment, praying that I didn't say any of that out loud.

"Quit chasing my best drinkers away," I tease, and she laughs, the sound vibrating through me.

"It's not my fault they can't handle me," she argues playfully. *You don't need to be handled.*

"Go watch the stage," I tell her, and she doesn't hesitate to find her way back into the chaos.

When I turn back to the kitchen, Kaia is standing by the exit door with her eyes on me and her jaw strung tight as her fingers rotate a small, shiny hunting knife between them. *This woman* enjoys *jail.*

"Tread lightly," she warns.

Sunday said that same thing.

At least now I have an idea of why they're all so careful with my sad girl.

"Get out, Kaia." I snap at her, and she narrows her eyes but pushes out of the door with her back and disappears into the night-soaked parking lot. With her busy outside, doing God only knows to the idiot's truck, I wade back into the busy section of the bar. Boone is waiting tables with some of the girls, and Judd is manning the bar by himself, completely drowning in orders.

I wander back around and start to help, watching Boone swipe the nearly full beer off the table in front of Miles as he starts to rub himself down with oil. These firefighters are full of themselves, but the female presence in the bar is blossoming more than on dance nights. When he turns back, he throws his hands up and starts accusing his friends of stealing it as they all get ready for their turn on stage.

Some radio personality with a stupid name is hosting, and before long, the Hollow's main floor is packed with drunk women screaming over shirtless men that parade around on the stage to horrible mainstream pop music.

Rhea's laughing with a few of the women who are around the front, and she says something to Judd as he passes by to collect drinks off the long, standing tables piled with dirty glasses. The firefighter she had been flirting with all night stomps across the stage, stripping from his damp uniform and kneeling across from her. She's standing just close enough for him to wrap it around her neck and pull her in tight to whisper something in her ear that makes her cheeks turn pink.

I'm going to break both his hands.

He kisses her cheek and straightens out as the host introduces him, and he flexes his muscles under the warm yellow lights for all the girls scream his name. *Never again.* The glass in my hand creeks uncomfortably as my fingers close around it tightly. Whatever Kaia is doing to Miles's truck better be worth the heart attack I'm having watching Rhea flirt with these assholes.

"Can I get some vodka shots to the back table?" one of them asks from my left, and I turn to see what table he's talking about with a nod. I fill nine glasses with vodka and then rim the other with it, but fill it with water. Just enough to smell like booze but give no buzz. I carry them over, tray high, to avoid spilling as the crowd parked around me.

I hand out the shots to them, personally giving Miles the water with a deadpan face. He lifts it to his lips without a word and takes back the water as it burns. I laugh to myself as I swing away back into the crowd.

Intermission has started, and the judges are being introduced on stage as ballots get passed around to outstretched hands to choose the people's favorite. I grab a water bottle and slip through the tightly packed bodies toward where she towers over a circle of women. They're looking at the extensive list on the ballot, and Rhea is pointing out certain names with a smile on her face.

"Hellcat," I call out and chuck the bottle as she looks up at me. She catches it without flinching, popping the top with a tiny thank you from her lips before she takes a drink. Just a moment of her attention— to remind me none of these douchebags matter. She comes home with me when the doors get locked.

She lives with you, asshole.

I can hear my brother in my head, reminding me about how stupid I'm being. But ever since she told me about her past, I can't help but buffer her from other men. Like she's triggered some possessive idiot that lives inside of me, the one I haven't met since my early years with feisty, loud-mouthed Riona Cody.

I grind my teeth together, calling her that. *She was Riona Black for so long until you ran her into the ground.* Every once in a while, I can still hear that laugh, see that girlish smile on her face, and I forget how badly it had gone wrong. I met Riona at a party that Boone had dragged me to. She was all blonde hair and glassy, predatory eyes, those long, sharp lashes fluttering at anyone who would look at her.

She was quick with her tongue and even faster with her insults, and I knew I needed to feel how good those sharp teeth felt in my skin. It was one night. One party. And she was mine forever. Her heart and everything that came next in the weeks that followed. Never leaving each other's side, the fear of finding out she was pregnant with Daisy, the fights, the worry, the sex, and the laughter.

She had years of school left, and I had no education and even less money.

So I joined the Marines with some stupid notion that they'd train me for real life, but instead I got a blood-stained soul, divorce, a daughter that hates me, and an aura void of any light. *"You're not very bright."* Her drunken words repeat in my head as my eyes catch Rhea, laughing brightly at something as the music grows louder again, and they prepare for the next round of contestants.

Maybe I could be.

"He's starting to get pissy," Kaia says, appearing at my side. I flinch. She's one of the only people that can sneak up on me.

"You're too quiet," I mutter with a scowl. She shrugs as I whip her up a whiskey sour and she settles onto the stool as Sunday and Cosy find their way to the bar. Boone is quick to steal three more beers right out from under Miles's nose, and Kaia is right, the more drunk his buddies get, the more he realizes what's happening.

"What the fuck is this?" He storms up to the bar. "My drinks have been weak or missing all night? Is this how you run a fucking business?"

"Watch your tone, fire-rat." I point to him as he nearly pushes Sunday off her stool to get to the bar. "Maybe you should be asking your friends, they seem twice as drunk as you."

"Harmless hazing, Miles." Kaia leans over the bar as she sips on her drink with a grin.

"Fuck off, Keegan. You're probably behind this," he sneers.

"If I were, you'd know it," she snaps. *This doesn't bode well.*

"Can I get something to drink that isn't water?" He ignores her and redirects his attention to me.

"What do you want?" I ask, cleaning my hands on the towel thrown over my shoulder.

"Vodka."

"We're out."

"Whiskey," he snaps.

I look around at the bar, eyes raking over the abundance of full bottles that are stored above my head. "Shit out of luck."

"Gin," he tries, and it's clear he's going to lose his shit any second, but he looks like an idiot without a shirt on, and his contest number is roughly finger-painted on one of his flabby pecs.

"Don't know what to tell you," I say, and I hear the girls snort into their drinks.

"I don't know what fucking game this is, but I know a lot of people who can make you hurt for this little stunt," he sneers, wagging a finger at me. I'm content to ignore him until he reaches out to take Sunday's full glass of sangria. Faster and working with the advantage of surprise, I catch him by the head and slam his face into the bar. Sunday is up out of her stool before the glass tips and shatters across the counter.

"Don't touch my sister," I warn him, holding his cheek to the surface.

"I wasn't going to!" He yells, and a few of the people around the crowded area have stopped to watch what's going on. "I just wanted a fucking drink!"

"Bri," Sunday's voice isn't quiet, but it's not commanding. I look up at her, and she smiles at me. "I'm alright, let him go."

"Get your shirt on and get out of my bar." I give him a shove, and he stumbles back, the side of his face red from the contact.

"You can't kick me out!" Miles argues, putting his hands out wide. The way he's talked about, I expected him to be bigger, tougher, maybe. But he's all binge drinking and no self-control.

"I don't have to," I say, nodding to who's behind him.

Rhea had appeared from the crowd shortly after the girls had funneled back into the bar, and she's watching now with her arms crossed behind Miles as he throws his hissy fit. She narrows her eyes at him, and for once, they aren't sad; instead, they're full of excitement and bright with hues of green and gold I've never seen before.

"He's shoving customers around and being rude." I cross my arms and watch as his face falls.

"Yeah," Rhea says. "That tracks. I've got plans tonight, so let's keep this parting clean of any drama." She smirks at him, and Kaia starts to laugh so hard she tips from her chair, and Cosy has to keep her upright.

"Are you seriously still salty?" Miles jokes over the sound of cheering as more firefighters roll onto the stage.

"Yeah," Rhea says. "I am." She smiles, sharp as a blade. "You got it wrong. I'm not only high maintenance—I'm petty, too."

She doesn't wait for him to respond; she just walks forward with intimidating height and every muscle in her arms flexing as Miles starts to stumble backwards. He yells a few more profanities, complains about his shirt, and tries to argue her out of it, but she never breaks.

"Here." I hand her a beer without looking at her as she leans her back against the bar, and the girls hype her up. Out of the corner of my eye, I watch her bring it to her lips with a tiny smirk on her face. Her pride and confidence were restored in one fell swoop. *That's my sad girl.*

"**H**ey, Hellcat," I call as I walk through the apartment. I heard her come home — singing some stupid song at the top of her lungs in the shower again. It's always something new, and she'll sing it until she's bored with it. Luckily for me, and the rest of the Hollow, she has a pretty decent voice, and it's kind of endearing. I look around, putting my hand on my hip, but she isn't in the kitchen, and her bedroom door is closed.

It creaks open, and she appears in a pair of black shorts and an oversized nineties-style shirt with a wrestler collage on the front of it. Her hair is pulled off her face in a ponytail, and she's surprisingly lacking any of the makeup she normally wears for work. She's staring at me like I'm insane, and she's got those filthy string headphones in again. I hate them. They're not even white anymore, are constantly tangled and the rubber around the ends has started to shred. She wears them around the apartment and can never hear anything. Half the time, she's talking to herself while she makes a mess in the kitchen for me to clean up later.

I step forward and gently tug them from her ears.

"What's up?" She leans against the frame and crosses her arms beneath her chest, but I keep my eyes on her face. I know I should step back, but I can't make myself even if I wanted to. I like being in her space and I like how she reacts to it.

"Uh—" I start and stop, unsure how to ask. "I'm calling in my favor."

"You are?" She perks up a little, almost like she has been waiting for me to do it and was losing hope that I ever would.

"I have a birthday party to go to, and the guys always bring their girl-friends and wives… and they—" I roll out my shoulders in the dark blue button-down shirt I'm wearing and push up the sleeves to the elbows as the temperature rises. "They always give me hell for not bringing anyone, and it would be nice to shut them up for once."

"Can I change?" she asks me.

"Please don't," I say quickly, and she freezes, looking down at herself. "That's perfect." *You're perfect.* "It's just bowling."

A squeal leaves her lips, and she grabs something off her dresser before shutting her door and sliding across the floor to the shoe closet. "I love bowling." The words come out in an excited string of mumbled mess as she pulls on a pair of sneakers and ties them. Somehow, the addition of her white socks and dad shoes makes everything even cuter, and I'm cursing myself for even suggesting this.

"You ready?" I ask her, and she springs up from the floor.

"Can I drive?" she asks, and I almost say yes because of the tone in her voice, and then I remember her Bronco is a war zone and shake my head. "Boo!" she teases, but follows me from the apartment to the street out front.

As I'm opening the door for her, a truck rolls by us, and something like a string of curse words leaves her lips before she climbs up, supporting herself on the roof of my truck as a loud, free laugh leaves her lips. I lift my hand to her lower back and stare as the truck stops at the stoplight at the end of the street. Miles' truck is covered in nasty claw marks and drawings that look like dicks all down the driver's side, and on the tailgate is bright orange spray paint that says BIG TRUCK, LITTLE DICK in scratchy letters that I recognize as Sunday's handwriting.

"I can't believe he's driving it around like that," she all but screams and looks down at me with the biggest smile I've ever seen. *I can.* I reported his truck stolen to every mechanic shop in town. If he wants it fixed, he has to go to Lorette.

"Even more unbelievable that they didn't get caught doing it," I say, putting my hand down before she can notice, and she sinks into the passenger seat.

"I never said thank you," she adds as I go to close the door. "You're a good friend, Brighton."

"I didn't do anything." I pat the doorframe with my fingers and close it over her. I climb in on my side and hand her my phone as I start the truck, and she finds music to listen to. "Oh uh—" I put my palm out, and she drops my phone back into it, her nails tickling the skin of my palm. I've never seen her with her nails done, and I furrow my brows at the sight of the clean, black talon-like length.

"We had staff photos," she says, scowling. "They're press-ons," she sticks her finger between her teeth and pops the acrylic off the base of her pinky finger. "See?" She drops it in my cup holder and starts to work on the rest of them with her mouth.

"You're disgusting," I groan. "Do not leave those there."

She stares at me for a moment before nodding to my phone, reminding me that I took it from her for a reason.

"I made you something..."

"You made me something?" She stops gnawing her thumb and leans closer as I turn the screen for her to see. "You made me a mixtape!" Her voice goes high, and her smile spreads like an infection across her face, making her cheeks turn pink and her eyes brighten.

"It's a playlist. Stuff we both listen to—so we can share." I try my hardest not to sound like an absolute idiot as I explain it to her. We regularly spent mornings fighting over what songs played on the stereo in the kitchen, and in the Hollow after close, and in my truck... "It's probably stupid."

She looks up at me like she's offended, I'd even say that, and gently takes the phone out of my hand again. "It's not stupid," she whispers, scrolling through the perfectly balanced list. It's all her favorites, all of mine, and some that I think she might like. "It's really nice."

Ignoring the way she looks at me, I put the truck in drive and pull out into traffic as she finds the perfect starter. The alley is across town, and Rhea goes through some of the playlist as she continues to chew on her hand like an animal. *You would pick the feral one.* I pull into the parking lot to unplug the phone, but she snatches it from me.

"Don't you dare," she warns, "you don't stop this one in the middle!"

I look at the dashboard, and it's one of the David Bowie songs that she's always singing around the apartment. She throws her head back and follows along at the top of her lungs as I watch her, trying not to laugh. *Trying not to fall for her.*

"Oh come on, Brighton, I know you know this song," she giggles and encourages me to join her with a shove. Part of me wants to say no, but I find myself parting my lips and shouting along with her as loud as I can. My cheeks hurt from smiling as the song fades out, and Rhea is breathless beside me. *It feels too good to relax.*

"Can we bowl now?" I ask her, drinking in her messy raven hair and flushed features. I never noticed the freckles across the bridge of her nose, or maybe it's because she always covers them, but I find them enticing. *What else are you hiding, Hellcat?*

I climb out, and she pops her door open, and I stop her from sliding out. "What did I tell you?"

She stares at me and sighs, "I can open my own door. I'm capable."

"It's good manners."

"It's high maintenance," she corrects.

"It's bare minimum," I say, and she stares me down for a second. Everything about Rhea Drake screams how little she sees herself as valuable, and it's infuriating.

"Just like you ordering my burgers without tomatoes?" She questions, I knew eventually she would.

"You don't like them," I say to her, my fingers flexing around the door frame. "So why not say that?"

"Because it's one more unnecessary thing Boone has to do when he's doing a hundred other things for other people." She brushes it off.

"That black bean burger is only on the menu *because* of you," I tell her.

"What?" Her brows furrow, and I want to smooth the lines between them with my finger. *Friendly, really friendly. Check yourself, Killjoy. You're losing your control.*

"Kaia told Boone you don't eat meat, so he made sure you had something you'd actually enjoy. You aren't a hassle asking for no tomato."

Rhea opens her mouth to argue and closes it again. Thinking about what she can say that validates her point. "I don't like to be a burden," she confesses.

"I know," I narrow my eyes at her. "Who told you that not liking tomatoes makes you a burden? I'll kick their ass."

That makes her laugh, finally, remembering our conversation from the night I taught her how to make the martini. She stretches out her legs and kicks my thigh gently. "Can we bowl now?" she asks, mocking me back.

"Yeah." I give her my hand, ignoring the tremor and how it stills when she presses her palm against mine as she hops from the truck to the cement. Inside, the bowling alley hasn't left the early two-thousands with its dirty, blue carpet and scuffed hardwood floors. Most of the lanes are empty except for three at the other end of the building, occupied by most of the guys from my old squad and a few from the group. "Come on."

"So, if I'm pretending to be your girlfriend, do we need a complicated backstory? We can say we met at the Hollow, you're clumsy, so you spilled a martini on me..."

There she goes again, poking the bear for fun. I turn from the kid behind the counter, handing out shoes, and growl at her, and she laughs. "Size eleven, please," she says, keeping her eyes off me.

"Ten," I say to him, "I have tiny feet for a guy my size, don't tease me." I don't look away as I try to deflect from how nervous she was to say that out loud in front of me.

"Scouts honor," she hums with a soft smile.

"You're my roommate tonight," I tell her. "No need to lie. These guys will see through it anyway." I lead her down toward the commotion that's happening at the end, and as we get closer, I hear them starting to take note that I've brought someone with me. "Don't back down," I warn.

"Military brat," she winks and wanders out in front of me to start greeting the guys without my introductions. I walk toward José, and he hands me a glass of beer I probably won't drink.

José Garza is one of the guys I actually served with, a skinny little kid barely twenty-five with a wife and two kids depending on him. He's funny, though; his humor is dry, and the best part of all is that he doesn't dig. He knows more of my past than anyone in the room, but he never brings it up, and he never uses it against me.

"Where's Sarge?" I ask, looking at him. Landon usually came around for these things when he was invited. Something about showing up for your community outside of hard times.

"Said he had something to do." He shrugs. "Who's the girl?" He asks, pointing to Rhea. She's introducing herself to José's wife and daughter while the rest of them toss me stupid looks.

"Rhea." I consider drinking the beer. It would be easier than trying to explain to them what we *are*. "She's my roommate. Guest room."

"She's pretty," he notes. "Didn't really think a scary dog was your type."

"Don't call her that," I say, shaking my head. "And there's no *type*. She's here as a friend to shut you all up."

"I do love it when a man dates the exact opposite of his ex-wife. You're really sticking it to Ri, here, Black." Josè comments and starts to wade into the conversation. Riona loved Josè, which only made the divorce harder when it came. Splitting up friends was just as bad as splitting up time with Daisy.

"Fuck you, Garza." I scowl and find an empty stool to pull on my bowling shoes. Rhea finds me eventually and starts to do the same. "Do you want a drink?" I ask her, but she's hyper-focused on trying to pull the knot free from her shoe. Her grunts of frustration grow, and the knot remains tight. "Rhea," I say, but she doesn't look up as she brings the shoe to her teeth. "Don't—" I grab the dirty shoe before she takes it between her teeth. She scowls at me as I start to loosen the knot before handing it back to her. "Do you want a drink?"

"Please," she says. "And a burger."

I nod, leaving her on her own to tie her shoes.

When I wander to the counter, I see Landon standing near the entrance with a birthday bag in his hand as he watches everyone at the other end of the building.

"Careful," I say. "You'll ruin the birthday with that ugly mug," I say, after ordering quickly. He doesn't respond to my joke, and it's pretty clear that his head is elsewhere as I approach him. "It was just a joke, Sarge, no need to get bent up about it."

"If you're here, the party's already ruined, Black." He snaps out of his fog and gives me a half-hearted smile.

"Josè said you weren't gonna make it." I stand next to him as he watches the party.

"Uh, yeah, I wasn't sure, so I didn't wanna disappoint anyone," he says.

"Well, you're here now." I clap my hand to his shoulder and start to walk back, thinking he's following, but I don't hear his footsteps, and he's exactly where I left him. "You coming?" I ask.

"Actually, I only came to drop this off," Landon says, holding out the bag. "Will you bring this over?" he asks.

"Yeah..." I step back and take the bag from him. "You sure you don't want to stay, just for a minute... I— I brought a date," I lie. It's not a date. Not really. But the way I want it to be is dangerous.

"The mystery girl, that makes the man of stone smile?" Landon inhales, and the lazy smile returns.

"You should come meet her," I say.

"Next time," he says quickly. "Say hello to the boys for me." Before I can convince him to stay, the front door is swinging open, and he's nothing but a shadow on the pavement. *Alright then.*

I palm the present and start back to the table, worried that Rhea might be overwhelmed, but by the time I've returned, she's completely taken over my friend group with her conversation. I set her drink down on the table and watch as she giggles with one of the girlfriends over funny names to pick for the scoreboard.

She fits into your life like she's always been there. Like she was made to fill the bullet holes in the wall you've been using as target practice your whole life with pure, unfiltered sunlight.

"We gave you Killjoy," she smiles at me.

"What?" I shake my head slightly.

"Killjoy, like your rugby call, I couldn't think of anything funny," she says, grabbing her drink. "I hope you know I'm a bowling assassin. It's actually a shame I have to kick your ass in front of everyone."

"Alright, Hellcat, put your money where your mouth is." I shake my head at her and walk past her to the lane.

The ball feels weightless as I send it down the lane and watch it crash into the pins, sending them all flying in a different direction. Rhea's bottom lip juts out in instant worry, her eyes trained on the back of the lane as her name flashes across the screen. After three turns, it's pretty clear that she was just talking shit, every ball she throws dies in the gutter, and she's joking around, asking for assisted lanes.

"Assassin, hey?" I laugh at her as she hugs a large ball in her tattooed arms.

"I'm rusty?" She shrugs, clearly tipsy from the drinks, but her eyes are glassy with enjoyment. "And hungry." She whines.

I point to the table behind her where two burgers sit, wandering around her as her eyes fall to the bright ring of red inside. Before she starts to eat it without complaint, I lift the lid, slide the tomatoes onto my plate, and swap in my pickles. Just like the girls always do for her.

She watches me carefully, doesn't say a word, and picks up the burger. Her face contorts, and for a second I think that maybe there's something wrong, but she finishes chewing and says. "Boone's are so much better," she sighs. I nod, and as she sets down the burger with a sad pout, I fill her plate with my French fries and take the burger from hers. "You don't—"

"After you've eaten pasta out of a bag, you'll eat anything," Josè says from our left.

"You've eaten pasta out of a bag?" Rhea looks like she's going to be sick as Josè starts to tell her the horror stories of field rations.

The whistle blows, and I lean over on my thighs to catch my breath as halftime starts. "Why the hell are they running so hard?" I huff, taking a water bottle from Margie.

"Whatever they're doing, it's working," Kaia looks up at the score-board with a scowl. Her dark braids are fuzzy, and she pops her mouth guard in and out of her mouth as she stares around the field, trying to figure out where we went wrong in the game. Down three tries, it was going to be brutal to claw back in seven minutes.

"Emma's taking that pocket between you and Margie—you're hand-ing it to her, and she's faster than any of us. We have to shut her down," Cosy says, looking over her shoulder at their star winger. "I'll handle Ava if she crosses, but Rhea, you need to get your arms around Emma before she hits that stride."

"Force the breakdown. Sunday and Kaia can do the rest," I say, our thoughts in unison.

"Good girl." Cosy slaps my side with her open palm in the huddle as the whistle fires off to start the second half. With a plan in our hands and the silent encouragement from each other, we line up and dig our heels into the turf. I close my eyes and listen to the buzz of the floodlights, and I inhale the sound of the crowd and the smell of the grass. *I can do this.*

My eyes are still closed when the kick goes up, and they fly open as my feet start to shuffle down the field. Margie is tight to my side, and just like predicted, Emma pockets the ball from her teammate on the right and tries to slip through the pocket. I step into Margie, close the gap, and drop my shoulder into her. Emma hits the ground hard, the ball popping from her grip and rolling across the ground toward her team, but Sunday is faster.

We stay tangled for a second, but Emma kicks her foot out as she goes to propel forward back into the action, and it grinds across the top of my hand hard enough that I cry out as something cracks.

I ignore the pain lancing up my arm, the skin across my left hand is tattered, and only my thumb curls in when I try to flex, but there's no time to worry about it. Sunday crosses the line with the ball, and we're thrown into another play immediately after the kick.

"Reaper," Cosy's eyes are on my hand as we file in and get ready, conversations flickering across both teams.

"It's chill, Bones. Just a scratch," I snap, still trying to uncurl my fingers to their full extent. A few tears spill from the corners of my eyes as I catch a girl by the waist and walk her back until she crumbles, and the breakdown forces a turnover of the ball. Kaia snags it, shuffling around a few defenders before she's forced out on the right side, and we have to start all over again. I can feel Cosy watching me like a hawk, but I continue to play, hiding the pain that thrums up through my muscles into the base of my shoulder and neck. *Something's dislocated—grinding on a nerve. Holy shit, it hurts.*

The ball snaps from hand to hand until it lands in mine, and I angle myself into their largest player. I may not be as fast as Kaia or as sneaky as Sunday, but my strength is my asset. I dig my cleats in and drive forward, my hand screaming and my thighs shaking as I overpower the girl trying to slow my path. Two more join her, hands and hair being slammed around as they team up on me. Cosy slams into my hips, doubling our drive and pushing me forward another few feet before my toe slips and the huddle crashes into the ground.

I push the ball out, protecting myself the best I can beneath the pile of bodies, and I feel it slip from my fingers. It's another ten seconds before I can confirm that Kaia has it and we've scored. Every Hillcat glances at the clock. One minute left.

It's enough.

I can hear them all say it as we scramble to find our composure.

Cosy claps her hands together loudly, signalling the ball release, and we take off. I keep my hand at my side as I try to focus on the field. Sunday cuts left, and Kaia follows as the ball slides into the winger's hands. Cosy chops a her down with a hard hit, and the two of them go down in a huddle, knocking the ball loose and ripe for Sunday.

She pops it out to Margie, wide right with a fat gap. Her eyes narrow on the goal posts, and I do my best to slow the chasers on her tail, pushing myself faster than I've played all day to throw my body at her as she gets held up at the line.

"I'm here," I call, driving at her hips until she's over and can curl into herself, aiming the ball for the ground. The whistle blows, and the ref is screaming as the clock winds down. The ball is clear, and we're only down the conversion. Margie kicks the ball out as fast as she can, sets it up, and it slips through the uprights perfectly.

I grab Kaia by the waist as we celebrate, trying to ignore the screaming pain at the base of my fingers as everyone cheers and high-fives.

Fuck.

An hour later, after a shower and a quiet cry, I leave my duffle in the Bronco, pull out my Hollow T-shirt, and wander through the back of the bar in search of a bucket to fill with ice before my shift. It's already starting to get busy as I shove the shirt into the pocket of my jeans and slip past Boone with my hand tucked out of sight. Brighton is talking to a couple in a booth across the room, and everyone else who might tattle is busy. *I just need ten minutes with it on ice, then I can work and sleep.*

I grab a bucket from under the bar and start to fill it with ice to the brim, tempted to stick my throbbing hand in it right there and then.

"What are you doing?" Brighton is too big to move that quietly.

"Getting ice." I turn to him with a fake smile, and his calm eyes rake over me like they always do after games, searching for damage. He used to only do it to Sunday, but lately it's become a new habit that makes my ears hot and my chest tight.

"For what?" His head cocks to the side as he crosses his arms, his biceps straining distractingly against the black fabric.

"One of the kitchen girls asked for it…" The words come out choppy, and I try to hide my confusion, but Brighton sighs.

"There's ice in the kitchen."

"Shit, there is?" I look over my shoulder at the kitchen and curse myself for not looking in there first when Brighton catches my wrist, and I hiss in pain.

"What did you do?" His fingers are tight on my wrist, but gentle at the same time. I gaze down between us at my swollen knuckles and the torn skin on my hand. Hiding it from coach was probably idiotic but I've been in too much trouble lately and figured I can sleep it off before practice tomorrow.

"Nothing. I'm fine," I say, and his grip tightens. "Got stepped on in the game today, it's just swollen—" Before I can finish the sentence, he slips his hand forward and presses his palm against mine, forcing my swollen fingers straight. I punch him in the chest with my good hand, and he grunts, baring his teeth from the contact, but he shakes his head. "That fucking hurts," my voice quivers, the pain vibrating up and out of my throat as I pull my hand back from his.

"You're going to the hospital." He turns from me and grabs the bucket of ice, only to dump it out in the sink.

"It's minor, Brighton. They're just gonna send me home with some ibuprofen." I shake my head.

"And that's their call, not yours," he says, moving toward the exit of the bar.

"I have a shift," I argue, and he rolls his eyes at me, stepping back into my space with two long strides.

"You're not working. They're dislocated, Rhea." He lowers his tone, and the use of my actual name and not the usual annoyed Hellcat makes me shiver.

"So relocate them." I scrunch my face up at him, and he just shakes his head. "Should be easy, you've probably done it lots in the field, right?"

"That'll hurt, it's dangerous..." He palms my hand again, and I try to hide how much it hurts right now. *Please stop doing that*, I think as his thumb draws a lazy circle over the inside of my wrist. "And I'm not a doctor."

"It'll hurt either way," I argue and he drops his head with his eyes closed, more arguments forming on his angry pout. "I'd rather it hurt with you." It rolls off my tongue brazenly but at least it's the truth.

Brighton steps forward again, staring at my hand as he gently inspects which fingers are the worst. *I can tell you, it's the ring finger and the middle finger. They feel like they're trying to claw their way off my wrist.* He looks up at me and his jaw ticks, but he doesn't let go of my hand.

"Did you know you've got freckles like the Little Dipper right here?" he asks me out of nowhere, and my brows furrow. "Right here, it's the cutest thing on your stubborn face." He nods to the left side. I open my mouth to question him, but a sharp, snapping pain radiates up into my elbow, and it takes everything in me not to cry out in pain. "Hospital. Now." His hand closes around my elbow as agony shoots through my hand—he's put them back. "*Please.*" It comes out rough, and the softness of the demand catches me off guard enough to nod.

"You know that was rude," I say as he lets go. "Lying to distract me."

Brighton stares at me, his icy glare rolling down my back as my temperature rises. "Go to the hospital before I call Kaia and make you go by ambulance."

"Fine," I groan, cradling the hand and leaving the bar, wondering why he didn't argue back. *And why I missed his skin on my skin.* "Shit," I holler as soon as the Bronco door slams shut.

Brighton

"What the hell was that earlier?" Boone asks, dropping two plates at a booth and spinning to catch up with me.

"What?" I ask, already avoiding the question he wants answered.

"Reaper looked upset." He moves around me so that he can see my face when I lie to him the second time.

"She got injured during the game. I was just helping her out so she could drive herself to the hospital." I slam the till closed and start stripping empty glasses from the bar.

"You made her drive herself?" Boone laughs, and I glare at him. "Something else is going on. It's making you... bristly."

"I'm not bristly." I roll my eyes and keep cleaning.

"You are, more so than usual, and I want to know why," he laughs, following me as I go. Sometimes having a twin who runs at the same frequency is a curse—it's like he feels the emotional wave before I do. He picks up on things faster when it comes to social cues and matters outside logic. Boone runs on emotion. It gets him in trouble, but it balances us. I've never known how to listen to my own heart.

"What's going on between the two of you?" Boone stops me as I try to take the tray to the kitchen.

"She's my roommate." I brush him off and keep moving to the door.

"No, no, no!" He slips in front of me again, hands locking around the tray. "It's something else."

"You're bored and making issues that don't exist," I explain to him, but he shakes that ruffled head of hair at me. His eyes light up at the deflection, and I know I've fucked it up because he smiles like an idiot.

"The crush on Reaper? It's getting worse, isn't it?" He swings around me as I force the tray from his grip and move the rest of the way into the kitchen. I slide the dirty dishes to the counter and lift the door to the dishwasher to start loading things. "Come on, Bri…"

"I do not have a crush on her," I say, but my shoulders clench—like my body knows the lie before my brain does.

"She got back ten minutes ago," Boone says, and I turn my head to look at him. Mistake two. "Went upstairs crying," he adds.

"She's probably sore," I grind my teeth together. "Her fingers were dislocated. She'll sleep it off," I say, too fast.

"Sure, but will *you*?" Boone questions, his eyes searching my face and finding everything he needs to win the argument without saying another word.

I turn back to the dishwasher, and he takes the hint that I'm done discussing it. It takes everything in me not to go upstairs and check on her. I busy myself with every stupid task I can think of. Cleaning the counters. The traps. The ice buckets. Checking cups for chips, pulling out menus that need replacing, and even fixing the felt on the pool table.

It's supposed to keep me busy, but I can't stop looking at the stairs, and halfway through the night, I break, climbing them two at a time to the apartment.

"Hellcat?" I nudge the door open gently with my foot, and before I even look around for her, I hear her crying in frustration from the bedroom. *How long has she been crying like this?* I inhale slowly, composing myself before knocking on her door. The crying dies down to a sniffle, and I hear her shift around on the bed before she answers me.

"What's up?" She tries to act casual. I pop open the door, and her sadness consumes me like a tidal wave. She wipes her cheek on the back of her uninjured hand and waves the splinted one in my face. "I went to the doctor. You can save your scolding for someone who deserves it."

"I know you aren't crying because of the pain," I say to her.

"Now he's a psychic and doctor," she groans.

"You didn't even cry when I popped them back in so what's wrong?" I ask her, not stepping into her room. *You're in here twice a week to get her laundry, why are you being a coward now?*

"I feel..." She trails off, chewing on her lip. "It's stupid. Go back to work."

"What's wrong?" I repeat myself a little more sternly.

"I feel gross, the hospital makes me feel *gross*. I got overwhelmed. I tried to relax, but because they wrapped it so I couldn't shower, and I snapped my headphones pulling them out of my backpack..." she points sadly to the headphones on the bedspread and almost starts crying harder. "I broke down, flipped out, and I took a shower anyway, managed to get my hair brushed, but it's damp, and I can't braid it or pull it back because..." she holds up her hand as she rambles faster.

"Move over." I walk into her room, careful not to disturb her calculated mess, and stand next to her bed. "Turn," I say, and help her balance on the bed with her back to me. "Brush," I say, holding out my hand.

"Brighton." She hesitates with a grumble.

"Give me the brush." I hold out my hand to her. She slaps into my palm and straightens out her shoulders, and I start to pull it gently through her hair. When the knots are gone, I hand it back to her and begin to braid it back.

"You've been practicing," she notes.

"YouTube." I clear my throat and try to concentrate on the strands of hair between my fingers, and do my best not to hurt her or pull it. "Too tight?" I ask.

Rhea laughs gently under her breath.

"What?" I pause.

"Nothing, it's fine. Keep going." She encourages.

"You're laughing at me," I scowl, but start braiding again until it becomes thin, and I put out my hand for one of those tiny elastics she leaves lying around the bathroom.

"I'm not," she responds quietly and looks around the bed for one. I spot it before her and lean over her to grab it between my fingers. Her body tenses at the sudden contact, and she turns her head towards mine, bringing our noses dangerously close together.

"Found it." I wait a second too long before pulling away. It's nearly impossible to look away from her at this distance, her brows scrunched, her eyes and cheeks red from crying. I tie it around the end of her hair without looking away and inhale the smell of her orange shampoo while she watches me like a hawk. "Feel better now?" I ask her, and she nods. "I'm getting you Tylenol. You're not leaving this bed."

"Okay," she nods again.

"Good." I let go of her hair and pull back from her begrudgingly, and force every step I take out of her room.

Rhea

Brighton sets the box of chips and cookies on the table where I pointed, then takes a moment to look around the gym. "Looks nice in here." He's wearing a dress shirt that's too tight on his throat because he keeps rolling around his head like it's going to loosen it up. He offered to chaperone the dance. I think it's mostly because he still doesn't trust the school to protect Daisy, and I don't blame him. And... It's just nice having him here.

His gaze turns on me as he rakes a hand through his hair and gives me a quiet *good job*. "I forgot you were a savant when it comes to high school dance decor," I tease and shake my head. I'd shimmied into my most appropriate dress, but I still feel exposed under Brighton's eyes. The thick straps feel too thin across my shoulders, and the loose, flowy fabric too tight around my hips.

"There's more food in the truck; Boone made too much. I'll go haul the rest in," he says.

"Let me help," I step forward, his eyes flickering to the splint on my hand with the shake of his head before he disappears from the gym. I refocus as best I can on the busy gym. Kids file in, laughing and shouting over each other as they take photos and flood the dance floor.

I spot Daisy before her dad gets back and smile at who she's with. Auggie looks cute in a dress shirt and red tie. His brown hair is starting to grow shaggy around his ears, and he's sporting a goofy, content smile. He's helping her carry a crate of records to the stage where Lori, the self-appointed DJ for the evening, picks out what she wants to play next.

"Who is that?" Brighton scares the shit out of me, leaning down to speak right into my ear over the music.

"Uh, Auggie," I tell him.

"What kind of name is Auggie?" His jaw goes tight, and his instant disdain for the kid makes me laugh. I cover my mouth and furrow my brows to stifle the enjoyment when Brighton tosses me an equally dirty look.

"They're having fun." I try to diffuse the situation.

"Yeah, about ten inches too close together," Brighton grumbles.

"This isn't a bible camp," I tease him.

"Do you know what happens when teenagers get that close?" He's two seconds from starting to pace, and I turn to him with a big smile on my face.

"Are you gonna give me the birds and the bees talk, Killjoy?" I raise an eyebrow just to get him more riled up.

"Do you need me to give you that talk, Hellcat?" His voice drops, and I realize my mistake because he's better at this game of riling than I am.

"Depends," I push, just a little, *just enough*. "Does it come with examples?"

Brighton chokes on his own spit, and I know I've won.

"Do you need water?" I start to laugh as another teacher summons me from across the room. "Leave Daisy alone, she's a smart girl. Don't be a helicopter parent, hand out drinks, food... keep busy." I warn him, and he scowls at me and asks me what that even means, but I'm too far away from him now to explain. I watch him watch *them* for most of the night.

It's a pretty low-key evening, with only one major fight that happened in the bathrooms, but it is dealt with almost immediately, thanks to Brighton's size. The boys take one look at him and think maybe they shouldn't start more crap.

"Thanks." I nudge him as we wander back to the gymnasium. "For a second there, I thought Boston was going to live in detention for the rest of his life."

"He probably still should," Brighton huffs, fussing with his sleeves. He'd rolled them up at some point during the evening, and every feral woman in the vicinity is eyeing him like a piece of meat.

"You know, I think half of them would faint if you asked them to dance." I look around at all of them staring at him while he watches Daisy and Auggie.

"What?" His brows pinch together, but he doesn't look away.

"You're fresh meat to these hyenas," I say.

"Cougars," he corrects. "You mean cougars."

"So you *have* noticed." I cross my arms, careful with my hand.

"The blonde in the neon blue tried to cop a feel by the punch bowl an hour ago." His lips curl into an amused smile.

"Lannah?" I gag. "She runs in a swingers circle—and not a good one. Her husband spends more time at the doctor's for his diseased junk than he does in their bedroom."

Brighton shakes his head at me.

"Casey is clean," I say. "But she sounds like her nose is constantly plugged."

"Oh yeah?" He looks down at me. "What does that sound like?"

I pinch my nose and moan—just loud enough to make him panic that someone heard, and he squeezes my side to get me to stop. His fingers linger, but only for a second before he pulls away.

"You asked." I shrug.

"How are you even allowed on school grounds?" he quips. "You're worse than a thirteen-year-old boy," he adds, his jaw clenching as the music slows down and Auggie's hands mold to Daisy's hips awkwardly.

"He's the most polite kid in this school," I tell him.

"Polite boys still think like pigs," Brighton argues.

I snort, the sound leaving me before I can stop it.

"What?" He huffs.

"You pride yourself on manners," I remind him. "So, on that fact, I can only make the assumption that you also think like a pig."

"Maybe I do." He's quick with it. "Makes me qualified to be pissed off when little boys touch my daughter inappropriately."

"He's not even roaming." I chuff and point to Auggie's stiff hands on her waist. "You're telling me you wouldn't have grabbed my ass by now if that were us?"

Brighton's head whips to me.

"I mean, if we were fourteen, awkwardly slow dancing at a school event," I try to slow his racing thoughts, the heated ones written all over his usually composed face.

"You're pushing buttons tonight, why?" he asks, and then lowers his voice. "Are you having fun?" For a second, I think I pushed too far—then a smile creeps onto his face.

"I am." I nod. He doesn't say anything further, but he steps out in front of me and extends his hands. "Don't be silly."

"Someone has to be a good role model for these animals." He grinds his teeth together, and the muscle in his jaw flexes.

Is that the point you're trying to make, Brighton Black? I stare at him, the lights dancing across his features and making him appear younger than he is just for a second. I let him pull me into the crowd of kids, a few of them recognize him from the day in the hall and whistle loudly, but he ignores them completely as he carefully wraps me up in the most respectful way he can.

"You know, this is the most I've slow-danced in my entire life," I say to him as he angles us to keep an eye on Daisy.

"Now who's telling lies about their high school experience?" he jabs.

"Not all of us were born looking like a god, Brighton. You probably came out of the womb with a glow." I roll my eyes.

He laughs. "I had braces well past graduation."

"No fucking way." I squeeze my hand in his and muffle the swear that falls from my lip by pressing my face into his shoulder.

"Serious," he says, his body tense. "Got them off two weeks before I met Riona." He leans closer, his lips in my hair and his breath on my skin, making every nerve tingle.

I look up at him, taking my eyes off the kids dancing awkwardly around us, and lean back so I can properly see his face. "You'd probably make braces look cool."

"Boone." He whispers his brothers name and nods in confirmation, "he made braces look cool. I looked like Andre the Giant had a baby with Steve Urkel." He teases himself, and I feel him relax.

"Okay, so maybe you weren't grabbing ass in high school." I'm very aware of where his hand is on my lower back. *Do it, I won't stop you.*

His eyes break from mine, and his brows furrow together tightly before whispering under his breath. "I'm going to kill little shit."

I hold on to him tighter, my eyes finding what his do. Auggie's hand is beneath Daisy's chin, and they're sharing the smallest of kisses. The kind that she'll remember for the rest of her life. "Brighton," I warn him. "She'll hate you forever if you interrupt that."

He turns his attention back to me. *You're adorable when you're all worked up, and it's fucking annoying.* I cock my head to the side, and we lock into a staring competition that feels endless. "Fine," he huffs, and I know I've won.

"Oh—I see the nerd now," I tease, and he shakes his head, annoyed. "What? It's there." I keep going until he spins me out, laughing.

Rhea

Brighton says goodnight to Daisy and drops onto the couch beside me, leaving a careful stretch of space between us. After the dance, we cleaned the gym with the committee, drove a few kids home, and finally landed back here. I kick my shoes off and curl my legs up beneath me with my head resting on the back of the couch. Brighton leans back, his hands on his thighs, and stares at the ceiling.

"Never again," he mutters.

"Pussy," I snort, and he scowls. "We throw four dances a year, not including Prom."

"Why?" A cross between a laugh and a scoff leaves his lips.

"Kids like to dance." I rake my fingers through my hair, then glance at my busted hand.

"Is it still sore?" he asks, and I don't know how he clocked that glance without even looking—but I hate that he did.

"Yeah, a little." I chew my lip, mad at myself for an unpreventable injury.

"How many games are you out for?" He asks, finally turning his head and prying one eye open to look at me.

"Five. Minimum. Until the brace is off." I try to move my fingers, but they're stiff, and a stubborn pain lingers beneath the surface around the joints. "I should get to bed. I still have to make six a.m. practice, and Coach will kill me if I'm exhausted and injured."

"Yeah," Brighton nods, "yeah, go."

He stares at me in the silence, and it feels like the apartment forgets how to breathe. I want to tell him to stop, but that would require me to explain why it feels like that and... *I just can't.*

I collect my stuff and wander to bed, crawling in and curling up under the blankets. Tonight the bed feels bigger than usual—and the apartment feels louder, too. I can hear every creak and groan the old building makes as the wind picks up outside, welcoming a storm to Harbor that we desperately need to quell the heat wave we've been under.

The analog clock Brighton keeps in the guest room ticks like it's wired to a speaker, and I can hear people laughing down the street as they stumble home from the bars on Main Street. I check my phone and nearly two sleepless hours have passed. *I'm so screwed for tomorrow.* Rolling onto my back, I look up at my ceiling and inhale sharply.

"Stars." Tons of glow-in-the-dark stars, stuck to the roof in different formations, and enough to count until I fall asleep. He stuck them all to my fucking ceiling. "Damn you," I swear, flipping back the blankets on a mission.

The second I open my door, my stomach drops—something's wrong. The apartment is dark as ever, with the street lamps outside pouring through the living room windows. The floorboards creak heavily at the end of the hallway, and I see Brighton's large frame shadowed against the wall. I open my mouth to complain about the stars in my room when his whole body jerks. *He's sleepwalking again.*

"Brighton," I call out to him, trying to draw him out toward me and away from Daisy's room before he wakes her, but he freezes, his head cocking to the side like he heard me but didn't register what I said. "Hey." I snap my fingers. His shoulders turn toward me. Something's wrong. It doesn't feel like last time.

He stalks down the hallway, his form seemingly growing in size with every heavy step he takes until he's standing two feet in front of me with a glazed-over look on his face. I try to think about what worked the first time. *Contact.*

I step forward, and his body tenses further as I reach out to touch him, but his hand snaps out and clamps around my wrist. It's clear in his movements that this is worse than before; he's stronger than me, even in his sleep, but I step into his space and try to coax his fingers off my skin as my heart rate beats up beneath my chest.

Stay calm. Panicking isn't going to help.

I repeat that to myself over and over again as he remains locked around me. *He's not your father; this isn't that. Take a deep breath.* I inhale and look up at him.

"Brighton?" My voice is shakier than before.

Nothing.

Daisy's door clicks open, and my worst fears play out like a burning roll of film before my eyes. She steps out, confusion painted on her sleepy face, and Brighton's entire body whips toward her. I don't know if it's fear or muscle memory, but my body moves between them in an instant.

"Daisy—back to your room," I say without turning.

"What's wrong with him?" she asks, and he starts to move forward.

"He's sleepwalking, just—"

Daisy flinches when he moves faster, and I extend my hand to her in comfort, ready to tell her to go back to her room again, but Brighton has other plans. He's too close now, and there's not enough space in the narrow hallway to go anywhere but back. I cover Daisy's body with my own; every muscle beneath my skin trembles, but I don't back down.

"Rhea..." Daisy's voice is quiet and terrified.

"It's okay. He won't hurt us. He's just sleeping." I tell her as I repeat it over and over again in my head.

He's sleepwalking; he won't hurt us.

"Slow. Back into your room. Lock the door," I tell her instinctively, and when I turn to make sure she hears me, Reid and Remi stare up at me, scared little kids with glassy eyes and bruises I couldn't prevent spattered across their faces. "Go back to bed, Daisy, he's okay," I tell her when she doesn't move.

She nods gently, squeezing my hand, and takes two slow steps before she's back in her room. The door locks behind her, and Brighton's head flinches toward the sound. *Contact.* My brain is running in circles trying to figure out how to wake him up this time, and I'm coming up blank. "Brighton," I say again, and he hears me, turning his head as I reach out and take his hand. If I can get him back into bed, maybe he'll stay there for the night. "Let's get you to bed."

I lace my fingers into his and tug gently until his feet start to move. His steps are syrupy and clumsy as he wanders through the dark into his room. I get him to bed and manage to force him down into the sheets. I dig around for one of the blankets, pulling it up around him and waiting a few seconds to make sure he's going to stay put before taking a step back.

"Stay," he huffs, the word still tangled in sleep.

I stare at him, and it's clear he's not awake, but he says it again clearly, and it's so desperate that I consider it for a second. I can wait until he's asleep properly and sneak from his bed before he even realizes any of this happened. *But Daisy.* I turn to the room and chew my lip, aiming to go back, sure she's alright, but he repeats himself.

"Don't leave me," his voice isn't his own, and it heaves at the barriers in my chest. Every logical thought I have is breaking down from the sound of it.

"Alright," I say out loud, even though he can't hear me. I wait another second, hoping that this decision doesn't backfire, before I crawl into his bed on the other side. I pull up a blanket and tuck it under my chin as I roll to my back, trying to keep the space between us that he works so hard to respect when he's lucid.

I sigh, seeing his ceiling. It's empty except for a group of exactly seven small glow-in-the-dark stars. "Is that the Little Dipper?" I whisper. My racing heart comes to a dead stop, and my mouth goes dry. *"Right here, it's the cutest thing on your stubborn face."*

He'd said it to distract me... but what if he wasn't lying?

Brighton rolls over in the bed, scaring me from the surprise, and presses his head against my shoulder with a small exhausted huff as his hand creeps beneath the blankets and finds a place splayed over my stomach, all before his body goes completely still.

I'm really sick of waking up to sheets that smell like Brighton.

My eyes fly open against his chest, and I hold my breath as I gently pull back to find him wrapped around me like a blanket. His hair is messy against his pillow, and there are none of the angry creases to his face that are normally there when he's awake. *Shit, shit, shit.*

I wiggle back, but his fingers dig into my back against the friction and keep me in place. He moves a little, his arms tightening around me as his body stirs from sleep. He freezes for what feels like an eternity before he slowly pulls back from me.

"Why are you in my bed?" His voice is caked with sleep that stirs up the butterflies asleep in the pit of my stomach.

Not the time, horny Rhea. You shouldn't be here.

"Why were you holding me like that?" I fire back, slipping from the bed to the floor. He cracks an eye open and stares at me, confused. He's trying to figure out why I'm here, and I don't blame him. Unable to wake him up from the episode last night, he has no idea what's going on.

"Well, I was asleep... I thought you were a pillow. You didn't answer why you were in here?" he asks again.

I scowl at him. "Why did you put all those stars on my ceiling?" I'm flustered and don't want to have to answer his questions, so I keep asking him more. He doesn't move, just lies there with the blanket draped around his waist and his expression thick with sleep.

Deep breaths, one: two, three, four... every part of his body is tight.

"Because you said they help you sleep. And you're my friend. I wanted to make you comfortable here." He says it so smoothly, I almost believe him.

"So what's that then?" I point to the ceiling. The seven perfectly placed stars on *his* ceiling.

"There were leftovers," he lies— and I watch him start to squirm.

"That you just happened to place up there in the shape of the Little Dipper?" I call him out.

"I don't know." His eyes flicker to it, "Maybe I just did it subconsciously."

"Likely." I scowl.

"Rhea," he huffs, "why were you in here?"

I stare at him, his eyes raking down my body, and I realize that I'm only wearing my underwear, and an oversized tank top longing for the trash bin that barely covers my thighs. I cross my arms over my chest and try to make myself less exposed. Brighton sits up in bed, pulling the sheets around his waist, and waits for an answer.

"You were sleepwalking again," I say.

"Daisy..." He moves out of bed.

"She's okay," I say, a tiny lie because I never checked. But she hadn't left her room in the time it'd taken me to fall asleep...

"Are you?" he asks next, and I nod.

"I couldn't wake you up, so I put you back in bed and... I guess I fell asleep, too," I admit, leaving out the part where he practically cried for me to stay. *He's got the Little Dipper on his ceiling. He's past the point of shame, Rhea.*

"Right." He shifts beside his bed in his thin pajama pants, and I try to keep my eyes on the wall behind his head. "I'm sorry."

"Does it usually happen *this* much?" I dare to ask.

"It's never happened with her home," he admits. "It's this time of the year... it..."

"You can tell me, I've heard it all," I say, and it's true. Dad used to wake us up in the middle of the night to tell us horror stories.

He shakes his head. "No. It's not for anyone to hear. I just... need a break." He inhales a large breath that sounds painful. "I need to get out of the city."

"Okay." I'm not sure what to say because he feels so scattered compared to how controlled he usually is about everything.

"Usually I go alone, but Daisy is here for two weeks, and you're here..." he says, trying to work out what he wants to do.

"I can watch Daisy. We can—"

"No, Rhea. I mean..." He swallows. "You can come. I want you to come." He cuts me off, steadies his thoughts and his body with a huff and tries again. "Do you want to go camping this weekend?"

"Camping?" I swallow hard. "I—"

"It'll be fun," he says. "I swear." He promises, but I'm not ready for his quiet plea, "I need it. Please."

I hate camping. The outdoors and I are mortal enemies, Brighton. This is a terrible fucking idea. His demeanor shifts so fast it's hard to say no, to tell him that I can't help him with this. My eyes flicker to the ceiling. *He's been helping you since you got here.* It's one thing, camping can't be that bad...

"Sure," I say, and hope I don't regret it.

Rhea

"It's my favorite art teacher!" Sunday bursts in, sliding into the quiet classroom. The few kids who usually spend lunch in here are gone today. School's almost over—no one wants to be inside, and I don't blame them.

"I'm the only art teacher you know, Sunny." I take my bag from her and pull it open. She always stops at my favorite sushi place and brings tempura veg with Boone's dipping sauce—sealed in the tiny container she never forgets. "I'm starving," I say, inhaling fryer oil straight into my soul.

"We haven't done this in a while. I was excited when you texted." Sunday sets up her spot and pulls a chair over from a student desk in her pink overalls and beige baby T. "You said you wanted to talk?"

Yeah. Your brother. And how you're going to kill me.

"We had lunch like four days ago," I laugh, and she shrugs.

"That's a while," she argues gently. "What's going on? You're being weird."

"I'm not being weird," I lie immediately, biting into a soft piece of sweet potato. "I—"

She lowers her chopsticks and stares at me curiously. I'm not typically one for losing my nerve. It'll come out eventually, most likely in a blur of words and a string of swears.

"Did you know that Brighton sleepwalks?" I ask her, careful not to approach any of my other feelings surrounding him.

"He has for a while," Sunday says quietly. "How do you know?" Her eyes narrow.

"It's happened a few times since I moved in," I explain. "Last night it happened while Daisy was there."

"Is she okay?" she asks, and I nod. I drove Daisy to school this morning and asked her how she was doing. I received a couple of grumbled responses, but for the most part, she wasn't affected by her Dad's episode. I thought *that's good because I can't shake the sticky feeling of my own trauma off my skin.*

"Yeah. Nothing happened." I hesitate. "Has he ever gone to therapy?"

Sunday shrugs, "We've tried. Our dad was kind of the man who believed therapy was useless for men. Talking about their emotions would make them soft. Brighton was exposed to a lot of the rants growing up, and I think it just stuck."

"That's stupid," I say. "Therapy is for everyone."

"Try telling Bri that." She stuffs another piece in her mouth and follows it with a sip of Coke. "He goes to group, though." I stare at her, confused, and she sets down her chopsticks. "Like group therapy—ex-military guys sitting around, swapping horror stories over bad coffee until they feel better?"

'It's not for anyone to hear.'

"Does he actually share?" I ask her.

"No clue. He won't let me go. Bobo went a couple of times in the beginning, but eventually Bri just started leaving him at home and going alone. He never mentioned anything about him being forthcoming with his trauma." Sunday explains, and everything is starting to make more sense, why Brighton is the way he is. "I do know it's bad," she says after a beat. "It's been bad for years, and he manages, but whatever he saw... messed him up. He's jumpy, his temper is shorter than ever, and he doesn't talk to anyone about it."

"He told me about the locks," I say, and Sunday looks up from her food with a sad expression. "I'm sorry—"

"He talked to you?" she says. For a second, I brace for her to be angry, but she's not; she's intrigued.

"Yeah. The first time it happened... he was trying to get into Daisy's room, but it was locked, and he was just standing there rattling the knob." The image is burned into my brain now.

"That's not new," she confesses. "I should have warned you..."

"You didn't owe me that. It's private." I tap the table with my finger to get her to look at me, and she offers a soft, Sunday-specific smile. "He told me what happened with you." I swallow. "The bathtub."

"Oh, man." Sunday sighs, her expression dropping. "Suddenly he's a motor mouth."

"I don't think I really gave him a choice. I kind of demanded an explanation," I admit.

"Reaper, you've never demanded a thing in your entire life, if he told you it's because he wanted to..." she says, "Brighton likes control. It's why he joined the military. He likes to say it was to support Riona and Daisy, but it's because he couldn't control our parents leaving, he couldn't control my seizures... He needed control, and the military offered that." Sunday explains between sips of her drink and bites of her lunch. "And frankly," she stops, setting down her pop. For a second, I'm sure she's about to call me out—or get mad I've gotten this close to him. I brace for the lecture, ready for it, and preparing a speech to assure her that I'd never cross those lines. *If she told me not to...* my mouth goes dry. "I'm just glad he's talking to someone."

I stare at her, confused by her lack of anger.

"Why do you look like you were expecting something else?" she asks.

"I feel like I'm going insane," I confess, trying to process everything she's said while still managing what's going on in my own mind. It's like bracing for a hurricane you're smack dab in the middle of, and you can't breathe or run. You just have to stand there and experience it, praying that you don't die. "Cabin fever. I've got cabin fever."

"What?" Sunday laughs. "Is this because you have a crush on him?"

I choke on the mushroom in my mouth, and my eyes water from the expected shock to my system. *I'm definitely dying.*

"I don't have a crush on him." I cough a little before taking a drink of water.

"We've been friends for almost ten years," Sunday points out. "I know when you like a guy."

"It's your brother. That's disgusting." I try to argue, but she just laughs.

"It's disgusting to *me*," she says, rolling her eyes. "You all act like I have nothing going on between my ears, but I'm not blind," she grumbles, "I know my brothers are attractive, they're also fucking idiots." She laughs. "And if there's any reason I'd keep you away from them, it's because I don't want *them* breaking *your* heart."

"But what about Kaia and Boone?" I ask her, my brows pinching. The story is as old as time, resurfacing any time I feel the need to deflect.

"You say that every single time. It's a terrible argument. I had no control over it." She shrugs. "She's the earth, and he's her moon. I'm just a girl, I can't compete against gravity."

I smile thinking about them, hoping one day they'll figure it out. That eventually Kaia will stop being so scared of the change and just let it happen. *That or we kill Christian, Goodbye Earl style, and don't tell Kaia we did it...*

"We aren't killing Christian." Sunday laughs, reading my mind. "It's too messy. And don't change the subject, we were talking about Brighton."

"We were?" I feign confusion, and she scoffs. "We're just friends, Sunny. That's all."

"Alright..." She doesn't believe me, but she's not winning the argument today, and she knows it.

"He wants to take Daisy and me camping this weekend," I say to her, closing the lid on my empty container as I finish.

"Wow," she mumbles. "He usually does that trip alone."

"What trip?" I ask, stomach dipping.

"Every year, he goes up into the park and camps by himself. Says it helps him *reset*," she mocks, "I think something happened overseas, I know it did. Boone knows, but neither of them will tell me. Something about this month marks an anniversary for something he won't share."

"Do you think it's a bad idea to go?" I chew on my bottom lip.

She stares at me for a second and ponders my question. "If Bri asked you, it means he needs you."

"Oh."

"It's a big ask, Rhea—especially since you *definitely* don't have romantic feelings for my brother," she smirks. "But if he's reaching out for help, please don't leave him hanging. Take his hand—because it doesn't happen very often that he offers it, and he could use all the friends he can get."

She sounds sad that he isn't reaching out to her, and I don't know how I feel about it, but I nod, trying to understand where she's coming from without letting the guilt eat at me.

Brighton

"What's your favorite song?" Rhea asks, focused on her phone as we drive out of the city.

The one you sing in the shower in the morning... the one that you sing at the top of your lungs. It's that one by Nine Days, Absolutely... or maybe it's called Story of A Girl. It's been stuck in your head for a week.

"Dunno. Probably something by the Eagles." I adjust my grip on the steering wheel, checking over my shoulder to make sure that Daisy still has her headphones in. It took some convincing, and none of it was me, but eventually we got her excited for the impromptu trip. Rhea's wearing shorts made of the thinnest fabric that rides up her tattooed thigh dangerously as she shifts in the seat and lets the wind push through her hair.

"Probably something by the Eagles," she mocks me with a crazy laugh. "Says the guy who has a playlist for brushing his teeth. What is it really?"

If I told you, it would make it substantially harder to keep my hands to myself.

"The Reason by Hoobastank," I tell her, it's not the truth, but it's so weird that she'll overlook the way my heart is pounding, pinned to my sleeve and bleeding down my arm.

"Hoobastank!" She laughs even harder, and the soft strands of her dark hair fall from the ponytail she has in, "I can see it, you've got an unhealthy obsession with early-2000s rock-pop. I've never met a man in the top one percent of Nickelback's Spotify fans."

"Don't diminish that. It was hard to earn that award." I scoff, and she smiles at me.

"I'm sure it was." Her tone softens as she goes back to scrolling through her phone for music to play. "Give me your phone," she asks, and I oblige. "You need to expand your musical tastes, Brighton Black. This is ridiculous."

"If you put any girl-pop on that playlist, I'll turn this truck around," I toss out the empty threat.

"How fast? Because Sabrina Carpenter is itching to make your ears bleed," she jokes, and her smile makes the lines around her eyes crinkle.

"At least three traffic violations will be made," I grumble, but it seems to satiate her need to push my buttons because she quiets for a little while, and so does my mind.

I hate how easily she does that without knowing. Like having her close is an interference to all the other noise around me. I swallow tightly, checking on her out of the corner of my eye just to see her. Distraction isn't healthy, but damn does she make it a comfortable place to be.

"How much further?" She doesn't look up, but it's clear she's giving herself access to the road trip playlist I made so she can fix things she doesn't like.

"We just left the city, Hellcat, don't do that." I sigh.

"Do what? Ask questions?" She laughs. Her hand is free of the splint now, but her fingers are still taped together for support. She's been antsy, pacing around the apartment like a caged animal because she hasn't been able to play or lift weights. I'm hoping that taking her out of the city does both of us some good.

She's mentioned more than once how much she hates camping, but most people say that until they're knee deep in it and having a good time in nature. She's packed an extra bag full of God-knows-what and crammed it into the back of my truck, even though I told her it wouldn't fit.

Just like I said she didn't fit into my life and yet...

"Are you even listening?" she asks.

"Nope."

She scowls and drops my phone back in the center console before kicking off her shoes and curling up her legs beneath her on the seat. "What's your favorite song?" I question after a beat of silence, and her face scrunches up in thought.

"Uh," she pauses, "maybe that song by Nine Days?" I try to hide the smile on my face.

"Story of a Girl?" I say like I don't know exactly which one she's talking about. "Is that your favorite or the song of the week?" I jab.

"Same thing." She shrugs.

She closes her eyes and pulls the large hoodie she has on up around her chin as she rests back on the seat and eventually falls asleep. The campsite is another two hours, and the silence that fills the truck is welcome as we pass small highway towns and rest stops, driving further into the wilderness. The smell of trees and fresh air fills my nose, and it's like balm to all the frayed nerves under my skin lately.

Rhea stirs a few times but never wakes, and as we pull into the campsite, I have to shake her shoulder gently to get her lucid. "We're here," I say quietly, reaching back to wake Daisy. "Sleepy head," I tease her as she sits up and yawns, looking around at her new surroundings.

"We are in the middle of nowhere..." Rhea says.

"There's no service out here, Dad," Daisy whines as she looks up from her phone.

"Okay, you two...You'll be alright for three days," I say to them, and Daisy chucks her phone into her backpack. "Who wants to help me set up a tent?" I ask them, and both stare at me like I've got two heads. "Right..."

I climb from the truck and take a second with the fresh air and the quiet nature to steady myself. So much has shifted in my life over the last few weeks that most days I feel completely sideways. Being out here resets everything. It always does. And when the breeze rustles through the trees, I feel them.

Hey boys.

My heart clenches for a moment, painfully so in my chest. Somewhere deep in the woods, the birds fight back and forth in the branches. The lake stirs, the soft sound of waves kissing the shore, and I feel it in my bones. This is a good decision. I breathe in the clean air, close my eyes, and root myself in the dirt before I start unloading.

Eventually, the two of them begin moving and start helping set everything out on the spot or on the nearby picnic table. Rhea and Daisy laugh as she flips out about a bug she can't identify, and I lay out the poles to the tent on the ground. Daisy wanders over eventually to aid me in my struggle, her hands a welcome help but pretty unexpected.

"Sorry, there's no service," I say to her as I thread a pole through the fabric.

"All my music is downloaded, it's chill." She hands me another and holds up the stiff side as I push the pole up and around. "Well, it wasn't, but...It's only a couple of days."

"That's my girl," I say to her and finish the third pole. "Hey uh..." I slow down, trying to come up with a way to word it that doesn't have her closing up on me. "So who's the boy?"

Daisy's head snaps up, and she looks entirely unimpressed.

Okay, so wrong approach.

"Dad, no." She shakes her head, "We are *not* having this talk."

"Why not?" I scoff, "I wanna hear about him," I say. *I really do not, but here we are.*

"No, you don't," she calls my bluff.

"Come on, I do. Tell me about him, what's his name?" I ask her, even though I already know, it's better to give the illusion of me being completely in the dark, so she can share what she wants and nothing more. Even though I'd prefer to hear everything...

"Auggie," she confesses gently, and it feels like I've won the lottery. *You got this. Keep her talking.*

"What kind of name is Auggie?" I pull the line out again, and she scowls, but I can see the amusement on her face and know that I have her attention.

"His name is August, its a nickname," she explains as she helps me flatten out the bottom of the tent. "He really likes music," she says next, and I'm surprised by the information. "All the stuff I like."

"Yeah?" I look up at her, and she's smiling softly as she lines up the Velcro. "So are you like..."

"Dad," she groans. "Please don't."

"Oh, come on, talk to me." It's not a plea, or a demand, and Daisy knows this because her body goes slack and she scratches the back of her neck. "I just wanna know what's going on in your life."

I'm trying. Please let me try.

"He hasn't asked me," she blurts.

He hasn't asked you, but he's kissed you... I hold my tongue, and in the distance, Rhea gives me a goofy thumbs up as she unpacks more stuff. It takes everything in me not to shake my head at her while Daisy has a teenage crisis in front of me.

"Have you talked about it?" I question, snapping the last pole in place. The tent pops up nicely, and Daisy hands me the rain cover from the bag.

"I can't just be like, 'Hey Auggie, so am I like your girlfriend or what?'" she says in a bundle of slang I barely catch. "That's so not smooth."

"So teenagers don't talk about their feelings anymore?" I'm confused, and I catch Rhea covering her mouth to stifle the laugh. When Daisy disappears around the tent, I shoot Rhea a death glare. She throws both hands up in surrender.

"Also embarrassing Dad," she whines. "We're friends..."

This time, when Rhea catches my eye, something stirs.

"Isn't that the best way to start something like that?" I swallow hard.

"Yeah, but what if it ruins it?" She proposes, and I can feel her worry. The fear that by bringing it up with Auggie, there's a chance she destroys the friendship she cherishes. Rhea pretends like she's not listening, but I see her pause briefly at the question, her shoulders roll back tightly before she starts piling the wood for a fire.

"If telling him how you feel ruins the friendship, then he isn't a very nice boy," I say, trying to avoid the thoughts that crawl around my subconscious. "Besides, he kissed you at that dance, didn't he…"

"Dad!" Daisy yells and throws a stick that she swipes off the ground in my direction. "Please stop talking now, maybe forever. Just never speak again!" She throws her hands in the air and stomps away to help Rhea, who's back to laughing.

Before long, the three of us have found a groove, and the campsite actually looks pretty livable, with lamps and a good fire burning in the middle. Rhea throws some blankets down on her air mattress inside the large tent and surveys the surroundings with pride.

"I still hate camping." She looks over at me, dead serious—except her cheeks are flushed and her eyes aren't sad, so I know she's lying.

"Mmhm," I say. I open my mouth to suggest we start dinner when she screams at the top of her lungs. "What, what?" I step closer as she swats at herself, still yipping as she checks herself over.

"Something fucking bit me, Brighton!" she snaps and keeps looking for the bug's location.

"It's probably just a mosquito," I say, reaching out to try to calm her down, but she's two seconds short of a full-blown mental breakdown with tears in her eyes as she rubs at her skin. "Rhea," I try not to laugh as she whips off her sweater. "You're alright."

"What if that was a poisonous spider? Or a hornet!" She panics further.

"It wasn't either of those things, it was probably a horse fly," I tell her, and realize my mistake when her brown eyes widen in shock. "They're not deadly, calm down."

"Stop laughing at me!" She shoves, and I catch her wrist.

"Let me look." I squeeze, and she finally inhales, her shoulders still tense and her eyes still searching around frantically. My eyes scan over her skin, searching between patches of ink for any sign of a bite that might actually be worrisome, but I don't find anything except for the fact that her body is more distracting than I remember.

"It was up here somewhere." She wiggles, pointing to her back.

"Turn around," I tell her. She shifts on her feet, and I brush my hand across her back to move her ponytail out of the way. Her skin is smooth and delicate beneath my rough, scarred hands. I inhale because now both of us are a little panicked for very different reasons, and inspect her skin to avoid the feelings kicking up in the base of my stomach.

"Right there," I say, finding a small red mark on her left shoulder blade. "It's just a horse fly bite," I confirm. "Stay here." I move to the truck and grab the first aid kit from the truck. When I return, Rhea is still searching around for the culprit, but she's not going to find it. If she finds anything, it'll be a bigger bug that scares her more, and I try not to laugh at her hatred of them.

"Hold still," I say to her, squeezing a little lotion onto my finger and massaging it into her skin.

"Are my limbs going to fall off?" she asks me nervously, and a chuckle leaves my throat.

"No, your arms and legs are safe. It might be itchy later, but this cream will help, and if you need more..." She turns to look at me as I finish.

"I *really* hate camping," she reiterates.

"I know, Hellcat." It takes everything in me not to fix the stray hairs that fly around her pretty face. I want to thank her for coming out here, even though she hates it. She's out here for me, and I recognize the effort, the care. It's whether or not she's out here as my friend that has me confused. Every line I make in the sand seems to get destroyed by her, stomping around and making a mess. "Hey, you want s'mores for dinner?"

"S'mores for dinner?" She narrows her eyes at me like I'm playing a trick on her. "That feels way too fun for you."

"It's a Boone special," I tell her and wander from the tent.

"That makes so much more sense," she scoffs. "How did he make s'mores special?"

"Grab the crackers from the bag," I tell Daisy, and her face lights up with excitement when she realizes what we're doing. I slide the cooler across the table and pop open the lid, digging inside for the two bags marked *s'mores* in Boone's disgusting handwriting.

I hand them to her, and she starts to dig inside with a confused face, "Where's the chocolate?" she asks, almost disappointed.

"Here," Daisy holds it up with a smile.

Inside the bags are packages of precut cheese and meats.

"Cheese and cracker s'mores?" she questions, finally catching on.

"Uncle B's favorite," Daisy coos, and hands me the box of crackers. "Dad doesn't like chocolate and complains a bunch about it, so we came up with this."

"I do not," I scowl at her, but she gives me a sharp glare that silently wins the argument.

"You don't like chocolate?" Rhea laughs, finding it all amusing.

"Nope." I take the bag from her and set everything out on a plate before stacking some of the ingredients together. I show her how to do it so the cheese melts around the meat and holds everything together. "Yeah, don't let it burn," I say to her as she starts chatting to Daisy without a care in the world for what she's doing.

"I need the bathroom," Daisy declares, swiping a lamp off the table, and Rhea offers to go with her, but she points to the shadows of the bathroom building in the distance. "It's close. I'll be okay."

Rhea nods, her worry dissipating as Daisy wanders off into the night and becomes nothing but a little firebug with her lantern in the distance. I wrap my hand around Rhea's and take it from her, pulling her skewer back from the fire. She watches me carefully as I tug it out of the cheese gently before putting my hand beneath it to prevent it from dripping on her skin as I hold it out to her.

"Careful," I warn, but she's not listening and burns her lip with a tiny inhale of pain. "Impatient." I scold, leaning in slowly to inspect her lip, I run my finger over it without thinking, and blow gently to apply some cool air to it. Rhea's eyes flicker to mine, the fire dancing behind them, and she freezes with a tiny smile.

"It's hot," she exhales, and a laugh trickles from her as she takes the smore, and my hand falls away from her face.

"Yeah, well, I warned you." I shake my head, our faces still close together.

"You said be careful," she teases, "that does not indicate that it's hot enough to burn me."

"That's exactly what that means, Hellcat." I scoff.

"Okay, well—next time talk to me like I'm a toddler," she purrs, her eyes trickling down my face to my lips so slowly it causes my heart to race uncomfortably.

"You are a toddler," I manage to say. *Don't kiss her, you idiot.*

Rhea licks her bottom lip to soothe the burn.

Okay, maybe kiss her...

The air is tight, and the sound of the fire cracking and popping in the distance is the only thing reminding me that the world is still spinning, and time hasn't completely stopped.

Just one. If she pushes you away, it's fine, you've just ruined the first real friendship you've made outside your siblings in the last ten years.

"Rhea," her name comes off my lips, and her entire body goes still at the sound.

If she doesn't push you away, it might just be the best thing you've ever done on impulse. Are we impulsive, though? No. Not about this.

"Yeah?" she whispers.

Do it. I lean in closer, prepared to make the biggest mistake of my life.

"You know it's pretty creepy out here in the dark!" Daisy's voice booms from the shadows, and we split apart into our camping chairs with a silent rustle.

The morning air feels good on my face as I run the path down and back up through the park. It's eerily quiet out, and my headphones are broken, leaving me alone with thoughts of Brighton's face inches from mine.

"Rhea?" I can hear him in my head, the way his voice dropped—the intention.

"He was going to kiss you," I pant, narrowly avoiding a stray root on the path with my sneaker. "Brighton Black was going to kiss you." My breathing is heavy against the quiet backdrop of the forest, and I'm stomping so loudly after mile three that the birds are rustling around in the tree above me in protest. "I'm sorry, I'm sorry." I lift my hands and cry out to them. "But I'm having an existential crisis here, and I have no cell phone service to call my friends!" I yell out in a frustrated whisper.

Brighton Black was going to kiss you.

"Fuck, fuck, fuck," I swear and push my legs faster into the run. *Maybe if I run fast enough, I can forget the way he smells after sweating his ass off setting up camp.*

"Probably not, though—ow!" A branch catches my cheek and leaves a stinging impression as I carry on through the forest. It's like everything that's been happening over the last months is sticking to my skin and demanding attention.

"Did I want him to kiss me?" The question comes out confused and stress-laden. I almost hit another tree thinking about the answer, but I hop to the left and manage to keep my pace.

"Do I want him to kiss me?" *Kinda.* I shake off the quick thought to focus on my run, curving back toward the campsite—and the lake.

"Oh...*shit.*" I skid to a stop, nearly tumbling down the hill, when I spot Brighton sitting by the lake alone, watching the sun rise over the horizon. "Go back to camp, Rhea," I hiss, as a squirrel yips overhead. "Yeah fuck you," I groan quietly.

Brighton sighs, his entire body shifting on the rock in the most gentle way. I've never seen him so still and quiet before, which is a wonder because that's basically who he is as a man. Listening to him talk to Daisy about Auggie reminded me of my conversation with Sunday, and now everything is tangled up in the most confusing way. *Are we still friends?*

"Don't be a coward," I whisper to myself.

After Daisy interrupted the tense moment between the two of us, we spent the rest of the night listening to her rank her favorite musicians in order. It's like without her phone, she was a completely different kid; she talked and talked. Thankfully, filling the silence and leaving no room for either of us to be awkward about what had almost happened.

But now you're alone.

I shake out my body, look around at the path that leads back to the campsite, and consider my options carefully. "Alright. Definitively: you're friends. It's not weird to join him for the sunrise." The birds above my head start singing a funny song that sounds like laughter. "Stop mocking me," I mutter.

"Who are you talking to?" Brighton's voice comes from ahead of me, and he's still staring at the lake, but I've definitely ruined any escape plan.

"The stupid birds," I grumble.

"You're fighting the wildlife?" He asks, confused. "That's a new low."

"Don't start, you'll ruin the sunrise." I roll my eyes.

"You're the one running around here like a bull in a china shop," he teases.

"Are you calling me fat, Brighton Black? Because we're alone in the woods, I listen to a lot of crime podcasts, and there are no witnesses." I warn him, and his shoulders shake with laughter.

He looks at me over his shoulder, with his dumb messy bedhead, in his *dumb* weather-worn hoodie, and a smile on his *dumb* handsome face.

My breath catches uncomfortably at the base of my throat.

I wish the birds were more helpful.

"What did you do to your cheek?" he asks, and I lift my fingers to the small scratch with a grumble.

"I was assaulted by nature, what else is new?" I groan, and he laughs, the sound almost startling against the serene backdrop.

"And why are you still standing back there?" he asks, and I don't know how to explain to him that being around him is confusing right now. And I don't want it to be confusing. I just want my friend.

"I'm sweaty. Didn't want to ruin your morning with my stench." He eyes me, unsatisfied with the answer, as his lips press into a thin line.

"Rhea," he scowls, and I think, *that's the Brighton I know.*

"Yeah," I huff. "Okay," I whisper, looking around, and do the next thing I can think of. I kick off my shoes, stripping from my socks. His face tenses in confusion as I leave them on the path to take off in a sprint. I whip past him, just hoping that the lake is decently deep before throwing myself off the rocky ledge, three feet down into the frigid water.

The water splashes up around me, and I can feel the wet, muddy earth beneath my toes and hold my breath for as long as I can just to avoid the look on his face. *Drowning feels like a more dignified option.* When my lungs start to burn uncomfortably, I push back up to the surface, and Brighton is cleaning his face with the bottom of his sweater. A habit he seems to have, and one that causes my temperature to rise. His stomach is tight and bare as he dries off his face. *Just let me die.* I sink back beneath the water as he drops the fabric from his hands, and his eyes narrow in on my face.

Be normal. For the love of God.

I break the surface and tread water out from the shore as Brighton takes another sip of coffee. "You're insane, you know that?" He says after a few minutes of welcoming, calming silence.

"Feels nice," I admit, the chilly water nips at my skin and refreshes me better than a cup of coffee would. "You should get in."

Why did I say that? Please just shut up.

"No thanks." He shakes his head.

"What, afraid you'll shrivel?" I tease.

Brighton glares at me, finding no humor in the joke. "I don't *shrivel.*"

Cool, now that I know that...

"Fine, you're just a chicken then." I splash water up at him.

"Just not a fan of leeches."

"Did you say leeches?" My brows furrow.

"The black bugs that stick to your skin, suck your blood?" He raises an eyebrow. The words come off his lips, and it takes a second to register what he's said, but I'm moving faster than I ever have toward the shore. Brighton is laughing, but he offers his hand to me and pulls me up from the water.

As soon as I'm on flat ground, I'm checking myself over and spinning in a circle to try to get a view of my back I'll never get. "Are there any on me?" I ask, my voice panicked as he continues to laugh quietly. "Brighton!" I hiss at him.

"Turn around," he says softly, wagging his finger in a circle as his eyes trace down me. "Nothing," he confirms after a minute or two.

"That's good." I breathe out in relief.

"Not surprising considering there are no leeches in this lake," he says with a smug look.

"Are you fucking serious? You're such a—" I step forward, but he doesn't move, with his back to the lake, it makes revenge for his little joke easy. Before he even realizes what I'm doing, I lay both hands flat to his chest and shove him backwards. He hits the water like a ton of bricks, and when he rights himself and breaks the surface, his expression is deadly.

"How fast can you run?" he snaps.

"Faster than you, I think we proved that." I cross my arms over my chest to control the way my entire body goosebumps in the cool air.

"You think you're so smooth," he groans, kicking to the shore. He hauls himself up on a few rocks and stalks toward me as I back away, still laughing and trying not to trip over anything.

"Don't you dare!" I yell as Brighton grabs the loose, wet fabric of my tank top at my stomach, pulling me closer to him as he shakes his head, sending water spraying all over my face. "Hey!" I cry out as the droplets hit me.

I shove against his chest and escape the unexpected shower with a loud gasp of laughter. When I clean the water from my eyes and face, he's stripping from his sweater, and I've realized the massive miscalculation. *Brighton's naked again.*

The water seems to stick to the tattoos and makes his skin shine under the warm light from the rising sun. And he's right, my eyes widen as they hit the dark fabric of his wet sweats, *he doesn't shrivel…* He inhales sharply as the cool morning air hits his damp muscles, and he throws his wet sweater over a nearby rock.

"I'm going to get swimmers' itch." He turns back to me and points to his wet sweatpants, and I can't help but snort at his concern.

"You can take them off," I say before I can think about the consequences of what that means.

"No," he sighs, "I actually can't."

He's not wearing anything under them. This just got so much worse.

"Right." I pull my bottom lip between my teeth and try to stifle the next laugh that follows at his misfortune. "At least we're even now…"

"And before six a.m.," he laughs. "Look at us go." The air around us is finally breathable, like all the tension from the night before had lightened just enough for us to enjoy the morning. He wanders around me back to his rock, before he pats the ground beneath his legs.

I stare at him for a second, confused by his actions.

"Your hair," he says, and I reach up to find my ponytail is barely hanging on and soaking wet.

An accurate representation of my mental state right now.

"I can fix it…" I say quickly. Trying to avoid contact with him.

"I need the practice," he says without breaking eye contact. I swallow my nerves and walk over. Once I find a comfy position between his legs, he gently pulls the hair from the elastic and tugs it over his wrist, even though I offer to hold it.

The feeling of his fingers in my hair is therapeutic, and I hate that it's becoming a habit. I feel myself lean back into his touch as my eyes close, and he gently brushes out any knots before starting the braid.

"You're getting really good at this," I mumble as his fingers loop around the next strand, tugging it just enough to make the braid tight, but not hurt me.

"I have a really patient teacher," he says, and I'm not sure if he means it to be as soft as it comes out, but it makes my cheeks warm. "Stop wiggling." The demand is laced with concentration.

"You're bossy this morning," I scowl, and he tugs a piece of my hair harder on purpose, causing me to laugh and turn my head up at him. It rests against his thigh as I stare at him upside down with a soft scowl on my face. "Ow."

He freezes, and that tense air rushes back in around us, only this time it feels encouraging. The breeze whispers through his damp, dark hair as all the birds go quiet and the world completely slows to a stop. Brighton's eyes watch me intently, his fingers still tangled in my hair. Last night was confusing, and it made me unsure about everything, but this morning? I can feel his intention; it radiates from him like sunbeams. His hand loosens its grip and dances across my throat until it's cupped gently beneath my chin, with his thumb caressing my jawline with the softest of touches.

I could die happy here.

When his lips part, I inhale, preparing myself for him to tell me that this is a bad idea. *And it is, it's a terrible fucking idea.* But he smells like the trees, and the fading apple and spice of his cologne, and my mind is dizzy with it, stumbling around, tripping on air, *over him.*

Brighton's lips meet mine in a kiss so gentle my whole body melts back against him. His fingers tighten at my throat just enough to expose his lack of control, and my eyes flutter closed as he deepens the connection. His body leans over mine, and a small, wondrous rumble leaves his chest as my hand cups the back of his head and tangles into the wet curls at the base of his neck.

He pulls away just as slow, almost begrudgingly, with a soft curse off his reddened lips, and his intense gaze meets mine as I finally open my eyes. *What the fuck was that?* His fingers loosen around my throat, but he doesn't remove them as I catch my breath.

Oh, we are so fucked.

Rhea

It was just a kiss.

One simple and quick kiss.

It meant nothing. *We were just out in the woods, alone—the mood was right.*

He hasn't spoken a word to me since unpacking the truck this morning.

My conscience was eating me alive.

"Earth to Reaper." Kaia snaps her fingers in my face. "Here," she says when I come back to earth. She has a martini in her hand and a scowl on her face. "What's going on with you?"

"Nothing," I say too quickly, and she narrows her judgmental brown eyes at me.

"Spill," she demands, taking my arm and leading me out onto Sunday's back porch. "Is it about the Terminator?"

"Don't call him that," I scoff.

"It is!" She pinches me gently and throws back her entire drink before setting it on the table beside her and pressuring me to finish mine. "All of it." She nudges the bottom of my glass, tipping it back so it burns down my throat until it's totally gone, and my stomach is full of vodka. "That's my girl."

"He kissed me." I blurt after a rough swallow. "I kissed him..."

"You touched faces. *Romantically*?" Kaia mocks me with a grin. "Holy shit. Was it good?"

"Yeah, really good," I breathe out. "But this is bad."

"Why is that bad?" She scrunches up her face. "Kissing is never bad."

"Kissing your best friend's brother is bad," I emphasize the issue, and Kaia shrugs her shoulders.

"Tell me what's bad about it?" She questions quickly, her eyes burning a hole through me.

"Sunday is going to flip out," I say.

"When have you ever seen Sunday *flip* out about anything?" She asks, crossing her arms. Sometimes, especially for how short she is, she looks fucking terrifying.

"This is different, it's her brother," I say.

"Okay, I'll catalog the one bad thing, even though it's flaky, but what was *good* about it?" Her tone changes.

"It doesn't matter that one bad thing outweighs the good," I respond. *I could really use about five more shots of vodka right now.*

"I'm the judge here, not you," she snaps.

"Judge, juror and executioner." I groan.

"Rhea." She pushes.

"You know when you kiss someone, and you can tell it's a means to an end?" I ask her and watch the recognition flicker across her face. "Like it's a kiss just to kiss someone?"

It takes her a moment to respond, but she nods, "Yeah, Reaper. I know."

"This wasn't that," I whisper, "it was like every kiss before this one was just a placeholder for something better, something that felt real."

Kaia's head tilts to the side as she processes what I've said, and her expression softens as a smile spreads across, puffing up her cheeks and lighting up her face.

"That was stupid. I sound like an idiot." A bark of laughter leaves me in a defeated echo.

"No," Kaia steps closer and cups my face. "You sound happy."

"Until Sunday finds out and roasts me over an open fire! She was chill at lunch, but she specifically emphasized that he needs a *friend!*" I panic a little.

"Well, you sure got friendly," she teases.

"Not funny." I huff.

"What are you two doing out here?" Sunday steps into the door frame, and Cosy hovers over her shoulder with a confused look on her face.

"Rhea kissed Brighton," Kaia blurts.

"Holy shit," Cosy gasps, and Sunday freezes.

"Is that why you've been spamming me with memes? You thought I'd be mad at you!" Sunday yells and steps out onto the back porch.

"Was it good?" Cosy interjects, and Kaia stifles a snort.

"That's what I asked," she whispers as Sunday stays firmly rooted in her shock.

"Well?" Sunday cocks her head to the side and glares at me. "Was kissing my brother good, Rhea?"

That is a trap. A big fat trap.

"Your silence is *so* guilty, Reap." Cosy giggles, hanging off Kaia.

"It was really good..." I wince, waiting for her to attack me, but Sunday just stands there.

"What happened?" She pushes, the wind kicking up her blonde hair around her face.

"Uh..." I chew on the inside of my mouth. "I went for a run. When I came back, Brighton was watching the sunrise and..."

"He was watching the sunrise," both Kaia and Cosy sing at the same time, and Sunday shushes them.

"Do these details really matter?" I ask her, and she nods. *Dead serious.* "I got in the lake for a swim... then got out."

"You got *in* the lake?" Cosy gasps. "*You*? You're terrified of open bodies of water."

"Did you skinny dip?" Kaia pipes up.

"No, I was in my..." I start and stop. "I got out, and he's been learning how to braid hair so he can help Daisy, and he's been practicing on me since I hurt my hand, so he was doing that..."

"Brighton Black braids hair?" Cosy looks at Kaia, who is just as surprised.

"He can braid my hair any day. Do you think we can hire him for pre-game gossip and hair?" Kaia teases. The two of them have the most contradictory expressions to Sunday's scowl.

"How exactly did you end up kissing him?" Sunday pushes, completely ignoring them.

"He pulled my hair, and I looked up at him, and it just happened?" I shrug.

"He pulled your hair like a little kid?" Sunday scowls.

"Wow, you made that sound earth-shattering romantic, Reaper. Ten out of ten," Kaia teases with a tiny laugh as she steals a sip of Cosy's beer.

"Okay, well, it's not the smoothest way to say it, but... it sort of was," I admit to Sunday. "Can you say something?"

"Do you like him?" she asks, her tone heavier than usual.

Did I? Do I?

"I like that he always makes my lunch, and leaves the little light in the bathroom on..." I say. Sunday watches me closely, "or that he labels everything in the fridge with his messy handwriting, picks up his phone on the first ring, and listens exclusively to music produced before two thousand and three."

Cosy snorts, and Kaia tries to settle her down. "This is like a fucking Nicholas Sparks movie," she whispers. "Please keep going."

"Yeah, don't stop now, Reaper," Kaia pushes.

"He takes the tomatoes off my burgers," I tell her, and she swallows tightly. "He takes care of me, Sunday." My voice drops because saying it out loud makes it real. Something about the sentence hits home. "I don't even know what this is," I admit. "It was just a kiss, but..."

"Rhea," Sunday responds, and I brace for her to tell me that I need to stay away from him, but she doesn't. "He's not exactly...stable."

"None of us are," I say, and both Cosy and Kaia agree quietly. "We're proof that it's better to be unstable together than apart."

"What if he ruins this?" Sunday's voice cracks, her finger pointing between the two of us.

"When hell freezes over, Sunny." I step forward, still unsure of everything happening between Brighton and me, but I gather her up in my arms and hug her tight until she returns the squeeze.

"I can't believe you weren't gonna tell me you kissed him!" She slaps my arm when I finally let her go.

"She wasn't going to tell any of us!" Kaia snitches.

"Can we kill monsters now?" I groan. "And I need more liquor."

"Yes, ma'am, but we want details." Cosy steps backward into the house, dragging a laughing Kaia with her.

"And you have to tell Addy!" Kaia yells over her shoulder ass I tip my head back in frustration and maybe a shred of relief.

The Hollow is dark except for a few lights when the Uber drops me off at the entrance. I'm not drunk, but I wasn't going to chance driving the Bronco and ending up in more debt than I already was. The condo association just kept emailing me about damage costs as if any of it was my fault, and I was starting to think that selling it back to them at half price was my only option. The vodka makes all the noise go quiet, but it doesn't do anything to fade the unfamiliar rhythm of Brighton's thrum beneath my chest.

I know he's inside somewhere, probably cleaning up before retreating upstairs to his room. *To the Little Dipper on his ceiling.*

I tap the glass with my finger; the sound echoes on the other side. Before long, he wanders to the main door and pops it open for me. "What are you doing?" he asks, *and I'm dying inside because those are the first words he's said to me in twelve hours.*

"I got a ride home," I say, holding my tongue on the first bit.

"Right, Dungeons and Dragons night." He nods. "How drunk are you?"

"Barely," I say, and at least that was honest.

"You smell like powdered sugar," he says when I slide past his chest and inside.

"Cosy made beignets, and I ate about four too many," I admit.

"And you didn't bring any home?" He scoffs, his tone teasing, but I'm stuck on the *home* part.

"You don't know me at all." I hold up a paper bag that's full of them, and he gives me a look that vibrates down my spine.

"Can I have one?" He asks, politely.

"I don't know, are you going to stop staring at me like you made a mistake?" I blurt, and his brow raises. When he doesn't answer me, I only assume that it's the truth. He regretted the kiss and me. I swallow roughly as he turns his back on me and wanders over to the music system beside the stage.

Soft music starts to play over the speakers as he moves through the room, flipping chairs up onto tables, before finding his way back to me. He takes the bag and sets it on the bar, taking my hand and spinning me in a circle gently. *Just talk to me.*

At first, the dance is stiff, the awkwardness that's coming off me ruining whatever moment Brighton is trying to have, but eventually I give in to his arms and follow his lead.

"Did I make a mistake, Rhea?" he asks in that same expectant and commanding tone he always has. He wants to know if I think he did, and for the last twelve hours, the answer has changed about a hundred times. Because if the answer is yes, it's a clean break. We can attempt to go back to being friends. I've pretended I'm fine in worse situations. But if the answer is no, it changes the entire dynamic of our relationship, and that's terrifying.

We're just friends.

Friends who kiss?

"What song is this?" My brows crumple.

Brighton inhales slowly, looking away from me for a second. "*Peach Tree*, by Ethan Regan, I think."

I smile at the side of his face as he thinks about it. "I thought you didn't listen to new music?" I whisper, and he looks back at me.

"Some annoying girl with big sad eyes told me I need to expand my musical horizons." He smiles back, softer than ever.

"She sounds smart," I respond.

"She can be," Brighton hums, and I scowl at him. "She's also stubborn, messy, and emotional."

"You forgot high maintenance," I add.

"And petty." He spins me in another circle.

"Very," I laugh.

"She has this bad habit of not answering questions when she thinks she's going to hurt someone's feelings," Brighton notes. He brings me back to him, my back against his chest, and his hand splayed out over my stomach. "Or when she feels like the answer might cause trouble."

I close my eyes and let him dance us around for another long moment.

"Did I ruin it?" His voice is more cautious than I've ever heard him be, and it stings like a papercut, causing me to angle my face up to his as we dance. "It felt impulsive," he adds.

"It was." Our faces are close again, and I can feel his breath on my face as he works through his own thoughts.

"Do you still want to be my friend?" he asks.

I shake my head no.

"Do you still want to be my roommate?" he asks next.

And I nod.

"What else do you want?" he asks.

"I want you to kiss me again," I say, watching his worry turn to contentment and maybe even happiness, which is a lot coming from Brighton. A softer, lazy smile forms on his lips, and before I can say anything else to convince him, he obliges my request.

"I'd also like you to take me upstairs now," I say to him as he pulls away.

"You've got about three too many vodka shots in you for that tonight, Hellcat." He grinds his jaw together and curls around me until his lips are back on mine, and he's stealing all my air.

"Killjoy," I whine.

"You think that'll work?" He challenges.

"How about... you carry me upstairs, bring the beignets, and we find out if dry-humping is as fun as I remember in high school." I change my tactic.

"Who the hell were you dry-humping in high school?" Brighton chuckles, obliging my first request without thought. He scoops me up against him with both arms and adjusts my legs around his waist so he can hold me securely with one of them.

"Are you jealous?" I wrap my arms around his neck, and he turns his face away from me, but his jaw tightens again, like it always does when he's pissed about something and trying to hide it. "You are!" I kiss the spot where the muscle flexes beneath the skin, and he doesn't hesitate to turn his face into the gesture, capturing my lips as he starts to move. "We can dry hump if you want. I bet you're *really* good at it."

He doesn't stop as he swipes the bag off the counter and carries me upstairs.

"You aren't eating these in my bed," he warns, breathless as he climbs each step.

"Yeah, I am," I argue, and it's clear he knows it's a losing fight because he doesn't say a single thing before popping the lock and letting us inside. He takes us down the hall and into his room, setting me down on the bed before disappearing from the space altogether. "You could have left them," I call out to him.

When he returns, he's free of his Hollow uniform, back into his loose pajama pants, and holding out a bottle of water for me.

"That's so unfair," I groan.

Brighton raises an eyebrow at me.

"Disposing of my treats, taking your shirt off, not letting me..." I trail off and stop talking because the things on my mind aren't appropriate.

"Are you done complaining?" he asks me, and I shrug.

"Probably not," I answer.

"I didn't dispose of your *treats*, and I wasn't sleeping in that shirt. It smells like booze and smoke," he explains. "I can find something else to wear if it's making you uncomfortable." He's so serious all the time, and all I can do is start laughing.

"You left out the most disappointing part." I pout.

"You aren't touching anything," he groans, "until you're sober. I need know it's what you want and that it's not the sugar high and vodka talking." He looks so sure of himself, I can't even argue.

"Please just get into bed, and give me my beignets back," I demand, and he listens to the first part, shooing me away from the edge so he can get comfortable on his side. He rests against the headboard with one of his knees bent, and I slide into the space between his thighs, wrapping my calves around his hips and resting my hands on his stomach.

I've been waiting to touch you for weeks.

"Sorry, what was that?" Brighton's brows furrow. "Weeks?"

Oh God.

"Did I say that out loud?" I slap my hand over my mouth.

"How many shots did you actually have?" he asks again.

"One too many, apparently," I giggle. "I was told the treats still exist, and if you lied to me, I'm going to dump you."

"Dump me?" he asks. "Moving a little fast there, Hellcat?" I can't tell if he's teasing me or not, and I freeze, trying to read him, but there's a little smirk on his face, and his eyes are the lightest shade of blue I've ever seen.

"We're working backwards here, I've already moved in..." I throw out the joke, and mid-sentence, he sits up, presses his hand into my hair, and takes my bottom lip between his. "About those beignets..." I say jokingly as he pulls back slightly, this warrants a long groan from his throat, but he reaches to the bedside table to grab them. I, too distracted and too drunk to notice he had even set them there, hum with excitement.

"Open up," he says, cradling the bowl in one hand and grabbing a beignet between his fingers with the other.

"You're gonna feed it to me?" I sit up a little straighter, hyperfixated on the way his eyes follow my every movement.

"It's the only way to ensure you don't get powdered sugar all over my bed," he says and holds it out to me. I wrap my lips around it without breaking eye contact, and I feel his whole body go taut. I chew the confection with a smile on my face as he steals the other half and cleans his fingers. "These are really good," he says, as I lick my bottom lip and look up at the stars on the ceiling.

"Did you do that on purpose?" I ask about them, brave with liquor and high on his gaze.

He nods.

"Hit me," I point to the bowl and ignore how warm his quiet confession makes me feel. "You know the girls—"

"I don't care, Rhea," Brighton cuts in. "Whatever they said about *this*. I don't care." It's not that he doesn't care about them or their opinions; it's that he holds what's going on between us in high regard. I see that. It's written all over his handsome face. "Even Day." He cuts off my thoughts as they come through. "You four share everything. Let me be selfish with you. Just for a little while, until we—"

"Figure this out?" I finish for him, and he grabs my chin with a stern nod. "Okay," I whisper as he kisses me gently, our bodies leaning against each other as it deepens and unlocks all the closed doors between us.

"You taste like vodka," he groans against my mouth.

"And sugar," I giggle and keep kissing him.

"*And sugar*," he confirms, tangling that hand back into my hair, setting the bowl aside, and pulling me down against him until there's no space between us anymore.

Brighton wanders into the apartment after dropping Daisy off at her mom's, scowling, a bag in his hand. "Here."

"Oh, hello to you too..." I dry my hands on the towel by the sink as he kicks his shoes off and puts them away.

"Open it." He points to the bag as he hangs his keys.

I roll my eyes at his dismissal and dig into the bag. "You didn't..." I pull the box out and hold it in my hands. "Brighton."

"You've been sulking around." He wanders away as I look at the headphone box and smile, my eyes lifting to find him disappearing down the hallway like the gift is no big deal. And maybe it's not to him, but to me, it means everything. When he returns, I've got them out of the box, they're sleek and dark purple and fit over my ears perfectly. "I couldn't find the stupid—" he motions up and down over his chest.

"It's okay, I love the purple. They're comfy too." I slip the headphones off and set them down. "You really didn't have to do this."

"Say thank you." He stares at me; it's not a demand, he doesn't even want the praise or the gratitude. He just wants me to stop fussing over his kindness.

"Thank you," I repeat back to him.

"What are you doing?" His eyes scan the kitchen across the mess I've made.

"Well... I *was* trying to cook you dinner, in a pathetic attempt to ask if you want a couch date with me?" I string the words together and straighten out to hide the mess with my body.

"Couch date?" His heavy brow furrows as he surveys the damage. "What's wrong with a real date?" I can see he's panicking, questioning whether or not we're even ready for that.

"It's quiet, less busy, no variables," I explain. "Just us."

"And what were you attempting to make?" He cocks his head to the side.

"Sushi, but the rice got too sticky, and the nori's gone soggy," I groan, raising my rice covered fingers in defeat. "I'm a mess."

"To your core, Hellcat." He agrees softly. "I'll clean up. You *order* sushi."

I nod, letting him shuffle me out of the way, but not before he steals the softest kiss. I'm still not used to the tenderness that follows around Brighton in the quietness of his own space. But I like it. *A lot.*

I do as I'm told, and Brighton has the kitchen clean before the sushi arrives. He gets us plates, disappearing downstairs for less than five minutes to make me a drink that tastes like Sprite but definitely isn't—baby-pink over ice, lemon slices clinking against the glass. He changes into his sweats and t-shirt that looks older than me before he settles into the cushions next to me.

"Okay," he says, settling in. "What's the next step of a couch date?" His hair is messy, and his smile lazy as I pull the blanket up around my lap.

"Wrestling," I say with a grin.

"Seriously?" Brighton sighs.

"Dead serious." I click on the start of the match and watch as he picks out the pieces of sushi he wants carefully. As we watch, he starts asking questions, and every time he does, it makes me feel warm and dizzy. *Okay, focus, we aren't starved for attention.*

"Who's that?" He points with his chopsticks at the TV.

"Roman Reigns," I explain his backstory, and Brighton shakes his head.

"And that?" he asks.

"That's Seth Rollins," I tell him.

"And who's your favorite?" he questions, handing me the last piece of roll without looking at me.

I sigh dramatically with a hazy smile. "CM Punk."

I watch him search his name in the browser, and he looks up from his phone with a scowl. He searches the name, then looks up with a scowl. "Rhea. That's an old man. What is wrong with you?" he groans, and I go full defense mode.

"He's the rebel of the wrestling community, he's a legend!"

"He could be your dad," Brighton scoffs.

"Oh, I have major Daddy issues, Brighton." I tease, and his eyes go wide. *So easily undone.*

"What about a grouchy, bossy, greying old guy is appealing?" He argues with a tight expression but it's soft and prodding.

"Did you stop to think that's the point? I need structure, Brighton." This only makes him scowl and causes me to laugh. "Oh, Daddy!" I cry out, and he gives me a shove on the couch.

"Stop it," he warns.

"Daddy Punk!" I giggle, "Show me your wrestling moves behind closed doors!"

"That's disgusting." He shakes his head and tries to ignore me.

After about an hour, he looks slightly interested, and he's still asking questions while he flinches at some of the moves and rolls his eyes at others. When he asks what my favorite moves are, all bets are off.

"No, up like this." I show him with my arms, two seconds from climbing up on the coffee table, and he stifles a laugh from the base of his throat. "What?" I look down at myself and have no idea what he finds amusing.

"Nothing." He presses his lips together in a thin line, his chin tilted up, watching me.

"You don't think I'll do it?" I snap, and he raises a brow.

"You just got that splint off, don't be an animal." His tone is cautious, shifting on the couch. He's relaxed but still wary, like he knows better than to let his guard down around me. It's hilarious and endearing. *He likes that you're unpredictable, even if he refuses to admit it.*

I toss my head back and laugh. Brighton calmy leans forward, stacking the empty plates to the side of the table as I step up onto it and stare down at him. "Just admit you're a coward."

"I'm not a coward, you're going to—"

Before he can say anything, I jump from the table, and he pushes back against the couch as my feet make contact on either side of his thighs. I go to throw a fake elbow at his shoulder, but he catches me around the middle and pulls me down into his lap.

Our faces come level with one another, and he scowls at me, but it doesn't last long because I steal a kiss from him, and when I pull back, his expression has softened into something else.

"Good catch," I whisper. He inhales slowly as his hands slide under my sleeveless T-shirt. It has been nothing but small stolen kisses, passing remarks, and the occasional ass grab that makes Brighton growly. "*You can't do that in the middle of the Hollow, Hellcat. You're going to get me reported to HR.*" I can hear him even now—followed by Sunday's inevitable loud gag and a quick reminder of, "*You are HR.*"

"Did you hurt yourself?" he asks, his eyes never leaving mine, and I shake my head.

"You softened the fall." I scrunch up my nose, and his fingers tighten on my hips. I lean forward, tugging at the collar of the old shirt around his throat. "Why do you still wear those?" I ask him about the dog tags. The chain is heavy over his skin, and I run my finger along the metal as my eyes drift to his tattoos beneath.

"Habit." He scowls.

He watches me with careful glances, and I don't ask as I tuck my fingers into the hem of his shirt and push it up his stomach. He lets me with a small grumble as he lifts his arms. Once free of his confines, I pull them in and hold them in my palm. They're beat up, but the engraving of his name is still strong and forever etched in the metal. I let them go gently, and they fall against his skin.

It feels silly to be so enamored by him, and he never takes his eyes off me, but I take my time to admire his impressively large frame. The broadness of his chest, the perfect combination of old muscle and new weight, he's rigid but soft. It's contradictory and *fucking hot*. I exhale quietly, letting out the sexual frustration that courses under my skin, and drop the shirt to put my hands on his stomach. He inhales a shaky breath as my fingers dance across the daisies tattooed on his chest.

"They're so delicate," I study them carefully, "any specific reason there's six?" I count them carefully and watch his throat bob uncomfortably as he shakes his head. I lean down and kiss the petal that crosses over his collarbone, where the silver chain rests. "And this one?" I point to a section on his bicep. The rest of his tattoos are so heavy in comparison to the stark design of the daisies.

"I like foxes," he says so simply that I snort. "What?"

"Nothing." I shake my head. It's an odd notion for him to just *enjoy* something when his entire personality is calculated.

"You're telling me that every single one of these means something?" His knuckles rake up my arm and over my shoulder before his finger hooks into my strap and pulls it down. "That one," he brushes his thumb over the jellyfish where the inky tentacles spread out and touch everything over my shoulder and tangle into a collection of ocean filler like seaweed and coral.

"It's a man-of-war jellyfish," I tell him. "They're pretty, and dangerous."

Brighton hums, "and that." He points to my chest, his fingers tingling over the ink just enough to make my body shiver. It's the biggest piece I have, an octopus painted in dark lines of black that cascades over my chest, its arms mixing with the rest of my tattoos.

"Octopuses are some of the smartest animals in the ocean; there's not a box you can trap them in that they can't get out of." His eyes flicker to meet mine. *Yeah, that means what you think it does.* He frowns and keeps exploring.

"What are these?" he asks, leaning in slowly to kiss my skin.

"Mantis shrimp, tiny little things, but their punch is comparable to a .22 caliber bullet," I say with excitement. "And these are dragon slugs. One of the most beautiful, but super poisonous. There's a vampire squid..." I lift my arm and flex to show him my bicep.

"You really like the ocean that much?" he asks me with a cautious expression.

"Oh, I'm terrified of the ocean. Won't even go in it," I admit, and it takes everything in him not to question me further. I can see it on his face as he opens his mouth and closes it again.

"Okay, tough guy. What's the meaning behind the scary raven?" I poked his chest.

"Death."

I inhale. *Alrighty then, there he is.* "And that?" There are a few other tattoos on his arm, but I'm more concerned about the scar that wraps around his torso.

"Caught on a piece of scrap metal fresh out of basic training, it was just a scratch." He shrugs like it means nothing, but it's rigid, feels like it was deep just by the way the skin healed in a corded river up his ribcage. It tells me that it was never just a scratch.

"And this?" My fingers brush against a tattoo that at first I thought was a butterfly, but upon closer inspection, it's a moth. I dip down to admire the way it tangles into the scarred skin in the most delicate way.

"It's a moth," he pauses, and I look up at him with my brows scrunched, "...for Ri." Her nickname is a surprise; I've never heard him call her that until today. He swallows tightly, clearly not knowing if he should lie or be honest, but I'm glad he told me the truth. I curl down further, pressing my lips to it and feel his body stutter beneath my touch.

"Okay, how about this?" He points to a small tattoo that screams Boone in a gentle deflection that gives him the chance to breathe again.

"Is that a worm?" I tuck down to get a better look at it as he pulls down his sweats over his hip. I lick my lips and try to concentrate on the ink and not the sharp lines of his pelvis, or the trail of dark hair that leads beneath the fabric. "What the hell does that mean?"

"Means don't make bets with Kaia Keegan." He raises an eyebrow.

"There's no way," I start to laugh, brushing my fingers over it, and Brighton's hips stir beneath me, making it very clear that I'm still sitting in his lap. "You're too smart for that shit."

"Drinking impairs intelligence, Hellcat."

He reaches up, pushing his hand into my hair and moving it out of the way of his lips. "What are these ones?" he asks–*the star, the sun, the moon, and the cloud.*

"Addy, Sunny, Kaia, and Cosy," I say to him, and our eyes lock for a brief moment before he smiles and kisses each one that trails along the base of my neck behind my ear. I try to hide the tiny yawn that leaves me, but he catches it and pulls back.

"Bedtime," he whispers as he kisses my jaw.

"Alright, but I want to know the story behind that worm," I giggle as he wraps himself around me and lifts me off the couch.

"Never going to happen," he tuts, turning off the kitchen light as he passes.

Brighton

"Hellcat, I don't think this is a good idea." I stand outside her family home — dusty blue paneling, white rose bushes framing the stone steps — completely filled with dread. Daisy is still sitting in the back of the truck, playing on her phone, completely ignorant of our conversation as Rhea fixes her hair in the mirror of the passenger door.

A week ago, we told Daisy about what was happening, transparency was important to Rhea, and that made it important to me. She's just as much a part of Daisy's life as I am, and we didn't want to sneak around behind her back.

"Why?" She stands up straight in her wrestling shirt and ripped jean shorts with a confused look on her face. I wore one of the three button-down shirts I have and feel extremely overdressed next to her, but she doesn't seem bothered in the slightest.

"We can just be friends in there. Roommates. If that's what you're worried about." She says it so casually, and it bothers me. *Because you aren't friends anymore. Idiot.*

"It's your family," I stress to her.

"Oh. Okay, well... family means something different to you than it does to me." She looks from me to the house and back again, "Be more afraid of making it out alive and less of what they think of you, and if Mom tries to show you a single baby picture, respectfully decline."

"You're out of your mind. My only reward for going in there *is* baby pictures. I'm not passing that up." I say to her, and she rolls her eyes. *I also don't want to spend two hours around you being respectful when all I wanna do is be in bed, where the world is quiet.*

"It's just dinner, Brighton. Gabe will make pasta, Reid will ignore you, Remi will give you the *'you hurt my sister'* speech, all while Mom yells." She explains. "Just don't leave your wallet anywhere because Toby has sticky fingers, and oh my god, don't sit on anything unless you wanna stain your pants."

"At least you come by being a raccoon honestly," I say to her.

"I'm taking that as a compliment," she coos as Daisy finally slides from the truck.

"Sorry, Mom called for a weekly update and wouldn't stop asking questions," she says, pulling out her headphones.

"Did you tell her about your boyfriend?" I ask.

"She loves Auggie," Daisy says.

Something about that gets under my skin, my jaw clenches, but I nod. "That's good." I offer. Daisy doesn't notice the clipped tone, but Rhea definitely does. She raises an eyebrow at me with a tiny smirk, but it helps calm the frustration that swims beneath.

We all head inside, and Rhea enters without knocking but kicks off her boots at the front door, which I find odd considering she stomps around our apartment in her dirty shoes every day. We follow suit and are immediately accosted by a small boy with fiery red hair and a wild look in his eyes, who I can only assume is Toby. He stares me down before his eyes flicker to Daisy, and a smile creeps on his face.

"This is Toby," Rhea says. "And that little wildin' is Shana." A tiny girl, similar to Toby, waves from her spot on the long, messy couch, barely breaking her focus on the book she's coloring in. Rhea moves on through the house, picking up toys and clothing as she goes, and Daisy gets distracted by Toby, leaving me standing alone in the hallway. *Since when does she clean?*

The wall opposite the staircase is scattered with pictures, all in different-sized frames, and clearly span decades of their lives. Rhea's graduation picture is adorable; her hair is cut short around her face, and she's still losing some of her stubborn baby fat from her cheeks. The one next to it is smaller, and it's obviously been ripped on the left side and tucked back into the frame without much care.

"I hate that one," she says. I look over at her, not realizing that she's backtracked to find me. "She's got a hundred other pictures of our family, but she refuses to take that down." Rhea points to it. "She says it's the only one of her and us she likes because Reid is actually smiling, but that's bullshit."

I frown, my eyes turning back to the picture.

"She keeps it up because she likes to cry about it," Rhea whispers. "This one is better." She points to a picture of the seven of them at Disneyland. "They took us to Disneyland for their honeymoon."

"Romantic," I say to her, and tangle my hand into hers with a thoughtful squeeze because her eyes are still locked on the ripped family photo. "Was he in it?"

"Once upon a time," she says. "Tearing him out means he doesn't exist." She means it to be a joke, but I can hear the sadness in her voice.

"I like this one," I point to one that's higher on the wall of her, and an older man, I'm guessing, is Gabe at an event. She's decked out in wrestling gear, couldn't be more than seventeen, and she's wearing a smile I've never seen before.

"That was the best day ever," she says.

"Alright, where are the embarrassing ones?" I tickle her side gently as she swats me away. I sneak a kiss on the top of her head as a girl comes around the corner. She's exactly how I picture Rhea, about ten years younger. I look between the two of them and extend my hand, "Remi?" I ask, and she nods.

"I'm sorry, I don't know who you are because Rhea doesn't talk about her life..." Remi hisses uncomfortably.

"This is Brighton," she says, making a face at her younger sister. "Don't be rude."

"You can call me Bright," I say. "I work with Rhea."

"Work?" Remi raises an eyebrow, "You're a teacher?"

"No," I chuckle. "I'm a bartender."

"Owner. He's an owner." Rhea is quick to correct me.

"Whatever he is, Reid's gonna be pissed he didn't know about it." Remi looks me up and down and disappears into the other parts of the house.

"What does that mean?" I tug on her hand as she goes to follow her sister.

"Reid doesn't trust very many men," she answers. "He'll be fine. She's being dramatic."

"You should have told me that," I say.

"It doesn't change anything," Rhea says. "He's going to be an ass either way, Brighton. You're just going to have to eat it."

"I would like tonight to go well." I stop her from walking away from me again with a gentle squeeze.

"Why? Are you trying to impress someone?" She teases, her humor sinking into the cracks of the tense situation.

"Rhea." I drop my tone. Her favorite form of deflection is when she's uncomfortable. I open my mouth to offer some kind of encouragement, but Daisy starts laughing from the living room at the top of her lungs, and Rhea smiles.

"It's already going well," she says.

For now.

"Come meet Gabe." She continues to tidy as we go, which is strange because I've never seen her clean a day in her life at the apartment. But she moves around the house silently, never disturbing anyone or causing a fuss. She exists between all her family members like a ghost.

As we enter the kitchen, I realize that they live the majority of their lives in this space. The round kitchen table is tucked into the corner booth style with a few spare chairs that don't match the rest of the set. It's covered in art, homework, and tools... everything is actually. The island, the chairs, there are piles of chaos in boxes here and there. It's like everything is set down and forgotten about.

Rhea never stops moving, and it's no wonder why. There's a pile of crap everywhere I look. Gabe looks exactly like he does in the pictures — short, round, and smiling.

He cleans his hands on a towel and extends one to me, "Gabe, you must be Brighton."

"Bright, and at least she told one of you I was coming." I tease, and Gabe laughs.

"Oh no, Remi just stomped through here." He laughs. "But that's Rhea," he nods, "little communication, lots of chaos. I hope you like vodka sauce!" He turns back to what he was focusing on.

"Sounds amazing," I say, keeping one eye on Rhea as she stops, arms full of stuff, and points to something that her sister is showing her. Her brows furrow, and she shifts the laundry in her arms so she can take the paper and read it properly. "Can I help with anything?" I ask.

Gabe turns, clearly surprised by the question, and points to a loaf of bread. "Rhea's favorite is garlic bread; if we forget about it, there will be hell to pay." He laughs and hands me a bowl of what looks like butter, spices, and herbs. It smells amazing, and once I get around him in the small kitchen, I set to work without another word, content to watch Rhea in her natural habitat. It's like she's a totally different person, a well-oiled machine keeping the threads of her family securely together in any way she can.

After a little while, the front door opens and slams shut again. The whole house seems to go still around us, even the long-winded conversation about construction that Gabe is locked in on dies down. Rhea's mother flies into the kitchen, throwing her purse on the floor by the island and instantly proving why I was warned.

"Amber," Gabe says. "We have a guest."

She spins on her heels, and I'm met with what I can only describe as a toxic ball of energy. It's like she sucks out all the air in the room and consumes it for nefarious purposes. It's instantly clear to me—*this is the woman who makes Rhea feel small.* I clean my hands and extend one to her, which she takes, but the shake is weak and quick before she crosses her arms.

"This is Bright," Gabe introduces me. "Rhea has been renting his spare bedroom," he explains. "He and his daughter Daisy came for dinner."

Before she can say anything, someone clears their throat from behind us. A kid, no older than seventeen maybe, stands in the narrow archway with a dirty look on his very familiar face. I swallow tightly as Rhea slides back into the kitchen just in time for everything to go to shit.

"Reid," she says, walking toward her brother. "This is—"

"Bright," he cuts her off. "Dad spilled the beans." His jaw tightens, but his eyes never leave mine. *I recognize those eyes, I just can't put my finger on why.* He looks to Rhea quickly, and his hands flex at his side. "Can I talk to you?" he asks her.

"I'll be right back," she says to me and follows her brother up the stairs and out of sight.

"Reid is a tough nut to crack, don't be offended," Gabe offers reassurance, but it means nothing to me because of the nervous sadness that had filled Rhea's face.

"How did Rhea come about renting your room?" Amber asks, cutting the tension with a hot knife.

"My younger sister is Sunday," I tell her.

"Who?" Amber raises an eyebrow at me, and it is very clear that Rhea either doesn't tell them anything or her mother just doesn't care to remember. *Both rub me the wrong way.*

"One of the girls that Rhea plays rugby with..." I see now why Rhea doesn't talk about her mother very much; she's squirrely and rude.

"Oh yes, yes. The little blonde one!" Gabe snaps as he remembers. "She's a sweetheart." *So it's not Rhea's fault you don't know.*

"That would be her." I nod and cross my arms over my chest, itching for Rhea to return and save me from this conversation.

"Sorry about that." Rhea appears in the kitchen doorway like my thoughts summoned her. Her mood has shifted; she's back to being tense, but she's doing a good job of hiding it to keep the peace. I'd question it, but this is the woman who would eat tomatoes so she didn't hurt Boone's feelings. "Reid is going to take his dinner in his room. I'm starving. Is it ready?" she asks, pushing to her tippy-toes to look over the group of us.

Daisy's screams pierce through the house, and my whole body tenses.

"Daisy?" I call out, aiming to move toward the source.

"I'm alright…" Her voice is shaky.

"I found Lady Gaga!" Toby screams from the living room, and Rhea starts to laugh awkwardly.

"Who is Lady Gaga?" I look around as Toby runs past Amber.

"Uh, that," Rhea snorts as Toby thrusts a massive snake into the air as high as he can.

"Touch it," Toby demands.

"No, thank you," I say.

"Chicken," he teases. *There's a first for everything, and today might be the day I hit a little kid.*

"You'd better touch the snake," Rhea says, stifling more laughter.

"I *really* don't want to touch the snake." It's taking everything in me not to step back from it as it wiggles between the kid's fingers.

"Touch. It."

"Fine." I reach out and pet the snake with one finger.

Rhea

I wait in the truck as Brighton drops Daisy off at Riona's, staring at the container of pasta in my lap. Dinner went as well as expected. Reid stayed in his room the entire time Brighton was there, but Daisy had fun with the kids while I fielded all the embarrassing questions about our situation.

He took every single jab from my mother without flinching.

That house is like a cage. I glazed over through the entire dinner, periodically remembering that there were other people in the room when Shana made Toby cry, or Mom tried to get under Remi's skin. I washed the dishes quietly, taking the chance to try to catch my breath after being interrogated. Brighton tried to help, but Gabe whisked him away to go through old albums, all while I convinced him that I was fine.

But his concerned expression is burned into my brain, and I just hope he doesn't ask me questions I'm not ready to answer. It was probably stupid to bring him there, to introduce him to that. I can't even imagine how I must look to him after all of that. I curl my fingers around the container, trying not to cry from the overwhelming wave that consumes me.

I turn my gaze on him, standing in the doorway with his arms crossed as Riona talks to him, her eyes flickering to me periodically. Brighton nods, backing away as she shuts the door, and I refocus my gaze on my lap as he climbs into the driver's seat.

"Sorry."

I laugh a little, and he scowls at me. "For what?" he asks.

"The wait," he says.

"Brighton, you just sat through what some might describe as an FBI torture technique seminar..." I tease, and it brings a small smirk to his lips. "Sitting in the car for two minutes doesn't bother me."

"Are you sure?" he asks, the truck still in park.

"Yeah," I sigh. It's not the waiting that's eating at me. Being in that house tends to make me a little frazzled; my brain's still catching up from playing mediator, maid, nanny, and therapist for three hours. I'm just lucky today; I didn't have to be a chef, too.

Brighton's smile drops, and his jaw ticks noticeably as he stares me down.

"I'm just tired." I lie easily. He might have signed up to kiss me now and again, but he certainly didn't sign up for me having a total meltdown about my family.

He moves the truck away from the curb slowly, driving back down toward the Hollow to take us back to the apartment. He's quiet all the way there, both hands wrapped tightly around the steering wheel and his gaze on the road. He parks down the street like always, helping me out and taking my hand without a word.

The Hollow is busier than usual, but he doesn't slow; he just weaves through the crowd, guiding me toward the stairs. His hulking frame parts people out of our way until we pop out at the base of the stairs. We've climbed them a hundred times in the last few weeks, but tonight I feel like I'm in trouble. Maybe my emotions are haywire, and I can't straighten myself out long enough to breathe, let alone decipher what he's thinking, too.

"Brighton," I say as we step inside, and he locks the door behind us. The sound of the bar beneath us is all-consuming today; it's like we're still in the middle of the chaos. But he moves around me, still silent, and wanders over to the living room.

Without explanation, he picks the coffee table up and moves it out of the way, creating space before he wanders back to me, takes the container, and throws it in the fridge.

"What are—"

He ignores me, disappearing down the hallway and returning with a stereo that he sets on the counter and plugs his phone into. He stands quietly, his focus on the screen for a few moments before inhaling slowly, tapping it once, and setting it down. He grabs my hand on the way by and pulls me into the space he created with such an effortless nature to his movements. I twist around and end up with my back against his chest. His chin rests against my head as the music drowns out all the noise in the apartment, even our breathing.

I inhale slowly, and he tightens his grip around me.

I could cry. It feels so good—for the life of me, I can't figure out why it works so well—but I exhale, and it's like all the muscles loosen in my body.

"Do it again," he instructs.

I take a deep breath, he holds me close, and I exhale all the stress. I start to laugh wildly, on the verge of tears, and sink my teeth into my bottom lip.

"Why does that feel so good?" My voice quivers.

"My favorite feeling in the world used to be our rucksacks." He explains. "The weight. Most of the guys hated it, but it helped me breathe."

"Like one of those blankets..." I laugh gently, and he nods.

"Yeah." He grunts. "You were overwhelmed."

"No, I wasn't," I lie again. He spins me gently to the music and brings me back chest to chest so he can stare me down. "I was... only a little."

"Why?" His eyes search mine.

"That house holds a lot," I swallow, "memories, anger, laughter, chaos. Everyone inside stayed the same. It's like a time capsule and I—"

He cocks his head to the side when I drop my gaze from his. I feel childish. Who complains about that kind of thing—a happy family, a big house? People crave that comfort, and it rubs me like sandpaper.

"I step inside, and it's like I'm back there. Just that seventeen-year-old girl with absolutely zero control over her life." I blurt. "It's disorientating, and infuriating. Sometimes I can't tell the difference between their happy, playful screaming. It's like I know it's Toby and Shana, but I hear Reid and Remi."

Brighton tenses, his hands tightening around me as we dance lazily.

"So why did we go for dinner then?" he asks, not making me feel stupid about all the other stuff.

"Because—" I huff, and he waits patiently for me to figure it out. "That's what people do. They meet each other's parents, suffer through family dinners, and look at embarrassing photos."

"Hellcat," his tone shifts so eloquently I barely notice the change until his lips curl to the side and his eyes soften on my face. "I like you."

"That's good news," I scoff, and he laughs gently.

"I mean, I like *you*." He repeats it with emphasis, but I'm still confused.

"Still kinda vague, Brighton." I stare up at him, and he nods, understanding that he's going to have to elaborate just a little more.

"You like me, right?" he asks.

"Probably too much," I confess, and he smiles brighter.

"Me?" he says, "I wasn't always this person." He stumbles over his words, and it's unusual because he's typically so calm and collected. "At seventeen, I was scared all the time, angry because my parents didn't want kids anymore, helpless and undereducated to care for Day."

I'm starting to understand what he's trying to convey.

"I'm older, smarter, less scared," he admits. "Can't say the anger got better, it's just weaponized now. I know that if I ever saw my parents again I'd fucking kill them." The honesty is terrifying, but he never breaks eye contact as he speaks. "I like *you*," he says.

"Me." I nod, understanding now.

"Yeah," he hums, "Hellcat. You." He kisses me gently, "Intelligent, funny, chaotic, messy and a little scary." He continues to pepper open-mouthed kisses down my jaw and throat. "I like that you keep me on my toes."

"That's a polite way of saying I'm crazy." I sigh, wrapping myself around him and resting my forehead against his chest.

"It is." Brighton agrees.

I snap my head up, and he catches my jaw between his hands, "but I like *you*."

"You keep saying that," I whisper.

"Do you believe me yet?" he asks, his lips brushing slowly against mine, softer than before. His nose traces upward, and he kisses my top lip and then my cheek and temple.

"You might have to say it a couple more times," I tease.

His mouth finds my ear lobe, his teeth tickling my skin, "I really like you." He pulls back to look at me as I lift my fingers to trace his lips, as I think about how serious he sounds. "Rhea," he whispers.

"You know you'd look really handsome with a mustache," I study his face as my brows come together. My brain is just blurting crap to keep from overloading on how I feel when he watches me like this. I can hear Kaia *climb him like a tree, but make sure that's all you do.*

"Never going to happen." He denies me without even cracking a smile. *Well, that prevents me from falling in love according to her list... easy.*

"Boo," I pout.

He takes advantage of it, dipping down and kissing me so hungrily that he has to steady me in his arms. My fingers push into his hair, and his tongue slides into my mouth. I pull gently and feel his smile grow against my lips as his hands roam up my back and press me flush to him.

Climb him like a tree.

"Hey, Brighton," I break the kiss to catch my breath. "How come you haven't..." I stumble over the words, "you know tried to—"

"Have sex with you?" He finishes my sentence. It's the perfect opportunity, the apartment is empty, every makeout gets closer and closer to us crossing that line, but he always slows down, pulls back, goes cold.

"Yeah," I swallow as his eyes flicker over my face.

"Sex ruins friendships," he pauses.

"I think we're past friendship, aren't we?" I hum impatiently.

"I just want to take it slow, make it right," he explains.

I stare at him, watching the way his jaw clenches, the muscle flicking tightly as he waits for my response. I understand what he's saying, but I'm so sick of crawling into bed alone when he's right here, and I'm begging to be touched just a little more.

But he's trying to be a gentleman, and if it were anyone else, I'd be pissed that all they wanted was in my pants. *I just can't think straight around him.*

"Alright," I agree. "But—" I curl my fingers into the collar of his shirt and bring him eye level with me. "I want a proper make-out tonight, hands wandering, lines crossed. Do you hear me?" I order. He scoops down, lifting me with such ease, and carries me to his room with a smug look on his face.

"I hear you, Hellcat." He laughs, kicking his door shut.

Brighton

"Did you see the girls won their game?" Boone chucks the ball at me, and I pocket it without looking as I stretch my thighs in the grass.

"Yeah, they're top of the league now." I lean forward and roll the ball out in front of me. "They have a real shot of taking it all this year."

"Maybe then people will start paying attention to them," he says, and joins me to stretch. When he comes eye level, his head angles to the side, and his eyes narrow on me.

"What?" I snap.

"Something's different." He stares at me, rolling over in the turf so he's on his knees, and he can stretch out his groin.

"Nothing's different." I move into the grass on my back and start to warm up my hips. Boone doesn't take that answer, though; he keeps inspecting me like he's going to find something physically wrong with me. "Can you fuck off?" I groan as my hip pops.

"Lovey," he calls, "come here."

Judd jogs over toward us, his hair cut shorter now that he's back on duty full-time. He looks between the two of us with a brow raised. "What?"

"Tell me you see it?" Boone points to me as Judd sinks into a squat. *They look like idiots, heads tilted, eyes narrowed.*

"You're not going to find anything," I grumble.

"He got laid," Judd says, a wicked smile forming on his face, and Boone lights up like a Christmas tree.

"I did not." I shake my head. *Not yet. But damn does she make it hard to take things slow.* All I can think about is how good it felt to have her in my lap.

"You did!" Boone snaps his fingers at me. "It was Reaper, wasn't it? Took you long enough."

"I didn't sleep with Rhea, shut up." I stare him down, but he's riled up today and looking for buttons to push.

"Oh, now it's *Rhea...*" Boone sings her name, and Judd whistles. "So what *did* happen then?" They're both watching me like I'm about to reveal some massive secret.

"There's been... kissing," I admit, and both of them start laughing at me.

"That's it? That's what you're hiding from us? Kissing!" Judd's accent is thick and breathy as he doubles over on his side. "Mate, you could have lied. We'd be none the wiser."

"Why would I lie?" I say, completely unimpressed.

"Was it good?" Boone asks next.

"It's none of your business, is what it was." I push off the ground as the ref blows the whistle to get the game started. Boone continues to broach the subject at every chance he gets, between whistles, at half, all through us getting our asses kicked in the second. I skipped my shower to avoid him, but he was waiting outside for me, ready for more fighting that carried on into the parking lot. I told him Judd could drive him home.

I had somewhere to be.

The Hollow is busy tonight, and after the rough game, I'm looking forward to a long shower and an even longer sleep. I adjust my bag as I push through the crowd toward the stairs. Sunday waves to me from behind the bar before turning back to customers with a smile on her face. Everything is alright. For once. *Try not to ruin it.*

I push open the door and drop my bag on the floor with an echoing thud before raising my eyes to see Rhea sitting on the counter in one of her silly wrestling shirts, eating ice cream out of my container of vanilla.

"That's mine." I cross my arms, and she looks up at me with the spoon between her lips.

"You're going to have to be more specific, Brighton," she teases as I stride forward, kicking off my shoes as I go. "Uh oh, he didn't put his sneakers away properly, I'm in trouble now," she giggles, watching the clumsy execution. My adrenaline is still pumping from the game, and there's something about a good workout that goes straight to my head. "You're not going to do three loads of laundry before bed?"

"Nope." I shake my head and slot myself between her legs. "I'm starving."

She digs out a spoonful of ice cream and holds it out to me. It melts on my tongue, and I don't take my eyes off her perfect face for a second. My chest squeezes at her soft smile as the spoon retreats, and she digs more out of the carton.

Is this what it feels like to be friends who kiss?

"How was your game?" she asks quietly.

"We got our asses kicked by the Cubs," I tell her, and she pouts.

"They're a tough team. You know if you switch up—"

"Coach me on rugby in the morning," I stop her and tap her wrist to get more ice cream.

"Oh, did you have other plans I wasn't aware of?" Rhea looks around with a phony confused look on her face. The ice cream on her spoon melts between us, and before I can get my mouth around the spoon, it drops onto her thigh, making her flinch from the sudden cold.

"Yeah," I slide her forward on the island, and my hands find her ass. She goes completely still as I dip down, running my tongue up her inner thigh to catch the drip, then I close my mouth around the rest of the spill. She inhales deeply and slowly as I pull back. "I did."

Her face changes when she realizes what I'm suggesting, her surprise evident.

"Put the ice cream down, please," I say. I can be a thousand things for Rhea Drake, but a man who allows melting dairy products in his bed is not one of them.

"Okay." She sets it down beside her on the counter, the spoon dangling from her lips as I pull her off the island and over my shoulder in one swift movement. She yelps from the contact, and I turn her toward the sink.

"Leave the spoon." A second later, it clatters into the sink. "Thank you."

"You don't want to wash it twice?" She teases, and I dig my fingers into her thigh. "I just don't want you thinking about that dirty spoon all—"

The teasing is cut short when I drop her on the bathroom counter and back away to run the shower. She leans back on the palms of her hands, and the hem of the shirt she's wearing rides up around her thighs as she watches me grab a clean towel.

I hear the tiny groan from her lips as I pull the sweaty shirt off and she leans over the counter to pop the lid of the basket for me, knowing that tossing it on the floor isn't an option, but it gives me a full view of the tiny boyshorts she's wearing. *Fuck me.*

"Do friends watch each other shower?" She asks me as I strip from my sweat pants and throw them in the same place.

"I don't know, you're the one whose friends have no boundaries," I smile at her, giving her full control of the situation. Her focus is elsewhere, and if I were a more modest man, I'd be blushing, but her eyes inspecting every dirty inch of skin only fuels the fire in the pit of my stomach.

"I—" she opens her mouth and closes it.

"Cat got your tongue?" I tease and step forward, my fingers ghosting the bottom of her shirt.

"Bear," she chokes out with a smile.

"How about we make an exception?" I ask her.

"Yeah, just this one time..." Her words trail off again as my lips find the base of her neck. "Friends can totally help friends shower," she mumbles as I lift the hem over her stomach. "I can...I can wash those stubborn spots on your back—" Every word is muffled or stuttered from her lips, but she lifts her arms and lets me remove her shirt. "Does this hurt?" She asks me, and I angle my face down to look at the bruise forming on my shoulder that she's focused on.

"No." I shake my head and go back to kissing her skin. Her fingers find my skin as my lips find her collarbone. The shower long forgotten, the bathroom fills with steam as my hands dig into her back and pull her against my chest.

"The water's going to get cold," she teases breathlessly.

I let out a low chuckle against her neck, "whose fault is that?" My hand trails down her sides as I continue to find places void of kisses. "You keep your hands to yourself, Hellcat," I warn as I step back and push down my boxers.

"Follow your own rules." She sticks her tongue out at me and follows suit, climbing into the shower after me.

I turn around and pull her into me, pressing her back against the cold tiles as the lukewarm water beats down on my shoulders. "I'm trying to be a good friend." My hands cup her jaw, and I tilt her face up to meet mine in a deep kiss. "But you're making it really hard."

Rhea giggles against my lips, and my whole body goes stiff from the sound.

"See what you're doing to me?" I whisper against her ear, my hands sliding down over her curves. "I pride myself on my control, Rhea." I turn her around gently, pressing against her back so she's under the water.

"Self-control is lame," she scoffs, leaning back against me as my hands rake over the soft skin on her stomach.

"It's necessary around you." My hands slip down to her hips as my teeth gently graze her shoulder.

"Not tonight." She presses back against me, melting our bodies together under the water. My breath catches as I wrap my arms around her, hands sliding up to her chest.

"You're distracting me from getting clean." My fingers play with one of her hardened nipples, and she turns to a dead weight in my arms as her body relaxes. "Turn around." I softly demand. I take my time with the soap, first Rhea and then myself. Making sure that I cover every inch of her skin and her patience kills me. "Lift your arms," I command, trying to maintain my composure despite the hardened pain between my legs.

"Thank you," she says, clearly trying to behave until I'm finished. I pull back from her because everything is suddenly very real and very warm. The adrenaline from the game is wearing off, and I realize how idiotic I'm being with her. *Rushing around and thinking with your dick got you in too much trouble the first time.*

"Mhmm," I respond, grinding my teeth together as I grab the shampoo to wash the feeling of mud and sweat from my hair. I avoid looking at her as best I can, knowing full well I'm seconds away from losing that control I boasted about. She watches me with heavy eyes as I quickly scrub my hair, my back muscles flexing tightly under her gaze. "You gotta stop staring at me like that," I whisper, rinsing it out as fast as I can.

"Too many rules, Brighton," she muses as I finish and shut off the water. I step out of the shower, extending a towel to her, and then wrap one around my waist.

"Rules exist for a reason," I say. "And we're already breaking a handful." I watch the water slide down her body, coating her tattoos in a slick shine.

"With that logic, breaking a few more won't hurt anyone," she argues softly, and I smile, shaking my head gently before running my fingers through my hair to release the knots. I wander out of the bathroom and to my room, waiting for the sound of her quiet footsteps.

"You have the logic of a thirteen-year-old boy," I grumble, digging around in my dresser as she enters the bedroom.

"I've been patient," Rhea says from behind me, and my muscles tense. "Please don't make me wait longer."

There's a need in her voice when she says it, one that I know I can't resist. When I turn, she's still in her towel, skin damp, eyes watching and waiting for me to make up my mind. Frustration and desire churn beneath my skin as I shift, hard at the sight of her. "I'm trying to be responsible, Rhea."

"Lame excuse," she says. "Ten minutes ago, you were flirting, cleaning up messes with your tongue, and making out with me like we're teenagers." She steps further into my room, "Where'd that Brighton go?"

My eyes follow her as she approaches. "I got carried away," I admit. *I was horny and an idiot. I wanted a release, but I don't want this to be just that.* I stare at her. "Look where it got us."

"I'm happier than I've ever been, right where I am," Rhea argues with those infuriatingly sad eyes. She means here, with me, and I'm just too stubborn to believe it. I know that. She does too, that's why she asks, "Aren't you?"

I had lost this fight the second she laid them on me that night in the Hollow. I'm not even sure I ever wanted to win the battle against her; it's just been easier to pretend I did. A grumble of frustration rumbles at the base of my throat as I stand and walk toward her.

"You know I am," I say with conviction and surprise myself.

"Then prove it," Rhea demands gently. She's through tiptoeing around my need to take it slow, around my manners and chivalry. She's sick of being friends who kiss.

Before I can even stop myself, I'm closing the distance between us. The towel around my waist slips to the ground as I pull her close. Our lips collide in a hungry kiss, so much more needy than before as I pull at her towel with one hand and dip down to raise her against my waist with the other.

Rhea tangles her fingers into my wet hair as I slam the door closed, keeping her lips on mine as I walk back to the bed and lay her down. My body presses against hers, hands roaming her body in a desperate need to memorize how it feels beneath me. She chases me with her lips as I break away, but I dip down against her neck, teeth grazing her skin just enough to make her body shudder against mine.

"That feels good," she encourages, and my body reacts like I've never touched a woman before. My grip tightens around her thigh, and her giggle turns to a throaty moan. I push her open with my knee, settling down between her as I continue to kiss over every inch.

"Tell me if I'm going too fast." I look up at her, and she's staring down at me, her breathing ragged and her lips red from mine.

"Brighton, you're going too slow," she says, and I nod.

I can take an order, and I take them well. Probably too well.

My movements slow only for a moment, my face pressing against her thigh as I breathe out heavily. Her voice, so needy and demanding, would be the death of me. I bite gently there, feeling her body react before continuing downward. I push her legs wider, making room for my shoulders, and pepper her damp skin with more kisses.

"Yeah," she breathes out, and I can tell she's fighting an inner monologue with herself. "You don't have to do that..."

"What?" I mumble against her skin.

"Go down on me..." she mumbles, and I grumble a string of curses between her legs.

"Rhea." I snap, "Do you want me to?" I ask, not looking up at her.

"I..." she clears her throat. "Do *you* want to?"

"Do I want to eat my ridiculously hot roommate out until she begs me to stop?" I smirk, kissing her thigh. "Yes."

"Oh..." She inhales. "Okay. Carry on."

"Thank you," I say before returning to what I was doing.

"Wait," she huffs. "Wait. Wait." She reaches down and cups my chin, angling my face up to her again and interrupting the string of gentle kisses and bites I'm dealing to her inner thigh.

"What?" I scowl.

"I just owe the girls money." She stares at me, realizing something she refuses to share.

Rhea please. The games are going to kill me. I shift uncomfortably against the bed, my fingers digging into her thigh tighter this time.

"The girls? Now? We're a little busy." I growl, my jaw clenching.

"No *later*," she laughs. "Cosy and Kaia said you'd be like this, and I didn't believe them," she keeps talking. *Why are you still fucking talking?* I lift higher and hover over her, willing to give her the conversation if that's what she needed, despite the way I throb for contact.

"Be like what?" I ask her.

"Um." Rhea chews her lip, and I reach out to stop her, pulling her bottom lip between my thumb and finger.

"Stop it," I warn. "Tell me what you expected."

"You're the Terminator... I expected you to be..." she starts and stops.

"Dominant?" I whisper and feel her body tense.

"Yeah." She watches for a reaction, but she isn't going to get one.

"And what did those little shits say?" I ask her, kissing her as a follow-up to keep her from panicking about the entire thing. Rhea lets go of a tiny laugh, her eyes flickering to the side and back again.

"Kaia said you were a dom in the streets, but a sub in sheets." She covers her face with both hands like she's embarrassed for even repeating it. *I'm annoyed, sexually frustrated and going to throttle Kaia the next time I see her for putting this nonsense in Rhea's head.*

"Okay." I clear my throat and grab her chin. "I'm going to say this once, and then all mentions of Kaia stay out of my bedroom. Understand?"

"Are you jealous of Kaia?" She laughs, and I scowl, grumbling a little before biting down on her bottom lip. "Rightfully so." She shrugs.

"Are you listening?" She nods in my grip, and I smile. *Good.* "For once in her God-forsaken life, Kaia is right."

Rhea

She's right.

"Okay, but... I'm not very good at being bossy," I admit, panic building that I won't be what he needs.

"Just ask for what you want," he says. "I'll give it to you." There's something about the way he stares at me that warms a strange place in my chest—something I didn't know existed. "Anything," he says when I don't answer.

"Okay," I say, trying to find the courage to be demanding. *Anything for you.*

"Can I continue what I was doing now?" Brighton's eyes are heavy, lust-filled, and searching mine for answers.

"Yeah," I choke out, still trying to process all the information.

"Thank you," he says, dipping back between my legs, and without warning, his tongue darts out over me.

"Fuck," I groan, trying to maintain composure, but he's unreasonably good at this. His teeth nip at my clit, causing the pressure to build faster than anticipated. I feel him smirk against me, pleased with the reaction. His tongue circles me before he sucks it into his mouth, applying just the right amount of pressure. One hand slides down to rub torturous circles at my entrance while the other holds my hip firmly against the bed.

"Keep going," I breathe, and his body shudders.

Brighton does as he's told, his tongue working faster as he slides one finger inside of me. I clamp around him, and his shoulders roll forward as he relieves some of the friction with the mattress, "Does that feel good?" he murmurs between licks.

"You're way too good at—" My words die on my lips as he slips another inside.

Brighton smirks up at me as I squeeze around his long fingers. He curls them slightly, hitting a spot inside of me that causes my back to arch off the bed. He knows exactly what he's doing, and he loves every second of it.

He adds a another, stretching me gently as he continues to suck and lick at my clit. Everything feels overwhelming and sensitive as he works. His hand moves up to play with one of my breasts, pinching at the nipple with his fingers.

"I want you to come," he says softly.

"That'll make a mess," I tease, already shaking.

"I'll clean it up." His eyes flicker up to mine as he bites down on my clit again. His fingers curl inside of me over and over as he hits that spot that makes my vision blur around the edges. "*Please*," he adds in desperation.

My body responds to his needy plea, bucking gently as I come undone around him. I clench tightly, digging my fingers into the sheets as my arousal leaks down his palm and wrist, still pumping inside of me.

Brighton groans loudly as I come, his face buried between my legs as he laps up every drop. He doesn't remove his fingers until I'm completely spent and desperately trying to catch my breath. He lifts them, eyes still on me, and brings them to his mouth to clean them.

"Lay down," I say to him, trying to navigate being bossy, but it's a learning curve I'm not sure I'm doing properly.

His eyes don't break from mine as I continue to guide him. I can tell he likes it because his body responds with a small twitch before he drops back to the bed without a word. He's hard, bobbing slightly against his stomach, and he spreads his legs slightly, putting himself entirely at my mercy. Before, I hadn't gotten a good look at him, and I have never been scared of a good time in my life, but Brighton Black was terrifying. Thick, prominent veins run the expanse, almost mocking my hesitation, and I swallow nervously.

"I'll go slow." His hand reaches for me. "Touch me? *Please.*"

I climb over him, not worrying about anything else but the sound of his need as I kiss him gently. He melts into it instantly, one hand automatically reaching up to tangle into my hair while the other slides around me to pull me closer. His body relaxes finally as he parts his lips to deepen the kiss, but his hips shift restlessly beneath me.

"Slow?" I ask, pulling back to feel him brush against my sensitive core.

"So slow it hurts," he admits, pressing his forehead against mine. His icy blue gaze is heavy-lidded with desire as he inhales me. "Take your time with me," he demands gently, like he wants to be tortured by it, and it lights an uncomfortable fire in my chest that tingles at my skin and makes me short of breath.

I straddle him slowly, using his chest for balance. I dig my fingers into his skin, and his body shivers beneath mine as I line him up. His eyes flutter closed as his hands move to my hips, gripping tightly but not guiding me down yet. I lick my bottom lip and nod before sinking down until the tip presses in—slow, deep, burning.

"Brighton," I whisper with worry.

His eyes snap open, filled with concern and desire as his hands tighten on my hips, holding me in place as he inhales deeply. "Inch by inch, Hellcat," he whispers. "Take it slow," he bites his lip, fighting the urge to raise his hips.

I huff in response, feeling like an inexperienced idiot, but my body craves so much more of him, and it drives me to lower further with a small pained gasp. He nods quickly, understanding the need to go slow. His hands slide down to my thighs, spreading me wider as he helps me sink another inch.

"I wish you could see this," he whispers, his eyes meeting mine. "It's—"

"Use your words, Brighton," I demand, needing to hear what he's thinking as I slide lower, every inch should be the last, but there's so much more.

"It's too much," he groans tightly. "Like you were made for me." His words slur slightly as he struggles to maintain his control. "Give me more?" he asks, and the sound breaks me down.

I nod as his hands guide me down further, stretching me open so deeply I can feel him pressing against every wall, twitching with impatience.

"Beg me for it," I say, finding the spark of courage to demand more of the needy, whiny Brighton from him. It turns me on more than I care to admit, and he knows it because he smiles up at me with pride.

"Please," he whines, tilting his chin up to me. "I'll be so good to you, but I need you to take it all."

The sight of him begging is enough to break the strongest of women. *And I am weak. The weakest of all the women to ever roam the earth.* I sink lower, letting him fill me completely until I physically cannot take anymore. He lets out a loud, guttural groan as I finally bottom out, his hands squeezing my thighs possessively.

When he sits up in the bed to hold me, cradling me in his lap tightly, it changes the angle and causes me to gasp loudly. I wrap around him tightly, digging my hands into his hair as his large hands splay out over my back and rib cage.

"Move, Brighton," I demand, my voice muffled against his neck.

He starts moving immediately, lifting his hips to thrust upwards in slow, shallow movements that hit the perfect spots inside of me. His arms stay firmly wrapped around me as he holds the gentle, rhythmic pace. His face buries in my neck, muffling the sounds of pleasure escaping him with each deep thrust.

"Good," I pant, digging my nails into the back of his neck. "That's really good."

His pace quickens slightly at the approval, his hips rolling higher and deeper. He kisses along my jawline and neck, marking me with gentle bites and sucks that only add to the tingly high I'm riding. His hands roam over my body possessively as he fucks me slowly in his lap, and I couldn't ask for more even if I tried.

Tiny, delicious moans of praise spill from me as he massages around the sore entrance with his fingers, as he continues to thrust up inside me, steady and unrelenting. He's quick to swallow the sounds, watching me closely, studying every noise and twitch. "You like that spot?" he groans against my lips, and I barely get the nod off as the desperate whine drips from me. He spreads my ass with his hands, angling his hips to hit that spot over and over again, still watching my face with intent. "Right there?"

"Yeah," I breathe out, unable to maintain control. "You're doing so good, baby."

His eyes light up at the praise, his movements becoming even more deliberate. He hits that spot over and over, dragging those breathy whimpers from my lips as his hands tighten on my ass. He moves slowly but intensely, making sure I feel every single thrust.

"Just a little longer," I whisper against his mouth. My own orgasm hits, and I tighten beneath his grip. His eyes snap to my face as his length becomes slick, my body demanding whatever he has left, and Brighton delivers tenfold. My toes curl tightly as he runs a hand up my sweaty spine and grips the back of my neck, pulling me back down on top of him as I try to retreat. His hips roll up to meet my ass, and I scream out his name in a slew of curse words in the aftershocks.

I tug on his dark curls to angle his head back so I can see his face when he falls apart, buried inside of me. "Come for me?" I whisper, biting his tense jaw before soothing the spot with a gentle suck.

"Rhea, I'm not wearing—"

"I'm good. You're good. Promise." I kiss him again between breathless pants, soothing the worry. Brighton's about as ready for another kid as I am for my first. His terror is palpable. *Birth control is quite possibly a girl's best friend.*

His eyes darken with a new hunger as he understands what I'm saying and exhales the breath he's holding. He nods, his movement becoming erratic as he chases his release and drags me to the edge with him. He throbs inside of me, and it sends delicious shockwaves through me and into my stomach and toes.

"Mmm," I moan, grabbing his jaw and rubbing my thumb over his bottom lip.

Brighton shivers hard, and his orgasm hits like a tidal wave. He buries himself deep inside of me and comes with a deep groan that bubbles up from the base of his throat. His hands dig into my skin hard enough to mark me with his fingertips for days to come, and he kisses me messily, swallowing my moans that follow. We tangle together as we both rock through the rest of the pleasure. Sloppy kisses are left against my throat, jaw, and sweaty temple as he rolls his hips up against me, slowly drawing out every single drop he can get from me until I'm nothing but a panting, boneless mess in his arms.

I pull on his hair again, harder this time, as his cock twitches inside of me, and he lets go of the most beautiful whimper.

"What was that for?" he growls and digs his fingers into my ass roughly.

"I needed to make sure you were real," I whisper in a shallow breath.

Brighton chuckles, "You hair-pulling, aggressive little monster." His fingers tickle my ribcage, and I start to laugh. Just when I think he's going to tell me that he doesn't like it, his chin tilts up, and he pulls me against his chest tightly, "do it again," he purrs in a tone that I didn't even know he could make.

"We're going to have to test out your boundaries," I say, brushing my nose against his with a smile as he gives me another tiny thrust, his cock already hardening for more.

"Oh yeah?" His eyes flutter closed. "Why's that, Miss *I'm-not-very-good-at-bossy?*" he asks with a small laugh, crackling an eye open as I kiss him.

I pull back just enough to speak, our lips brushing together as I do. "Because that was the hottest thing a man could ever do."

Brighton's eyes light up, and he nods eagerly, like I mean right this second, his hips rolling up against mine slowly. He flips me over in the bed, warranting a tiny yelp as he hovers over me and kisses me gently. "That was just the practice, Hellcat," he warns, and crashes down on top of me. "You should see me come game time."

"Please." I laugh at how serious he is and tug him back for more kissing.

"I told you I'd be good to you," he whispers against my mouth, and I think I might die.

What a damn good way to go.

Brighton

"Where are we going?" Rhea asks as I open the passenger door for her.

"Do you understand the definition of a surprise, Hellcat?" I help her out onto the concrete and exhale a breath at the sight of her.

"Eight-hour drives are not surprises, they're road trips. If we're camping again, I'm going to kill you," she warns, and I scoff.

"In that outfit?" I look at her in disbelief. I told her to dress up, and what I had in mind wasn't even in competition with how she looked. Her strong thighs in the tiniest leather skirt, that barely covered her ass, and those boots she was wearing the night she hurt her hand—*the ones that hug her perfect calves*. "I'm going to jail tonight," I grumble under my breath, and she laughs.

"What, you don't like my skirt?" she asks, fluffing the pleats with her ring-laden hands and showing off the red underwear she has on beneath it.

"Cut it out, or we won't even make it inside," I demand, and she gives me a tiny shrug.

"Killjoy," she grumbles, and I tap her ass as she wanders in front of me. "There better be a good reason you dragged me all the way out here."

"Read." I point to the sign about the stadium.

Her eyes scan the big letters that say WWE in bright white, and then her head snaps to me as I hold out two passes in my hand. She grabs one, reads it over, and looks up at me with glassy eyes.

I laugh, caught off guard by her reaction. "Why are you crying?" I step forward, using my thumb to catch the tear that falls and threatens to ruin her pretty, dark makeup.

"This is really nice," her voice shakes.

"It's just SmackDown, Hellcat." I inspect her face to make sure there are no more tears before stepping back and helping her put the access badge over her head.

"It's *ringside* SmackDown," she says, staring up at me with her brows pinched tight. "These must have cost a fortune, Brighton!"

And every bit is worth that look on your face.

"Nope," I say. "Come on, before we're late."

"Do you even like wrestling?" She slips her hand in mine and catches up to match her step to mine. "For real?"

"I like you," I respond without skipping a beat. *For real.*

Rhea doesn't say anything else because when we enter the stadium, she's completely silenced by her shock. It's busy, really busy, and just about every fucker that passes us puts his eyes on her legs. I squeeze her hand in mine because I can't help the possession that floods me at the thought of someone else touching her. *Ever.*

Having sex was instantly a bad idea. I knew it then. I know it now. It just makes every feeling I have for her stronger. Her laugh derails me; her smile has me walking into walls. Last week, I nearly dropped a tray of glasses on the floor because she was flirting with some cops as she kicked them out of the Hollow and into cabs. It took me the rest of the shift, two hours of making her scream my name, and a cold shower to remind myself that she was doing her job.

Idiot.

I'm consumed—and happy to be stuck in her quicksand.

"Okay, you need a shirt," she declares and drags me through the stadium.

"I really don't," I groan, but let her drag me. Tonight is all about her, and I will do anything she asks of me because it means there's a smile on her face. "Slow down, Hellcat."

It's a wondrous thing to watch a woman so strong turn into such a little kid at the hint of something she loves. Every day, she gives reason to find joy in life despite all of the horrible things going on around her—and in her mind. She looks over her shoulder at me to make sure I'm still behind her, and even though the sadness is still there, it's tangled with unbridled excitement.

"You pick one you like, and I'll tell you if it's acceptable," she says. Her giggle is enough to get me to shut my mouth as she drags us into a line for merch.

I scowl at her before looking up at the selection they have displayed. I know nothing about wrestling and even less about the people on the shirts. "Is there anything plain?" I ask her, and she snorts.

"Don't be a buzzkill," she groans.

"Alright uh…" My eyes scan the shirts, trying to find the least offensive one on my eyes, and come up short. "That one," I point to a black shirt at the end with some guy's face all over it.

"Oof," Rhea scoffs, "no. Try again."

"Who's that and why is he a no?" I ask.

"Just move on," she pokes. Another group of guys wanders behind us, and one of them points to her skirt, but she's none the wiser as she continues to talk in circles about the different wrestlers.

I slide in behind her and press my chest to her back, "What about that one?" I point over her shoulder.

"Much better. I approve." She doesn't skip a beat. "I need a CM Punk shirt, mine got destroyed in the condo." She points to one with that old man on it, and I look down at her with a dirty look on my face.

"Yeah, yeah." I kiss the back of her head as we move in line. "Is that the only one you want?"

"Oh no." She shakes her head. "I'm buying them. You've done enough for the day."

"Rhea." I stare at her, and she opens her mouth to say something about making it even. I know her better than she cares to admit. She hates this. But I lean down and pull her chin toward me with a finger, kissing her gently once before retreating. "Don't argue with me in public, you won't win."

"Okay." She falls silent and turns her attention back to the line.

"It's also your birthday," I whisper to her, and she whips around.

"Who told you that?" She glares at me, and I don't think I've ever seen her mad face, at least not directed at me. It's as cute as it is terrifying.

"I'm offended you think I didn't dig," I respond with a smirk. *I'm not scared of you, Hellcat. Nice try.*

"You shouldn't have dug." She rolls her eyes. After pulling up just about every single social media page she has, I couldn't find anything about her birthday. Not even a post. So I went to the source, *Sunday.*

I cornered her in the bar last week.

"Did you ask Rhea?" She hops slightly to reach a cup hanging just out of her reach behind the bar.

"I'm asking you." I follow her and the stupid 'please don't ask me for my number' shirt out of the bar and across the crowded floor to the back wall of booths.

"How is that, by the way? She barely talks about you because she thinks it'll gross me out, which it would, but... I still want to know what's going on." Sunday yells over the music as she hands the girl a fresh cup and pours her some water.

"It's fine." I shrug, and Sunday gives me a dirty look. "I like her," I admit, unable to defend myself from the glare. "A lot."

"It's in two weeks, on the thirteenth," Sunday says, like she's ready with the information. "She hates her birthday, though, she spends them cleaning up after her siblings in that stupid fucking house where her Mom rarely remembers, and when Gabe does, he makes fucking pasta. Do you know how much Rhea hates pasta?"

"She hates pasta?"

She had eaten two bowls that night with a smile on her face and let Gabe pack her leftovers for her lunch the rest of the week. Actually, every time she comes back to the apartment, there's a container of pasta in the fridge the next morning. But now that I think about it... She never touches it. It goes bad, and I throw it out a week later.

"Listen, Bri, birthdays sting for Rhea." *The severity of the situation is driven home by the tone in Sunday's voice when she stops moving and stares me down.*

"It's on your employee form," I lie, and her brows furrow.

"No, it's not," she says as the line moves. "I put a different date every time I apply for a job."

"Isn't that illegal?" I shake my head at her.

"Maybe," she muses. We're only a few bodies back from the main counter now. "Which one of the *little shits* snitched on me?" She teases, and the memory of that night floods back in.

"Day," I laugh, directing her focus. "Go pick your shirts." I lift her chin with a finger so she makes eye contact, "and pick two."

I'm wandering down the hallway at school when I hear a commotion coming from Mr. Disson's class. I slow my steps and tuck my papers under my arm, intending to help, but it's Riona who barrels out of the classroom. Her hair hangs in blonde waves around her sharp features.

"Oh," I open my mouth and shut it again.

"Ms. Drake," Riona inhales slowly, righting herself.

"Are you alright?" I ask, against my better judgment. I don't know how much she knows about everything, and I'm nervous that her opinion of me has changed. But her expression shifts, and it's clear she's overwhelmed.

"No," she swallows.

"The art room is empty," I say, pointing back to my room, and Riona takes a second but follows me. As we enter, I shut the door behind us, and she sets her bag down on the desk. "Mr. *Dick*son can be a real prick."

"That's a good name for him," she compliments. "And yes, he is a prick."

"Are you here about Daisy?" I question as she wanders around the art room, taking it all in.

"Did you do all this?" she asks about the paintings that decorate the walls instead of answering me.

"No, students," I answer honestly.

"Freedom to express is important at this age. It fosters emotional independence," Riona says, laughing at one of the paintings that Lori has done. It's a polar bear in a Speedo.

"So I've heard," I say, and she looks over her shoulder at me. "Daisy says stuff like that all the time; it's pretty obvious she doesn't get that emotional independence from her dad."

This makes her laugh, genuinely, her shoulders relax a bit, but I can tell she's still on guard.

"She's been doing well, if that's why you're here. Although she's been spending a lot more time in the music room." I tell her.

"Auggie." Riona swallows tightly. "If someone told me fourteen years ago my daughter would crush on Silas Shore's son, I'd have throat-punched them." Silas Shore is a retired Hornet's baseball player, his father is Charles Shore. A filthy rich idiot currently on trial for a lot of fraud, tax evasion and money laundering. The connection to Riona is a little rattling. I didn't take her for the bat bunny type.

"Oh?" I raise an eyebrow.

"Don't judge me," she laughs, "he was a work of art back then."

"I was going to say you have good taste in men." I give her a look, and she rolls her eyes.

"I had. I think I'm sick of athletes." She corrects me.

"You're being liberal calling Brighton an athlete," I tease and she laughs gently with a small nod.

"He's different with you." Anyone else might have taken it as an insult, but there's a softness to the way she says it. Something that makes me believe she's genuinely happy about it. "He thinks I don't see it, but I do."

I open my mouth to argue that he's not different; their relationship is, but she shakes her head softly. Riona spent her life with him; she's got the upper hand.

"I think trauma had a hand in that," I say, refusing to take the credit.

"They warned me that he'd come home differently. I took classes, sat in group therapy, and did everything I could to prepare myself for it. I thought if anyone could ground him in reality, it's me," she sighs quietly. "I thought he'd come back with pieces of himself. Instead, he came home hollow."

The bar. I should've known it was something that was said to him at some point.

"Yeah, Boone thinks that's hilarious, too." Riona sighs, tracking my expression. "I didn't come in here to act as I know him and warn you away or anything." She tells me, picking up her bag again. "Bright's a good dad. He loves Daisy. Sometimes, I think it's all he has room to do. So if he's making room for you," she stops at the door, hand on the knob, "utilize it. Because the man I loved would burn the world down for the people he cares about, and that's a big way to love. It's not something you just forget how to do."

A week later, I'm dragging Brighton along on the thousands of errands I have to do. I'd much rather be spending my Saturday in bed with him, ignoring the world, but unfortunately, my Mom is at work, and Hockey doesn't stop for anyone. The arena is a lot colder than I expect, and the raw stench of cold sweat hits my nose like a tidal wave as Brighton holds the door open for me.

"You want this?" he asks, pulling off his hat, and already half out of the hoodie he's wearing, like he knows I'm going to refuse and he's not going to let me. The long sleeve he's wearing beneath is tight and clings to his oversized body like it was stretched around him a size too small.

It's unfair that he looks that good, clothed and naked.

"Rhea," he chuckles, waving it in my face as I stare. I take it as he smooths out his hair back under the hat and watches me.

"Thank you." I pull it over my head, expecting to fit it like it's mine, but it hits my body like a blanket, roomy in every way possible. I tuck my chin inside the collar, and Brighton smiles at me, pleased with himself.

"What's his number?" He asks, following me up into the stands.

"Seventy-one," I point to where Reid warms up with a few of his teammates. He currently plays for an AA team, but his skills are growing and developing so fast that he'll just keep climbing through the ranks.

"Why seventy-one?" Brighton slides onto the stone bleacher beside me.

"Uh..." I try to remember the player's name. "He's always been obsessed with the Penguins? I don't know the guy's name."

Brighton just nods, his eyes trailing the ice as Reid moves back and forth between the boards, getting faster with each lap until his team starts to circle back to the bench to get a word from their coach.

"Is he going to be pissed you brought me here?" Brighton asks. Mostly because when the game starts, Reid turns his head to look over at us, and his expression is cold.

"He wasn't even mad you came for dinner," I say—which is a lie. That's just Reid.

"You're full of shit, Hellcat. You forget I'm *that* brother," he turns to look at me, and his glare is knowing.

"He was upset I didn't tell him, not that you were there," I correct myself. "He's just protective for all the wrong reasons. He was so little when it all happened, and he spends every day trying to prove he's not a victim anymore."

Brighton's jaw tightens at the mention of what happened. For a while, I thought maybe he'd forgotten what I told him. He was a little dazed that night, and there was a chance he didn't retain anything but that strained tick tells me he does. Every single detail.

"I still wish you had warned me," he says. "Having me show up there couldn't have been easy on him."

"He had a few choice words about your size." I laugh at the look Brighton gives me. "I don't know if you noticed, but Gabe isn't exactly what someone would consider the man of the house."

"You and I both know you're the man of that house," Brighton teases.

"But I let Reid believe it's him, and unfortunately, that was a little threatened. He's fine now. I think…" I shrug and turn my eyes back to the game.

"Teenagers are terrifying."

"You're telling me," I scoff.

Reid moves down the ice with precision, and I watch as he slots through the legs of a defenseman, regains complete control of the puck, and pockets it into the top left corner of the net, completely bypassing the goalie without breaking a sweat.

I jump up, screaming as loud as I can for him, and don't stop screaming until he turns to me with his stick extended and a stupid grin on his face. He doesn't wear that one as much anymore, and it's always nice to see it.

"I understand better now," Brighton says after the first goal is scored.

"What?" I ask, sitting back down.

"Why you are the way you are," he says, like it's supposed to clear up the confusion. He chuckles because he can see my expression out of the corner of his eye while he watches the game. "You're so content being the last priority because it's always meant that the people you love are the first."

I scoff, both because he's not wrong but because the statement comes out of nowhere.

"Sunday said they never show up and yet…" he nods to the ice. "You're always trailing behind them, making sure they never feel that way. Why?" He finally looks at me when he asks.

"Because they didn't ask for any of this. They're just kids," I say as Reid scores his second goal of the game and the crowd surges.

"Neither did you." He argues gently.

"I have the power to make sure they don't feel the way I do," I explain to him. "Showing up is the bottom line." I whisper, the tears pricking at the corners of my eyes because it's true.

"Hey." He hooks his finger into the collar of my hoodie and pulls me toward him until our noses are touching. The sudden show of public affection set me off balance a little, but he doesn't even blink when he says, "Every game, if I can't be there, it goes on the big TV."

I smile as my eyes fill with more uncontrollable tears. "Even when the Huskies play?" I ask quietly.

"Especially when the Huskies play."

"Why?" I ask him.

"Because I have the power to make sure you don't feel like that anymore either." His tone isn't harsh; it's the same as the voice he used the night I was nervous to wear my heels. I nod, only because if I open my mouth to agree, I'll cry harder, and we are still very much in public. "Good."

He pulls the hood over my head, kissing my temple as he pulls me into his side so I can stop what tears are falling without anyone paying attention to me, and we watch the rest of the game like that. Brighton even starts cheering with me for Reid every time he makes a play, and for the first time in a long time, it doesn't feel like I'm burdening anyone. We're just here, enjoying the game and the afternoon.

When the game finishes, Brighton waits with me by the locker rooms as Reid showers and collects his bag.

"Why's he here?" is the first thing out of his mouth when he steps into the tunnel.

"Good game, Reid." I sigh.

He looks at me, and all I see is the anger behind those green eyes, but it fades as he takes in my expression. He turns to Brighton and unclenches his jaw.

"Sorry," he clips.

"Can I take that?" Brighton points to his hockey bag, and Reid questions his motives for a second but drops it on the floor. Brighton bends down and scoops it up as Reid throws his hand through the damp, dark hair on his head.

"You did really well today," I say, trying to diffuse the tension.

Neither of them is paying attention to me, though. My brother is too busy trying to find things he hates about my— about Brighton. *Is he my boyfriend? We've never had that conversation... Oh god, Rhea. Every turn you stumble around like Bambi in the dark.*

Brighton looks at the sticks Reid carries, three, all identical. "Right down to the stick," he says, and Reid gives him a dirty look as we wander out to the parking lot.

"What?" He scowls.

"Seventy-one. These are expensive. You really like the one-ten flex?" he asks, and my brother turns into a different person I've never seen before in my life. "You can't be more than one-eighty."

"I'm one-fifty-two, but the one-ten flex has a better give to it than what they recommend for my size. So yeah," he says as Brighton throws the bag into the back of his truck.

"Evgeni barely handles a one-ten, and he's twice your size." Brighton shrugs and closes the cover as he turns back to Reid.

"Geno is the best hockey player of this generation," Reid defends with a wicked grin on his face. "Don't tell me, you're an Ovechkin fan boy. Ree... who the hell is this guy?"

I raise my hands in the air because the way Brighton is talking, I barely know.

"Now you're just insulting me," Brighton laughs. "Jagr is who you should idolize," he says. "That's a next-level Russian superstar. Geno is just following pace."

Reid inhales, and his smile grows. "Alright, alright," he nods. "That's better than I expected. I can work with that."

"You hungry?" Brighton asks him.

"Fucking starving," he swears, and I scowl. "I'm practically eighteen, Ree," he waves me off and climbs into the back seat of the truck. Brighton walks me over to the passenger side and palms the handle.

"That was impressive," I say, and Brighton smirks at me.

"I own a sports bar, Hellcat. It's my job."

"Right. Well, still, he's not the easiest. He definitely bites." I joke.

"So do you," he teases, popping the door for me.

"You're a sadist." I roll my eyes. When I climb in, I turn to Reid in the back seat, and he just shrugs in approval, which is more than I was expecting to get today.

Brighton

Daisy sits next to me in the truck, half awake and scrolling through her phone as something plays over her headphones, and I sit with the music softer in the cab. It's one of Rhea's playlists, and I won't admit it to her, but I love every song on it. They're all stringy guitars and no drums, but there's still so much feeling in them. I hate that she's so easily able to change all of my habits.

Infuriating.

I pull up the trail and put the truck in park in the small, dirt parking lot before I offload the canoe and get it set up in the water. Daisy carries down the box and hands it to me with a little grumbly sigh as she realizes the service is crap this far from the city. I wish I could say it's an accident, but it's really just a way to get her to talk to me without the buffer of the screen between us.

It takes us a second, and she argues about what side she wants to sit on, but once we're on the water, I row us to the middle of the lake and stow the paddle inside.

"Dad." Daisy squints at me from across the canoe. "I just want you to know I hate fishing more than I hate when Mom hosts study parties for every test I have."

I stifle the laugh that forms in the base of my throat; *of course, Riona throws parties around studying.*

"Seriously, if this is some sick plan to teach me discipline, or... I don't know, patience. It's not going to work." She crosses her arms.

"I didn't bring you out here to fish, Squish." I set the pole between my legs as the sun starts to come up over the trees.

"Okay, well…" she shrugs, pointing to the fishing rod with a scowl on her face that I can't even get mad at because I gave it to her. "It's five am on a Saturday, and if you didn't bring me out here to fish, what are we doing?"

"You brought your book?" I ask her, my eyes drifting to the bag between her feet. I know she did, I watch her put the ratty sketch journal in there every morning before school. She nods, "Take it out, I'll fish, you draw."

Daisy studies my expression for a long moment before tucking a chunk of her unruly blonde hair behind her ear and doing what she's told. She balances the book on her lap alongside the container of pencils she has.

"Fish aren't really my area of inspiration," she admits.

"Not the fish, Daisy." I laugh, and the canoe rumbles beneath us. "Just look around you, find something. Birds, trees, wildlife, flowers," I give her plenty of examples, and she starts to get the idea. "Look," I direct her eye line to the shore where a doe steps out of the tree line with her fawn.

"Wow," Daisy whispers, her fingers gently moving the pages without taking her eyes off the deer. "Okay, that's cool, you win," she mumbles. "This time," she adds quietly, and the scratch of her pencils fills the air, tangling with the soft ripples of the water.

I don't even like fishing. But I don't tell her that. There's something methodical about it; cast it out, reel it in. I actually don't even really like the taste of fish. But I needed the quiet, and it's been too long since Daisy, and I just did something together. Sometimes I stare at her and can't figure out where the time has gone. I remember when she was barely able to stand; her diaper was always lopsided, matching that big, goofy, toothless smile. Riona used to pull her hair into these tiny little pig tails that were all thin curls and stuck off the top of her head.

Now she's a teenager.

Her hair falls in her face as she keeps one eye on the deer and the other on her book. She kept that goofy smile, even though I don't get to see it as much anymore, but she has gained so much more. She's her own personality now, and some days it feels like I missed her figuring out what that looks like.

The guilt is violent. The scales feel unbalanced.

You left so you could give her this, versus *you left*.

It's hard to explain to your toddler why you're leaving, rationalizing abandonment for the betterment of her life. It wouldn't have made sense to her; it barely makes sense to her now. Riona and I were two halves of a whole once. An unshakeable team. If you told twenty-year-old me that Riona Cody couldn't even look at me anymore, I'd scorch the earth to prove you wrong. But I'd left with my half, promising to return it to her—then it came home in a coffin. Nothing but ash. And not even Riona could fix that.

"You know your mom deserves a little more credit, even if she is a nerd," I huff, and Daisy's brows pinch together as a tiny smile forms on her lips, but she doesn't look up from her book as I reel in air on the line. *Again.*

"I dare you to say that to her face," Daisy snorts.

"I've called your mom a nerd to her face."

Daisy looks up at me with a raised brow.

"Okay, maybe not to her face," I backtrack. "But I'm serious, lame study parties aside. She's done all she can to make sure you have every-thing you need."

She continues to stare at me, obviously suspicious of the conversa-tion.

"Are you sick?" She blurts the question.

"No," I grumble with a chuckle. "But you're proving my point," I say. "That attitude you have is all your mom. It's going to come in handy later in life, just quit aiming it at me."

"Mom's too strict." Daisy rolls her eyes.

"She's just trying to make sure you stay on track, with school and your responsibilities." I say, "It's important."

"She could ease up a little," Daisy grunts.

"If you say this behind her back, what the hell are you saying about me?" I laugh in disbelief.

"You're always late for meetings, you hover like I'm going to be kidnapped right in front of you, and you get angry over nothing..." she says without hesitation.

"Fair," I sigh. "I don't hover..."

"You do." Daisy shakes her head, "Everyone is afraid of you and Mom. That's why Auggie won't come over," she confesses.

"You were going to bring him over?" I stop her, ignoring the first bit.

"Yeah, but you scare him," she scoffs.

"Me? Your mom is way scarier..." I groan.

"Yeah, but she's friends with Dr. Shore, and that's Auggie's Dad, or step-dad, I guess..." She shrugs and goes back to her sketch.

I cock my head to the side. Is *it now...*

Silas Shore is a cockroach. A year before Daisy was born, Silas Shore bulldozed into our lives a fucking frat party and it seems like no matter what I do, I can't get rid of him. He was always there, haunting me, on the back of Riona's mind. A living, breathing what-if that never seemed to let it go. The universe is cruel and Daisy having a crush on his son is a joke.

"Right," I nod, looking out over the water. *These Hornets are starting to get on my fucking nerves.* "Well, what if Auggie brings over his Mom and step-dad for dinner. Uncle B can cook whatever you want."

Daisy looks back up at me. "Really?"

"Yeah, Sunny and Kaia can come too if you want," I suggest.

"What about C?" she pushes. My hand flexes around the fishing pole, the words *hell no* on my lips, but she stares at me with those big green eyes and quietly waits for me to say yes.

"If you want him there, he can come." I grind out. *And I can always choke him out in the service closet downstairs, where no one will ever find his body.*

"Okay," she agrees. "Will Rhea be there?" She asks.

"Sure," I say, knowing that it'll cause trouble. But if I have to deal with that blond fuckhead, then I'll need backup.

Rhea

Brighton is slamming things around in an empty bar, grumbling and grunting about something as I try to mark art assignments from the students' journals.

"Hey, grumpy," I say to get his attention. "You slam those bottles any harder, I'm going to get jealous."

Brighton stops, a tight laugh tumbling from him, and turns his head to look at me. There's clearly something bothering him, but he's not the type to just talk about it. If I want to know what's going on, I have to pry the information from him with a crowbar.

"Are you okay?" I ask him.

"Fine." His smile drops, and he goes back to roughing up top-shelf liquor.

"So like," I set down my pen and shift in my chair. "This might seem insane, but I can see the difference between a normal grumpy mood and whatever this is…"

He sighs and plants his hands on the bar top as his head hangs between his arms in defeat. "Nothing's wrong," he says, but doesn't make eye contact, and I can feel that he's lying in my bones.

"Brighton," I whisper.

He tilts his head to look at me.

"I'll work it out," he says.

"Oh come on, that only makes me wanna know more," I push. It's quiet in the bar, everyone is gone, and I'm starting to get used to it just being the two of us after close.

"I don't want to talk about my ex-wife with my—" he swallows hard, and I narrow my eyes at him.

"I thought everything had settled down?" I ask, trying to ignore the way the word died on his lips. *Say it, Brighton. You big, handsome coward.*

"I thought so, but..." He pats his hand on the counter and stands up straight. "Daisy wants this dinner, and Riona nearly chewed off my head for planning it without asking her first. It just seems like no matter what I do, I'm still in the wrong."

"Well, you probably are," I say, and he scowls at me. "Just listen," I laugh at his expression. "Everything I know about Riona is second-hand, from you, Daisy, Sunday. I don't know what happened between you, but I can say from experience that when someone you love comes home different after being gone for a long time, it's a hard pill to swallow."

Brighton stares at me, and I know I've hit a chord, but there's no turning back now.

"I talked to her..." I admit and the muscle in his jaw ticks violently. "I just—I can't imagine loving someone enough to have a child with them and then having them come home completely changed," I continue, and his expression pulls taught as his eyes grow dark. "I didn't know you before, I'm just starting to get to know you now," I say and offer him a nervous smile. "But Brighton, maybe she's just adjusting?"

"I've been home a long time, Rhea." His words are tight, but not angry.

"I can't imagine seeing you around all the time is easy for her," I advocate. "If it were me, having you, losing you, and watching you find your way back... that would hurt. It would make me resentful too, especially if things ended badly."

"Do you want to know what happened?" His tone shifts. I know that I'm in trouble. "I came home and couldn't look at her, couldn't touch her without shaking, and everything I said started a fight. I couldn't hold Daisy without crying, I couldn't even look Boone in the eyes without feeling like—" he stops, collecting himself.

I don't move a muscle. I've never seen him string together that many sentences and in such an honest way before. It's unnerving and overwhelming.

"I know why she resents me, and I don't hate her for it. She earned that right." He confirms, and something twists in my heart. His lack of self-awareness of how important he is to so many people is devastating. "I don't love her anymore," he assures me, misreading the look on my face, but I don't have it in me to stop him now that he's started. "Not like that. But she's the mother of my child, and I hate that no matter what I do, she still pushes back. I can't seem to make it right."

"Have you told her that?" I ask him, and it causes him to pause.

"She wouldn't want to hear it. Not now, it wouldn't mean anything." He seems sure of that, but from what I know about Riona, that doesn't sound like her. Riona took the shards of her broken heart and strung them into a suncatcher, the raw edges of her pain on display in the most beautiful way. Brighton's just confused because he's trying to put together the old pieces and keeps getting cut. I want to tell him to quit trying to destroy her art and instead admire it, but he wouldn't understand the analogy even if I tried.

"So fixing the past isn't how you make it right," I push.

"No." He admits.

"So what *are* you doing?" I question, and he paces away from me behind the bar, staring out the wide front windows that line the Hollow and give a view into the darkness of Harbor after midnight.

"Everything I can for Daisy," he says after a moment. "It's all for her." *Paving a future she can be proud of.*

I smile at him even if he can't see it. All the tension eases from between his shoulder blades, and when he turns to look at me over his shoulder, there's a lightness to those soft blue eyes I haven't seen all day.

"You're a good Dad, Brighton," I whisper. "Remember that." I know from experience what makes someone worthy of the title, and despite everyone constantly making him question that, he tries, and that's all that matters. I don't think Riona hates him. Even if he believes that's true, I think she *misses* him. And I don't blame her, because once I got past all the walls he built, there was a simple man behind them, just wandering around in the dark trying to find his way back. The heavy realization hits me that I'd miss him, too, if I lost him like that. In the most vicious, resentful way.

Brighton just doesn't understand that's the effect he has on people. He watches me, lips pressed into a tight line, his head nodding in agreement. The stretch of quiet that follows settles over us in a soft way, as if saying it out loud helped him release a little of the pent of rage he was feeling. I just hope I didn't push him too far.

"Are you almost done?" he asks after another beat, folding his arms over his chest.

"Yeah, why?" I relax a little, easing away the heavy conversation.

"Because after blurting out all the ways I fucked up my last relationship, I'd like to remind you how much I like *you*." He says it with the same straight, hardened expression he always has, but it makes my chest warm. "If that's alright with you?"

"It's hard to forget," I say, leaning over the school work on my elbows. *I've been walking funny for weeks.*

"Answer the question, Hellcat." He shifts in the tight Hollow t-shirt, and it stretches across his chest, giving away how nervous he really is to ask.

"Right here?" I raise an eyebrow.

"Seriously?" He stumbles.

"If I want you..." I push up from the stool, sliding onto the bar and swinging my legs around to face him again, "right here in the Hollow, right now..."

His jaw ticks.

"Will you give it to me?" I ask, *consider it testing my boundaries.*

"I need you to know that you ask for whatever you want, and if you really want it..." He steps forward, his eyes dropping to my thighs in the gym shorts I'm wearing. "Then yeah, I'll give it to you."

A chill runs down my spine.

"You have to ask," Brighton reminds me, separating my legs and stepping between them.

"Even with all those windows?" I question, not really believing that he'd go that far.

"Rhea," he groans softly. "Ask."

It's just us; his hands on my thighs are warm, and it's making it easy to be brazen. He leans across the bar, hitting the remote that controls the audio system, and music plays over us just loud enough to be heard. Submissive Brighton is a wild animal, and I can't help myself as my teeth sink into my bottom lip thinking about it.

"Will you show me, right here in the bar?" I finally ask him.

"I'll do anything you want if you keep looking at me like that, Hellcat." His eyes flicker between mine, and his thumbs trace the hem of my shirt.

"Help me out of these?" I ask, snapping the fabric of my shorts around my thigh.

He pulls off each sneaker first, setting them to the side and then the socks, tickling the bottom of my feet with his knuckles as he works. I watch him intently, sitting still as his fingers curl into the hem at my hips. I push up on my palms, lifting off the counter enough for him to roll them out from under me and down my thighs. He sinks to his knees as he pulls them down my calves.

Brighton's hands grip me firmly as he kneels before me. The position is submissive, his strong jaw lifted to meet mine in a heavy-lidded gaze filled with raw hunger and obedience. A muscle tightens in his cheek as he waits for my next command.

"You're overdressed, Killjoy." I poke his chest with my foot, and he raises an eyebrow before rolling the shirt up his chest and setting it with my shoes on the bar floor. When he returns to his position, he tucks his hands behind his back, and it forces the muscles in his shoulders and chest to ripple beneath the heavy ink of his tattoos.

His soft abs contract as he sits back on his heels. "How's that?"

"Flawless," I whisper.

My eyes scan the wall of windows as my heart races in my chest.

"Do you think anyone will walk by?" I ask him.

His focus is on my hips. "The windows are tinted. They can't see in unless they're right up against the glass." He spreads his knees wider on the floor, making his shoulders look even broader. He watches me intently, memorizing every small movement. "Do you like being watched, Rhea?"

"Only by you," I admit.

Brighton's eyes darken with that familiar possessive shade, but there's a tenderness there. It's clear he's antsy to touch, but he won't unless I ask him to. I lean back on my elbows, my eyes never leaving his. "Do you want to touch me, Brighton?"

"More than anything." His voice is husky as his eyes flicker across my body spread out on the bar. He swallows tightly before they meet my gaze again, "Can I?" His biceps flex as his hands itch for contact behind his back.

"Not yet," I tell him, enjoying the control for a little while longer. I let my head fall against my shoulder, just enough, but so I can still see his reaction as my hand finds a slow path down my stomach. I push the shirt I'm wearing up to expose the underwear beneath. Brighton inhales a sharp breath as my fingers work the fabric to the side carefully, slipping into a familiar rhythm I knew long before meeting him.

Brighton's eyes are glued to my hand as it moves between my legs. He watches with an intense focus, his chest rising and falling with restrained breath. A low, desperate whimper escapes him as he sees my fingers moving inside of me. The combination makes my body shudder, and I didn't realize until now just how much I enjoyed driving him insane.

His body vibrates, every muscle in his torso is tight as he holds himself back, waiting for permission to touch. Seeing him completely at a loss is exhilarating, and it only fuels the tingling feeling between my legs as I work a finger deep inside. A tiny gasp leaves my lips, and I watch as he rises off his heels, the reaction completely involuntary.

"Be patient," I huff, my eyes fluttering closed.

Brighton clenches, and I can see how hard he is beneath his jeans. He thrives on the feeling of being turned on and completely out of control. Seeing me touch myself while he's forced to watch is driving him to the brink.

"Please." The word slips from him, and after it does, his jaw clenches tightly.

"Please, what?" I tease, sinking another finger in and letting another moan slip from me.

Brighton groans loudly; the sound is painful and desperate.

"Either make me leave, Rhea, or let me touch you because I can't just fucking watch this." His hips shift forward in search of friction. "You're going to make me come in my pants like a teenager." His panic is loud, and it makes me smile.

"Oh?" I sit up a little further so I can really look at him. Every inch hardened in wait.

"I've never been so fucking hard in my life," he snaps. "And you won't even let me use my hands." It's not a whine that leaves him, but it's close. And it's hot.

"Prove it," I dare him, still paused in my efforts to drive him nuts. He spreads his knees wider, the expression on his face proving just how uncomfortably hard he is. He uses a hand to undo his jeans, shifting slightly to push them down enough to expose the grey boxers, darkened by him during the wait. "All for me?" I smile lazily.

"Only for you," he confirms darkly, his hips jerking slightly. "Put me out of my misery, Hellcat." He swallows, on the edge of begging, when his mouth parts again. "*Please?*"

"Alright." I pull my hand out, and before I can use it to steady myself, he's surging forward and capturing my wrist, sucking the fingers into his mouth.

His tongue swirls around them, releasing it with a wet pop, and immediately crashes his lips against mine in a rough, hungry kiss. He grabs my face roughly as he slips his tongue into my mouth. I can feel every inch of him against my thigh and groan against his mouth, needy and desperate in my own way.

"You turn me into an idiot," he laughs between kisses, the sound frustrated and amused all at once. He presses his hips forward deliberately, letting me feel how hard he is, and I help him push the boxers and jeans down over his ass to free him.

"All this power is going to my head." I bite down on his bottom lip and push my fingers into his hair, tugging gently.

"Let it." He breathes out a strained laugh that turns into a moan as I pull on his hair. He springs free, pressing urgently against my thigh. "Open up," he begs as his hand digs into my hip.

I help him line up with me, pulling my underwear out of the way and hooking my leg around his hip. The head of his cock catches against my entrance, and he stops talking completely, his eyes falling shut as he tries to hold back. He's so hard that it feels like he's ripping me open, and he hasn't even started.

I tug on his hair harder. "If this is you reminding me how much you like me, I'm disappointed," I tease.

"Rhea," he snaps, but there's no heat behind it. "I'm trying not to hurt you right now." He pressed forward slightly, just an inch into my wetness. "You're so tight and—" he pauses.

"A little pain never did anyone any harm," I whisper slowly.

That's all he needs to hear. With a dark groan, he snaps his hips forward, burying himself completely inside of me with one brutal thrust. A sound I've never heard before leaves my lips as my head falls back against the bar, and he starts to pick up his pace. He pants heavily, hands gripping my hips hard enough to bruise.

"Brighton," I cry. "That's so good, so, so good..." The back of the bar digs into my back, but my sole focus is on the aching pain between my legs as he rocks forward. The plea does nothing; he doesn't hold back. He fucks me like he's been starved of it. Every thrust is brutal and lifts me off the bar slightly as his teeth find my neck and collarbone.

"You can take it, baby," he praises, and just like that, the roles are reversed. He reaches between us, pressing his thumb against my clit as he continues in bursts.

"Brighton," I gasp this time, exposing my throat to him. He takes the silent direction, his hand snakes up my body, cupping it with ease. He doesn't squeeze, but he holds me in place as he fucks me on the bar top with reckless abandon. His lips find mine in a hungry kiss as I clench around him and try not to fall apart on him before he's ready.

"Rhea," he warns, "if you do that again..." his words are cut off as I squeeze around his shaft and urge him forward, locking my legs around him tighter. The feeling forces his eyes to roll into the back of his head and his thumb to pause its relentless circling.

"Don't you dare stop," I warn him, so fucking close I can feel the air being stolen from my lungs.

He smirks at the warning, knowing that he's won the game of tug of war and I'm completely at his mercy. With a final circle of my clit he starts to rock even harder, his hips slapping against mine as he pushes me through my orgasm.

"I want to feel it," he pants roughly. My body trembles uncontrollably under his touch, every inch of me on fire as he chases his own release.

I fall apart beneath him, and it's enough to push him over the edge completely. He watches my body writhe beneath him and feels me flutter around his length. He swallows hard, his Adam's apple bobbing roughly as he fights with himself. His hips spread me wider as he drives into me harder, making the glasses above the bar clink together loudly.

"That's it," I praise, and it does him in. He growls deeply, slamming into me one last time. His cock pulses and twitches as he fills me up, his release triggering a hot wave of pleasure through my body. Brighton huffs, completely out of breath as his thrusts slow and his kisses become apologies on my sweaty skin. "I definitely feel well adored..." I giggle.

"Good," he murmurs against my throat as he slips out from between me.

"Although I don't think I'll ever look at the bar the same," I tease as he collects himself. He turns with a lazy smile, his hair sticking to the back of his neck in sweaty, limp waves. "What?"

"Next time I'll show you the other useful things it can do." He adjusts himself in his jeans, shaking them up over his hips, and leans down to find my shorts for me. He says it with such nonchalance I almost don't catch the tone in his voice.

"Wait—" I lean forward, hiding the ache I feel between my legs. His eyes narrow at my expression. "Do you dream of bending me over things?" I tease.

"Every. Fucking. Day." Brighton shakes his head, the euphoria gone and replaced with his routine casual annoyance for me.

"Is this really a smart idea?" Sunday helps me push some of the tables together downstairs. We were closing the Hollow for the evening for a private event. One that should be the funeral of Cael Cody and Silas Shore—my two least-favorite people in Harbor.

"It'll be fine, and Daisy is excited." I push until the table clicks together and stand back. "Boone is making some extravagant French five-course meal to impress Ri, and Rhea is upstairs helping Daisy do her hair." I groan.

"You're a good Dad," she says to me, wiping her hands on her jeans as she moves around the table to start setting it.

"I'm a tolerant Dad," I correct her, and she laughs.

"You were always a good Dad," she argues, her eyes meeting mine.

Yeah, I know, Sunny. She's pointing out the fact that I've been doing this longer than just Daisy—and with much higher stakes. I look away from her because she's burning a hole in my heart with her glare.

"Auggie is a really sweet kid, and this means a lot to Daisy." She continues to talk as she moves around the table.

"I keep forgetting that he's met everyone else at this fucking party," I grumble and hand her cups as she goes.

"That's why he hasn't met you," Sunday groans. "Curb the attitude."

"There's no attitude," I sigh as the kitchen door clangs open and Boone starts excitedly yelling around. "They're here..." I swallow tightly and shift around in my shirt uncomfortably. It's going to take every ounce of patience I have to get through this dinner.

"You're a better man than anyone in Harbor," Sunday stares at me like she can hear me panicking. "Just be yourself."

"That's the problem, isn't it?" I joke, and she shakes her head, wandering past me.

I follow her into the kitchen, and Boone already has a little redhead with a spoon between her lips, tasting the food he's making. Silas Shore stands rigid with his hand in his pocket and his eyes on the girl.

There's not a man in Harbor that gets under my skin quite as easily as him. At first it was nothing, he was simply someone who helped Riona relax. I might be a little more possessive now but if Riona wanted it, she got it. And back then she wanted Silas. So I swallowed the venom and made them comfortable. But he changed something in her, rewired a part of her I couldn't untangle and I resent him for it. Vocally. And as often as I can.

Cael, Riona's nephew, brought his girlfriend—Clementine, I think—and she's already causing trouble. Kaia is in tow, all three are getting scolded by Riona, who wears the most unfamiliar smile I've ever seen on her face.

The most surprising addition to the evening is Ryan. I haven't seen him in a while, and he looks old but still as grouchy and as sharp as ever. *Great, this night just went down the drain.*

"I'll go get Daisy," I announce, but Sunday stops me with a glare.

"I'll go, *behave*." She warns before disappearing up the stairs.

"Brighton," Silas nods, and Riona turns her head.

"Silas," I give him a tight smile and then toss Riona a dirty look with a smile on my face. "Riona."

"It smells wonderful in here, Boone," she says to him instead of acknowledging me. She's still pissed off about the way things were handled with Daisy and Ricky's kid, but that's life. She's likely more upset that it was out of her control.

"It's Boeuf Bourguignon," he tells her, bringing her over.

I point to the redhead, and Silas inhales slowly, "Drew, this is Brighton Black, Daisy's father and Riona's ex." *That makes two of us, you spineless shit.*

It's like a bad joke. What do you get when your ex-wife, her ex-boytoy, his current wife walk into a bar?

"Oh." Drew sidesteps Riona in her sundress and holds out her tiny hand to me to shake. "It's nice to finally meet you. They all act like you're scary. I even got a rundown of things not to bring up, but you look harmless to me."

I grind my teeth together and force a polite smile to my face.

"Give him ten minutes, Drew." Riona snaps.

"An hour, minimum," I correct her jab, and Drew starts to laugh.

"I see why you two got along..." she jokes.

"Like oil and water," I grumble as Auggie wanders in the back door and Daisy enters from the kitchen. I clear my throat and step aside as Rhea comes in behind her with Sunday on her tail. Daisy's hair is curled around the ends, and I'm pretty sure she's wearing mascara. I turn with the intention of saying something to Rhea, but she's smiling across the kitchen at them as they nervously say hi, and I realize the truth in what she said. *Daisy isn't just yours.* I look around the kitchen and swallow my discomfort when I see how everyone is here for her, for them. *I was the problem.*

Auggie didn't want to meet *me.*

I flex my hands to rid them of the shake, but it does nothing, so I go to tuck them in my jeans, but Rhea pushes her hand into mine and squeezes.

"Breathe," she whispers, "look at that smile."

I follow her eye line to Daisy, who's dragging Auggie across the kitchen to show him the ridiculous dessert that Boone made for after dinner. I can do this. For her.

We all find our seats, and I'm instantly tested when Kaia sits across from Cael, who's purposely trying to start shit to see me explode. Ryan grabs the bun that's being tossed back and forth, giving them both a look that makes them stop.

"How's the season?" I ask Ryan because the tension that floats over the table is violent.

"A lot of rookies, a lot of mistakes." He takes the platter from his sister and spoons himself some food before handing it to me. "How's... this?"

I scoff. "Fine. It pays the bills."

"Listening to you two talk is like two robots trying to learn human emotions," Kaia jabs, and Cael starts losing it laughing.

"At least they aren't choking each other out," he snorts. "Remember Daze's second birthday?" Cael asks, and Riona looks like she's ready to commit murder.

"Don't start," Ryan snaps, and Cael shrugs.

"That sounds like a fun story," Clementine says, and Cael nods.

I remember it like it was yesterday. It's when I proposed to her. They had all made the trip to Harbor for the occasion, and it ended up with Ryan in lockup.

I swear, Riona married me just to piss him off.

"This is delicious, Boone," Drew speaks up to cut the tension. She's a sweet woman, a little quiet, and nothing like I expected Silas to marry. I guess once you've had your fill of a woman like Riona, you actively seek out the opposite. I turn to check on Rhea, who's listening to all the conversations intently but not really saying much. Her brown eyes watch every interaction with caution as it goes around the conversation and lands on Boone.

"What do you think, Aug?" he asks the kid, but he's too busy whispering something to Daisy. Rhea's hand finds my thigh under the table, and I look over at her to calm down the vicious urge to start shit with everyone at the table except her.

"It's great, I could use more salt," Auggie finally responds, and Boone just laughs at him.

"I like that kid," he nods. "Honesty is a good trait to have."

"It's true, the world has enough liars." Riona's words are venom.

I'll love you until the day we die, Bright. What's mine is yours. For always.

Only it wasn't true. Not for her.

But I died the day I stepped foot on home soil, alone...

"How long have you all known each other?" Drew asks, looking between Riona and me.

"College," Riona answers dryly. "There was a time way back when Silas was quite the party animal."

"You?" Drew laughs, and Silas just shakes his head of greying hair at her.

"They're lying. If anyone was a party animal, it was Bright," Silas jabs.

"Once upon a time." I clip and stare him down.

"You were in the military?" She asks next, and the table goes still.

"Yeah. Medical," I say.

"So like Silas?" She asks, she's so polite, and every question is pointed without her even knowing. I keep my eyes locked on Silas, ignoring how hot I feel inside and how little room I start to feel.

"A little more dangerous." I offer her a tight smile.

"I'd say so," Clementine hums.

"Auggie," Rhea calls out to the other end of the table, and he looks up from his food to her, "tell them what you're doing for your art project."

He starts to explain begrudgingly after being put on the spot, but I'm grateful to Rhea for ending the conversation about me. I was starting to run out of air. Daisy looks over at me, and for a second, her grateful smile calms me down, but I can feel Riona's glare, and I can hear every single piece of criticism that will come down on my head later for being rude to Drew.

"We should do more of those rugby games," Cael suggests to Kaia, who's picking the olives off Boone's plate as he talks to Silas.

"The Hogs are cowards, you'll never get them to do that again," Kaia groans, and Sunday laughs at the scowl on my face.

"Aw, come on," Daisy chimes in, "I wasn't invited last time!"

"Yeah, me either," Clementine adds.

"It was too late for you to come," I say to Daisy.

"Yeah, but I want to watch Auntie K, kick Uncle B's ass," Daisy swears, and Riona chokes on her wine.

"Daze!" Boone makes a motion for her to stop, an amused smile on his face.

"It was pretty entertaining, and the Hillcat burger sells more than the Boone Burger ever did." Kaia hums.

"You have a burger named after you?" Ryan questions gruffly.

"He *did*," Kaia snorts. "Past tense."

The conversation seems to be flowing back to a more comfortable place, and I think I'm doing okay until Sunday accidentally drops her fork, and Riona shoves her chair back to reach for it. The two sharp sounds hit at once, pulsing through me like electricity. I push from the table and excuse myself to wander out to the back parking lot for a moment of air that I wasn't going to get sitting at that table. *Enemies. Those people are there to mock you.*

"What are you doing?" Riona's voice is a gunshot. I flinch at the sound, refusing to turn my head to look at her.

"Behaving." I repeat back Sunday's word.

"By storming off?" She questions. "Mature."

"It's better than strangling Silas at the dinner table," I say, my lip curling up in amusement when a soft chuckle falls from her.

"You'll traumatize the new wife," Riona teases.

"What you don't get along?" I ask.

"She's a mouse." The insult almost makes me laugh.

"Not everyone can be a predator, Ri." I finally look at her and she's staring up at the night sky, no doubt looking for the stars but the lights are too bright. "She'd love this."

"She would not," Riona's voice is strangled but the laughter that pours from her is warm and bright.

"She loved the chaos more than anyone, it's where that little fucker gets it from." I sigh. Cael's mother, Daisy's aunt Lorraine was special. I square my shoulders to keep myself together as Riona wraps her arms around herself in thought.

"You don't have to feel guilty anymore, you know?" She says, her body turning back into the Hollow.

"For what?" I ask. There's too much to feel guilt for, even if I wanted to I wouldn't be able to pin down the exact reason for her statement.

"For everything," she says. "I know I give you a hard time, but if I don't, who will?" She teases gently.

I open my mouth to respond but she slips back inside and I'd be lying if I said that it didn't rattle me a little. I stare down at the shakiness of my hands and hiss at how pathetic it feels. *"You walk yourself in a circle long enough, Bright, you'll start tripping over your own steps."* Sarge's voice plays in my head, mocking me.

"Dad?" Daisy snaps me from the moment of weakness, and I turn to see her standing in the door.

"What's up, Squish?" I put on a brave face, one that doesn't give away how uncomfortable I am with all of this.

"Are you alright?" she asks.

"Yeah," I smile. "Just ate too much. Needed a hit of fresh air," I lie.

"Thanks for doing this today. Auggie's having lots of fun." She smiles at me, and I stuff down everything to keep it on her face. "Do you think you can take us bowling next week?"

"Just the three of us?" I ask her, and she nods.

"Deal." I nod. "Let's go eat the dessert before Uncle B can serve it."

"Are you sure?" The smile on her face grows. "Very rebellious, Dad."

"Yeah, yeah, hurry before we get caught." I shoo her inside.

Brighton

It's five in the morning when my phone starts ringing on the table beside my head. The screen light illuminates everything, including Rhea's sleepy face as she rolls away from me and curls into a ball like a cat on the other side of the bed.

I reach for my phone and bring it to my ear, closing my eyes as I answer. "Hello?" I groan.

"Hey," José sounds far away and loud all at once. "Sorry, I waited as long as I could to call."

"What's going on, Garza?" I sit up in bed. We hadn't gotten to sleep until three, and I can still feel the exhaustion that lingers in my muscles.

One of our group rules is that if your phone rings, you answer it. When it comes to PTSD, there is no control. There's no telling when it will show up to destroy your life, and even if I don't talk about mine in group, I'll always answer the phone.

"Man, I hate to be the one making this phone call."

Someone is dead.

"Terell is gone," he says.

My throat gets tight at the mention of him. Harvey Terell. An old guy who retired way too late, because when he finally did, he had nothing but the military left. His wife was long gone, and his kids hated him. The army was his family.

"How?" I clear my throat, and Rhea stretches awake beside me, her eyes still sleepy as she stares up at me in bed.

"I don't know, I can't get any information out of anyone. It's buttoned up tight," José sounds exhausted and frankly pretty heartbroken. *He was a dad to all of us, man, I get it. This sucks.*

"I'll get dressed. Have you called Sarge? The guys might need a meeting," I say, just trying to keep myself calm for José.

"Yeah, he said to call you." He huffs.

"I have Terell's funeral directives somewhere. I'll dig them out and bring them down to the church. Keep trying to figure out what happened," I order. *It's going to matter.* Unfortunately, in our line of work, open caskets weren't usually possible.

"You gonna be alright?" He asks me before I hang up the phone.

"Call Leon, and get him to call Robert," I tell him, "they'll wanna know."

"Done," José confirms. "Sorry for waking you up with this."

"That's what the phone is for, man, don't be sorry. Go call the guys," I say, and hang up this time before he can say anything else to me.

"Are you okay?" She asks. I hear it, but my chest hurts so much I can't form the words to tell her I am. That I have to be. I flip the blankets back off my legs and try to get up *I need to get dressed,* I think. One foot in front of the other.

I don't get far. My legs feel like Jell-O, and my hands tangle into the sheets as my body gives way to the news. *Get up, you have shit to do.* I push off my feet, straightening my shaking legs. I feel Rhea reach for me, but I move to the dresser while she sits up on her knees and watches me move around in the dark.

"Brighton?" Her voice is like a siren song, *Come back to bed, be sad here with me.* I rub the tear that escapes me with the back of my hand and yank on the drawer so hard it snaps on its hinges. I pull out the massive lockbox, setting it on the top of the dresser, and pop it open.

My jaw grinds at the sight of my dog tags, the old ones, the ones that were replaced with what I wear now. Clean and not stained with my mistakes... but I push them aside for the envelope with my name on it. I take it out with my shaky hands, set it on the dresser, and start to find clean clothes. *You need to get your dress blues pressed.* I stare at the dark closet thinking about the last time I wore them, and a shudder runs through my body.

They reek of death.

Fuck.

I can hear her shuffle on the bed, and when I look back to the mattress, she's gone. But I can't be worried about whatever the hell she's doing. I pull on a clean pair of jeans and dig through my dresser without care for a shirt.

I stuff the envelope in my back pocket without opening it, and my phone starts to vibrate again. *Shit.*

"Hello?" I answer.

"Major," Landon says. He sounds just as exhausted as José did.

"You're a coward for making him break the news to me." I snap at him.

"We all have our faults, Bright," he says, moving around in the background.

"He killed himself, didn't he?" I ask, knowing that Landon is the only one who will be honest with me.

"Found out last week that Laura's getting remarried," he says. "The claws of despair are rough, kid."

"You should have told me; I could have talked to him," I say, not angry with Landon, but at the situation as a whole.

"Yeah, because you're so forthcoming in a conversation." He jokes, and I don't laugh.

"I could have done something, made him feel not so alone," I argue.

"We're all alone, kid. That's life," he sounds different, like his years of therapy are chipping away. *He's sad, too, you asshole. Harvey was his friend.* "He didn't want to talk, Bright. He wanted to die, honor that." It comes off Landon's mouth as an order, and my body tightens subconsciously.

"I'm sick of honoring rules made to kill us," I grumble, and the line goes quiet for a minute. "I have his funeral stuff, I'll bring it by the church in an hour. I have to stop at the dry cleaner."

"You know better than to let your blues get dusty, Major," he scolds with a light tone.

"We're lucky I didn't burn them after the last time," I say, my jaw tightening.

November

A few weeks after medical discharge

Six coffins. *There should be seven.*

My bones cried out to join them, six feet under.

Soon.

I've been shaking hands for the last two hours, completely checked out from my surroundings with the eerie feeling of being watched. *You are being watched.* The crutch under my arm burns my skin, and the collar of my dress clothes eats into my throat, desperate to strangle me. *Let it.*

I didn't deserve to be standing here with these people.

Their families.

Grant, Noah, John, Wyatt, Penn, and Bennet shouldn't be dead.

I shouldn't be alive.

I can't breathe.

The lack of oxygen makes my eyes water, but I keep shaking hands, cold touch after cold touch, telling me that I'm lucky, I'm alive, I should buy a lottery ticket.

I bought a gun instead.

An older man stands in front of me, his eyes cold and tight. "Mr. Henry." Wyatt's father. "I'm sorry for your loss." I choke out.

"Go home to your daughter, Major." There's a venom in his voice, a resentment that I deserve to shoulder. *There should be seven.* The sentence echoes in the back of my head. "Hold her tight." *Daisy.*

A child cries nearby, and I turn my head to see Noah Wales' wife... *widow*, trying to calm down their toddler. He looks so much like Noah, it makes me sick to my stomach. I need out of here. I can't do this.

I move on hobbled steps, my ankle screaming at me to slow down, but the walls are closing in on me, and there's nothing I can do to stop them. I push out of the church doors, and the air hits me like a ton of bricks, but it does nothing. The vomit rises faster than I can stop it, and the nearby bushes that line the steps fall victim to what little food is in my stomach. Pure acid rolls up my throat over and over until I'm dry heaving and nothing but spit is spilling from my lips.

I use the planter to steady myself as I inhale slowly, trying to get air into my lungs that doesn't feel like ice.

"Here." I turn my crutch on the voice, ready to hit him, and he steps back, the cloth in his hand still extended out. "Careful with that," he says, and I lower the steel back beneath my armpit. He stares at me with the most intense green eyes I've ever seen on a person, and he's on guard, unsure of what I might do. "It's just a napkin, kid."

"Thanks," I grunt, taking it from him and wiping the spit from under my lip. "Sorry about your bushes."

"I'm sure they've seen their fair share of puke," he says, shoving his hands into his pockets. He's dressed in casual jeans and a t-shirt, his graying hair pushed back off his face. *He's out of place.*

"Sorry, I didn't catch your name," I say to him.

"Sergeant Landon Gaboury," he nods. "And you're Major Brighton Black," he says before I can introduce myself. "I'm part of the military's effort to help soldiers acclimate after traumatic events."

"They sent a shrink to the funeral?" I bark out a hollow laugh.

"I'm not a therapist, I'm a veteran." He shakes his head at me and digs in his pocket before holding out a business card. "I offer group sessions in this very church for guys like you, *guys like me.*" He adds.

"Yeah? You ever watch your best friends be gunned down like fish in a barrel by a bunch of kids?" I snapped at him. He flinches. *One by one. Your hands are covered in their blood. You should have saved them.* "I didn't think so."

He watches me for a few more seconds, studying my anger, and I hate it. I feel like an animal in a cage, and there's nothing I can do about it.

What are you going to do? Fight some old man with one good ankle? Tough guy.

"Take the card, kid," he says, not breaking eye contact. I put my fingers around it, but he doesn't let go right away. "My number is on there. Before you kill yourself tonight, call me. I'll tell you a story."

Fuck you.

He lets go of the card, and I look down to inspect it.

"I don't need a bedtime story," I say, looking back up, but the church door slams closed, and I realize I'm alone again.

Brighton storms into the kitchen while I'm running my fingers through my hair, socks clenched between my teeth, halfway through pulling on tights and a sweatshirt.

"Go back to bed," he says in a tone I don't recognize—and don't like. He grabs his keys and shoves his feet into a pair of boots, clumsy and frantic.

"No." I slip my socks on and then a pair of sneakers. "Wherever you're going, you need a friend," I snap, and he stares at me for a long, tense moment. For a second, I think he might argue further, but he pops open the front door and waits for me to lead him out.

The truck ride is silent. Neither of us says a word. I don't even bother to put on music. Brighton pulls the truck into a dark, empty parking lot of a massive church I've never seen before and shuts off the engine.

"Someone very important to me took his life last night." He says. "I have to go inside and deal with a bunch of questions, and I don't have answers for them."

His jaw tightens uncomfortably, and it's pretty clear that he's trying to keep himself together. Whether it's for me or for himself, I don't know, but either way, I hate it.

"Okay, give me the keys," I say. "You're all going to want coffee."

He stares at me for a moment and hands the keys over.

"I'll be right back." I offer, watching him climb from the truck and wander off into the darkness, waiting until light spills from the church door as he steps inside before I climb over the console and start the engine.

It's not uncommon for men like Brighton to get too familiar with death. More often than not, they spent their time at funerals because if active duty didn't kill them, home soil sometimes finished the job, but I knew the sound of a man who meant it when he said he wanted to die.

I'd still be able to tell his footsteps just from the sound.

I inhale slowly and pull out of the parking lot to find the closest coffee shop. I have zero information about who will be there, so I grab whatever I can and hope it's enough. I linger outside a liquor store, debating if they'd also want that, but I've never seen Brighton drink and would feel weird about bringing it into a church. When I pull into the lot, José swings in from the opposite side and brings his jeep up beside me.

"Need some help?" He asks, hopping from his seat and grabbing the bag I'm balancing on top of the donut box. He looks exhausted, and his shirt is buttoned wrong, crooked all the way up.

"Thanks." I shoulder the rest, grab the two boxes of coffee, and let José close the door behind me as we start inside.

"Where's Bright?"

"Inside," I say, not having anything else to offer him. He eyes me for a second, shifting his grip on the bag he's carrying to open the church door.

"Don't take it personally," he says after a minute. "Brighton doesn't even talk in groups."

"He doesn't?" I question as he leads me over to a table.

"Never." José shakes his head. "I know he's one of the best guys to be stationed with, and I know that he did everything he could to save those boys in his squad." He mentions, and I tense.

His squad?

"He never talks about them," I push, just to see if I can learn something new that might help him through whatever grief he was about to tackle.

"They call them 'The Six, '" he says while he helps me set out the food and cups. "It was a tragedy, really. Bad ops had them marching through a town they shouldn't have been in. Child Soldiers."

"It was kids?" I do everything I can to keep my face neutral.

"Ambushed them in an alley, killed everyone. Brighton had stopped to help some old lady on the side of the road, and by the time he found them, three were dead, and the other three bled out. Brighton kept them going for twelve hours until evac came, but it was too late." José explains. "I couldn't imagine the guilt he feels, but there was nothing he could do. If he weren't so damn kind, he would have never helped her and would have walked into the same ambush. I think that's why he doesn't talk about it, because he still thinks it's his fault they're gone. Like he wasn't enough, so he doesn't get to share their stories."

"He's punishing himself," I whisper, and José nods. "He just doesn't talk to anyone?"

"Maybe, Sarge, but never in front—" he trails off as the door opens and more guys file in.

"Hey," Brighton calls from the other end of the room. He looks so tired and sad. "In here."

They all follow the sound of his voice and leave me alone with the story of Brighton's past, haunting me. I sit on a bench and open my phone. The Six. I type it into the search bar and a few articles from 2017 pop up in the results. He had been twenty-five when it happened. I clench my jaw and scroll through the article. There's a lot of information I don't understand, and even more that breaks my heart. Most of them were dads with young kids, just like Brighton. My nose stings as I try to keep the tears at bay, but when I see the photo of them together, smiling with their arms around each other, I break.

Major Brighton Black's efforts will not go unnoticed. The twenty-five-year-old combat medic lasted twelve hours bouncing between the bodies of his remaining squad members, doing whatever he could to bring them home alive.

The photo below rewires how I see him.

He's being escorted off a plane in some desert location following what looks like six gurneys, his gear soaked and stained in blood around the knees and torso. My stomach churns. *"Is there a reason there's six?" I had asked him about those daisies.* For twelve hours, he had knelt in the blood of his friends. I set the phone down and wipe my tears on the back of my sweater sleeve with shaky hands.

I inhale, taking a walk to clear my head. I couldn't let the information eat at me, not because it shouldn't, but because Brighton needed me to be the strong one for the two of us. Even if he doesn't want me to be. I busy my hands and brain, finish setting up the food and wander closer to the door where most of them disappeared through to listen to the plans, but I only hear José and Brighton arguing.

"What do you mean he's not coming?" Brighton snaps.

"I called him on the way over here to see if he wanted a ride, and he told me that he couldn't make it," José explains.

"This isn't optional." Brighton's voice is exhausted and strained. "He was one of Harvey's best friends. I shouldn't even be holding this!" Something gets thrown across the room, a chair maybe, and a loud sigh leaves José, "I'm sorry."

"Annie said she'll handle the food, and Leon's girl can help set up a group to contact anyone who might wanna come to the funeral. Let us handle it. I know this is hard."

"It's not hard, it's bullshit." He swears before stomping away.

I tried to convince Brighton that working is a terrible idea, but he storms around the Hollow like a black cloud. There's so much electricity coursing beneath his skin that he's ready to blow at any second.

"Is he alright?" Boone asks, tossing me a look as he gives a nearby table their food.

"One of his military friends committed suicide." I swallow tightly.

"Why the hell is he working?" Boone asks, crossing his arms over his chest. It's moments like this that it's clear they're twins. They share the same scowl, but Boone uses it so sparingly that it can be easy to forget they are.

"I begged him to go back to bed, but he refused. Said he had too much to do today," I say.

"I'll keep my eye on him, see if I can use some Jedi mind trick..." He nudges me, and I give him a pathetic smile in return. I do my rounds, keeping an eye on some rowdy people at the back of the Hollow, and end up at the table where Kaia is sitting with guys from her station.

"He's still crying about that!" Lee says, leaning on Kaia. "He had to take his truck to Lorette to get them to service it."

"I hope he transfers out of our district. He's such a pussy," Kaia shakes her head and pounds back a shot of tequila.

"He didn't deserve an angel like Rhea anyway," Lee flirts. I try to ignore him.

"Shut up, Ramos, you're too much of a coward to ask her out. It's the only reason she ended up on a date with that chode." One of the other guys teases. Lee Ramos is handsome, all dark hair and tawny skin with sharp green eyes and a smile that makes women weak in the knees. But he's goofy and a player. Even if he had, I would have told him to fuck off.

"Rhea." He pushes up out of the booth and leans against the wall next to me as I try to watch the crowd for trouble. "What do you say?" He's trying to be cute, but he's yelling over the music, and my interest is in the way Brighton watches like a hawk.

"Lee, sit down before you get put through a wall," Kaia warns, but he doesn't listen.

"Oh, come on, Rhea, just one date. I'll show you how a real man treats a woman," he inches closer, but I don't dare take my eyes off Brighton. He's gone completely still—like a predator.

"This idiot is being stalked like a field mouse, and he has no idea," Kaia barks out a string of laughter.

"What the hell are you talking about?" He scoffs and makes the mistake of touching my arm. I blink, a groan leaving my lips, and when I open them, Brighton is gone. *Shit.*

"Flirting with Reaper is a death wish," Kaia stands up and backs away from the table. I know what she's doing because I'm doing the same thing.

"Is that supposed to be cryptic, Keegan?" Lee laughs.

"Nope, that's a literal problem you're about to have," she whips her head around and spots Boone before I do. She cups her hands over her face, and at the same time as she yells his name, Brighton comes out of the crowd, and without warning, sucker punches Lee in the side of the face. Lee crumbles to the ground, and I try to lay hands on Brighton, but he's got blinders on and drives a boot into his side.

"He was just flirting, he's drunk!" I say loudly, hoping it gets him to stop.

Boone is moving towards us as fast as he can, but the crowd is becoming tight around the commotion, and Brighton is already hauling Lee up by the collar, completely unfazed by the amount of eyes on him.

"Let him go, it was innocent, he wasn't getting anywhere with it!" I do my best to get between them, but Brighton turns his back on me walking Lee backwards through the sea of bodies toward the front door. "Brighton!" I yell, chasing after them as Lee's boots scrape clumsily across the floor.

"Shit!" Boone flies out of the crowd from the left and manages to duck beneath his brother's arm, successfully placing himself between them. "Let go of him, Bri. You know you're not angry at this little weasel. You're just tired, man," he urges him to listen. "Brighton!" He snaps when the calm technique doesn't work. "Cut it out!" Something about the phrase makes him stop, and his grip loosens on Lee.

"You out," Kaia moves fast, cutting Lee off before he can say anything idiotic that might relight the fire that's been put out. "Now, come on, move your stupid ass."

Boone works Brighton back and gets him into the kitchen away from everyone's gaze as Judd screams over the sound of whispers and music that everyone gets a free round.

What the actual fuck just happened?

Brighton

I don't know how or when Boone got me upstairs, but I'm sitting on my bedroom floor against the wall, and he's standing in the doorway wearing his best scary look.

"What the hell was that?" He asks.

"I saw red," I say, using the palms of my hand to clear my vision.

"You don't get to do that—not here," Boone sighs. "We need the Hollow, Bri. And if you start swinging on every guy that hits on our bouncer, we're going to get shut down."

"My—" I start to argue. *She's mine.* I don't know how to explain to him that Rhea fixes something that I thought was irreparable. "Just because she's the bouncer doesn't mean she has to put up with harassment."

"Oh fuck off, that wasn't harassment, and you know it. You saw your girlfriend getting hit on and went full asshole because you're in a bad mood." Boone says. It's rare he speaks to me like this, because he walks on eggshells to keep things like tonight from happening. The guilt eats at me, knowing that I'm a burden to them even when I think I'm doing good. PTSD doesn't warn you before it destroys your life—it just does.

"I wouldn't call a friend dying a bad mood, Boone." I scowl.

"You've been in a knot for weeks, this was just the catalyst," he says, "she told Sunday that you've been sleepwalking again."

"Fuck—"

"Yeah, how often?" He asks.

"Once a week, maybe," I snap. "Less when she's home," I admit, and Boone nods.

"Okay," he sinks to his heels in a squat and stares at me. "So tonight?"

"Lucid—but he touched her, and..." *I flipped out like an animal.* The anger had been building since this morning, and I knew eventually it would snap. I just didn't think it would look like this. "Is she mad?" I ask quietly.

"She's fine, working the bar with Kaia." He shrugs it off. "Can I trust you to be alone with her?"

"Wow," I scoff.

"It's a legitimate question, Bri, if you're not in control..."

I'd never lay a hand on her.

"We'll be fine."

"Not what I asked," he retorts.

"You can trust me," I sighed.

"You aren't alone." He stands and taps the door frame. "I just wish you'd figure that out because it's getting exhausting banging on closed doors, Bri."

"Try living behind them." I drop my head between my knees as he disappears, I don't breathe properly again until I hear the front door open and close. I don't know how much time passes before I open my eyes again, but I hear the bathroom door shut, and I know Rhea has finished closing up downstairs. I check my watch, and it flashes two am in my face like it's laughing at me. She could have come upstairs at any point to talk, *but she didn't because you're an idiot.*

I push off the carpet, stripping from the Hollow t-shirt and tossing it on the floor. It's only then that I look around and see the mess I made this morning. Everything is tossed about and misplaced. I start cleaning my mess, piece by piece, until the room is back in order and I can breathe again.

Just go talk to her, coward.

What if that was the straw? What if that aggression drives her out of reach? I only knew what she wanted me to know about her dad, but I know he was rough on her. On all of them. And tonight I proved that that monster resides somewhere in me. *She's probably terrified of you.*

I pull on a hoodie and walk down the hall, hesitating before I knock on the bathroom door. The water isn't running, and I know she's behind it, but she doesn't answer.

"Hellcat…" I try her nickname first, trying to sound gentle instead of guilty. *I'm a hot head, I know. Just don't ignore me.* "Hey." I knock again and wait. "I shouldn't have done that tonight. Can you just… open the door?" I ask, wrapping my hand around the knob with the intention to go inside anyway. If she wouldn't come to me, I'd make her to look me in the eye and tell me that she's done.

But it's locked.

I breathe in, trying it again.

Still locked.

"Rhea." I press my head against the wooden door and try it again, but it doesn't budge under my advances. I knock again, only to be met with more silence. "Don't do this," the plea is quiet. There's nothing to stop the panic that surges up through me, and any other day, I might be able to curb it, but I'm walking on a tight rope with little to no balance left.

I'm not mentally equipped to deal with a locked door today.

"Rhea," I say again, louder this time, and bang on the door with my hand. It heaves under the weight but doesn't open, and she's still silent on the other side. My hand shakes against the door, and I try to focus on the sound behind it as my memories flicker dangerously around in my mind. It's like a wall is breaking and every single suffocating memory is seeping back into my consciousness with remorse. I can feel the tub overflowing and drenching the carpet under my feet, and I can smell the blood on my skin weeks after returning home. My whole body tenses.

Sunday would have taken your place as the seventh.

I bang again.

"Rhea, come on! Open the door, please." My voice cracks, but it doesn't budge.

You would have let that happen because you weren't strong enough.

I hit the door with my shoulder before a rational thought can form.

And you aren't strong enough now.

You can't even get to her through a door. What if she's in actual danger?

My friends are dying, my daughter avoids me, my brother doesn't trust me, and Rhea is afraid of me. The gunshots ring out, and I can't seem to get to them; every memory I run through is dark and endless. *You'll never get to them in time.* To her.

Bang.

Bang.

Bang.

Bang.

Bang.

Bang.

"Whoa!" The bathroom door whips open, and Brighton stands there with glazed eyes. I pull off my headphones and set them slowly on the counter. "Brighton?" I stare at him, not daring to move an inch because he's not focusing on anything.

His breathing is ragged—chest heaving like he can't catch it. The door is split at the top, wood splintered in a jagged crack down the center, and his hands are bloodied, no doubt from hitting it.

"Hey," I say, putting my hands up. "Hey," I whisper, stepping forward.

I've never seen him so far gone, but it's not scary, it's heartbreaking. The tears are pouring from him like he can't stop them, and his entire body is shaking violently. I move toward him, each step more terrifying than the last. I have no idea what he'll do. This isn't sleepwalking.

He's awake—just not here.

My phone is in my back pocket.

Call Boone.

My brain screams at me, but every muscle in my body tells me differently, *Don't do that.* I step forward, and Brighton doesn't move. His hair is damp around his collar, and it's so clear he's in distress, but I don't know how to help him out of this. It's not the same.

"Help me out here, Brighton." I chew on my lip and step forward again. His hand swings out. I step back just in time—close enough to feel the air of it, but it shakes me. Worse, it puts us off balance, and I'm still cornered in the bathroom. His foot jitters. He's counting himself down—seven taps, a long pause, then again.

I tried to remember all the conversations I had in therapy, every time my therapist told me that it wasn't my problem to solve. That my father's trauma was his own. All I can do is prepare, watch for the signs, understand the trauma, and be aware.

The Six. *Brighton was the only survivor.* It should have been seven.

Ever since he took that call this morning, he's been bent, different. He hasn't been himself. And he isn't now. Something along the way triggered this.

Nausea hits hard. Gun oil and freshly cut grass flood my nose, and suddenly I'm not here anymore. Stuck rewatching my worst nightmare happening just out of reach.

"Control your movements. Inhale before you take the shot." Dad sits at the shabby picnic table in the backyard while Reid swings his hockey stick, sending pucks flying one after another. They hit the back of the net with delicate swoosh sounds as Dad pulled apart his shotgun.

"Like that?" Reid asks, barely big enough for the stick he was bought, and Dad nods with pride. It's a good day. But I know what happens next, I've watched it play out a million times. Reid pulls back, and instead of the puck hitting the net, it smashes hard against the shed, and Dad's on his feet.

He stomps across the grass toward him, and before Reid understands that it's not Dad anymore, he's in the grass beneath him, gasping for breath. He claws at the ground as Dad screams about the enemy. "Run, Rhea!" he yells at me, and my body seizes. Reid is turning blue, his green eyes so vibrant before they lose their light for good.

Do something, Rhea. Do something! Protect yourself!

Bang.

It might be a mistake—but it feels good. *You aren't small anymore, Rhea, you made sure of that. You never have to be small again.*

I step forward, using both hands, and shove him as hard as I can.

"Wake up, Brighton!" I scream, shoving him again—again—until he gives ground. "Wake the fuck up!" I yell, over and over until we're pushed so far back that I'm free of the tiny bathroom and have room to breathe. Once the crying starts, it doesn't stop. I can't control it. I don't want to do it, but it starts. I push on his chest again, harder this time.

"You know where you are," I whisper, tears streaming. I don't shove that time, I wrap my arms around him. I squeeze tightly, trying to slow down his breathing enough for him to regulate his mind. "Please, Brighton," I beg. "Come back."

I sound pathetic, I can hear the whine in my voice, but trying to convince myself that he's okay is getting harder and harder. The barriers between him and what happened all those years ago start to break down.

"Please." I press my face against his chest and feel his legs give out as he buries his face into my hair, and we collapse to the living-room floor in a tangle of limbs and breath. His hands wrap around me tightly, and he pulls me as close as I can get.

I can hear him repeating himself over and over, his voice hoarse and muffled against my head, and his fingers dig into my skin like he's trying to ground himself. I inhale, finding whatever courage I have left, and pull back from his chest.

Seeing him like this, so small and broken. I feel the second my heart shatters like glass.

He reaches up with a hand and stops, his eyes widening on the blood, and he freezes before he starts frantically looking me over.

Stop, stop, stop. I grab his face, making him tense in my grip and look me in the eyes. "Are you okay?" I ask him, and he flinches.

"Me?" His heavy brows furrow. Brighton sets me to the floor, breaking contact completely, and slides back until he's against the wall. He looks over at the door and starts to piece together what happened. The door was a goner, it hangs funny on the hinges, and there are tiny pieces of wood splintered across the bathroom floor.

Brighton's hands are still bleeding, and he looks down at them with a shaky lip. His hair falls against his forehead, and I can see him trying to gain control of the shallow breaths without results.

"Brighton?" I reach out across the floor, giving my hand to him.

He continues to stare at his own, his jaw grinding as he silently reasons with himself. *Talk to me.* My heart is racing unevenly in my chest, and the color of my shirt feels suffocating around my throat as I wait in silence for him to do something, do anything. I feel like an idiot waiting for him to reach out for me.

"Bri," I whisper, half his name broken on my lips.

"Don't call me that." He goes rigid. "Not you."

I feel like a scolded child.

"He was right." Brighton tries to shuffle to his feet, but his body is still weak, and he stumbles a little before sliding back down against the wall.

"Who was right?" I ask him, trying to ignore how jittery I feel. Any sharp movement he makes turns me rigid and makes me flinch. *He'd never hurt you. Very convincing.*

"He doesn't trust me, and he shouldn't," Brighton grumbles.

"I don't understand…" I say, I shift to my knees and put both hands flat on the floor.

"You don't need to," he snaps, looking up at me. "It doesn't matter." *That stings.*

"What the hell do you mean it doesn't matter?" I stare at him without blinking.

"It doesn't fucking matter, Rhea. Any of it. This—" When he finally looks up, the pain I feel is worse than anything I've ever experienced. *He means us. You.*

I inhale slowly, trying to control my thoughts as they whip around my subconscious like a hundred tennis balls. "Will you just talk to me?" I grind out.

"There's nothing to talk about." He shakes his head.

"No, you don't get to do that to me!" I cry out. "You're going to tell me what is going on right now!"

"It won't change anything!" His hand shoots out, and I flinch. *Even worse*, he catches it. His head cocks to the side, and he swallows tightly. "See."

"I—"

"What am I supposed to say that takes it back?" His bottom lip trembles like he's working his hardest to shove down everything else. "Sorry?" he huffs. "It's done, Rhea. You know it."

"I'm asking you to talk to me!" I slam my hand on the ground, and the sound echoes out in the silence around us. "Just talk to me!" I repeat myself.

"I can't," he whispers.

"Yes, you can," I snap at him, and he tenses. "You don't want to."

Brighton's eyes darken, and his tongue darts out over his bottom lip. *He's shutting down on you. You lost this fight the second it started.*

"I know about them," I say, aware that it's not my finest moment. "The Six."

"Don't you dare." He shows his teeth—strangled, feral. His eyes are completely void of light again, and my heart clenches painfully. For a little while there, his stupid eyes were so reflective and blue. Now there's nothing.

"Today, with your friend dying."

"Rhea." His voice is a warning. *Stop pushing.*

"It was too much for you to carry alone," I say, ignoring the tone.

"I shouldn't have hit that guy," Brighton says. "I'm sorry."

"It's not about that idiot!" I point to the door he's destroyed. "You'd rather do that then..."

He looks at the door and closes his eyes.

"But I'm right here, and you won't even talk to me. I thought..."

Brighton stares at me, and the look on his face makes me want to cry. *I'm never going to win this.*

"No." He gives his head a soft shake. "I saw it that day, I see it now..." his jaw clenches. "You absorb everything from everyone, it's exhausting just to watch."

"I do not," I scowl.

"You do!" He raises his voice at me, and my body goes rigid. "With your friends, with your family. You've been nurtured by this toxic need to fix everything for everyone, because if you don't, you might get in trouble." He swallows hard. "I won't let you fix this. It's not yours to fix."

I settle on my heels, completely defeated.

"Alright." I nod, feeling like a burden. *He's trying to protect you.* It feels a hell of a lot like an eviction notice. I push to my feet, my legs feel like jello, and I'm doing everything I can to keep from crying. I move toward my room with the intention of collecting a bag and dragging it over to Kaia's, but I stop.

I turn back to look at him. "You don't have to shove me away, Brighton," I remind him. "This isn't what scares me." I point to the destruction. "Today—when you got that call—what I saw wasn't grief, Brighton."

His eyes are so blue it stings as he rakes his eyes up to mine, locking our gaze.

"It was jealousy."

Recognition crosses his face, and his trembling hands flex at his side. He knows I'm right, and it's why he doesn't respond.

"You know what I said to Sunday?" I say to him, and he looks up at me. "When she asked why I like you?"

He doesn't say a word.

"I..." I swallow the need to cry again. "I told her that you take care of me. Like that was some huge romantic gesture. She looked at me like I was insane." I let go of a heartbreaking laugh that turns into tears. "Maybe I am." I shrug. "I need you to find someone to take care of you. And if you refuse to let me, at least find someone."

I don't wait for him to speak because the chances of him actually doing it are low. I wander to my room and grab my duffle, stuffing it with just enough for the night. When I return to the living room, he's gone, and it takes everything in me not to go searching for him. The worry gnaws at me violently as I grab my keys.

Just go. He doesn't want you here.

On the way out to the Bronco, I text Kaia, and she responds instantly with a phone call.

"*Come to Boone's.*" She drops the pin, and I start the Bronco.

"He's okay," I say as the apartment door swings open and Boone waits on the other side. Kaia shoves him aside and hauls me in. Crosby greets me—Boone's senior German shepherd he is absolutely, illegally keeping in this apartment. But the instant my fingers dig into that wiry fur, I take a deep breath and feel my body regulating.

I don't even speak. I just drop to the floor and let him crawl into my lap.

"Cros—"

"Don't," Kaia snaps. "Leave them alone."

"Are you alright?" are the next words out of Boone's mouth, and I nod. Physically, I'm fine; emotionally, it's a lie. "I mean, did he hurt you..."

"That's what the nod was for," Kaia explains, "can you make her some food?"

"I'm not hungry," I say.

"Make her food," she repeats, "please."

Boone leaves the entrance of the apartment, disappearing into the kitchen and leaving Kaia and me alone in the echoes of Crosby's metal collar shaking gently as I continue to pet him.

"What happened?" She asks after a few minutes of me staring at the wall with tears streaming down my face. Kaia senses him first, her fingers creeping across the floor as Boone appears in the doorway to listen.

"I thought he was sleepwalking but..." I trail off.

"It's a dissociative episode," Boone says quietly. "He has had one before," he says, clearing his throat. Boone tugs at his collar. Kaia and I clock the long scar on his neck. "Sunday doesn't know," he adds quickly. "It was a few weeks after the funeral, and he wouldn't let me go with him, but I knew the basics. He was wandering around like a shell of a human, and we got drunk because I thought whiskey would open him up. Maybe he'd talk to me about it. The bottle hit the floor, and when I looked back up, he was a totally different person." Boone's jaw tightens as he tells the story. "Are you sure he didn't hurt you? You can tell us."

"He didn't touch me," I say without hesitation. "I promise."

"I've never seen that," Kaia whispers, her eyes flickering from the ink-covered scar to his face.

"It's not really one I'm proud of," he grumbles. "I had to punch him to get him out of it."

"There might have been some shoving," I admit. "From my end."

"You couldn't hurt that brick wall even if you tried. He'll be fine, just sore in the morning," Boone brushes it off. "Did he say anything?"

"I'm here, aren't I?" I sigh.

"That tracks," Boone huffs.

"Can one of you fill in the gaps here? I feel left out," Kaia grumbles.

"Brighton's last tour ended badly; six guys died, three because he couldn't save them. It fucked him up pretty badly; he doesn't talk about it. Sunday doesn't even know. He made me swear complete secrecy, and if you tell her..." Boone says.

"I won't," Kaia confirms.

"His buddy took his life yesterday," Boone swallows.

"It triggered everything for the rest of the day," I whisper.

"Him punching Lee?" Kaia asks with a small nod. "That explains his lack of control. He's a hot head but he's not a loose cannon."

"He needs help, Boone," I say. "Real help."

"I've tried." He shrugs, "short of dragging him to a nuthouse."

"Drag him to the nuthouse," I snap, and Kaia's expression changes.

"Something else happened..." She leans forward.

"You didn't see the look on his face, Boone. He's going to do something stupid. When José called to tell him about Harvey..." I trail off.

"What?" Boone shifts on his feet nervously.

"It was like he was jealous Harvey had the guts to do it." I choke back another wave of tears. "I'm scared that he might do something stupid."

Boone reaches across the hallway, pulling his hoodie off the hook. "There's pizza in the oven, three more minutes. Take it out, give it two minutes to set, Kaia Keegan." He points at her like he's trying to get ahead of her impatience. "Sleep here, in the guest room, until I get this figured out." He looks at me, and I nod as he disappears out the front door.

"What's he gonna do?" I ask.

"Weird twin shit probably." She shrugs. Kaia presses her hand to my face. "You're really brave, Ree," she whispers. "It's hard to love people that don't think they deserve it, and you do it every day."

"I don't know if we were in love," I scoff. "We were still calling each other friends who kiss."

Kaia tilts her head, "Him, us, yourself. You've got the biggest, most selfless heart of us all, and you walk around with it on your sleeve, trusting the world to protect it." She pinches my cheek.

"You're being too nice. I'm going to cry. Say something mean," I give her a half-hearted smile.

"You got your heart broken for some good dick," she pats my cheek roughly.

"Really good dick," I pout, and it doesn't make me less sad, but the sting doesn't feel as bad.

"Let's burn our tongues on pizza, and you can keep talking."

I nod and let her pull me off the floor.

Waking up in Boone's spare room the next morning feels like hell. The faint reminder of Brighton is there, but it feels so far away, and it only makes it all hurt worse. The only thing that helps is that Crosby is curled up at the end of the mattress, keeping my feet warm. I pull back the sheets and force myself to shower, only to spend ten minutes crying while I braid my hair. We have a game in three hours, and I have a shift at the Hollow later, but I'm not even sure if I'm welcome there, so I cry some more.

"Reaper." A tiny knock taps the door before Boone opens it. "Sorry, he sleeps with Kaia in here… I couldn't keep him out." He pats Crosby as the dog hobbles out into the living room.

"It was nice to have company," I say softly.

"There's food out here, and I have an update," he says, and my heart flinches. I grab my bag and follow him out into the delicious smell of cinnamon buns.

"Was he okay?" I ask as Boone slides a mug of coffee in my direction.

"He's messed up, but he's alive. It was a long night," he explains.

"Did he say anything?" I ask, pulling off a piece of the bun. It's warm and melts on my tongue, and it hits me—Boone came home and baked instead of sleeping. I scowl at him gently, worried about both twins now instead of just one.

"No," Boone sighs, "avoided the topic. By the time I got there, the bathroom door was in the dumpster downstairs, and the apartment was immaculate. He was in bed like nothing happened, Reaper."

"Bastard." I shake my head. "Please believe me," my voice gets shaky.

"I do." He assures me, "Bri and I are pretty opposite, but I know my brother down to the blood in his veins, and something is off. I'll keep my eye on him."

"Keep both," I warn, and he nods with a small smile.

"Rhea," Boone says as I start to clean up to get out the door. I stop at the sound of my name. "He needs you too, you know that, right?"

Doesn't really feel like he does.

"Questionable," I say.

"My brother is a creature of habit. He gets up, he makes breakfast, he does admin, he takes Daisy to school and on the days he doesn't have her, makes her lunch and brings it to her before the bell rings." Boone explains, rolling his fingers through the air, listing it like it's engraved into him, "he comes back, cleans the Hollow, opens it for lunch. Closes it, preps for the evening, rugby on a rotating schedule. Then he closes the front doors, goes upstairs, showers, does one load of laundry, and goes to bed."

I swallow tightly. *Not a moment out of place.*

"He's up by six am every morning, and in bed by two thirty. It's been that way since he returned home; nothing has ever changed." He stares at me. "Until you. School dances, new drink menus, bowling, sleeping in."

The tears are threatening to return.

"You take care of him, just as much as he takes care of you."

Kaia's a snitch.

I nod, "I think this time it's out of my capabilities, Boone."

"He wants you to believe that so you don't go through the trouble," he responds. "So keep making a mess."

The hit I take is brutal. I collide with the ground like a bag of bricks, and my head gets fuzzy as I roll to my stomach to collect myself. Blood drips from my forehead into my eye.

"You have to sub out," Cosy says, looking at it. "Bring in Jessie," she waves to the sidelines.

Fuck. Nothing today is going right.

I want to be home, in bed, with Brighton.

Stupid.

I kick the grass and meet the medical girl halfway so she can take a look at it as I watch Sunday play tag with a few of the other attackers until she finds a lane. We're up four tries. It should feel comforting, but everything is out of whack, and nothing feels safe anymore.

The bruises forming on my knees from earlier are nasty against my pale skin, and my head is still a little dizzy from the tackle. I need a hot bath. I wish I could say that my head was in the game, but it's not. I still have a shift to work at the Hollow, and Boone convinced me I was still employed, but something about it felt strained.

Kaia stops before the whistle blows, and I follow her eyeline to where Boone is coming across the base of the stone bleachers. She looks at me as I stand.

Something's wrong.

When it does finally echo through the air, I move past the celebration huddle toward Boone.

"What happened?" I ask him before he even opens his mouth.

"He's gone." Boone's shrug looks wrong on him.

"What do you mean he's gone?" My voice trembles as more than one emotion bubbles up. Fear, anger, abandonment.

"Riona called me, losing her mind because he sent her some text saying to keep Daisy safe and he'll be back as soon as he can." Boone shakes his head and looks over my shoulder at the girls standing and watching. "Now, when I call his phone, it goes to voicemail."

"Okay— uh, there's a list in the top drawer of the kitchen cupboard, beside the fridge. It has a few numbers on it that I'm pretty sure are guys from group. Call them."

"Rhea," he says, reaching out.

"Just go," I snap—then wince. "I'm sorry. Call them, thank you."

Boone nods and starts back toward the parking lot.

"Everything okay?" Kaia asks as I turn and storm back across the field. I need a cold shower and to strangle a grown man with my bare hands.

"It's chill." I slam through the locker room door and ignored them chasing after me.

Rhea

"I thought Mom was supposed to get me?" Reid climbs into the Bronco with a scowl on his face.

"What's that from?" I ask him, pointing to the black eye.

"Got in a fight after a dirty hit." He brushes me off as I pull from the curb. "What's that from?" He points to the gash above my eye. "Answer the question, Ree." He pushes when I stay silent.

"Bad tackle. and I don't know. She called in a panic—said she couldn't be here—so I came. But I have to go to the condo, and you're coming with me," I say to him and merge into traffic.

"The swamp?" he teases, but I don't find it amusing today. "Whoa, what's up your ass today?" He asks, his tone changing a little when he sees my reaction.

"Nothing," I say. He drops it, but I can tell that all he wants to do is keep asking questions. I just don't have answers for him right now. Two weeks ago, we were laughing in the Hollow after Brighton lost in a game of pool and drank a mystery smoothie as the loser.

Now we can't find Brighton, my life is back to being nothing but a never-ending mess, and I can't seem to collect the pieces fast enough to put it all back together. When we arrive, some asshole with a lifted truck is parked in my spot, and I almost lose my mind, but I pull into the visitor space instead.

"Come on." I climb out and head for my front door. Even from outside, I can smell the mold crawling up the walls, and it threatens tears. *You can do this.* I unlock the front door, and Reid gags from the wet dog smell that rolls from the hallway. "They fucking closed all the windows," I swear, stepping inside.

It's worse than I could have imagined, and there's not a shot in hell that it's an easy fix. Water damage wraps around most of the main space—two to three feet up the walls—grey patches of peeling paint and warped baseboards. My couch is destroyed and is the source of the foul smell.

"Damn, Ree," Reid stands next to me with his sweater up over his nose. "Can you even live here anymore?"

Yes, and turn into a heartless swamp monster that never speaks to anyone and never loves a thing again.

"Probably not," I say instead. "I just need to see if there's anything I can salvage. They want to clean it out next week, and whatever I don't take now is going to the dump."

"That's rough," he says, nudging the crusty leg of my coffee table with his shoe. I didn't really have it in me to have small talk with him, so I start moving around the condo in silence, collecting what wasn't totally ruined and throwing it in a pile.

"There are two bins in the back of the Bronco. Grab them," I tell him, and he nods, jogging out to the parking lot. I wander into my room and survey the mess. If I were tidier, the ruined clothes matted to the muddy carpet would have been in the dresser or hanging in the closet.

Brighton would have put them away.

I clench my jaw and stare at them, pushing away the tears with the back of my hand before I start to pull what I can up. Out of the corner of my eye, I spot my old CM Punk shirt, and I move toward it, stuck halfway under my bed. It's crusted to the couch leg, and I yank on it, but the fabric rips clean down the center.

The sudden give sends me stumbling backwards, and I hit my head on the dresser, knocking over a few picture frames. I stare down at the destroyed t-shirt, and I should be upset that it's ruined, but all I can think about is Brighton, and it only makes everything worse. The tears start, and I can't stop them this time. I shove myself up and fling the shreds away.

I look around, pissed off at the room; everything feels so foreign now.

This isn't my home anymore.

I hate it here.

I spin and swipe every picture off the dresser, sending them flying against the wall, before grabbing the lamp and throwing that too. It feels good to destroy something, to have control of that distraught rage that's coursing through me, and once I start, I just can't stop. I grab the back of the dresser and rock it as hard as I can until it crashes over. I slam my boot into the back of it over and over until the flimsy particle board snaps.

I don't even give a shit about the posters on the wall that aren't ruined; they get torn down, too. Glass shatters as I chuck them across the room and scream at the top of my lungs.

It's not until Reid barrels into the bedroom with a scared look on his face that it hits me like a freight train.

"Are you okay?" he asks quietly, and I shake my head before I sink back to my knees in the glass and try to catch my breath. Reid kneels next to me, completely silent and unsure what to do as I cry out the rest of the air in my lungs.

"Hey, Ree?" he says after a few minutes. "Will you tell me what's going on, cause that was…"

"I shouldn't have… I just—" I try to explain myself, but nothing comes out, and he nods.

"I get it," he blurts and rolls back so he's sitting with his arms wrapped around his knees. He looks like a little kid again, and it's been a long time since I saw his face so soft and sad. "You should see the inside of the shed."

"In the back yard?" I question.

He nods. "Sometimes when I feel scared, I lock myself in there with a hockey stick and tee off on the walls."

"Reid." My mouth falls open in surprise.

"Did you know it went through him?" he says quietly, and my brows furrow in confusion. "The bullet. It's in the shed."

"What?" I sit straighter, my muscles going tense.

"Yeah, it's stuck between two boards in there. Sometimes I think about prying it out with pliers, but I kind of like seeing it." Reid explains. "Makes me feel less crazy because I know it happened, what wakes me up at night wasn't just a nightmare, it's real life."

"Of course it's real." I reach out to him and tug on the hair at the back of his neck so he looks at me. "It was you and me that day, it was real."

"Sometimes it feels like he's a fictional monster, and it doesn't help that Mom fans the flames any chance she can, kid. She's made him into a figure of shadows that I can't shake." He inhales slowly, and my heart squeezes in my chest.

"I was there, Reid. He's made of blood and bone just like you and me," I remind him, and don't break eye contact. "Look." I climb to my feet, turn off the light, and close the door so he can see. "I still need them."

The old glow-in-the-dark stars I put up the day I moved in are faded and peeling, but they glow all the same. Reid chuckles, the sound defeated and sad, but it's better than the silence. I stare at them, and even though I put them up in random patterns, my eyes trace the Little Dipper in a cluster near the left corner above my bed.

Of course, I find you when I don't want you here.

"Brighton left," I blurt, and Reid's expression shifts in the dim light. "He uh—"

"You don't have to say it," he says, "I looked him up after dinner that night because I wanted to know more about the guy that had my sister all tangled up."

"I wasn't tangled," I scoff, but the smile that slips out is small and pathetic.

"I could hear you giggling from my room. All through dinner," he argues and stares at me. "I know he's ex-military. Like Dad."

"He's not like Dad." I'm quick to stop him.

"Okay, then why are you so sad?" he challenges.

"Some things happened, and Brighton took off. We can't find him, and I'm worried." I chew on my lip and sink to the mattress across from him on the floor still.

"You think he..." Reid trails off.

"No," I whisper, shaking my head. "I think he just needed to clear his head, but it's scary all the same."

"You really like him?" Reid asks.

"I really do." I nod.

"Then fight for it." He stares at me with those glassy green eyes that remind me so much of our Dad; it's scary, and I can't breathe.

"When did you become a Brighton advocate?" I laugh because it's all I can do to keep from crying.

"He makes my sister smile," Reid says, "and he's not so bad... I guess. But if he doesn't figure himself out soon, I'm going to kick his ass."

"I'd pay to see that," I laugh. "Now let's fill these bins and get out of here before the black mold kills us both."

Brighton

I bang on the apartment door and wait. I drove around Harbor for three hours before the vibrations started—mostly Riona and Boone. I turned my phone off after the third call and chucked it on the floor before figuring out where I needed to go.

"Major?" Landon opens the door, half-awake, and I glance down at my watch.

"It's four in the afternoon. Why are you asleep?" I snap.

"It's four in the morning, Black," he says back with a scowl. I check my watch again—he's right.

"Where the hell have you been?" I ask him, and he sighs. "What's more important than Harvey dying?"

"Hey now," Landon warns, "you're in the hall screaming like a lunatic."

"Right," I walk inside as he steps back. I've never actually been inside his apartment, but it's exactly how I picture it. It looks like mine before Rhea. Neat, simple, boring, and clean. I crave the mess she brings, and it stings like papercuts in vinegar. "Now answer my question."

"I knew you could handle it," is what he says to me.

"That's a load of shit, Sarge."

"Do you want water?" he asks me, and I nod, finding a spot to sit on the couch. He doesn't have a TV, but there's a wall of bookshelves crammed with more books than I've ever seen.

"You read?" I ask, confused and still very pissed off at him.

"I never used to, but it helps pass the time." He hands me a glass, but I don't drink it. I just hold onto it like it's going to save my life. "Why are you here, Bright?" he asks.

"Because you've been avoiding us, and I want to know why," I demand.

"Why are you actually here?" He tries again, and all I can do is fall silent. Anger twists around all my other emotions and makes it hard to decipher what's real and what's not.

"I need to talk."

He stares at me like he's been waiting for this moment for the last five years.

"Okay," he says, "let me make a coffee."

He takes his time, and soon enough, the apartment smells like I made a terrible decision. I shouldn't have come here with this. I shouldn't have bothered him. I can handle this on my own.

"Don't even think about it," he warns and sets the cup down on the table. "You're such a bolter," he sighs and mumbles, "worse than a street cat."

"I can figure it out on my own. I didn't mean to bug you." I stare at the cup on the table.

"You needed to, it's different. Tell me what's going on," he encourages as he drinks his coffee. I explain what happened overseas, and talk of the trauma I brought home. How I can still hear them begging me to save them.

Twelve hours of Noah crying that I'd get him home to his baby.

I promised him that I would.

A lifetime of regretting that promise and reminding myself that I was the reason his son is growing up without a dad. I tell him that sometimes I look at Daisy, and the guilt is so bad that I throw up everything in my stomach. There are still days when I want to make the scales even because I don't deserve to see Daisy grow up.

Then I tell him what happened after leaving the church—every single detail of the episode that followed. I avoid using her name because hearing it out loud makes my whole body shiver.

The look on her face when she walked away from me was worse than any nightmare I've ever experienced. *And you let her go.* Boone had come to check on me, and I knew she had gone to Kaia, which made everything worse. Once he left, I got out of bed and got in the truck.

"Alright," Landon sets his mug down. "My turn."

"What?" I say.

"That's how group works, Brighton. You tell a story, you listen to a story. Then you find the points where your stories touch, and you use them to solve your problem. It's why you're still a tangled mess. You've never admitted you are." Landon raises an eyebrow at me.

"Okay."

"I came home from my thirteenth tour, discharged from service because I nearly blew myself up cleaning my own weapon. After the eighth tour, I was drunk more than I was sober and really good at hiding it. Having something like that happen is enough to scare you sober, but it also opens the doors for the sober nightmares." Landon explains. "They came on with a vengeance. I had been suppressing them for years, taking them out on people who didn't deserve it a lot of the time. Luckily, I was in a place where no one ever asked questions."

"Until you weren't." I finish his sentence.

"I was home for a week when the episodes started. I thought I wasn't a man, Bright. Talking to people made my crimes okay, forgave me for my sins. But I didn't want to be forgiven, I wanted to feel the punishment for those crimes."

I've heard this story a hundred times. Told it to myself.

"Unfortunately, I was not the man I prided myself on. I was a coward, I was sick, and it created a ripple effect that I will never be able to undo." Landon swallows tightly. "I need you to listen to the next part all the way before you interrupt."

"Alright," I say, digging my heels into the carpet.

"I was home alone with my oldest daughter and my son after convincing my wife that I would be able to handle it for an hour while she took our youngest to the doctor." He inhales slowly. "I wasn't always the best father, and every tour made it harder to be one. I got mean, Brighton. I'm ashamed to admit that, but I don't omit it from my life because it's the truth."

My brows furrow, and my palms are sweaty against my thighs.

"That day, my son was hitting pucks; he loves hockey." Landon smiles to himself. "He's gonna be huge one day, he's talented." The reminiscing makes me sick to my stomach as the wall of realization hits me.

I recognize those eyes.

Sure, more tired, less vibrant. But the same deep green and angry shape.

Please don't.

"I was cleaning my guns in the backyard, and in hindsight I should have never even been allowed to own them..." he trails off. "He was doing great, the sun was out, and he never misses the net even at that age. My daughter's painting—maybe drawing, I don't know—the details get fuzzy because I hear a gunshot. Loud and clear. And I'm back there. Staring down the barrel of a gun. Ten feet in front of me in the grass is a man with a gun. Threatening everything. I move in quick, tactical steps and snuff out the threat. But I'm not fast enough, and there's a second gunman."

Landon pulls up his shirt to show me an ugly scar on the side of his stomach.

I can't.

I want to get up from the couch so badly, I need to. I need out of here, away from him. Rhea's devastated eyes flicker across my memory, and I grind my jaw together to keep from moving or saying anything.

"The pain knocked me from the episode, and she was standing there, her tiny hands shaking around the gun, and my son is unconscious beside me in the grass," he says, and I shoot from the couch. "Sit down, Bright."

"You knew," I bark. "You knew that day at the bowling alley. It's why you've been avoiding me. Avoiding the guys. You saw her."

"I did. It was the first time in thirteen years I'd seen her, but I'd never forget that face." He stands to match me. "I just don't know if it's the right time to—"

He raises both hands when I charge and slam him back against the bookshelf. It rattles under the blow, and a few books fall to the floor. "I should fucking kill you." My voice is low and violent.

Her voice still shakes when she tells stories about you—like she can feel your hands on her, like she can still smell the gunpowder on her skin. I'm vibrating with unchecked rage. I don't know what to do with it.

Landon doesn't even flinch. "You should."

The omission is worse than him trying to talk his way out of it. It means every horrible thing he did to them, to her, is true.

"Does she know you're still in Harbor?" I ask him next, and he shakes his head. "Listen to me right now," I say, and tighten my grip on his shoulder, pressing my forearm into his throat. "I don't know what the fucking point is in telling me that story. What twisted game you're play-ing, but if you ever even contemplate the idea of *ever* going near Rhea, I will make sure it's the last time you ever do."

"I'm not that man anymore, Bright," Landon says. "You know me."

"I don't know you," I snarl. "Were you going to use me to get to her?"

He doesn't say anything, and I scoff.

"If I'm being honest, I don't know. But I had to make sure you were a better man than me," he finally says.

"That's the problem. All you've taught me tonight is that I'm no better than you. We're a mirror. Rhea's better off without either of us." I spit.

"That's not true." Landon shakes his head and tries to get air, but I push harder. "You came here ready to talk after how long? And you did it for her."

"Don't you fucking play some moral high ground bullshit with me," I bark.

"I might not deserve a second chance," he says, and I shove him.

"You won't get one," I remind him.

"But you do," he says. "Don't let my daughter think she failed a second man. Protect her from this, from me." He whispers the last part, and I realize how serious he is about it.

"This is a fucking joke. She didn't fail me, and she can protect herself. She's been doing it long before I barrelled into her life." I snap. "She told me about you, she barely sleeps..."

"Are you going to tell her about this?"

"She has a hard enough time moving through the mess you made without having to look over her shoulder, so no." I can barely look at him anymore. "I trusted you."

"Trust that you'll never become me." He tries, but it just pisses me off even more.

"Stay away from her, Landon," I let him go finally, backing away toward his front door. "And me."

He nods, his jaw ticking shut tightly as I reach for the doorknob.

"Fuck." My entire body wracks with tremors as I shut the door and storm back to my truck. I dig my phone out from where I threw it earlier and turn it on to dial a number I should've forgotten a long time ago. They answer after the first ring. "Hey, you wanna meet up for a drink?"

"Do you remember when Huxley tossed that grenade at Noah and he thought it was unpinned and wrote him up?" Jackson rolls back in his chair, drunk off about six too many shots and teasing everyone he can think of.

"Noah didn't even look in his direction for a month," I laugh, slamming back another shot. I lick the whiskey off my bottom lip and shake the burning aftertaste down.

Jack had been a troublemaker with a secondary squad on my last tour. He was one of the only guys in the area who knew the boys that I had. The only problem was that his only hobby was drinking. I hadn't touched an ounce of liquor since getting sober, but I couldn't erase the way Rhea looked from my mind. I knew Jack would be down to get day-drunk with me if I called.

"Man, those were the days," Jack recalls. "What have you been doing these days?"

"Boone and I own the Hollow in Harbor," I tell him.

"No shit," he slaps the table, "I'll have to come by!"

"Please don't ever come to my bar," I start laughing again as Jack slides me another shot.

"I'm offended, Bri!" He fakes it and takes back the shot. "You got a girl?"

And just like that, she's back.

I see her, standing there, staring at me with those sad brown eyes and disappointed frown, and I wonder what God I pissed off to have her so briefly and lose her so violently.

"Yeah," I hear myself say, the whiskey lingers on my tongue. "You should see her. She's the most beautiful woman I've ever seen, Jack. Tall, covered in tattoos, with big brown eyes and a mouth on her. Fuck." I swallow tightly. *I miss her.* "She's an angel of death," I say, and he laughs.

"You sound like you're in love," he jokes. I raise my dizzy gaze to look at him, and I can hear the laughter growing louder, but I'm tripping over his blurted statement like he's tied a wire around my ankles.

My head snaps to the song playing from the jukebox, and I start to lose it, laughing as *Absolutely* pours out of it and over the bar. *Yeah fuck you too*, I say to the ceiling, talking to anyone who will listen.

"Is your little sister still hot?" Jack interrupts my thoughts.

"Yup—and my hands still fit around your neck," I remind him, and he shakes his head.

"She's gotta have some pretty little friends you can introduce me to," he pokes.

"I gotta be real sick in the head to let you near any of them, Jack. Stick with your cougars, they respond better to your bullshit." I slap his face, and he rolls his eyes before he calls the waitress over. He took me to some small shitty dive bar in Lorette, and I don't care where we end up, as long as it's far away from Harbor. She leans over the table, and Jack's hand teases the back of her skirt as she talks to him, but there are two guys at the bar watching angrily.

"Might wanna keep your hands to yourself," I warn him, and he only pushes it up higher. The second problem, Jack loves to fight.

"There's no fun in behaving," he smirks at me as the two men slide from their stools.

I'm drunk enough that his enthusiasm hits.

"Fuck it," I laugh as they charge us, spewing sentences of bullshit. The girl rushes back from the table as my hand connects with the face of the first guy. Jack doubles over, taking a shot to the stomach, and I kick my foot out, catching the bigger of the two in the knee. We're both too drunk to be fighting. Our movements are clumsy, and I take a hard, closed fist to the side of the face as they get the upper hand.

"Duck!" Jack slurs and smashes a beer bottle over the top of the guy's head as I charge the other. I wrap him around the middle, slamming him hard against a nearby table, and he swings on me, clipping me in the ribs before I can tip him over to the ground. We both end up rolling around on the floor until the front of the pub is lit up with red and blue lights.

We sit in the drunk tank for six hours before they let either of us make a phone call, and it's a lot of pained groaning from Jack as he rolls to his feet to call his friend. I stare at the phone, knowing that Boone's going to kill me, but I shrug, too drunk to care, mind quiet for once.

I feel unchained from the nightmares.

I dial the number to the Hollow.

"Boone speaking." It sounds busy, and I swallow my pride.

"Can you come get me?" I slur.

"**I** found him." Boone hangs up the phone behind the bar.

"Where?" I ask.

"You'll never guess, not in a million years," he says as he moves around the bar to come out and wander into the kitchen. Kaia is helping pick up the slack, running food to tables as Boone double works the bar and the kitchen. We tried to convince him that we could close the kitchen to big orders for the night, but he insisted it would be fine, and Kaia backed him.

So now we're all scrambling to keep the Hollow running the way Brighton does—without even breaking a sweat.

"He's in lock up," Kaia barks, laughing. "I swear to everything holy, Boonie, if you don't bring me back a mug shot of Brighton Black, I will never speak to you again."

"You told her first?" I say, completely offended.

"I've been trying to figure out how to sneak out of here to go get him." Boone throws his hands up.

"Let him rot for a night," Kaia snaps and grabs more plates.

"I'll go," I say to him, and he instantly shakes his head at me. "I'm not leaving him there."

"He's drunk, Rhea, really drunk," Boone warns.

"It's fine, he can be drunk out of jail." I groan and hand him the radio I usually wear in my ear to talk to Sunday behind the bar when I'm at the front door.

I fish my keys out and wander to the parking lot, taking my time to find a playlist, only to notice there's a new one queued up in my list.

A Happy Playlist for My Sad Girl.

"You're a fucking prick," I swear, plugging in my phone and hitting play on it only to cry the entire way to Lorette. Every single song on the playlist is happy in rhythm with the saddest possible lyrics I've ever heard. And I hate him every single time a new one starts. It's so far out of his wheelhouse that it must have taken him hours—maybe days.

I slam my hands on the steering wheel, and the Bronco swerves a little, scaring me enough to slow down.

"I hate you!" I scream at the empty highway.

By the time I get to the station, my head is throbbing, and my chest is sore from screaming, but I don't feel so wound up and am a little more confident about coming face to face with him.

You can do this. You're a brave little toaster.

I exhale and push through the doors. It smells like bleach, booze, and blood inside, and my stomach churns. It was a lot easier doing this the first time when Brighton was at my back, not the one needing to be bailed out.

"I'm here to pick up Brighton Black," I say to the girl behind the counter, and she starts the paperwork.

I hear him before I see him. He's laughing with the cop escorting him out like they're old friends, and it's infuriating.

"Say hi to Lovey for me. He hasn't been around much lately. He's turning into a homebody!" The cop shakes Brighton's hand and gives me a tiny nod.

Brighton turns, stopping dead in his clumsy, drunk tracks when he sees me standing there with my arms crossed. "Why are you here?" He asks, his gaze glassy, a small smile on his face. "What did you do?" He steps forward, reaching out to the small bandage on my forehead, but I step back and don't answer his second question.

He scowls.

There you are.

"Boone is trying to keep the Hollow from burning down in your absence. I'm the only one who could leave to bring you home from your joy ride." I snap. "Did you have fun?" I ask him, and his jaw tightens. "Good," I whisper.

I don't waste time trying to convince him to follow. I just walk out to the Bronco, and before I can open my door, he does it for me. I don't look at him as I climb inside and start the engine.

"Hey, you got the playlist!" He smiles at me and feels like someone presses my heart into a bowl of broken glass. "Wow, it's clean in here," he says, looking around. I hate how easy-going he is when he's drunk. I want my Brighton. Not whoever this is.

You cleaned... You took it to the cleaners!

I want to scream.

"Shut up," I tell him and turn the stereo off. "Here." I hand him a water. "Drink."

"Grumpy." He reaches out, and his fingers tap the volume back up. I keep my eyes on the road, but I can feel him staring at me because it burns like the sun.

At least with the music on, I can't hear him breathing.

I'm so upset with him I could cry. But simultaneously, I'm so glad he's not dead. *This could have been a lot worse.* It's another twenty minutes before he opens his mouth again.

"You're mad at me."

"Take a nap or something," I huff.

"Talk to me."

Are you serious?

I whip the wheel to the side and slam on the brakes.

"Get out."

"We're still half an hour from Harbor," he says. "Oh, don't be like that."

"Maybe the walk will sober you up," I say.

He pops the top on the water bottle, staring me directly in the eyes and drinks the entire thing without blinking before he tosses it on the floor.

"Wow," I click my teeth together.

"It was getting too tidy in here," he smirks.

"Ha, ha." I shake my head and inhale a shaky breath before closing my eyes and leaning my forehead against the steering wheel. After a couple of minutes, I turn my head to look at him. "I can't do this, Brighton."

"Bright," he corrects.

"It's not funny." My bottom lip shakes as I hold back the tears. "You've been a liability for forty-eight hours and... You scared me."

His face goes cold. "I couldn't find the control. I'm sorry. It won't happen again."

"No," I sigh, "today, you scared me." I argue gently, "When Boone showed up at the game and said you were gone... that no one could get a hold of you." The tears fall before I can stop them, and the muscle in his jaw tightens.

"I wouldn't do that," he says roughly. *I want to believe you.*

"We couldn't find you," I choke out, and he reaches out to touch my face, but I pull back, and he drops his hand. "You turned your phone off. You had Riona calling hospitals for your *body*," I hiss at him.

"Who would make you and Daisy lunch?" he teases with a shaky voice.

"Don't just take off," I demand, even though I have no right. I'm just trying to survive how sad he looks and failing spectacularly at it. "Please."

"Alright. I'm sorry." He apologizes again.

I take it, bank it, and pull off the side of the road and take us back to Harbor. He falls asleep for a bit, thankfully, but the second he feels the Bronco cross the rough divot leading into the Hollow lot, he's wide awake and looking green.

"If you puke in here, you're cleaning it," I warn, and it makes him chuckle, but he flips open the door the second it's in park and hurls up what's left of his stomach on the concrete.

I get out and help him up straight, the feeling of his skin on mine like a sunburn I didn't ask for when he takes my hand and pushes me away. "I'm okay, Reaper."

I flinch like I've been slapped, and he knows why.

"I didn't... shit, Rhea!" He calls after me as I pop the lock on the kitchen door and walk inside. The Hollow is still packed, and Boone finds me instantly with a worried look. I roll my eyes but step to the side to show him, Brighton following behind me with calculated steps. I point to the stairs, guiding him up and walking behind him closely so I know he isn't going to fall.

Brighton turns to the side on the stairs, his shoulder leaning against the door, and I slide in beside him to unlock it. Before I can, he leans in close and inhales slowly, closing his eyes and pressing his forehead against mine. We had been here once before, months ago, before the word roommate, before the word friend.

When I was simply *Sunday's best friend,* and he was *Killjoy.*

So much carnage in so little time.

"Don't leave tonight," he whispers, his lips so close to mine I can feel every word. The plea is quiet but violent, and my entire body curls into the sound of it as a guarantee that I won't.

But I have to.

I will not be my mother's daughter.

I cannot stand around until it's too late.

"Get in bed," I say. His body tenses—but it's enough to get him moving.

He starts to strip the second he's beyond the threshold, and I put both his shoes on the mat where he likes them, collect his socks, shirt, and pants to put them in the basket. I fill a glass of water for him and start the washing machine with tears in my eyes before wandering back to his room to find him sleeping in bed on top of the sheets.

It's nearly impossible to be mad at him when he looks this small.

I set the water on his nightstand and kneel next to the bed to brush the perfect dark strand of hair off his forehead. "You're right, Brighton,"

I whisper, "it's not mine to fix." I search all the harsh lines of his face before looking up at the stars on the ceiling, my heart breaking because all I want to do is crawl into that bed with him.

I kiss his cheek, lingering just to feel his skin. "I just want to be-friends-who-kiss with you forever," I whisper. "But I need your help."

Brighton

It's not mine to fix.

The ultimatum rings in my ears as I roll over in bed. She didn't stay. I shouldn't have asked her to, but I couldn't help it.

I need your help.

Sounds like you're in love.

You scared me today.

Protect her from this.

The worst of them all is that I can see Rhea, just out of reach, and with her is Landon. The rage is unbearable, but the fear it's all-consuming. Drunk, it was easier to process the surprise. Sober, it feels like someone is taking a jackhammer to my chest.

He's been here. He knows where she is.

I still can't tell if he wants to approach her. I think I scared him out of it, but it feels wrong. He asked me if I would tell her, and I told him no, that much I did right. She doesn't need to know about all of this. About the tangled connection—the sinister thread that knots us together.

Leave her out of it.

I can handle the disappointment of losing two friends at once, on my own.

Conversations all bleed together, and I can't pinpoint exactly which one gets me out of bed, but my feet are on the ground, and I'm running the shower. I leave it cold and let it shock my system back to life, puke twice, and leave the bathroom in better shape than I entered. I look around the apartment for a sign of her, but find nothing. The shoes are neatly put away, and there are no dishes in the sink or cups on the island.

The blanket on the couch she loves so much is folded the way I left it, and it feels... *cold.*

She was just supposed to be temporary. Here until she could get her feet on the ground. It was never long-term. So why does this feel like I'm walking on glass?

I stare at my phone with the intention to call her, the picture of us at Daisy's dance stares up at us, and I hate how nauseous I feel staring at it. She was a little older than Daisy is now, but everything that went down that day... Daisy and I could very easily become Rhea and Landon—with one small misstep.

I can't let that happen again.

I need to protect them from me.

I pull on clean clothes, calling José while I do, and then Boone. Both arrive at the apartment an hour later. José has coffee, and Boone has food.

"Eat something," he says to me, and I nod.

"I'm sorry I took off," I apologize to him, but Boone doesn't look me in the eye, and I know I've fucked up badly. Whatever is in the sandwich he made me cures me from the inside out, the dull throb in the back of my skull fades to nothing but a tingle, and I'm ready to clean up the mess I made.

"Harvey's dying triggered an episode," I tell José to get him up to speed. "I flipped out, couldn't get control. I made a mess of everything, and I need your help."

Boone looks up from his coffee like he's shocked I even asked, but he nods.

"Whatever is going on in my head... I can't fix it, at least not on my own. I haven't been able to for a long time, but I can't risk it." I shake my head in shame. *Protect her.*

"What do you mean, risk it?" José asks.

"I can't risk snapping like that again. What if next time Daisy's home? Or Rhea? And I don't just break a door?"

"Is she okay?" Is his next question.

"I didn't touch her. Thank God. I can live with what I did this time—" I trail off, and both of them understand.

"So what do you need from us?" Boone interjects into my dark thoughts.

"I need you to keep this place standing," I say to him, and his brows furrow.

"That doesn't fix the problem, Bri," he warns.

"Yeah, I know, it's just for a bit. There's a facility in Pittsburgh."

José nods; he knows exactly what the plan is. "We talk about it sometimes in group with the guys that really need extra support. It's an assisted living and therapy placement."

"The program is eighteen weeks long," I say to Boone.

"That's a long time." He swallows tightly.

"It is, but I've been gone longer for stupider reasons; this is important." I stare at him. "I ran because the idea of hurting her, hurting them... it pushed me to a place I didn't want to be."

"Alright." He agrees—without any more arguing.

"What do you need from me?" José asks.

"I need you to take over group sessions for a bit," I say, the next breath is deep, to keep me from saying something I shouldn't. "Sarge is taking a step back. He wanted me to do it—but you're the only person I trust to take care of the guys. You think you can do that?"

"Of course," he nods, watching me closely for a tell that might give away more, but I'm locked down. *No one can know about Landon.* "I need to get to work, but keep me updated and email me all the shit for the church on your drive." He slaps the island, says goodbye to Boone, and the front door slams shut.

"There's something else," Boone says instantly. "And don't try that military mind voodoo shit on me. You're hiding something, I can feel it."

He hates this. All of it. I know that, it's obvious enough. He's mad that it's something he can't fix, something that I have to get from someone else after all these years.

He's never been one to get jealous; it's just not him. We used to joke that I took it all, leaving Boone to be so easygoing and carefree. But that's not the truth either. Boone is just as dark as I am on the inside; he just hides it better.

"I need you to keep an eye on Rhea," I say to him.

"There it is. You're not telling her." He narrows his eyes at me, sharp and judgmental.

"No." I confirm. *I can't face her, not like this. I'll call her once I'm there.* The unspoken truth is that if I hear her voice, I might not go at all. Leaving her and Daisy is going to kill me.

"You know better than anyone that Rhea can take care of herself."

"It's not about her taking care of herself," I sigh.

I know she can do that; she was doing it long before I came around.

"Just…" I stop to think about my words. "Make sure she's not alone. She gets sad, and she hides it really well, but don't let her be sad and alone with this. She's going to hate me for it, she'll probably make excuses for me, she's definitely going to think it's her fault."

Boone chuckles darkly and nods in agreement.

"Don't let her do that stuff alone."

"I hear you."

"Thank you," I choke out. "And I'm sorry that I scared you. That I scared everyone."

"I knew you wouldn't do it," Boone smirks, and I furrow my brows at him. "You'd never abandon us like that even if you thought you wanted to. The Brighton I grew up with would put up a fight."

My nose itches, and my hands get shaky again.

"This feels like I'm running," I say to him.

"You're not. This is fighting." He taps the counter with his hand. "I'll drive you. When do we leave?" Boone asks before I can argue that I can drive myself.

"Tomorrow."

"Yeah, that one," I say as Kaia throws the dark purple blanket into the cart Boone's pushing around the homeware store. Sunday sits inside it, and Cosy trails behind me, double-checking I'm not leaving anything good behind.

"So you can get back in on Monday to get more of your stuff?" Sunday asks.

"Yeah, and the apartment I'm subletting is nice. It's only five minutes from the school; hopefully, with the insurance payout, I can start looking at houses next summer." I chew my lip and feel through more of the blankets. Pretty much everything that was left at the condo succumbed to mold, and I was having to buy new...*everything*.

Staying with Boone isn't ideal. Crosby is sweet, but the apartment is too small for two large humans and a large dog. I just need my own space again, and frankly, being around Boone just makes me miss Brighton.

The day after the drunk tank, Boone took Brighton to a facility in Pittsburgh. It specializes in Military PTSD, and everything Boone told me about it seems nice. Brighton has his own apartment there; it's basically assisted living. He does therapy twice a day, calls Daisy with his one phone call, and keeps his head down.

But I miss him.

So much so that sometimes Boone catches my eye and I think it's him. My brain ignores the different color in his eyes and the shift in the tattoos. It aches for what we lost, and it shows me what I want just to silence the screaming in the rest of my body.

I get excited, and I end up crying upstairs in the empty apartment for half my shift when my brain finally realizes that it's not. Last time it happened, I left my key on the island and haven't been back since.

I bring Daisy lunch from Boone every morning, and I can tell it's taking a toll on her. She's retreating into the shell she was in at the start of the year, and she's becoming more secretive about her art again. It's frustrating watching it happen without the ability to stop it.

"You alright?" Cosy asks as we round a corner into an aisle full of pillows.

"Yeah, just you know..." I shrug. "Missing Brighton."

Kaia groans as loudly as she can. Between them and the girls, at least I'm not alone and sad. They take turns doing shit with me, and since Kaia started coming to family dinners, I started getting invited less, which is a blessing in disguise. But also, eating leftovers from the Hollow at the bar is getting old, especially when there's no one around to tell Boone I don't like tomatoes.

Rugby off-season will be the death of me; it's all low-intensity work-outs and strength training. I could really use an outlet that involves tossing people around, but there are another couple of months until we get back on the field.

"He's home, Reaper," Boone says off the cuff.

"Excuse me." Kaia puts both hands on the end of the cart, stopping Boone so sharply that he groans and Sunday slides forward. "Ow," he hisses at her, and Sunday starts laughing.

"What do you mean he's home?" I inhale sharply, and the air stings.

"He got home last week," Boone looks between all of us, his green eyes searching for forgiveness. "I didn't realize he hadn't come to see you."

He doesn't want to.

You sent him away.

"He's probably just respecting my space. You know, Brighton." I press my lips together, trying not to chew the inside of my mouth raw.

"Yeah, but..." Cosy says quietly, "You'd think."

They all stare at me, and the longer they do, the hotter I get and the more uncomfortable I feel. "Okay, stop," I snap at them, and they jump.

They all fall quiet, and Boone is the first to man up. "What do you want to do?" he asks.

"Curl up into a ball and die," I throw my head back and pray for the fluorescent lighting to kill me. "Wait." I look down at Sunday. "Did you know?"

"I had no idea he was home," she says, "I'm just as surprised as you are."

"Daisy hasn't said anything," I sigh, pushing my hands through my hair. "He hasn't been working?"

"He got home Monday, said he had shit to take care of before he got back to it," Boone explains. "He wouldn't tell me anything else."

"Good to know he's still buttoned up," I try to joke, but my bottom lip trembles.

"Oh, Reap." Sunday pushes to her knees. "He's an idiot, give him some time."

"He's been gone five months, Sunny..." I swallow the disappointment. "I think a point comes when a girl just gives up on the Nicholas Sparks movie ending."

Cosy tosses her arm around my waist and presses her cheek to my shoulder. "Wanna go play DND and get sushi?" she asks.

"Can I come?" Boone interjects, and all three girls simultaneously deny him access to girls' night. "Yeah, fine, whatever. Make Boone drive around town, but don't invite him to the fun stuff. You guys suck," he groans, and Kaia pinches him, which starts them fighting, but the air returns to normal, and everyone starts shopping again.

I pull my phone out, staring at the lock screen.

Idiot.

I never changed it from the photo we took at WWE. Brighton's got the biggest smile on his face, staring down at me, and every time I look at it, the butterflies stir in my chest. But today, an anvil sits there.

He's been home for a week.

By the time I get home that night, I'm so sick of people waiting for me to explode that I barely greet Crosby as he pads to the open apartment door. He follows me down the hall and into the bedroom, taking his spot on the bed and waiting for me to join him.

"You'd come see me, right?" I flip the blankets back, and he moves up, putting his head on my chest. "If you didn't see me for five months, would I be one of your first stops?" I ask him, pressing my fingers between his ears for a good scratch. "I mean, yeah, things ended rocky, but..."

Crosby lifts his head.

"Well, not that rocky," I argue with the sound of silence. "Just like... a rough break."

I reach over and pull out my phone, hitting play, knowing that the playlist was loaded and letting the sound of stupid pop music and its stupid, sad lyrics flood the quiet. In the morning, my lunch is sitting beside Daisy's, and I can hear Boone in the shower. Usually, I'd wait to thank him, but I don't need him asking me if I'm okay again, so I slip out before the water stops.

Today is going to be long. Even more so now that I know Brighton is within reach and doesn't want to see me. I'm in the Bronco on the way to school when I get the text from the group chat.

BONES:

> 911. Meet at the field.

SUNNY:

> Seriously?

KILLER:

> Can it wait?

BONES:

911 literally means an emergency…

I sigh, messaging the principal that I have a family emergency, and turn myself around back toward the field to meet the girls. Only their cars are in the parking lot when I arrive, and I kill the engine, leaving my phone behind.

"This better be quick," I yell as I stomp across the grass. It's still that pretty pink color outside—the one that happens when the sun just starts to touch the clouds, and the field is fucking empty.

I fucking hate these girls.

I dig my boots into the grass and spin around in my dress. I put it on this morning because it's the only thing in my closet that brings me any joy right now. It's delicate and fun, with applique glitter stars, moons, and flowers. It makes me feel like a witch, and it blows in the morning breeze. But all that joy is gone, and now I'm just annoyed.

"Where the hell are you guys?" I holler, looking around to see if they're on the benches or if the lights of the locker room are on. "This is *really* fucking hilarious, you guys! Some of us have work!" *Maybe I read the text wrong?* I pat myself down and curse myself for leaving my phone in the Bronco. "You're a fucking idiot," I snap and turn to walk back to the parking lot.

"Are you arguing with *yourself*?" His voice is low, sending a shiver down my spine. "That's a new low."

"Don't start," I huff, trying to ignore the profound effect he has on me as I burn a hole in the side of the locker room building. "You'll ruin the day." I do my best to hide the shake in my voice.

"Hellcat," he says, begging me to turn around.

"Go away," I whisper, my eyes trained on the parking lot as I try to decide if I want to walk away. "This is a mean trick, and now I have to be mad at you *and* the girls."

"It's not mean," he fights gently. "Don't be mad at them. I asked for help."

I drop my head, and silence fills the gaps between our breathing. I have a million questions I want to ask him, but I don't know where to start, and all of them feel childish.

Most I know the answer to.

You told him to do something about it, and he did. You don't get to complain now.

"Rhea," he says, like he can read my mind, and at this point, he probably can. "You said that out loud," he whispers.

I really need to get this inner monologue shit under control.

"It's the truth," I shrug.

"It is," he agrees, "but you can complain about it."

"No." I shake my head. "It's a situation I created. I have to deal with what comes with that."

"So life kicks you around, and you just keep your mouth shut about it, doesn't sound very fair," he says, his voice gets closer, and I know he's coming toward me, but I can't figure out how to make my feet move.

"Complaining has never once solved a problem," I huff, picking at one of the silver stars.

"It's not about solving the problem," Brighton groans. "It's about acknowledging the hurt."

"Therapy brainwashed you," I snort, because I can't pinpoint what I'm feeling, and I'm a second away from crying. "I have no reason to be hurt," I say. "Roommates help each other. You helped me when I needed it, and I helped you. It's fine."

"You've never once said it's fine, and it's meant that, Rhea Drake. Yell at me, tell me all the reasons you hate me, give me something to go on here."

"I don't hate you," I respond. I *probably couldn't even if I tried. That's the problem.*

"So you just feel nothing at all? Completely disconnected?" he asks.

No, Brighton, my head is spinning, my hands are sweaty, my heart is racing, and I want to cry every time you open your mouth.

"We're friends, Brighton. I'm glad you're home, but I have to get to work," I say. He groans, a few choice swear words leave his lips, and I can picture the scowl on his handsome face.

"Will you stop for two seconds?" he asks, but I shake my head no and force my feet to start moving.

I can hear him thinking, trying to find an avenue that might help him keep talking to me, but he stops following me altogether. *Good.*

When the music starts, my brain doesn't know what to do with itself. *You fucking asshole.*

I turn around, taking him in, and try not to cry. He feels sturdy again; the small man from the night I last saw him is gone, replaced with the man I've been missing so much. His hair is shorter, but the stubborn strand still leans gently against his forehead, begging to be tugged. And he's wearing a suit, a fully tailored dark suit that I've never seen before, but it rises and falls with his nervous breathing in the most beautiful way. His blue eyes are alive again, and it makes me exhale quietly.

"You've got to be kidding me," I hiss.

He looks me over, then extends his hand.

Brighton

I shouldn't have given Kaia control of my phone, because she turns on the playlist Rhea affectionately calls *Songs to Get Dirty To*. I know it the second the first song starts. It's mostly trash. A combination of rap, country, and mainstream pop music that she considers worth adding, but there's one specific song I know Rhea loves. It pours over the field from every speaker they've got. Loud. Consuming. And it puts a smile on her face.

Her hair is loose around her sharp jaw, and her eyes are bigger and sadder than I remember. She's in a dress I've never seen—she must've bought it while I was gone — and it hugs her chest and her waist. It's soft, and it makes it hard not to touch her, but I keep my other hand in my pocket until she's ready.

It's been weeks. *She's nervous, angry, and sad — and she doesn't believe we're just friends. She doesn't. Give her a second to catch up.*

But I miss the way she smells, and being patient with her is the worst pain imaginable.

"Come on, Hellcat," I say gently. "We have our best conversations when we're dancing."

"The girls are here somewhere," she huffs. "If you think they left, you're delusional."

"I promised them a romance movie moment. Here it is." I smile more widely at her.

It was a whole fight when I called them together. They were pissed at me, and I let them berate me for nearly an hour before they finally agreed to help me get my sad girl back. Cosy was the first to cave and made her demands very clear.

Go big or go home.

Reaper deserves the drama.

"Are you serious right now?" She looks around, confused.

"Quit acting like you don't love the attention." I smile at her, praying to whoever will listen to get her to cooperate. *Just for one song.* "You can be high maintenance and petty over here, with me."

I step forward when she doesn't move, and she crosses her arms over her chest. I breathe her in, the orange in her shampoo, the subtle smell of her favorite lotion. I slip my hand between her arms and grab her wrist until I can tangle my fingers into hers, and I spin her in a soft circle that makes her fight to keep the serious look on her face.

"What song is this?" she asks me, and I shrug even though I know. "Is this the 'Get Dirty' playlist?" she asks, her eyes flickering up to mine.

"It is," I say, guiding her back into my steps as my hand finds her back and her fingers rest gently on my shoulder blade. Her touch makes my entire body shiver.

"You've been home a whole week, Brighton." Her sad accusation isn't a lie, but it pinches at my nervous system, and I nod to confirm it.

"I fixed it," I say to her, and she looks at me with a confused expression.

"Brighton…" She opens her mouth to argue something, and I shake my head.

"I came too close to losing everything that night, Rhea," I tell her. *You, Daisy.* Even a friend I thought would be in my life. For every step. Someone who understood me better than anyone. And it was a lie.

"I was here," she whispers.

"You're the only reason I'm *here*." I tell her, "You and Daisy."

"I have nothing to do with that." Rhea shakes her head. "There's no forcing you to do anything you don't want to do, Brighton."

"That morning, waking up, remembering what I did. How I treated you when you were just trying to help me. I stripped myself of my pride and got help. It's not perfect. There's so much medication my head spins, but I'm in control," I tell her, confident in my actions, in myself. "I couldn't do this back then, I didn't have it in me. I didn't know I could. But I'm stronger now, and I had to make things right, with more than one person this week. Daisy, Riona, and my siblings. I had to prove to myself that I could handle this without an outburst. The stress, the guilt."

She stares at me like I'm talking too fast, and it's taking everything in me not to kiss the look off her face. "I couldn't make my last stop until I knew that I was the man you needed."

"Oh," she exhales.

The man you deserve.

"You're it for me. I don't know what I need to say to you to convince you to forgive me. Maybe you never do, but I'll do anything." She tenses in my grip, and I know she's conflicted. This is all a lot, and she's been bombarded.

"Brighton," she sighs, and her teeth sink into her bottom lip.

"I'll stick glow-in-the-dark stars to every surface in the apartment, eat all your tomatoes, learn all the wrestling moves, never make you eat pasta ever again," I whisper as the song comes to a soft conclusion and the next one is a loud, trap song that cracks a smile on her face. "Hell, I'll even relinquish music privileges in the truck as long as you promise to never make me listen to this song ever again."

Rhea starts to laugh and shakes her head, "I don't even know what this song is."

"Seriously?" I scowl.

"I added a bunch to the playlist without listening to them to see if you actually played them all the way through without complaining," she admits.

"You're a terror—" I shake my head and bite my tongue.

"You sure you want me back as a roommate? It was such a hard adjustment period the first time." She smiles, and I think every muscle in my body tightens in excitement. *There you are, my emotional, sad girl.*

"I never thought I'd say this, but the apartment is too clean," I tell her, and her smile grows. "There's no hair ties in the sink, week-old leftovers growing mold in the fridge, or energy drink cans in my truck."

"I don't like to litter," she says weakly. "And if I can't find a garbage can, what am I supposed to do? Throw it out the window—" I stop her, dropping her hands to cup her face and bring it close to mine. I groan and lift her face to meet mine in a long kiss that feels like heaven. Five months of missing her, waiting for this exact moment. The feeling of her in my arms again was enough to get me through every single second of therapy, and now that I have her—

I never want to let go.

I push my hands into her hair and pull her closer to deepen the kiss as fingers dig into my shoulders to mold us together. I can feel how much she missed me, and every worry fades into the background around us. She tangles her hand into the front of my suit, pulling me harder against her, and somewhere in the distance, the cheers of three very proud friends echo into the morning air.

"They are insufferable," I groan, and she smiles against my lips.

I kiss her again, unable to get enough as the music shifts again and her brows furrow in the funniest way. "This song is really horrible," she laughs as she pulls back.

"It really is," I breathe finally, inhaling her completely. "I missed you," I tell her when I refocus on her face. "A lot."

It's a weird feeling to be so happy and simultaneously so wrong about something, because when I really look at her this time, I see it. Rhea Drake glows the prettiest shade of purple.

"What does purple mean?" I ask her, and she furrows her brows. "Your color trick," I chuckle, "what does the color purple mean?"

"Uh," she straightens out, "it's love, empathy, balance."

"Glad we got that figured out," I whisper. *Love.* "Is mine still dark red?" *Almost black—it's so dark*, I remember her telling me.

"I can only do it when I'm drunk," she confesses, and I shake my head at her.

"Pretty sure that's just blurred vision, Hellcat..." I sigh, but she starts to laugh like a wild thing, and I gravitate toward the sound, peppering her jaw with kisses. "Thank you," I say to her. "For taking care of Daisy while I was gone. She told me that you kept taking her to school when you could and watched out for her. You didn't have to do that."

"She's not just yours, Brighton," Rhea reminds me.

"No, she's not, is she?" I realize that now more than ever. "I found this," I say, and pull her key from my pocket.

"I..." she trails off, "I've been staying with your brother. I have an apartment lined up."

"No." I shake my head. "No," I repeat. "Absolutely not." *I didn't do all of this work to lose you again.*

"Me living there is what got us into this situation," Rhea hums, and all I hear is her telling me she doesn't want to be around me anymore. "Maybe it's just best we—"

"Come home and make a mess, Hellcat." I press my forehead against hers, and she responds by tangling a hand into the front of my shirt. "*Please.*"

"So we can go back to being friends?" she asks me after a long moment of silence that kills me with every passing second.

"Don't ever use that word around me again," I snap and kiss her hard, reminding her that we stopped being friends-who-kiss a long time ago.

Epilogue

BRIGHTON

"We're going to be late, Dad." Daisy tugs on my arm as I lock the truck and follow her into the stadium. It's busier than usual. During the off-season, the girls started getting more attention, and now the Hillcats get played on the big TV at the Hollow—even during hockey games. "I want a Drake jersey!" Daisy points to the line.

"Yeah, alright," I say to her and hand her my card. She starts toward the line when I call out, "Get me one too."

Daisy nods quickly and turns toward the line. I stare up at the mural on the wall of the sports complex with pride. There's a framed photo of the Hillcats from last season, and any chance I get to see that smile, I take it. Rhea has her arm around Kaia and Addy, grinning ear to ear in her rugby jersey.

God, I love that sad girl so much it hurts.

"Here," Daisy returns and hands me the jersey. I look at the tag and sigh. "It's the only size they had left," she hollers before running to the bathroom. I follow her, changing out of my shirt and into the jersey that's two sizes too small. It pulls tight around my ribcage and chest, but it makes Daisy laugh, and Rhea is going to think it's hilarious.

"You're going to have to cut me out of this," I tell her as she drags me toward our seats.

"What the hell are you wearing?" Boone's voice is loud as I settle down into my chair next to him, Loveday, and Boone's best friend, Wren.

"And what the hell is on your face?" Judd grimaces.

399

"It's the only size they had left, and Rhea likes it…" I say to them, running my hand over the mustache, she asked very politely for me to grow, but they're all losing it laughing. "Yeah, laugh it up, assholes. So funny."

The girls come out on the field, and we all stand to cheer for them. I cross my arms over my chest uncomfortably as they line up for the national anthem, and I wait for her to find us in the crowd. She's nervous about today—her first time as captain, and her first tournament at this scale—but it doesn't show. Her hair is braided into two buns, and her face looks so plain without her piercings, but her eyes are bright and scanning the crowd.

Daisy waves beside me as Boone whistles loudly. Kaia taps her on the arm and points in our direction. Rhea smiles nervously, and I turn so she can see the back of the jersey, and it turns into full-blown laughter as I turn back to her. She shakes her head gently and scrunches up her nose at me.

The game starts, and the Hillcats move fast; they don't waste a second of the clock before they're scoring. Sunday manages to hurdle a player and dive over the line for an electric start to the game. I think I hold my breath every time Rhea takes possession, but true to her nickname, she's Death on the field. She moves like a shadow, graceful and powerful. It's insane to watch.

When she scores, she points to us in the stands and flexes to Daisy, who does it in return with that goofy smile on her face that I love so much. *My girls.*

"She's an animal." Wren shakes his head in disbelief. "I'd grow a mustache for her, too, Bri." He leans over with a stupid grin on his face.

"She'd tear you to shreds if you said that to her face," Boone laughs.

Wren looks horrified, and it only makes me laugh. *She's not scary*; that thought has remained true. She jogs down the field, her feet moving faster than the girl next to her as Kaia launches the ball backwards to Cosy, who skips it to Sunday and out to another girl. Watching them move together in tandem is like moving art. It's flawless, and even if one stumbles, the others pick up the slack.

"Women terrify me," Wren mumbles, and Judd laughs in agreement.

Kaia tips the ball off just as the clock runs down and brings them into the half. Seven minutes down, and the Hillcats are up two tries. Boone and the guys run to get beers during the quick break, leaving Daisy and me in silence.

"Hey, I signed you up for some classes down at the rec center," I say to her, and she scowls at me. "Yeah, I know how much you love fishing, so..."

"Dad!" She groans.

"Guitar classes, Squish," I confess, and she lights up like a Christmas tree.

"Really?" She turns in her seat and throws herself at me for a hug. "I need to text Lori and Auggie," she squeals, pulling out her phone.

The excitement in her voice is enough to keep me smiling the rest of the game, and by the end of the second half, the girls have won their first match. They just have to do the same thing for the rest of the weekend.

Every game is stressful, and slowly but surely the crowd starts to thin, leaving the die-hards and the family members cheering on who they can, when they can. By the last game, Daisy is asleep with her head on my shoulder, and I'm doing everything I can not to move around, but Rhea takes a hard tackle, and my whole body tenses when she gets up slowly.

"Come on, Reaper," Boone whispers from beside me as he slides forward in his chair. "You're tougher than that."

When she pushes off the ground and starts moving, I exhale the breath I'm holding, and Boone nods in approval. They've got two minutes left on the clock to score a try that wins them the game, but Kansas matches pace, and they'll be lucky to break the defence.

"Sunday's gassed," Boone grumbles.

"No, look," Judd snaps his fingers, and Cosy pulls up for relief. Sunday rifles the ball back to her left. The second the ball leaves her hands, she loops around to back up Kaia, who trails Cosy. Rhea is trying, but it's clear she's dizzy from the hit because she's moving more slowly than usual. Kaia's screaming out orders, and the girls are filing into a line for one last push.

"Come on," I urge them under my breath. "One more good play."

Boone flinches beside me as Kaia gets thrown to the bottom of a pile, but Rhea is there to protect, pushing it back to a stable position as the ball comes loose and Sunday pockets it. She chucks it to Margie, who snaps it back to Cosy and out to Rhea, who has repositioned.

"Atta girl, Hellcat." I sit up a little straighter with every step she takes, and Daisy stirs against me.

"There it is," Judd huffs, and Rhea throws herself across the line with a defender attached to her waist, tapping the ball into the turf with a wild smile on her flushed face.

Everyone explodes, scaring Daisy awake, but I don't move. I let her get both eyes open, and when she realizes what happened, she's on her feet. As the tournament winds down, we wait for the girls outside. It feels like forever, and I just wanna see her so I know that she didn't get too banged up over the last ten hours. When the doors push open, I hear her before I see her, and she's laughing with the girls as they wander over to us.

When she turns her back to say something to Kaia, my eyes catch the lettering on the back of her shirt. *Who's a good boy?*

"What the hell is that?" I choke, and she looks down at her shirt.

"Boone got me a new Hollow shirt?" She looks at it like it's no big deal, but she has that infuriating little smirk on her lips.

"Oh, did he?" I narrow my eyes on her face, and she just smiles brighter. *I'm going to kill that fucker.*

I choose not to start a fight with her, knowing she'll win, and instead let my eyes scan her. The loose sweats she wears are definitely mine, and the sweater she quickly pulls on is covering most of the damage, but there's a pretty nasty grass rash on her throat where she got hung up in game three with another centre.

"You alright?" I ask, my hand coming up to her face so she'll show me her neck.

"Gonna be sore for tomorrow but fine," she admits.

"I hate to be the bearer of bad news, but the mustache has to go, Hellcat."

"What, no!" she whines and narrows her eyes at me.

"I can't take the shit, I'm not man enough," I huff, and it makes her laugh.

"Can I get one last ride tonight?" she says under her breath.

"Then you have to help me get rid of it." I kiss her gently, and she hums in agreement against my lips.

"It tickles too much anyway." She pouts. "Where's Daisy?" she asks, looking around.

"Boone took her to Riona's," I say quietly as my eyes inspect the bruising, irritated red area.

"Empty apartment?" She stares at me.

"Very," I hum and tug her closer, my fingers curling around the back of her neck. "Good games today," I congratulate the rest of them over the top of her head as she wraps her arm around my middle.

"Nice jersey," Kaia teases as she pulls her hair up into a bun. "A little snug though, Killjoy."

"I like it," Rhea laughs and digs her fingers into my side. She tips her head up to look at me with a soft, tired smile. "Take me home."

"First round's on me," I tell them, and they all start cheering as they pile out of the arena.

RHEA

"In the washing machine," he says as we enter the apartment, and I start stripping off the dirty clothes.

"Or what?" I turn, pulling the shirt over my sore chest and dropping it on the floor just to see what he does.

"Hellcat," he hums, dropping my bag on the floor. "Don't start."

"Too late," I shrug, tugging my sports bra off and throwing that too.

"You'll be the death of me," he grumbles.

"Better make this quick, then." I kick off my sweats as I make my way back to the bedroom.

I hear him behind me, mumbling every word as he goes, but when he reaches the bedroom and finds me lying back on the bed in nothing but dark underwear, his mood shifts again.

"Your turn to make a mess." I stare up at him, and his jaw ticks as he crosses the room and crawls over me. His lips crash against mine as the dirty clothes get left on the floor, and his body overrides his need to clean.

The kiss is needy, a frantic game of back and forth with our lips as I work at his belt between us. He sits up, pulling at the hem of the jersey and groans loudly through kiss-bitten lips.

"What?" I laugh, staring up at him, my chest heaving.

"I uh—" he huffs, "I can't get out of it."

"Sorry, what?" I laugh.

"It's not funny." He clears his throat, standing up tall, and stretches the collar of the jersey with both hands. "It's stuck."

I sit up on the bed on my elbows and watch him struggle with the impossibly tight fabric of the rugby jersey. "That's unfortunate." I stifle the laughter at the base of my throat.

"Laugh it up, Hellcat," he says, but there's no real anger in his voice.

"You could always just live in it," I tease him, hooking my fingers into the front of his jeans to pull him back between my legs as he continues to stretch out the collar with two hands. "Become, 'Mr. Rhea Drake, *super fan.*'" I laugh.

"Mmm," he grins slightly, "you'd love that." He yanks at the collar again, and every muscle in his body tightens.

"It would be hilarious for a little while," I say, and push a hand beneath the fabric against his stomach, "but I'm kind of attached to what's underneath it."

He lets out a low chuckle and freezes as my hand moves up his abs. "Yeah?" He glances down at me for a split second before going back to stretch out the collar with a new urgency.

"Yeah," I confirm and pop the button on his jeans, helping him out of them as he struggles with the tight fabric.

"Hey," he mutters under his breath as my hands start wandering. "Not helping with the jersey situation here." His voice comes out breathless. "Stop distracting me."

"Get it off, Brighton," I demand, and watch his body harden. It's like everything shifts in the bedroom, his enjoyment of following orders takes over, and he thrives under the smallest of them. His breath hitches at the command, immediately responding to the authority.

When he pulls at the jersey this time, it's with a renewed force in an effort to obey the request. "Yes, Ma'am," he clips, and I hear the fabric tear as my hand dips into the front of his boxers.

Brighton tears the jersey down the front with a heavy grunt as my hand finds his shaft. "Good boy," I whisper, staring up at him.

It's new, but his eyes flutter closed briefly at the praise, a soft whimper escaping his lips. The fabric, once restrictive, now falls open completely, revealing his bare chest that rises and falls rapidly with each breath. His hips push forward slightly, seeking more contact with my hand, and I smile with every tiny reaction.

"Feel better?" I ask, leaning forward and kissing his hip as my hand wraps around him. I lick my tongue up his stomach just to feel his body shudder from the contact. His hand tightens as I kiss his skin, rock hard in my palm. The possessive touches and soft commands are slowly undoing him, and we haven't even gotten anywhere.

"Mhm," he hums, nodding slightly, but his eyes never leave me.

"What else do you need?" I ask.

His breath catches at the questions. His eyes fluttered closed at the small touches before opening again, filled with need and desperation. "Don't stop touching me," he admits quietly, his fingers tightening. "And talk to me like that."

"Like what?" I ask, my thumb rubs over his tip, and I use the other hand to push away the boxers from his hips as he shucks out of the ruined jersey and tosses it aside. There's something about needy, pleading Brighton that does things to my nervous system. I know what he wants, but I *like* to hear him say it.

"Like you're in charge." He swallows hard as my thumb circles him again. His boxers slide to the floor, leaving him completely naked and hard. "As if you own me," he adds softly, not breaking eye contact. His hips buck into my touch without permission. "Please," he whispers. "Take what you want."

"I don't know," I smile lazily, "I'm pretty sore from the game. Do you think you could be gentle with me tonight?" I ask in a soft tone, watching him through my lashes as he inhales shakily.

Those blue eyes widen, and he nods, his hand immediately moving to frame my face gently. "Of course I can be gentle, Hellcat," he promises softly, his thumbs brushing over my cheeks. "I'll be so careful," he whispers, leaning down to place soft kisses along my jaw.

"I'm going to miss this," I huff, and rub my fingers in the stupid mustache that covers his top lip.

"Make your peace with it," his voice is stern. There's no way I'll convince him to keep it at this rate.

"Oh, I will," I giggle.

We move back across the bed, and Brighton continues his onslaught of tender kisses and even softer touches. His mouth moves down my neck, sucking gently at the sensitive skin. His fingers brush over my collarbone, down between my breasts, and along my ribs. He's so gentle it's almost torture, his touch so feathered and his gaze so hot.

Just make sure that's all you do.

Fuck. I laugh gently, the sound vibrating from me.

"Brighton," I wait until he's looking at me again, "I love you," I say to him. I probably shouldn't—it's not the time, but there's something in him that begs for the words. That lends to a comfort that makes them mean more than anything.

His lips pause, his breath hitching at the confession.

It's true, I do. I stare at him.

"I love *you*," he whispers back urgently, his voice cracking slightly. The air in the room gets quiet and tight.

"Did I ruin it?" I ask, the mood, the night. "It was impulsive."

"It was." He wets his bottom lip. "But you didn't ruin it."

I nod, even though we both know it wasn't.

"I didn't?" I question.

"If anything, I'm having a pretty tough time keeping it together right now," he huffs, and his fingertips dig into my hips.

"Oh." I exhale nervously, truly unsure if I had screwed everything up in the heat of the moment.

"Rhea, I don't know how to explain to you how hard I am without turning into a horny teenager, so can you just kiss me some more?" he asks, and the smile on his face is euphoric when I grab his jaw and pull him back to me.

"I kind of like the sound of horny out of control, Brighton," I giggle against his mouth.

He groans into the kiss, hands tightening on my hips as he hovers above me. His kisses turn messy and desperate, his tongue pushing into my mouth as my hands find his hair. "You want out of control?" he breathes when he breaks the kiss.

"I do," I gasp as he rolls his hips down into me.

"I don't know, Rhea." His body shudders. "You're sore and..."

"Brighton Black, I'm giving you permission to lose control." I grab his chin and squeeze.

Something shifts in his eyes, and a smile grows on his face. "Will you beg me?"

"Do you need me to?" There's no hesitation as the warmth pools between my legs, and he nods.

"I'm begging you," I whisper, leaning on the bed just enough to brush my lips over his. "Please, Brighton. *Please.*"

He buries his face in my neck, the mustache tickling before he bites down on the skin there as he starts to grind against me harder, his hands possessively roaming my skin. His fingers make easy work of the underwear I'm wearing, and I lift my hips to meet his as he returns, his mouth finding a nipple. He releases it with a pop and kisses up my chest to capture my mouth again, biting my bottom lip softly.

"Don't stop," I dig my nails into his biceps.

He smirks at the command, lining himself up at my entrance, and rocks into me hard without warning. I cry out, burying my face against his chest, and he starts moving immediately, hard and rougher than he's ever been. *Out of control Brighton is a different animal.*

"Fuck." He peers down between us with a devilish grin. His hips snap forward harder at the sight of us coming together, and my back arches off the bed. "I'm going to tear you apart," he pants, reaching down to spread my legs wider.

"*Please?*" I don't mean to beg, but his lack of control is turning my rational thoughts into putty. His eyes harden at the desperate pleas, his hand presses down on my stomach, and I can feel every single thrust he makes.

The pain is delicious and nips at every sensitive nerve and curls my toes as I wrap my legs around his hips. He leans down, sucking a nipple into his mouth and biting hard enough to leave a mark with his teeth as he rocks deeper. The groan that leaves him is loud against the sound of skin slapping against skin as he grips my thighs and pulls me down over him roughly. I cry out from the pain, my hips arching off the bed, so he hits that spot buried deep inside of me that blurs my vision.

Brighton loses it completely when the cry leaves my lips. He slams into that spot over and over, his movements turning animalistic as he chases his release. Without warning, he pulls out, and I gasp loudly as he flips me onto my stomach and pulls me back against his hips with a slick intrusion. "Brighton!" I scream out, and he chuckles darkly as his fingers tangle into the back of my hair.

"You begged for this," he reminds me, tugging my hair gently as he fucks me from behind with wild abandon. His other hand reaches around to rub rough circles on my clit, making me cry out his name again and again. The room fills with the sounds of raw sex and desperate moans for more. "Take it. All of it."

"I don't think I can," I moan, my fingers digging into the sheets as he slams into me relentlessly.

He ignores the plea, his hips snapping as he fucks me mercilessly. His fingers on my clit become brutal, almost punishing, as he tries to coax the orgasm out of me. "Rhea, I need to slap your ass." His fingers dig into the skin there, and I look over my shoulder at him with a weak nod. His lips are wet, and his pupils dilated as he rubs the skin gently, having zero regard for how rough he's being. It's an intense sight I didn't expect to love, but it makes me clench around his cock tightly, and he shudders on his next thrust.

Brighton doesn't prepare me; he just brings his hand back, and the sting is euphoric as his tip pops out roughly and slides back in just as smoothly. "Time to make a mess," he says, his hand soothing the spot before he lays another hard slap to the skin. "I need you to come for me, or else I'll stay here forever," he groans and picks up his pace.

I yelp as his hand comes across my ass harder than before, but it shocks my body, and I tense with a surge of adrenaline. The tingle of the orgasm starts in the pit of my stomach and grows without care up through my body until I can't breathe.

"That's it, baby. All over me," he demands against my skin as my body tenses.

Brighton wraps his arm around me as my body is wracked with pleasure and turns me into nothing but a quivering mess. I clench around him, and he groans deeply, using his other arm to steady us as my orgasm triggers his own, and he buries himself deep inside. He comes hard, and it fills every space before it mixes and leaks down my thighs.

He continues to rock gently, softening inside of me as he catches his breath. One hand remains around me as the other slides down to feel the release against my sore thighs. "Look at that." He leans closer and kisses the back of my sweaty neck. Whatever animal possessed Brighton is long gone as he collapses gently beside me, kissing my shoulder and jaw.

"So does this make you a switch?" I pant out and angle my head back so he can kiss my throat with a tiny rumble of laughter.

"Don't start, Hellcat," he groans and wraps his sweaty body around mine.

Acknowledgements

First of all, this book was massive and I'm sorry. There's something about these two that apparently turn me into a yappy little thing. But also, I'm not sorry ha ha.

A lot of heart went into these pages, into this book. Growing up not a lot of things we're permanent in my life, we moved a decent amount, changed schools, made friends, lost them. Much like Rhea I was also a military brat, well I became one when my Mom married my step-dad, who is affectionally and gratefully, just Dad now. So our house was pretty chaotic at every single turn. But I had music, I had bad CW shows like Supernatural and I had sports. Hockey at first, go pens go, but then I was introduced to the world of Women's Rugby when I started high school. I fell in love that day with the sport and have never looked back. There is something so empowering about rugby that unless you have the opportunity to play a match you can never truly understand. The smell of the dirt, the feeling of the wind on your flushed face, the adrenaline and the soreness of your muscles after every game. You play rugby with your heart, body and soul. You have too, it demands that full experience every single match. I also believe that it's inspiring. And not just for women, for everyone. It's important in media for us to be exposed to that sort of raw, beautiful strength that these players have and the world should be paying more attention.

This book was my ode to that love, to that sport, to these women. I wanted something that screamed early 2000s romcoms, the kind that when someone brings up Sandra Bullock you know exactly what rom-com you love her from, *Hope Floats. No notes.* I wanted it to have the humor of our favorite adult sitcoms, Golden Girls, Sex in the City, Girls. That chaotic, funny and sometimes heartbreaking reality of what it means to be growing up and finding your place in the world. These are young women still stumbling through love, life, sex and trauma but they're doing it together. Anyway, that's enough of that, if you read it, you know what I mean. And thank you, for doing that. Always.

Husband first, husband always. Aaron you carry so much weight so I can live my dream and I don't think you'll ever understand how much that means to me. Brighton's love for Rhea is so furious and so easy at the same time because you taught me that love exists. That there is someone out there that will always put you first, no matter what. So thank you for being my Brighton. For taking care of me without question, for always making sure no blueberries get in my yogurt, for never making me eat leftovers, and reminding me to brush my teeth and take my vitamins. Without you there would be no Bright or Rhea. This sad girl will love you in every lifetime.

A massive thank you to my Alphas and Betas. MK, JJ, Delaney, Cyenna, Sarah, Netty, Lizzy, Beth, Jasmin, Aislin, Courtney, Mattie. Fucking superstars, every single one of you. For your feedback, your encouragement, your excitement and your hearts. No one understands how much work you guys put in for me and I wish that every indie author had a team like you guys. You do this unpaid, and you do it with your entire souls. So thank you, from now until the end of time, for doing this with me, two steps at a time.

Bec, editing wizard, love of my life, mother from across the ocean. 2025 was a fucking doozy. But you still managed to power through, write only God knows how many books, publish a handful of them and still found time to be our favorite witchy mother and my editor. So thank you, for your patience and your kindness. I couldn't do this without you.

Rory, goddess of my life, creative star shine. Eddie to my Steve. You are a saint. You put up with so much shit from me and half the time probably want to kick my ass for changing shit but I couldn't ask for a better person to create these covers. It's insane to think this will be our second series together and you still haven't walked to Winnipeg and throttled me yet. I love you so much (plus .69cents), and I'm going to work my ass off to make sure that everyone knows how special and talented you are.

Mattie, Red. You were a crucial component in this story, you were a sounding board to the smallest most intimate of moments that shaped Bright and Rhea into what they are today. There are no words to describe how grateful I am for you being a space I can vent, rant, brainstorm. You wake up everyday, and it never matters how shit your night was, or the day before was, you're always there to remind me of what friendship is. So thank you, for inspiring me on a daily basis with your compassion and empathy. I love you.

Killer, our corner is a fucking rave at this point. 2025 was our bitch, 2026 is a new animal but we got this. Four books between us up to this point since declaring that last year and we aren't slowing down any time soon. Thank you for always being the strength I need when I feel a little wobbly. For always being a little mean after being too sappy to bring me back to reality and for always believing in me, especially when I don't believe in myself. You really are the Kaia to my Rhea. You are a complicated little badass and I wish the rest of the world understood what that meant, because you are so kind and you work so hard for so many people. I love your happy moods, but thank you for trusting me enough to see the queen bitch depressed energy. I love her. You are my moon, for always.

And as always, last but not least. My drunk duck, twinkle toes. Jess, it has been what feels like forever and not enough time all at once since we met and every day since you've brought such warmth and hilarity into my life. I cannot say that middle school Aubrey would ever believe she has a country music artist in her top five on Spotify wrapped but here we are. You did that. I am so grateful for your willingness to love me in all forms, and your undying love for me and my ridiculousness. Please never lose your light for the things you love, Dinosaurs, the ocean, extreme fishing shows and grizzly bear men. You are an inspiration, you are beautiful and you are so fucking intelligent. Don't ever let anyone take that from you.

And honestly, to me because I grew up a sad girl, forever crying, overwhelmingly empathic and always people-pleasing. I survived that, grew inside of it. Despite it. I'm still a sad girl, I still cry at everything and still passionately empathic to the underdog, a lover girl at heart just wanting to be heard and seen. However I no longer allow myself to be quieted by the noise around me and that's on personal growth. I now have the freedom to use those emotions to create stories that touch the hearts of others and make space for those who desperately need it.

In the true theme of this book I want every reader to understand that this group of women above, and the ones I didn't have space to mention. My friends, my family, my community. These women are why I get to write girlhood in its rawest form. They are why I understand how strong women are, how brilliant we can be while still being compassionate and kind. They are the muse for these books, the backbone to the Hillcats. **They are the reason I know girlhood exists.**

About the ^Author

AUBREY TAYLOR

Aubrey Taylor is a 33-year-old mom living in chilly Canada with her two kids and wonderful husband. Raised by Dean Winchester, Percy Jackson, and horror movies. She's a loud, nerdy, sarcastic lover of stories. Her favourites always including chosen families and adventure. She has been writing and creating stories from her dreams ever since she could remember. With massive emotions of her own, she puts her entire heart into her characters and stories. Aubrey's favorite genres are fantasy, reverse harem romance, and contemporary romance!

Also by Aubrey:
THE HORNETS NEST SERIES
BAD HONEY

AUBREY TAYLOR

Honey Pot
So Long, Honey (Novella)
Honeysuckle
True Honey
Honey Undone
All I Need, Honey (Novella)
The Whiskey River Series
With Jessica Norton
Huckleberry
Cowboy
Standalones
The Manor on Orchid Lane
With Rowan Stone